Modern Man:
Life's Like That

By

Jon Co

Contents

1. Out of the Starting Blocks 4

2. A Degree of Progress 11

3. Motive, Means and Opportunity 28

4. Visiting Uncle Sam 49

5. All the Right Moves 79

6. Flights of Fancy 107

7. A Supporting Role 132

8. The Final Countdown 146

9. The Inner Child 165

10.   Part Time Single Parent 177

11.   A Bump in the Road 191

1. Out of the Starting Blocks

Modern Man was coming to terms with news that wasn't easy to take head on. He had always thought he was pretty good at dealing with tough situations in a measured and reasonable manner. He wasn't prone to panic and yell, 'Why me?' or unload his troubles on a total stranger in a public place. He was inclined to become withdrawn and opt for solitude whilst trying to figure out how to move forward with his life.

The news he'd recently received made moving forward that much more difficult because it was his actual life that may not continue for much longer. Could he really be dying? The doctor had been infuriatingly vague and lapsed into complex medical terminology. The underlying message was clear enough though. This was serious and surgery was inevitable. Tests would be required and the picture would be clearer after the results were known.

Modern Man had only seen the Consultant twice. To be fair to the man, giving this kind of information on a regular basis must be difficult. The Consultant had no way of knowing how his patient would react to this news but he would still have to explain how he intended to proceed. Modern Man was immediately confused. Why was he feeling sorry for the guy who had dropped this ticking bomb in his lap? The only comfort being that the Consultant and his team might be able to defuse it but they weren't making any promises at this stage.

Modern Man was a fairly ordinary chap. He didn't have any super-powers, nor was he an evil genius with an ambition for world domination. In fact, he had never entertained any political aspirations at all. He was a regular guy trying to make his way in the world with his innate capabilities and the skills he'd picked up along the way.

Up to this moment in time he had enjoyed good health and a reasonable standard of living. He'd never been a smoker and only drank to excess when the circumstances demanded it. And they had from time to time.

Modern Man was born in the early 1960's in the north of England. His formative years had been spent in a big village, or was it a small town? He wasn't sure which. As a tail-ender to the post war baby boom generation, he grew up during an era of rapid population expansion and new houses seemed to pop up faster than dandelions in the back garden. He did the usual things most boys do, and got away with it more often than not. He also had a really good circle of close friends, for whom he would always be there, as they would be for him. That sounded rather sentimental when he was young but grew in importance as an adult.

He was the archetypal 'average bloke' for most of his life. Good at some things, rubbish at others. The things he was good at tended to be practical rather than theoretical or philosophical. Overall he reckoned he'd achieved an 'above average' passing grade in life skills.

He'd learned a few domestic plumbing and electrical wiring techniques. Mainly to avoid paying registered tradesmen substantial call-out and labour rates to do what appeared to be some relatively simple tasks. However, some of his earliest DIY jobs wouldn't have passed critical scrutiny. He would advise anyone he cared about not to buy the first house he'd owned, 'Just in case...' He'd learned and moved on, in every sense.

Modern Man walked the country lanes near his home. Physically, he felt fine. Mentally, he was in bits. He wasn't the kind of guy who mistook heartburn for a massive coronary or a bit of a headache for cerebral haemorrhage. He had a fairly good understanding of the scale of pain. This was usually as a result of his own stupidity and bad luck.

He walked and he let his mind run free. He had no choice. He couldn't rein it in. He'd been trying for a few hours and it simply wasn't happening. His brain was running through all its recorded events for his entire life trying to find something that could reasonably be attributed as a cause of his present condition. Modern Man did a quick mental scan, throwing apparently random images onto a virtual big screen in his subconscious. There were some quick flickers and others that lingered for a few seconds before being replaced by some vague half-memory from times long gone by.

Was it Darwin at work? Was he being removed from the gene pool because he was too stupid to live? Did his progeny have the potential to destroy the human race? Was that actually possible? He'd met people he considered to be a danger to all life forms. For instance, there was the guy who drove his pick up truck straight down the slipway into the harbour until his vehicle was almost totally submerged. Any sensible person would have reversed down the slipway and floated his boat off the trailer. Not this guy.

Modern Man had done daft stuff. Sure, who hadn't? There was that one time, when he was a kid, and super glue was a fascinating new product. He was curious whether this marvellous invention really could stick skin to so many other materials.

He had a few more scars from any number of skirmishes with the laws of physics. Initially his parents had encouraged him to be an inquisitive child, although as his imagination developed this was quickly amended to active discouragement and much closer supervision. The family dog, Oscar, should have been named Beaker after Bunsen Honeydew's petrified lab technician in *The Muppets Show*. The dog was an equally unwilling participant in potentially risky experiments. Oscar developed a nervous twitch every time a match was struck but could still run faster than the boy. Oscar also found some ingenious hiding places to shelter until the danger passed.

No, this wasn't Darwin's theories of survival of the fittest. Maybe it was genetic. He didn't know much about his family history. His old man had done some research into his side of the family tree. Dad had found some old photographs in the attic and as far as Modern Man could tell, there were no hunchbacks or vestigial tails to be seen. Not that a physical deformity would necessarily have a direct link to his problem. It may indicate dodgy DNA, he supposed, but there was no evidence and therefore it was moot.

The male line showed a history of mainly dependable, rather than outstanding, engineers and scientists. No Nobel Prizes or ground-breaking discoveries to brag about. Maybe the female line held the clue to his problem. Clearly that would be much harder to trace as every marriage would mean a change of surname. Parish records were making their way onto the internet but even so, it would be a tough job for a naff prize.

In the end, all he discovered was that most of his ancestors lived normal lives and died at about the right age for the period in which they lived. Of the handful that didn't, one died in the Boer War and two were taken by the flu epidemic of 1918. The only other untimely death was that of great uncle Walter on his father's side.

Modern Man remembered his dad once told him the story about Walter. He cast his mind back to his late teens when the tale had been used as a warning to him about the dangers of drinking alcohol. The memory came into sharp focus and he relived it.

Great uncle Walter had enjoyed many hours in numerous pubs over the years. What he never did was learn to swim. He was drunk, he fell into the canal and not surprisingly, he drowned. End of story.

It was an interesting anecdote regarding the frailties of his forebears and, as usual, the moral had been rammed home with typical north-country subtlety. However, it was an isolated incident and threw no new light on his present predicament. Besides, Modern man had learned to swim.

Once again his brain went into over-drive processing memories.

Modern Man's gran, on his mother's side, had been a bit of a character. He had stayed with her a few times during school holidays when he was younger. She had lived in a small village in Somerset where almost nothing happened on a daily basis. The village was an encapsulation of quaint old England. There was a pub, post office and one shop next to a patch of grass they called the big green. The little green was by the bus stop, right next to the big green.

The boundary between the big green and the little green wasn't clearly defined and had been a talking point in the village for years. Some claimed the boundary was the imaginary line between the north wall of the pub and the site of the Lightning Tree, a huge oak tree that had been hit by lightening and burned to the ground in the great storm of '57. Even though the roots had been removed and the site grassed over in '59, it was still known locally as the Lightning Tree. 'Like it was yesterday,' they said. Others rubbished that as total nonsense and the debate continued.

There was almost nothing for a young boy to do in the village. Gran didn't have a dog and the neighbour's cat was nowhere near as gullible as the average mutt, so he couldn't do any experiments on those trips to the country.

He and Gran would have days out to the bigger towns and cities in the area. It would take two or three different buses to complete the journey to the major conurbations but that turned the excursion into an adventure. He desperately needed some excitement in his young life, what with the restrictions being put on him at home.

Gran liked Bath. She often spoke about the beautiful architecture and the history of the city. For Modern Man, it was the street entertainers in the Abbey Square. There was always something interesting to watch. He particularly liked the fire eaters.

Exeter and Bristol were bigger and therefore had more things to do. They also had bigger toyshops and playgrounds. He really liked going to Bristol Zoo. That was brilliant. There were lots of animals there that he could imagine as his test specimens. He never intended to hurt any of them. He was merely curious.

The highlight of the day would be when Gran sneaked him into the pub so she could have a sherry before they caught the bus home. He'd have fizzy pop and a bag of crisps. The barman would turn a blind eye to his presence as he and Gran always left before the office workers piled in for a quick one on their way home. Gran had been a regular in the pub since the current landlord's father ran the place and the kid didn't bother anyone. No harm done and business was business.

Primary school was also a small village affair with only one teacher and an average of twenty children aged between five and eleven. Perhaps his situation had its roots in Miss Laidlaw's frequent and literal banging of heads together.

She was referred to, by the gossiping classes, as the spinster of the parish and clearly had issues. Shouting was her first but not her only release of the pent up frustration she harboured. She had once been overheard in the hairdresser's salon attempting to justify her Victorian attitudes. 'If a good talking to doesn't change the wicked behaviour of small children then I'll mend their evil ways by knocking some sense into those boys and girls,' she said whilst cocooned under a huge hairdryer and unaware how loudly she'd spoken. Had these violent acts planted the seed of destruction that Modern Man was now contemplating?

His high school years had also been tough. Probably no worse than most people's and he'd avoided serious trouble and great academic achievement in equal measure. Modern Man attended lessons and absorbed what information he could. He never went looking for trouble. Although, it did occasionally bump into him in the corridor and stitch him up. He really couldn't master the role of innocent bystander. The temptation to be involved on some level was far too great. The consequences were never serious enough to threaten expulsion. His parents were never hauled in to hear of his misdeeds, thankfully.

Neither was he one of the anonymous herd and by the time he reached fifth year he was beginning to realise that perhaps he should toe the line more often. Modern Man didn't want five years of his teenage life to have passed by unnoticed but he had to avoid serious trouble. A paradox indeed. He had only recently become aware that the school was obliged to keep him until the age of sixteen but after that it was their choice.

He passed his exams by a slim margin. He now had to show some aptitude and enthusiasm for the three subjects he had chosen to take in the sixth year. The stumbling block was to convince the deputy headmaster that he was capable of achieving the required standard.

Modern Man had made promises about effort and application. Neither he nor the deputy headmaster believed in his declarations of intended endeavour but his eloquence under pressure won the day and Modern Man was enrolled on his selected courses. This was partly due to Modern Man's choice to take the sciences with geography.

Far too many of his contemporaries had chosen what they mistakenly thought were the easier arts subjects. They were soon horrified by the required reading lists and the need to research topics thoroughly before writing essays. No more winging it or copying huge chunks of text directly from a library book.

The threat of real research and the need for intelligent and balanced arguments was an almighty shock. Worst of all, they would have to list the sources they had used at the end of their essays, which meant actually reading these books. Nightmare!

Geography was Modern Man's downfall as that also came with the obligatory background reading. Physics did have some advised texts but the interpretation of 'advised' was 'optional' and the very idea of a maths textbook was ludicrous to him. Maths was hard enough without adding the confusion of explaining the thinking behind calculus or any of the other stuff he had to look forward to.

Whilst two years of hard labour was staring him in the face, a spark of an idea grew into an imaginative game he and his mates could play at the start of term. The school library was run by a woman. The lads were almost certain she was a woman, despite her best efforts at an androgynous appearance. She specialised in long shapeless trousers and baggy cardigans with huge buttons. Her hairstyle, although style couldn't possibly be the right word, was mannish and cosmetics played no part in her life. Modern Man didn't know her very well as he had avoided all contact with the library during years one to five.

The game was simple genius. Armed with their reading lists for the coming term, he and his mates embarked on a modified form of hide and seek. One person read out the title of a book on their reading list, without divulging the subject. The others had to race around the library looking for it. The first to find the book scored a point and then read out one of the titles on their list. As an added twist to annoy the librarian the books were never put back in the right place. The Library Game wasn't exactly Quidditch but it was better than being depressed about the workload being forced upon them.

The guys only managed to play this for about half an hour before they were caught. The punishment for this 'crime' was severe. Everyone in the group was hauled out of classes and summoned to the headmaster's office. A vicious interrogation to identify the ring leader revealed nothing more than one weak bladder and the release of a little previously trapped wind here and there.

This was followed by a pointless lecture on developing the level of responsibility and maturity expected of sixth year students. The ante was raised to a new and frightening level when one of the defendants implied that a physical relationship with a sexual dynamic existed between the headmaster and the librarian.

Modern Man knew this could only end badly and being expelled was a real possibility. He tried various non-verbal communication techniques to encourage his former friend to shut up. Mainly in the form of pop-eyed staring and hand gestures to indicate that this guy was not speaking for the whole group. The headmaster was instantly transformed from furious to incandescent with rage when it was postulated that a BDSM element to the alleged relationship also existed. In the face of this barrage it became obvious that his office floor would need a more thorough cleaning regime than usual. Bladder weakness had become endemic, along with brief instances of trembling and cold clammy skin. Thankfully none of them fainted. Apart from the embarrassment, the floor was awash with bodily fluids.

When the headmaster regained some self-control he sent all the defendants back to their classes except the one boy who had no idea when to shut up. None of the lads wanted to leave their friend in the hands of the enemy. Nor did they have the courage or stupidity to back him up. Reckless Ted was left to take the punishment alone. They had their own problems, mainly in the form of sitting through two more lessons in soiled underwear.

Looking back on this event, Modern Man wondered if the fear and humiliation he endured were enough to trigger some sort of chemical reaction in his brain. Could all that have been stored away to produce a devastating physical effect years later? He wasn't sure but it seemed highly unlikely.

Parents' evenings and school reports came and went. At the end of the lower sixth year he had failed to impress on any academic level. The fact that he wasn't disruptive in class and was putting in a reasonable effort, most of the time, counted in his favour. The question of whether he was up to the task still had to be faced. When his parents suggested they engage a tutor to help him, his attitude completely changed. He was confused at first. Were they thinking of taking him out of school and having someone come to the house and teach him one-to-one? Surely not, that would be really expensive.

No. What they were suggesting was that after a full day at school, he should then sit down with a retired or out-of-work teacher. Did they expect him to study for even more hours of his precious time? Were they not aware that he already had a mountain of homework? All this extra work seemed to be the prize for passing his previous exams. It didn't make sense.

Modern Man never did figure out if they were serious or had devised a plan so cunning that he would actually knuckle down and work harder without any intervention.

That was one of the many strange things about his parents. He never knew whether they had a plan for every eventuality or were bumbling along, dealing with each challenge in a rather haphazard spur-of-the-moment kind of way.

Sometimes he would get off fairly lightly when he expected serious trouble. Yet on other occasions he would take so much heat for what he considered to be very minor infringements of the rules. Parents were odd. They had no sense of an appropriate response and were totally inconsistent.

Maybe it would help if they drank to excess occasionally. Perhaps then they'd understand. He certainly didn't need any more stories from their whiter-than-white, butter-wouldn't-melt-in-their-mouths boring youth. Hearing those stories was punishment enough. They didn't need to add to his list of domestic chores. Tasks that were supposed to, 'Refocus his mind on what was acceptable behaviour,' as they phrased it.

Modern Man continued to muse how and why his present predicament had been instigated as his life unfolded. There had to be a reason, there just had to be. Otherwise, what was the point of it all…?

2. A Degree of Progress

The real down side of being a deputy anything is you are bound to pick up all the crap jobs that the principal doesn't want to do but still have to be done all the same. In high school it was no different. The deputy headmaster was less than enthusiastic about interviewing all final year students regarding their transition into higher education or the world of employment.

Some of these interviews were fairly straightforward. The academic superstars applied to Oxford and Cambridge. The big decision for those students was whether to sit an exam set by the college or let everything rest on the A level results. They obsessed about it, naturally, but the deputy's job was to help them decide on the best course of action.

Those at the bottom of the academic food chain were nudged towards the military and emergency services. If they hadn't played any sports during their school lives it was banks or insurance for them. That left the large middle ground. This was where the deputy's problems usually lay. As a school, they had a policy of encouraging progression to university because it looked good at County Hall. The vast majority of sixth years applied to five universities. The students had interviews and normally at least one or two conditional offers. The condition being that they achieve the required grades in their A levels. All the interviews and offers had taken place in the first term of their final year.

Six months later, with the mock exam results to ponder, a number of these plans needed to be reviewed. The deputy head had to introduce reality into the equation. Some of his students reacted as if they had just been informed by their parents that they were, in fact, adopted at birth. They had no need for harsh reality; they were still kids, despite occasional attempts at maturity.

Others were more stoic and Modern Man was one of them. The deputy head recalled the meetings they'd had regarding his progression into sixth year and couldn't deny that the lad had grafted. There was the one incident regarding the Library Game but the deputy head didn't see that as serious. Anyway, since his office was next door to the headmaster's, he'd heard every word of the disciplinary rant meted out by his immediate superior. He'd particularly enjoyed the accusation of an affair with the librarian, mainly because he knew there was some truth in it. The pompous ass had been exposed. 'The librarian? Really? So often it's the quiet ones,' he thought to himself.

Coming back to the point of the meeting, he advised Modern Man to apply to a polytechnic, as a kind of safety net. 'They do degree courses as well but they usually accept lower grades. They run courses over four years that include job placements. That way you get some work experience into the bargain.'

The deputy chose not to add that some employers considered having a polytechnic degree as academically equivalent to a Cub Scout merit badge. The real world had to be introduced slowly on a need-to-know basis.

When the time came, Modern Man was right on the money with his exam results. He passed all three subjects at the skin-of-his-teeth end of the spectrum. No need to trouble the university admissions staff any further. He much preferred the certainty of a polytechnic place than the desperate grab for something through the clearing process.

Clearing was a kind of academic end of season sale. Universities had some places available on a few less popular courses. Applicants who had under-performed in the exams had an opportunity to rebuild their self-esteem. It was a *Get Out of Jail Free* card for sixth formers who had bragged about their university place before exam results sealed the deal.

Going away to college was inevitably a big milestone. Packing up and moving on, to a certain extent. It wasn't really moving out because the bedroom wouldn't be converted into a gym or office as soon as term started. It would be there for the Christmas holidays and Easter and possibly forever. Some parents simply can't come to terms with the absence of offspring.

Modern Man wasn't sure how his parents would take it. He knew he was ready. He'd been ready to move out for at least a couple of years. It was only the lack of somewhere to move into that had stopped him fleeing the nest before. Packing had been a strange experience. For reasons unknown, the unlikeliest of people wanted to contribute in some small way. The woman across the road gave him an egg poaching pan and a pair of brass candle sticks. The church warden gave him a desk diary. Had the essentials of college life only one generation previously been so different? Doubtful!

With the car loaded they headed for the hills: trans-Pennine. Modern Man had accepted the polytechnic's offer the day his results came out. By accepting the offer straight away he was given the bonus of being allocated a room in the halls of residence. It turned out to be a rather grand title for a block of flats full of students. On the upside, it was a single room. On the downside, it was next to the kitchen. The kitchen that would become the focal point for ten of them in this self-catering establishment.

Modern Man was on the ninth floor. The lift was small and about a hundred new tenants arrived within a few hours of each other. Consequently, unloading the car took quite a while. It also required delicate diplomacy as no one wanted to unwittingly pick a fight with anyone. It would be very unfortunate if they turned out to be sharing the same room.

There was stress, fatigue and a few tears as most parents managed to embarrass their teenage children one way or another, before leaving them to their own devices. For Modern Man, it was time to put his stuff away and investigate the place. Unpacking was very quick. He didn't own much and that was a blessing because there was hardly any space in his room to stow stuff, anyway. The fixtures and fittings were pretty basic. The en-suite facilities in this five star establishment amounted to a wash basin behind the door. The other essentials were along the corridor beyond the kitchen.

Once he was organised he made himself a coffee, propped open his door and waited for another student to move into one of the adjacent rooms. Having been the first to arrive in this section of the ninth floor landing, he took it upon himself to act as an established resident. He welcomed new arrivals in the manner of an experienced old hand. After a couple of warm handshakes he realised this made him look like a total pillock and he changed his approach.

Each kitchen was the hub of all social activity and there were up to three kitchens on each floor in the halls of residence. The ten guys assigned to Modern Man's kitchen were new first years. For some reason they were called Freshers by the educational establishment. Clearly the person who coined that title had never been downwind of an eighteen year old boy on a warm summer's day. Nevertheless, they gelled as a group almost immediately.

As with any collection of young males thrown together by circumstance, there was some serious sizing up to be done. Testosterone had to be measured and a pecking order established. Points could be scored in a number of technical disciplines.

Modern Man took an early lead by correctly identifying an oven and a fridge. These wouldn't normally count for much but staring down the barrel of nine months having to cook for themselves added gravitas to this kind of knowledge. A slight swagger and self-satisfied smile made a brief appearance. This was short-lived as one of the others produced a couple of pre-chilled six-packs of beer.

No one was ready to raise the stakes after that master stroke of advanced planning. Jack-Six-Pack was duly elected ninth floor captain and alpha male. Modern Man was officially recognised as his sergeant and the other eight were clearly marked out as 'other ranks.'

JSP, as he quickly became known, made his first proclamation. 'We must establish our territory.' He went on to state that they had to identify other potentially hostile groups of males. He pressed the point that it was essential to quickly locate a herd of friendly females with whom to mate as often as possible. Aware that his plan was not unique, JSP recommended an early start and decided to give his new friends a pep talk before the marauding began.

Looking each young hopeful in the eye, he told them that whatever had gone before was history. They were starting here with a clean slate. No one knew anything of their previous embarrassing mistakes, awkward fumbling or early finishes. If indeed they had ever had the opportunity to start, let alone finish.

A few heads went down at this point but JSP raised their spirits with the fact, 'Yes, it is a proven fact,' he informed them, 'all first year girls at college are absolutely gagging for it. They're away from their over-protective parents and ready to get down and dirty with us guys.' All the heads were up again and ready for action.

Too revved up to wait for the lift, they piled down the staircase and reconvened at the front door ready to hit the town. Being northern lads, they had given little thought to what they were wearing, the state of their hair or any other aspect of personal hygiene. Aftershave was for poufs and southerners, or were they the same thing?

The first pub they went into was sparsely populated with old men and the barmaid was showing more cleavage than was strictly necessary for a woman of her age. She smiled as they walked in but nicotine stained teeth didn't do it for any of them and they left straightaway. The next two pubs were not much better and the boys quickly realised they were in the wrong part of town.

Eventually things improved. They found themselves in a smart place with real ale and a tasty young lass behind the bar. As each of them went up to buy his round he tried his best chat up line on her.

Over the course of the next two hours they built up a dossier of information about the girl. Her name was Julie and yes, she came here often, since it was her job to serve behind the bar. She wasn't a student and she had a boy friend called Spike. He had recently been released from jail after serving two years for GBH. He was also insanely jealous and happened to be standing at the other end of the bar watching and listening to the guys hit on his woman. That final nugget was the clincher. They all stood up, downed their pints and quickly left the pub.

The town was clearly a hostile place and the lads made a policy decision to try the Students Union bar next. It was cheap, it was hot and it was heaving. There was a lot of hugging going on between senior students. Many of them were returning for their final year after spending the last twelve months on industrial placements around the country. Second years were desperately trying to look cool because they weren't first years anymore. First years were trying to look cool so they wouldn't be taken for first years, who were obviously starry-eyed morons.

A few minutes surveying the assembled hoards resulted in the startling fact that about 80% of the people in there were blokes. Of the 20% that were women, half could pass for a bloke and the remaining few were surrounded by blokes. Anyway, the beer was cheap and they were back on campus and too drunk by now to have initiated a meaningful thirty minute relationship.

The lads had bonded as a group, or so they thought. A quick check on numbers revealed that they had lost a few mates along the way. Two were found puking in the toilet but Matt was not in the building. Between them, they couldn't remember seeing him since they left the pub where the lovely Julie worked behind the bar. Could he have gone back there to continue with a lost cause coupled with the probability of an imminent and painful death? They certainly weren't going to go back and look for him. After all they'd only known him for a few hours. It wasn't like they were life-long friends, duty bound to protect each other when lust won out over logic. Nah, stuff him. He deserved to die, the horny bastard.

The first week of college was called Fresher's Week. It involved filling in the same information on lots of different forms and attending numerous 'Welcome' meetings for various clubs and societies. None of it was scheduled for too early in the morning. Years of experience had taught the administrators that new students weren't very good at mornings. A significant number of them were only barely familiar with afternoons and they were the ones unlikely to extend their student life beyond year one.

A real chance to find where the college stood in the world rankings was the Fresher's Ball. There was always a live band playing and the bigger the band the greater the kudos of the college. The slightly ironic thing about booking a band for the Fresher's Ball was that it was usually the final act of the outgoing entertainments committee chairman. A one-year elected post, paid for by the Students Union. The irony being that all the plaudits for booking a great band would go to the current chairman who had nothing to do with it. Similarly, all the hostility for putting on a bunch of useless unknowns would effectively torpedo the chairman's year in office before it had really begun.

Modern Man wasn't too bothered about who was playing. He had never been to a live gig before and didn't worship at the altar of the pop charts every Sunday afternoon. Even so, this was a new experience and that was a major part of what going to college was about. The guys all went along together and got gloriously drunk again. The band did their thing. As it was too loud to talk and too hot not to sweat a great deal, none of them even attempted to pull a girl. They kept to the sidelines and tried to look cool.

Having co-existed for a week by this time, those among them who possessed a personality found time to unpack it and try it on for size. Those who didn't, over compensated at regular intervals and frequently behaved like total dickheads. A split in the group was inevitable. The dickheads were evidently discouraging the girls from approaching the studs.

Matt hadn't been seen for three days. As he had the other single room on the landing, he was able to avoid people quite easily when he wanted to. He was the only one in the group on a business studies degree course and had a different timetable to the rest of them.

Modern Man and a shy nerdy lad, called Philip, were on the same engineering course. JSP and Alex were doing architecture and two others were doing biochemistry; whatever that was. One music student and two sociologists made up the group.

When Matt finally put in an appearance he was immediately interrogated about the first night out. He neither confirmed nor denied that he had gone back to the pub to try his luck with the hot barmaid. He deftly side-stepped questions he didn't want to answer and was impressively vague on several details.

Meanwhile JSP's position as natural leader was already under pressure as he had failed to come good with the ladies. His efforts to hang on to his status had become increasingly desperate as the first week drew to a close. To their immense disappointment, it was clear that not one single girl on campus was gagging for it. Not with any of them anyway. It would only make it worse if they discovered everyone else was seeing some action.

Modern Man had always liked his food, so basic cooking held some interest for him. He had no ambitions to be a chef but wasn't ready to live off beans-on-toast for three years either. Within a few weeks he had established a sustainable routine of catering for himself. However, with one four-ring cooker, one kettle and nine other people massacring processed gunge, he kept out of the kitchen at peak times.

What he found particularly odd was that even though every one of the group knew they were going to be living in a self-catering set up, none of them had the faintest idea how to cook anything. This led to some bizarre experiments involving cans of spaghetti hoops, frozen peas and fried eggs. Any or all of which would then be slapped between two slices of bread. As this was a few years before microwave ovens came on the scene, there were no 'ready meals', as such. The closest thing at that time was dehydrated stuff that took a lot of effort to make and was rarely worth the trouble.

He had no chance of keeping his unusual skills a secret and before long he was sharing what knowledge he had with his new mates. Some took to it, others quickly gave up. A few persisted with their strange combinations from tins, numerous and various. They insisted that their creations were both nutritious and flavoursome. Modern Man declined the offer of a free tasting and in doing so, threw up a fairly significant social barrier between them. It wasn't intentional but the lads who were prepared to do no more than 'buy it and fry it' effectively labelled themselves as an underclass within the group.

As time went on the gap widened and whilst there was no direct hostility there was plenty of territorial one-upmanship. There were accusations of failing to wash up shared pans and utensils. The final straw was when a forgotten frying pan burst into flames. Of course this set off the smoke alarm, which, in turn triggered the main fire alarm that was linked directly to the fire station. The student hall being a large residential building in the town centre, five fire engines were on the scene in a few short minutes. At almost midnight there wasn't much traffic to hold them up and they had made the journey many times before.

The fact that it was a mixed hall was common knowledge. It was equally well known that each corridor was either all boys' rooms or all girls' rooms. The evacuated students stood around on the other side of the street waiting to be told what to do next. Alex, the one studying architecture, explained that each corridor had to have its own fire door and exit route. Muster points were equally spaced along the road. Most of the folks were still dressed when the alarm went off but a few were shivering in dressing gowns of varying degrees of naffness.

In amongst a group, which should have been made up entirely of girls, was Matt. He was trying to blend in with those around him and doing a reasonable job since he had on a pink satin robe and matching slippers. He had long hair which helped, but he also had broad shoulders and at 5'11" should have been noticeably taller than all the girls around him. Matt was crouching down and that's what gave him away. His shoulders were hunched and his hairy knees could be seen quite easily. That and the loud speculation as to which room he had come out of during the evacuation. Whilst he wasn't bad looking, with the scrutiny of their peers at such close quarters, none of the girls was ready to claim him.

That wasn't really Matt's biggest concern at that moment. What he was worried about was how he was going to recover his clothes from this girl's room. A girl that needed serious alcohol induced coercion to let him into her room in the first place. She had now apparently sobered up sufficiently to see it as a mistake. His clothes, wallet and room key were all out of reach.

When the chief fire officer declared the building safe, everyone started drifting back towards the lift. Matt held back and sidled up to Modern Man and JSP. Deliberately ignoring all the predictable jibes about how pink suited him, how they never suspected he was gay or the subtlety of his make up, yadda, yadda, yadda; Matt asked, and then pleaded for help. Modern Man and JSP were only too pleased to give assistance. There would be a price to pay. They wanted to know who he'd been with that evening and all about his missing three days in Fresher's Week.

Modern Man took off his over sized greatcoat and gave it to Matt. The coat was a bargain he'd picked up from the Army and Navy stores. Essential as soon as he realised how cold and wet it could be in the early autumn in Yorkshire. After crossing the road, Matt took off the slippers and put them in the huge pockets of the greatcoat. He was then able to blend in with the tail end of the returning masses. Modern Man wasn't the only person to see the benefits of military tailoring. At least a dozen others had bought similar greatcoats from the same shop.

Back in the relative safety of their kitchen, JSP said he would recover Matt's stuff. Modern Man offered his room until Jack returned. He was ready to wheedle out all the details while JSP was out of the way. Matt wanted to know how he was going to get his clothes back but JSP just winked and said, 'Trust me.' Neither Matt nor Modern Man knew him particularly well. Although, they both knew by now that when he said "trust me," it meant he didn't have a plan. Maybe he had a plan that was worse than not having a plan. This increased the tension Matt was experiencing. Would he ever see his stuff again? At this point Modern Man realised he was in with a chance of a successful interrogation.

He was also desperate to know which girl on the seventh floor was a 'possible.' Whilst none of the girls was an absolute stunner, they were all a lot better looking than The Dogs of Desperation down on the sixth.

That was a group of improbably shaped and aesthetically disadvantaged young women that even a skin-full of beer couldn't make attractive. Some of them knew it and were openly hostile to any man who so much as acknowledged their existence. Others were in denial and abused the privilege to be plug-ugly in countless ways, primarily through hideous clothes and inappropriate use of cosmetics. Even the Goths in the shopping centre gave them a wide berth. It couldn't have been a coincidence that they had all been roomed on one floor. Someone in the administration department had decided to corral these individuals together, for the safety and security of everyone.

JSP went down to the seventh floor corridor armed with nothing more than an A4 sized piece of cardboard and a packet of bin liners. He rolled the cardboard into a funnel shape and used it as a loud hailer to make his quickly prepared speech.

'Ladies of the seventh floor. Behind one of your closed doors lie some of my friend's possessions. He's keen to have them back. It's apparent that you wish to remain anonymous and I respect that. To this end I shall push a bin liner under each door and then I'll sit in your kitchen for five minutes.'

He went on to announce 'After this time I shall return and expect to find one bin liner in this corridor with Matt's stuff in it. If this doesn't happen I shall come back with my boys and one by one we'll kick your doors in and find his stuff that way. The choice is yours.'

What JSP hadn't anticipated was that whilst he and the guys had been doing their male bonding thing, the sisters here, had been sharing their feelings in a very girly way. Whilst they didn't approve of any one of them bringing a lad back to her room without him being properly vetted first, they accepted her mitigation of a wine induced mistake.

They didn't take to the idea of their doors being kicked in by a bunch of morons and decided that they would have to take this upstart down while he was alone and on their turf. Being girls, they hatched a plan that was far more devious, more humiliating and complicated than any man could have come up with.

Amanda was grudgingly recognised by the others as 'the sexy one' so she was the main player in the subterfuge that was to follow. Initially nervous but quickly warming to the role, she slinked into the kitchen in a short silk dressing gown and sat down across the table from JSP. Leaning forward she revealed a measured amount of cleavage. The exact unit of measurement was unclear but it was enough to put JSP into a sort of hypnotic trance.

Without a word, she took his hand and led him back to what he supposed was her room. Still without saying anything, communicating only with her eyes, he took the hint and started to undress. Part way through, he made a lunge for her, only to be silently rebuffed but not discouraged. When he was down to his pants she nodded at the bed and he threw the sheet aside. From nowhere, she produced two pairs of fluffy handcuffs and secured his writs to the top of the bed frame. His enthusiasm for what he was expecting to happen was clear. Still without speaking she produced a couple of silk scarves and gently but firmly secured his ankles to the bottom of the bed. Then she left him spread-eagled and optimistic.

A few minutes passed and his anticipation was approaching its peak. When Amanda returned there was good news and bad news. The good news was that she was not alone. The bad news was that she was fully dressed and so were the other girls in the room. The really bad news was yet to come. The bed was on castors and moved easily with three girls pulling and three more pushing. It took a bit of effort to force it through the door. By tipping it on its side and scraping his skin on the woodwork, they managed it. Once in the corridor it was a straightforward glide along to the lift. The main doors were much wider and even the mud on the grass verge was not a problem.

Manoeuvring the bed into the centre of the roundabout was a challenge but these were very determined ladies. Once he was in position, floodlit by street lights and more than a little concerned about his immediate future, the final flourish was administered. A bottle of water was splashed over his last remaining item of clothing, making his underpants totally transparent. He was very cold and just when he thought it couldn't get any worse, it did. With nimble fingers and a pair of very sharp scissors, his final defences were shredded and he was left with very little to show for his adventure.

The girls left him to reassess his role in the grand scheme of things and the police arrived about half an hour later. Initially, it was one copper on foot but he decided that the bed might be booby-trapped so called for back up. An area car showed up and they called in a dog handler and tactical firearms unit, just in case. Regional Crime Squad was tipped off and a helicopter was put in the air. SOCOs took about a hundred photographs and Jack-Six-Pack kept the same initials but for a whole new name that he was far less proud of. Matt's clothes were found in a bin liner in the boy's kitchen.

For a while things returned to normal. People went to lectures, wrote essays and even visited the library. It was a large building full of books that Modern Man deliberately avoided. In his limited experience, academic books asked more questions than they ever answered. They toyed with the reader by dangling facts in front of them, only to introduce other ideas that supported their hypotheses. Yet they still managed to introduce an element of doubt. They widened the scope of the subject even further. In his mind, once he started reading academic texts, he would have to continue for the rest of his life and he wasn't a fast reader anyway.

The guys that shared the ninth floor kitchen managed to get along reasonably well after the fire alarm incident. Those that didn't like each other so much avoided direct contact. Most, but not all of them, improved their cooking skills and Modern Man found a kindred spirit in David Beech, one of the biochemistry lads. Modern Man's first impression of him was that he was very shy and that was an issue for David.

One evening Modern Man and David were talking in the kitchen and it turned out he was from South Wales, a keen rugby player and lifelong Llanelli supporter. Being from that part of the world, all his mates called him Dai. This presented a real problem when introducing himself to any girl he fancied. When the mere act of stating his name sounded to her like, 'Die Bitch,' he was already dead in the water.

He was looking for a fresh start and had come north to try to achieve it. Although he didn't say much, he listened to everyone intently. He decided that the local accent was worth adopting. He put a lot of effort into copying what he heard the locals say, despite having no idea what they were talking about most of the time. He was a work-in-progress and would remain in that limbo state for most of his three years at college. The lads who came from the area helped in the way that lads do. They mercilessly ripped into him at every opportunity.

When the winter weather set in the central heating was switched off. Apparently it was too expensive to heat the building all the time. Consequently, from early

November through to late February the heating was set to prevent the pipes freezing but not the residents. This brought a real Dunkirk Spirit to the ninth floor kitchen. If indeed the troops waiting to be plucked off the beach sat around shivering and complaining about being abandoned to the elements. The lads did figure out what to do with the oven at that time of need.

As a few of them had tried cooking things in it, they were aware that if you figured out which knob to turn, the oven would heat up. Over the next few weeks they invented several ways of making the most of this thermal energy. The simplest was to sit around the oven with the door open. This raised the ambient temperature but did little for the mood. Keeping the oven door shut until it was up to temperature then briefly opening the door gave a bit of a rush. When they were bored with that, they sat around the open oven and waggled their feet in front of it. It was the best way to warm up their extremities.

By late November the students were all short of money and were painfully aware that the run up to Christmas ought to be party time and that would cost. The sociology boys had so few lectures and tutorials that they could have taken full time work but they couldn't be bothered. They shared one of the double rooms and rarely set foot outside the door before mid-afternoon. The cleaners refused to enter their room because of the smell. Since the boys had recently resorted to living off dodgy Chinese take-aways the pong was much worse. The Ming Palace became known as the Minge Phallus after that.

Some of the others asked their parents for money but most relied on the friendly manager at the campus branch of a once respectable High Street bank. He was an overweight, middle-aged man with a reputation as a bit of a perv. This was based mainly on the simple fact that he favoured female students. If they wore something short at the bottom and plunging at the top he would usually see a way to help them out of a tight situation. It was a bit tougher for the guys. They had to work much harder for their overdrafts and were still hammered with account charges.

There was a rumour that one of the Dogs of Desperation had lived up to her name and performed what the media always referred to as 'a sex act' in return for an unlimited overdraft. The man from the bank that liked to say yes, was reported to have said, 'Yes,' quite a lot and very emphatically. In fact the exact quote from an innocent passer-by was, 'Yes. Yes. YES! OH GOD, YES!' It seems the walls of the bank didn't offer much protection. Sadly for her, neither did he, but a course of penicillin cleared the infection up fairly quickly.

Modern Man arranged his overdraft by more conventional means and was solvent for the last few weeks of term. His intention was to live life to the full but his lecturers had other ideas. They decided that after nine weeks of teaching it was time to see what their aspiring engineers had really learned and set a series of assessment tests.

No one was going to be thrown off the course if they failed these tests but they would certainly receive some serious grief from their tutor.

All the tests were scheduled for the first week in December. This gave the lecturers time to mark and return the papers before the Christmas holidays. There were seven individual subjects and two months of lecture notes for each one. Having sat in a daze through most of his classes Modern Man was blissfully unaware how much he had actually written down since the start of term. He was therefore stunned by exactly how much revision would be required for these tests.

One week before the tests were due to take place, all the engineers were given a presentation about their first industrial placement. They were scheduled to spend the summer months working in a proper engineering job and this would form part of their final qualification. Over the four years of the degree course they would have to amass a minimum of twelve months of relevant work.

The college had connections with a number of local businesses who were prepared to take students for a while. First years were notoriously difficult to place because they knew so little as to be almost useless. All they were able to do was join the apprentice program if it was a large company or shadow an experienced engineer in the smaller businesses.

Modern Man was letting his mind drift when the kicker was delivered.

'How well you do in test week will determine how much effort goes in to placing you this summer. Usually about a third of first years fail their exams, so we don't need to find work for them. Of those who will be returning, we find positions for about half. You will not be awarded a degree at the end of the course if you haven't completed the required time in industry. If the department hasn't been able to place you then you will need to find something suitable yourself. '

It was a very intense seven days leading up to test week. Modern Man put off all offers of pubs and parties. None of the other ninth floor boys had tests and were chasing women every night. He had left himself far too much to do and didn't have the kind of retentive brain that could absorb technical detail at first reading. As a result, he went into his first test short on sleep and filled with dread.

An hour later he came out of it wondering what the employment market was like for students who didn't progress past the first year. This only darkened his mood further and it took all his will power to walk past the union bar rather than into it. The rest of the week was more of the same. By Friday night he was seriously considering writing a CV and buying a suit for interviews. What was he thinking? He wouldn't get any interviews. This was a complete disaster.

His friend Dai had gone home to south Wales for the weekend. Llanelli had a top-of-the-table clash with Cardiff and Dai never missed that big game. Sitting alone in a surprisingly quiet union bar, Modern Man was lost in thought and seriously depressed. Whilst he had no illusions of being the greatest engineer, or greatest anything, come to that, he couldn't face the idea of absolute failure. The humiliation would be unbearable.

Having nursed the same pint for almost an hour, even getting drunk seemed to be beyond him. So when Seventh Floor Amanda came over and sat down opposite, he hardly noticed. It wasn't until she spoke to him that he was actually aware that she was alone and had made a conscious effort to join him.

'Why so sad?' she asked. She looked amazing. Hair, make up, clothes. If it wasn't for the brummy accent she'd be fantastic.

'Where are all your mates?' Modern Man asked with trepidation. JSP's treatment was folklore and he wasn't keen to follow him into the history books.

'Most have gone home for the weekend and a couple of them have gone to a party. I'm supposed to be meeting Janice here.'

Janice was blond on the inside. 'Nice girl wrong planet' and, it turned out, was the one Matt had been with when the fire alarm went off. That detail had only come out long after the event. She'd apparently decided it hadn't been such a big mistake after all and had been seen leaving Matt's room in the early hours one morning.

Amanda seemed happy enough in Modern Man's company. At least until her friend arrived. Janice was in a real mood when she eventually bumbled through the door. 'Where have you been? I've been waiting for you in the White Lion,' she said.

'So', Modern Man muttered under his breath, 'The wrong pub and the wrong planet.'

Amanda masked her amusement by taking a huge mouthful of wine but the glass wasn't wide enough to conceal her smile and Jan interpreted it as laughing at her. By way of riposte she accused Amanda of standing her up so she could meet up with, 'some guy,' instead. Before any response could be uttered Jan had wandered off.

Modern Man had no previous history of being spontaneous with girls, so he was surprised to hear himself strike up a conversation that didn't start with a lame chat up line. When there was a lull he went off to the bar and bought her another drink and a pint for himself. His mood was lightening a little and Amanda seemed to be putting some serious effort into cheering him up. This was another first. Most of his mates would have told him to stop being so effing miserable.

When the union bar closed they walked back across the campus together. Modern Man was desperately trying to decide whether he should make a move on her when she took his hand and manoeuvred him into an alcove. The kissing was tentative at first. Once they figured out that their noses were in the way and it was bit sore when they cracked together, they got deep and meaningful with each other. They stopped a couple more times on the way back to the flats and things were looking promising.

The clincher would come when they entered the lift. Amanda knew his room was on the ninth floor. If she pressed seven and nine it would be a major disappointment but there could be an opportunity to take things further on another occasion. Preferably the next day, while so many people were away for the weekend. She didn't press nine but he did. It was habit, that's all.

When the doors opened on the seventh floor he followed her out. She took his hand and they ran down the corridor. Modern Man didn't know whether this was because she didn't want anyone to see them together or because she was keen to have him in her room as soon as possible. Then he gave himself a mental slapping for even caring what her motivation was. Even he was pretty sure he knew where things were going and he had absolutely no experience to base this on.

Once behind closed doors it was hard to tell who was more nervous or more enthusiastic. Neither of them knew that it was the first time for both of them. Buttons and zips were sacrificed in the name of lust and they each started and finished more quickly than they would have liked. Not deterred by this, they filled the short intermissions by talking dirty to each other.

After three trips to the end zone Modern Man was ready for the half time hooter. The room was a mess of his clothes, her clothes and tangled bedclothes, so they adjourned to the kitchen for tea and biscuits. How frightfully British, he thought to himself.

The second half was all about consolidation and trying to second guess whether this would turn out to be a one night stand or the beginning of something. There was no easy way of asking the question, so it stood in the corner of the room like an unwelcome guest cramping their style. Even though physically exhausted, sleep was fitful for them. Single beds are really only for one person. The clue's in the name.

By mid morning they had given up hope of having any more rest. Although Modern Man was up for a bit more action Amanda just kissed him on the end of his nose and said, 'Get dressed, you're leaving.' She was vague about her plans for the rest of the weekend and Modern Man realised there was no point pushing it.

When the corridor was declared clear, he slipped out and hurried along to the lift. Once he was inside, his victory dance started. Even though he was only ascending two floors, his enthusiastic jumping up and down and slapping the walls was enough to trigger a fault in the winding mechanism. He'd broken the lift. Granted it was a small lift, maximum load six persons.

He never understood why people became persons when they boarded any form of public transport. All the buses clearly stated the number of persons allowed to stand while the vehicle was in motion. Since it was a weekend he would probably have plenty of time to ponder that quirk of the English language.

Modern Man opened the hatch, picked up the emergency phone and listened for a dial tone. Why, he wasn't quite sure. It wasn't as if he could choose whom to call. In fact he couldn't call anyone. The thing was broken. He battered on the doors and yelled through the narrow gap between the doors, 'Help, I'm stuck in the lift.'

About ten minutes later he heard a wheezy, out-of-breath voice coming from somewhere near his ankles. It was the security guard. He had hauled his immense frame up several flights of steps and sounded as if he was about to be in need of emergency assistance rather than provide it.

In between deep breaths and hacking coughs the guard managed to communicate that he had called the lift company and an engineer would be with them as soon as possible. In the meantime Modern Man should stay put. From somewhere in the back of the guard's mind he remembered to ask Modern Man if he suffered from any acute medical conditions. Modern Man said that he didn't but he did need to pee rather urgently. The guard laughed and wandered off back to his cosy nook by the main entrance.

In a surprisingly short space of time the lift doors were prised open and Modern Man could understand why the voice of the guard had been where it was. He was between the eighth and ninth floors. He climbed out then moon-walked along to his room.

No one was around so he made himself some breakfast and sat in the kitchen staring into space with a part happy, part stupid expression on his face. If he'd been a smoker he'd be on his second packet by now, such was the exhilaration. The knowledge that he wouldn't be faking next time the lads were talking about their sexual adventures was a huge relief.

When the endorphin rush finally subsided he remembered how it all started. He was drowning his sorrows. It was a near certainty that the upcoming test results would mark him down as a probable fail at the end of the first year. The mood had well and truly swung back from euphoria to despair. There was no other option than to work like crazy and hope for the best. It wasn't a fool proof strategy but it had taken him to where he was now. Probably best not to look at it that way, though. Maybe a better motto would be, 'It has saved the day before and would do so again.' That had a more positive spin on it.

The test results were better than expected. It was another close run thing but an overall passing grade. Unfortunately, it wasn't enough to secure him the guaranteed industrial placement. Now he had to figure out how he would sort that out as well as prepare for the exams at the end of the year. His tutor was no help either. This prophet of doom went to great lengths to explain how much harder he would have to work. Adding, as an afterthought and with his best stab at sincerity, 'Do you have any personal problems you want to share? After all, I'm not only a senior lecturer, I'm your friend and mentor as well.'

Modern Man and Amanda didn't see much of each other after that. It wasn't through any animosity or emotional distress on either side. They both seemed to realise instinctively that it had been a one-off event that had been special but wouldn't be repeated. The strangest thing was that each of them was okay with it. Neither felt used by the other and no one else knew about it. They carried on as before. Modern Man decided that this must represent some kind of emotional maturity and that was worth something. It didn't hold him back from being totally childish in other ways though. This growing up deal had to be taken one baby step at a time. It was a whole new territory to be entered into with extreme caution.

By the time the end of year exams arrived, Modern Man was as prepared as he could be. He had been through several years of previous exam questions. He had completed all his assignments on time and to the best of his ability. However, he still lived in the relegation zone of his year group. He had managed to secure an industrial placement for the summer through a friend of his parents. He would be spending three months with a firm of consulting engineers who had recently won a big contract and were feeling unusually philanthropic.

As expected, one third of the first year engineers failed their exams and became immediately available for employment. A further third had to re-take one or two exams and pass them, to be allowed to continue. To everyone's amazement, Modern Man was among the select few who passed all subjects at the first attempt. Not merely passed but passed with good grades in several areas.

He was prepared to publicly admit that on this occasion hard graft had taken him from the bottom third to the top third. That didn't mean it was the only way to survive the exams. He would continue to try other methods in future. It wasn't that he objected to hard work, it was just that it was so tiring. There had to be an easier way. He would channel the same energy that he had dedicated to the grafting hypothesis, into finding an alternative.

Second year came and went in the blink of an eye. He shared a house with a bunch of other lads and they did the usual loud, drunken, unsociable, unhygienic and occasionally dangerous stuff that young men do when at college. He slipped back into the bottom third of the slimmed down class and barely kept his head above water, academically speaking. He left it too late to prepare for exams properly and had to re-take a couple during the holidays. He passed those and was back on track for year three.

The third year was only two terms in college and the remainder out on placement. Once again, he had to find his own job because the college didn't come up with anything in time. The consultancy company he had spent time with in the first year was happy to have him back. As it was for a reasonable length of time they gave him a project to work on by himself. It wasn't especially exciting but they paid him and it was an easy commute from his parents' house which meant he had almost no living expenses.

The fourth and final year was intense academically and not as much fun as he had hoped. The work load increased dramatically. For the lucky few there would be job interviews for the daunting period that came next: The Real World. Despite considerable effort researching alternatives to hard work, Modern Man hadn't come up with anything. He was forced to resort to the only approach that had shown any real success.

It was time to graft again, like he did last summer, he grafted again, it was his final year. Bop; bop; bop, bop.

Modern Man continued to stroll through the country lanes and amble through his memories, some vivid, some vague. Despite the torment, he seriously doubted whether anything that happened so long ago could lie dormant in his body and flare up now.

At the main road he turned right and wandered through the small business park that did a reasonable job of fitting in with its rural surroundings. It was a mish-mash of neat office buildings and single storey industrial units. He wasn't there for the view, it was a direct route into the woods but it did remind him of his early career.

3. Motive, Means and Opportunity

As a newly qualified graduate engineer, Modern Man was practically unemployable in a recession. And it was a serious recession that greeted this generation of college leavers. It was a time of political conflict, industrial unrest and the death throes of the Cold War.

The British economy was being driven away from the traditional manufacturing to something called a 'service based' economy. To the small minority who knew what that meant, there was a phenomenal amount of money to be made in an incredibly short period of time. For most of the population it was the agony of change and uncertainty.

Modern Man had a little over a year's experience in different jobs related to engineering in one way or another. That should have been an advantage when applying for jobs. He soon found out that he would have had more chance if he had gone straight from school to work, as three to five years real experience was worth more than a certificate. Lesser men would have wept, thinking about how they were encouraged to work so diligently to secure a place at college. He hadn't, so no wasted effort on his part there.

He was facing the hard facts that he needed two things pretty quickly: he needed somewhere to live and he needed a paying job. He had managed to navigate his way through his college years without building up a massive mountain of debt. This was partly through the industrial placements being salaried positions and partly by living in abject squalor for his entire student life. That was no real hardship and something he had been practising throughout his teenage years in the privacy of his bedroom. Once he realised that a certain level of filth ensured no visitors, he had adopted this as his personal standard of hygiene.

He had two over-riding requirements in his quest for accommodation and income. He wasn't staying in his college town and he wasn't going back to the area where he grew up. His parents had said that there would always be a bed for him at home but frankly, his room was a tip. He didn't want to be one of those sad types who go off to college then come back to their old haunts. The only thing worse than going back was staying put. College had been a brilliant life-changing experience but he saw too much evidence of people who didn't know when to move on. They still hung out in student pubs and clubs.

The economic policies of the British Government at that time created something called the 'North-South Divide.' That in itself was a misnomer. It should have been called the 'Home Counties Haven for the Smugly Self-Satisfied' because the wealth and opportunities certainly seemed to be restricted to the already prosperous south east corner of the country.

Modern Man was a proud northerner but not so proud that he was prepared to be unemployed up north when he could be working and living well down south. The road to London was well trodden by generations before him, as well as by several of his mates from school and college days. As a result, it wasn't hard for him to find somewhere he could doss down for a few days until he found his own place. He was overflowing with the optimism of youth and didn't think for a minute that he would have any trouble finding a job and a flat in about a week.

After a month and a half of looking at hideous bed-sits and writing dozens of give-me-a-job begging letters, his cash card was swallowed up by a hole-in-the-wall machine. His mates were also letting him know that his novelty value had worn off. He was now officially a parasite.

In the depths of despair Modern Man realised he was doing it all wrong. He had been applying for jobs that didn't exist with companies that were shrinking, not growing. He had looked at flats and bed-sits for one person but they were tiny rat holes in the skirting board. It was time for a different approach. It was time for a different attitude and it was time for a pint. So he went to the pub to drink about his future. He had to change his strategy, adopt a 'can do' attitude and put clear blue water between himself and the three million other people who were unemployed at that time.

Modern Man remembered the advice he been given at school when filling in the university application form. Embellishment is OK, blatant lies will catch you out. With this in mind he started to rewrite his CV with a more positive spin on his brief work experience.

In the first placement he had spent three months shadowing an experienced engineer at a consultancy company. They were overseeing the building of a new British Embassy in Eastern Europe. One of the many requirements of the government contract was to distribute updates and revisions of documents to the many businesses involved in the project. This necessitated a lot of repetitive clerical work. It was exactly the right job for a keen-but-green student engineer in an office with minimal secretarial support.

Modern Man spent three weeks on that task and nothing else. By the end of his time there he knew more than most about toner cartridges and paper jams. Not once was he tempted to photocopy his genitals and include the image with the technical documents he was posting out. He proudly saw this as a sign of maturity. Albeit slightly offset by his tendency to kick the machine when the document feeder didn't work properly.

As a task, it had been incredibly boring. As a supplement to his formal education, it had added little of value. As an entry on his CV, it was elevated to the impressive status of, 'Documentation Engineer responsible for the management of requirements of sub-contract suppliers to a major government contract overseas.'

In his second year he had worked in the drawing office of an air conditioning company. This was one of the businesses on the embassy contract and Modern Man had blatantly and repeatedly asked for the job while he'd been working at the consultancy. Although he had no previous experience of design or air conditioning systems, the company were finding themselves bogged down in paperwork. They had also put in a desperately low bid to secure the work. If they hadn't been successful they would have had to start laying off employees. The harsh reality was that they couldn't afford to take on extra staff. However, a student on a six month placement was a technical risk worth taking. Cheap, but risky.

For Modern Man this was a stark contrast to the consultancy where he'd worked the previous summer. Calm and professional were two words that would never be used to describe this office. The tension was palpable and it ran from the top down. The boss swore at everyone and the 'f word' was universally used as a form of phonetic punctuation. It was an incredibly versatile word as an adjective, as a comma while they drew breath or as a verb in the present tense. It was also a powerful exclamation or instruction and in the past tense, it was a statement of fact. They were, totally....

Finding a positive spin for the CV from this was going to be a bit harder. What Modern Man had actually done was difficult to define. He had started every day with no clear role, or responsibility, and had been poached by one person after another to do what they should have done, several months ago. He had frequently been chewed out for not completing the work as they had expected, even though no one had actually taken the time to explain what it was they wanted. Modern Man was not surprised that this company was in trouble. He eloquently enhanced his actual role as general dog's body to that of 'Project Engineer.'

Modern Man's Year Three placement was with the consultancy once again. Older, more worldly wise, he had been given a small project on a different contract. Having seen and heard enough of the embassy, he was glad to move on to something else.

The consultancy partners were obsessed with efficiency so Modern Man was given the task of investigating the processes that were used in the management of projects. It was a way of involving him in the business but not on anything that was critically important. At worst, he would be interrupting people to ask them about their jobs. He'd been doing that the last time he worked there anyway, simply because he was bored and had nothing else to do. The best outcome would be if, having no preconceptions, he was able to spot something that no one else had.

Without really having the slightest idea what he was supposed to be doing, Modern Man set about the task with as much enthusiasm as he could muster. Some people were quite helpful and provided useful insights into how projects could be better managed, whereas others were openly hostile to a student 'investigating' their work practices.

By the end of his placement Modern Man had hacked together a report. It contained sizeable chunks of plagiarised text from a business management book. These were interspersed with a handful of keen observations that he had been handed on a plate by a disenchanted project leader on the verge of retirement. This was all bound up in what Modern Man thought was cutting edge business language. None of the partners ever read his report. They were simply helping the college by taking a few students each summer to massage their own egos and slightly reduce their tax liability.

Modern Man reinterpreted that experience as an in-depth study into working practices in a cutting edge engineering consultancy. He awarded himself the job title of 'Trouble Shooter' on his revamped CV.

His next master stroke was to apply for jobs he didn't want. In fact, he applied for every vacancy in the Job Centre. It seems unlikely that anyone can be barred from a Job Centre but Modern Man came as close as humanly possible to that eventuality. The staff members were sick of the sight of him. One minute he wanted to be a trainee hairdresser but at the same time apply for the position of night shift manager in a shoe factory. All he really wanted was to have interviews and lots of them.

After a few days his plan started to work. His first interview was with a direct sales company, whatever that was. Modern Man was to see a Mr Henderson at six in the evening at the company office. The premises were located in one of many small industrial estates in the area. Six o'clock seemed rather late for an interview but he guessed the guy must have a full schedule and this was the only time available.

Mr Henderson was thin and quite small. He wore a shirt that was too big for him and although his tie was snug to the collar it was still a good inch away from his scrawny neck. His suit jacket hung loosely off his shoulders and he looked about twelve years old. He introduced himself as the sales manager of Double Digit Kitchens and, without blinking or drawing breath, offered Modern Man a seat, cigarette and tea or coffee.

Modern Man only accepted the seat and young Henderson launched into a speech he had made several hundred times before. He painted a verbal picture of his sales team working as a well oiled machine. He explained how they worked hard and partied harder. They were living the lives of successful sales executives.

Modern man couldn't help but be carried along with it. He saw himself driving a flash car with a gorgeous girl at his side. He couldn't wait to start hanging out in the casino and dining in smart restaurants. Naturally, he'd be living in a fantastic flat in the heart of the West End.

The speech ended with the phrase, 'On target earnings in your first year are £50,000. You start tomorrow evening. Be here at seven sharp.'

Modern Man quickly rewound the tape in his head and searched for the part where he had been offered and accepted the job. He couldn't find it but it must have happened because he had a fifty grand job starting the next day.

He also had another three interviews lined up over the next few days. As these were all during normal office hours he wouldn't have to cancel any of them and may also be able to rustle up more job offers. This was a good day and he was about to start making big money.

Over the next twenty-four hours Modern Man had mentally spent about £3 million on bare essentials and a few luxuries as well. Maybe he'd have a few drinks with the lads from Chelsea or Arsenal. Those footballers seemed to know how to have a good time.

He was still living in that bubble when he wandered into the building later the next evening. His induction was nearly as quick as his interview. It consisted of him being given a brief history of the company from its inception eighteen months ago to its current standing as the leading fitted kitchen company in the London Borough of Hammersmith and Fulham. All hail the mighty Double Digit Kitchens.

Modern Man was given a sales script and strict instructions not to make up his own patter. After being shown to a booth containing only a small desk and a phone, he was handed a list of names and phone numbers and an order pad.

'Here's the deal,' said Mr Henderson. 'If you make ten or more appointments tonight, you go out and see those people over the next two days and sell them a fantastic new Double Digit kitchen. Less than ten appointments and you're back in here tomorrow night making calls. Any questions?'

'What if I make nine appointments? What happens then?' Modern Man asked.

'Those appointments are split up between the people who did make their target and they go out and see the punters. Got that?'

Modern Man had another question, 'Do I get the commission if one of my appointments turns into a sale?'

'No. You have three hours and you just wasted five minutes asking stupid questions. Pick up the phone. There are people out there who need a new kitchen.'

Henderson stalked off to bring a little sunshine into someone else's world and left Modern Man with his list, phone and order pad. When Modern Man looked at the list he noticed almost immediately that the names were in alphabetical order and all started with the letter P. There were three columns of surnames, addresses and numbers, pages and pages of them. Just like a telephone directory - spooky.

Modern Man picked up the phone and dialled the first number. It was answered within a couple of seconds. 'Yes, what do you want?'

Modern Man launched into his script, 'Good evening sir or madam. Great News! You have won third prize in a competition, a massive discount on a brand new fitted kitchen. Can you confirm your name and address please?' he enthused.

'Who are you? What do you want?' replied a voice of indeterminate age or gender.

'Double Digit Kitchens will install, totally free of charge, a fantastic new fitted kitchen at your place of residence,' continued Modern Man.

'Why? What have I done wrong?' was the rather odd response.

Not wavering from the script, Modern Man ploughed on with the features and benefits of the marvellous, superb, first class, cutting edge, beautiful and lovely kitchens and eventually nailed his first appointment for the following day.

Buoyed with confidence he picked up the phone again and called his next prospect. A man answered, that much he could tell almost immediately. Modern Man recited his speech again. Part way through his second sentence the guy said, 'Not interested.' Modern Man ignored it and kept going. The frequency of, 'Not interested,' responses increased rapidly and eventually Modern Man completed his pitch. There was silence for a moment then, 'My God, you're persistent.'

Without knowing where it came from, Modern Man replied, 'Persistent, is my middle name. No really, it is. My parents were Quakers. And yes, it is a burden but it could have been much worse. If I'd been a girl it would have been Ebullient.' He didn't get an appointment but he did feel he had won that small battle of wits.

His next three calls went unanswered and, after an hour on the phone, he had been verbally abused seven times, hung up on eight times and chatted up once by a very drunk woman. What the hell, he got an appointment out of her. When the evening shift was finally over Modern Man had five appointments spread over the next couple of days.

Henderson appeared from his office and yelled at the dozen or so people, 'You lot are the most useless bunch of pathetic losers I have ever met! None of you have met your target for tonight, you morons!' This was the opening gambit of his inspirational speech to round off the day. He continued, 'However, because I am such a nice guy, I have decided to let those of you with five or more appointments keep them. The two of you who made none are fired. Leave now. The rest are back in here tomorrow.' One of the two ex-employees ran out in tears and the other shrugged his shoulders and seemed to be relieved it was finally over.

The successful three would be going out on sales calls the next day. This was good, in that it wasn't another night on the phones but bad because he had to stay for another half hour. He still had to collect his samples and brochures and endure a short training session with Mr Henderson.

In the sales training, Henderson told him how the Double Digit system worked. 'You told them they had won a prize, yeh? Course you did, it's in the script, in'it? What you said was, they would get a brand new kitchen fitted totally free, right? FITTED FREE! They've still got to buy it don't they, otherwise we can't fit it, can we?'

Modern Man was totally blown away by the cunning of this evil genius.

'So,' Henderson went on, 'You 'elps them choose the kitchen they want and draw them a little picture of it. You fill out the order pad and get their credit card details. If they won't give you the details, force them to buy a finance deal. We make more on the finance deal but we can benefit from having their credit card details as well. So, it's swings and roundabouts, yeh? One more thing, right? Do not leave any appointment without an order. That's an order. Got it?'

Inevitably, Modern Man had a question. 'Is this ethical? As in legal?'

'You don't need to worry about that my son, your face ain't going to be on Crime Watch any time soon.'

Modern Man left the building with a heavy heart. He needed a pint and, as if by magic, a pub appeared around the next corner. As it was almost time for last orders, he bought a couple of pints. The first one went down without touching the sides and the second was the pick-me-up he really needed.

'You did well tonight,' said a vaguely familiar voice. It was Darren, one of the other two successful telephone sales operatives.

Denise was standing right behind him and nodded in agreement. 'Most people don't last more than an hour on their first night on the phones,' she added. She had a voice like a rusty bicycle, presumably from smoking. Having said that, she had a pretty face and a body that would encourage any red blooded male to sign whatever piece of paper she put in front of them.

Darren noticed him noticing her and chimed in with, 'Denise is the top sales agent in the company.'

She added, 'You'd be amazed what the right clothes can do to close a sale.'

'Or the lack of them, you tart.' Darren said.

'Don't underestimate it. It might even work for you one day, if you ever get an appointment with a short-sighted nymphomaniac, or my sister.'

Darren and Denise had presumably run this little double act before and it did lift Modern Man's spirits a bit, although most of the credit had to be given to the beer on that score. His first appointment as a Double Digit Kitchens sales executive was the following morning. He had another script to work with, brochures and samples. He had to learn this script off by heart as he could hardly stand in front of a prospective customer and read it to them. He briefly toyed with the idea of leaving them in the living room and reading it to them from their kitchen while he measured up, but he couldn't see that working either.

He would have to travel to his appointments on the tube since he had failed to mention that he didn't actually have a car. He had said he had access to one and in a sense he had. Anyone could use a taxi, which was a car. Without a car he wouldn't have secured this incredible job at all.

The drunk woman, from the previous evening, had sobered up and didn't remember making the appointment. As he tried to remind her, things got out of hand. Voices were raised and after a few net curtains had twitched, the police were called. The concerned neighbour didn't particularly like this woman and her affinity with alcohol but she was still a woman alone with a stranger trying to force his way into her home. Modern Man was let off with a serious ticking off from the police constable and left the scene rather embarrassed. At least no one on that street knew who he was.

His next appointment was with a young couple who had a baby. They lived in a tiny bed-sit in a converted Victorian terrace. As Modern Man went through his sales script, he realised they were seriously interested. They really wanted a kitchen to replace the crumbling mess they were currently using. The baby was five months old and that meant it would be crawling soon, the mother told him. Modern Man had no knowledge or understanding of babies and there was no reason why he should.

The couple picked the cheapest kitchen in the brochure but that was still £2,000 and they didn't have a credit card. They would have to finance it. The fact that the couple were both at home during the day was a fairly strong indication that neither of them had a job. Nevertheless, the couple would still be eligible for a finance deal. Henderson had made that very clear; he called everyone with personal circumstances like that a Ninja. No Income, No Job or Assets. Why a finance company would lend under those conditions was a mystery but apparently some of them did.

The commission on a £2,000 kitchen including the finance deal was £150 and Modern Man needed money more than he needed air to breathe at that time in his life. He couldn't do it though. He couldn't let these people saddle themselves with more debt in exchange for six feet of pretend marble worktop, a few cupboards and wall units and a one-and-a-half bowl sink and drainer.

Darren would probably have suggested the girl sell one of her kidneys for the sake of her child. Denise would have split them up and seduced the guy into buying the top of the range kitchen at £20,000. Thus netting herself £1,500 commission as a result.

Modern Man could do neither of these things and was about to leave when the guy asked if he could apply for a job selling kitchens for Double Digit. Modern Man told him he would be better off selling his soul to the Devil and left them to ponder what that meant.

After a bad cup of coffee in a dirty cafe he phoned his remaining appointments and cancelled them. No one was disappointed when he explained that these were probably the worst kitchens in the world. He returned his samples and paperwork early in the afternoon and told Henderson he had been offered a job as a rep for a wine importer in Saudi Arabia and would be leaving immediately.

With a mixture of relief and concern, he prepared for his next interview. The details in the job centre had claimed unlimited earnings potential in an exciting and fast-growing sector of the leisure industry. Full training given and no sales experience required. It also said 'commission only' but Modern Man wasn't sure what that meant so he didn't let it worry him.

The interview was in a hotel, which he thought was strange. When he arrived, there were about twenty other people attending the same interview at the same time. They were all shown into a small function room and after a few minutes a middle aged man strode in purposefully and started talking, loudly and quickly. He exuded self-confidence and made sure everyone noticed his Rolex watch. After a brief introduction, he launched into a speech about travel to exotic locations. He focussed on the lifestyles of the rich and famous with their holiday homes in the Caribbean and Indian Ocean. Then he slapped the desk so hard a couple of the women screamed involuntarily, then blushed and apologised repeatedly.

The speaker had tried many times to use this shock tactic and so far it had never worked the way he wanted it to. It had this time! Anyone daydreaming of white sandy beaches was yanked back to reality by the scruff of the neck. When his audience regained their collective composure, he proceeded to make his point. 'This is the lifestyle that everybody wants but almost nobody can afford. You are going to sell the dream of owning a holiday home in the tropics to Dean and Rochelle from Billericay.'

The presentation went on for half an hour. If he sold the dream once, he sold it a dozen times in twelve different ways. Everyone in the room wanted it and he was going to show them how to get it. The next stage of his presentation was a walk through of ways to promote the idea.

'Sell the sizzle, not the steak. Make sure you convince them that they'll be able to travel the world and live in luxury for the rest of their lives. All this for less than the price of a new car. Holiday Ownership,' he continued. 'No one calls it timeshare anymore. It brings caviar to Camden and champagne to Carshalton. The real bonus is that if you give enough people what they want, you can have absolutely anything you want. There is no limit to the amount of money you can earn selling Holiday Ownership. Who, in this room, wants unlimited earnings? Anybody? Everybody!'

On this cue a number of assistants moved in with contracts and everyone was encouraged to sign up. A few people declined and were escorted out of the room immediately. Clearly negativity was not to be tolerated in this happy place filled with dreams.

With an over-bearing individual invading his personal space, Modern Man felt compelled to put his autograph on the dotted line without actually reading what he was committing himself to. The document ran to three pages of small print, crafted in the finest legal terminology by a professionally discredited solicitor.

Modern Man knew that it was a bad idea to sign something he hadn't read. After three laps through the first couple of paragraphs, he realised that he wouldn't understand it anyway. No matter how long they gave him to study the text, he'd still be baffled by the jargon. Besides, how bad could it be? These were business people. They wore suits and carried briefcases.

There was a bit of a 'situation' when one of the interviewees insisted on reading the document in full. The over-eager assistant became impatient and started muttering under his breath, 'Sign it, stop wasting time and sign it. Sign it you stupid cow or I'll never get out of here.'

The Main Guy picked up on the atmosphere and was over to intervene in a heart beat. He stood between the assistant and his newest recruit. He gave a death stare to his assistant and gentle reassurance to the interviewee. She eventually signed the contract and the recruitment process returned to its well choreographed script.

The Main Guy returned to the front of the room and started to describe in detail, how their product was to be sold. He told them that only the bottom 5% of the adult population, in terms of income would not be able to afford at least one week each year in a resort somewhere, and that some of their owners were amongst the richest in the country. He painted more mental pictures and the new recruits wrote notes and listened, open-mouthed at times, while he described the financial miracle that was Holiday Ownership.

Modern Man wanted to be sceptical, it was in his nature, but he so wanted this to work out, after his dismal experience with that kitchen job. He wrote copious notes and tried to understand the principle. He didn't ask any questions, his ego was still a bit raw from being chewed out the day before.

There were fifteen new guys in the room; three were women and twelve were men. The age range was school leavers to mid-fifties he guessed and this seemed to please the Main Guy enormously. He told them that as an agent there was no barrier to age, race or gender. That buoyed the confidence level in the room even more.

'So,' he said, 'are you ready to start getting rich? Are you ready to make some people's holiday dreams come true?' His next statement took them all by surprise. 'Next door are fifteen couples who have been watching a film about holiday ownership. They are very excited and eager to buy, so go and sign them up now.' There was stunned silence for about three seconds, which is a long time for nothing to happen in a busy room.

Assistants appeared again, this time armed with sales contracts and each new recruit was escorted from that meeting room to another one down the corridor. Before they had time to take in what was going on they were seated with a prospective buyer.

Modern Man's clients were in their early thirties, well dressed, in a chain store kind of way and clearly interpreted the situation differently. The woman was keen. She leaned forward with bright wide-open eyes and an engaging smile. The man was a subtle combination of bored and slightly hostile. It was almost as if he had been tricked into being there.

Modern Man took this in and reflected back to the client that he didn't know the half of it. Modern Man introduced himself, first name only. The short training session he'd received had made that point clear. Apparently it was friendlier and not done to protect their identity.

Modern Man recited his presentation text exactly as he had been instructed and nearly word perfect. When he came to the close, the bit where salesmen encourage clients to commit to the purchase, he stumbled a bit. The woman was all for it but the man was still holding back. It looked like the man was the sole wage earner in the partnership and she was an accomplished spender.

After a little negotiation they found some common ground and Modern Man made the sale. The assistant looked incredibly relieved and this appeared odd to Modern Man. He could only assume that there was some kind of commission paid to the assistant or maybe it was just reflected glory.

When the paperwork was done and the clients who had signed up were taken to the hotel bar for a celebratory reception, the Main Guy strode into the room. The bonhomie didn't join him this time. He had a face like an erupting volcano and it didn't take long for the molten grit to hit the fan above his head. Only five couples had signed up and this was unacceptable. Modern Man thought it sounded like a good result but what did he know? By now, he knew enough to keep his opinions to himself. That much he had learned. The Main Guy spewed red hot lava over them for about ten minutes then ran out of steam. The kicker was still to come and it arrived when someone tried to leave during a secondary tirade.

One of the people who had sold a deal wanted his commission and wanted out.

'Read your contract,' was the robust reply. 'You'll get your commission for this sale when you make your next one and you'll get your commission for that one when you make the one after that.' There was a collective exhalation in the room as everyone realised they had been shafted.

The guy who wanted out was furious. 'Stuff your commission, I'm leaving anyway.'

Kicker number two was delivered with a self-satisfied smile from the Main Guy. 'If you leave now, you have to repay your tuition fees. Which, coincidently, are exactly double the commission you thought you had just earned.'

The Main Guy went on to explain that when they'd given their bank details in the paperwork, it wasn't solely for them to be paid directly into their accounts. It also enabled any outstanding costs to be recouped, should they be in breach of contract. They were each handed a copy of the contracts they had signed earlier, the relevant section now highlighted a garish pink.

'There are presentations twice each week; you will have another chance to sell on Saturday afternoon. If any of you fail to show up for work on Saturday, you will be in breach of contract. If you wish to resign from the company then you must sign up a replacement. The only way you can do that is by coming to a sales and recruitment day like this and encourage an interviewee to become an employee, as you were earlier today. Any questions?'

So there it was. Twice in a week Modern Man had, in a nutshell, been stitched up, conned and ripped off. His self-esteem was plummeting and he wasn't too far away from jacking it all in and heading for the northbound mainline railway stations.

He was depressed. Not in a clinical sense, where you collect a regular prescription and knowing looks from the pharmacist. It was more a sort of deeply fed up with the aroma of total despair subtly fused with seeds of failed potential. Dark clouds were gathering overhead and he could see no way out of the approaching storm. This wasn't deeper self-diagnosis, it really was raining and he was becoming very wet. It was time to drink about his future again, pint in hand, brain in gear.

Modern Man found a different pub and bought himself a lager. He was hungry too. He hadn't realised how hungry until the waitress shimmied past him, carrying a couple of plates piled high with burgers, barbecue sauce and chips. He was sure it was no accident that she was holding them at eye level making sure he caught the sight and the aroma. The wink she gave him closed the deal.

He found a table and caught her eye as she was returning to the kitchen. She told him he should order at the bar. Modern Man pointed out he was on his own and if he left the table even for a minute, someone else would grab it. She was quite a flirt and he enjoyed the chat they had. She took his order but declined to give him her phone number. He took the slight rejection with good grace and in the full knowledge that he knew where to find her when he was ready to try again. Part of him liked the idea that she wasn't a push-over. He managed to let that part of his brain overrule the caveman within him and channelled those thoughts towards an erotic fantasy that he would probably flesh out later.

That small yet positive interaction with an attractive member of the opposite sex picked up his confidence and gave a boost to his self-esteem. While riding on the endorphin wave of almost chatting up a pretty girl, Modern Man reviewed the last few days in a more positive light. He had completed two interviews and been offered both positions. He had also secured appointments from cold calls and made some sales. Not bad for a first attempt. He wasn't about to pretend that sales was his life but there was no denying he had a natural talent for it. The key was to find the right product and the best company to work for. The snag was he hadn't a clue what either of those might be. It was time for some more 'blue-sky thinking.'

Beer was obviously excellent brain food. The more he drank the more confident he became in his ability to sell performance cars, luxury accommodation and any number of other big ticket items with spectacular commission payments. That was the essential element. Commission, and lots of it. Unlimited earnings had a nice sound to it. It made anything possible.

Modern Man was able to nurture this positive energy through the night and into the next day. He woke with a determination to throw off the shackles of limiting beliefs and realise his full potential. He couldn't be the working class kid who rose to the top because he had never been working class. He wasn't one of those strange individuals who tried to pretend they grew up on a rough council estate. No. Modern Man was middle class and it didn't bother him a jot. He didn't flaunt it; what was there to flaunt about being neither frightfully rich nor embarrassingly poor? He was what he was and accepted it.

What he was that morning was inspired. He was also optimistic and energised. Bright and early, well, before midday, he set out to secure his future. He'd had enough of the Job Centre and all its public sector negative hostility towards him. Modern Man was going private from now on. There were loads of recruitment companies that were dynamic and pro-active and things that sounded good but he didn't really know what they meant.

Whatever. They were the catalyst he would use to rise to the top and be all he could be. Smartly dressed and armed with several copies of his CV, he hit the streets.

Some recruitment agencies were really high street job shops and not that different to the Job Centre he now despised. The ones he wanted to make contact with were hidden away in back street basements and office buildings. They were worth finding because they had the professional positions with swanky titles. Why be a sales rep when you could be a Territory Manager? He soon discovered that it was considered bad form to show up without an appointment. Somehow they always happened to have someone available to see him, though. He took this as another sign that his luck was changing.

Modern Man had never been interviewed by a recruitment company before and didn't know how it all worked. It wasn't the same as talking to the person who actually had the job to offer you. Yet these people projected an air of superiority that he felt was rather misplaced. The agent took his CV and asked the usual questions to verify that there was at least a thread of truth in the document and that he had a reasonable idea what it contained.

When Modern Man queried this approach he was told in no uncertain terms that a significant number of applicants had not written nor even read the CVs they sent out. That guaranteed a short and pointless meeting with a few home truths thrown in for wasting his time. Modern Man shared his disdain for the ignorant plebs and they moved on with the interview. His technical qualifications and brief experience in direct sales led the recruitment guy to a swift conclusion. He said, 'I have the perfect job for you,' and with that he left the room.

Modern Man had heard about these unusual interview techniques where they throw unexpected scenarios at you. He half expected the guy to return dressed in martial arts gear and kick the crap out of him but thankfully that didn't happen. After about ten minutes he returned with an older and considerably fatter guy who explained that Modern Man had the perfect skills and experience to be a recruitment consultant. Modern Man was not ready for this twist at all and without thinking asked, 'What the hell would I want to do that for?'

The interview almost fell apart at that point. With patience and a little humility, the owner of the recruitment company explained that it was really a specialised form of technical sales on a number of levels. 'We sell our company services to engineering firms who want to recruit. These are small and medium sized companies that don't have the resources to handle hundreds of under-qualified and time wasting applicants. That brings in the vacancies.'

'We then find the candidates by advertising the positions and handle the responses. We carry out the preliminary interviews and forward a short list to the client company. The next stage is to convince the client to offer a position to the best candidates. Finally we sell the new job to the chosen candidate.'

'As you can see, it's a fairly complex set of steps and we think you have the qualities we are looking for.'

Modern Man had been schmoozed into two hideous sales jobs already that week and had no hesitation in telling this guy that he wasn't interested. After all he still had to figure out how to extricate himself from Timeshare Hell.

He was now certain in his own mind that if he was going to sell something for a living, it had to be something real that he could touch and demonstrate and become excited about. He was an engineer and engineers dealt with reality not airy-fairy conceptual intangibles. He wasn't about to sell his soul to an organisation that called a spade an earth inverting horticultural implement.

As he left their rather faux looking offices he realised that despite the fact that he had turned down a job, he actually felt better about himself. His self esteem was buoyed and he had a clearer idea of where he was heading.

The next agency he visited must have had the same decorators as the last one but thankfully, they were fully staffed and listened to what Modern Man wanted to do with his life. They had a number of vacancies and were fairly upbeat about his CV and his chances of securing one or two interviews in the next week or two. Modern Man was also encouraged to hear that being available immediately was a good thing because a pay cheque couldn't come too soon in his opinion.

Modern Man wandered back to his latest temporary abode; yet another couch residing in a dingy flat leased by a friend of a friend. There were no nightingales singing and it was a long way from Berkeley Square but even so, to find a tramp sleeping in your doorway was not what he expected. As Modern Man approached with caution the figure began to stir and then suddenly jumped up and grinned at him from behind a pathetic attempt at a beard. It took a moment to register but then the dishevelled individual spoke and that confirmed his identity. It was his old pal from first year in college, Jack-Six-Pack.

'How the hell did you find me?' was all Modern Man could manage to say in his state of shock and confusion.

'Not much of a welcome, that,' said Jack.

It didn't take a genius to work out that Jack was hoping to stay in the flat which he thought was Modern Man's place. Jack had come down on the train and was en route to the States to work on a kids' summer camp a couple of hours drive north of New York. He had a few days to kill before his flight and was looking for a good time with a budget of about £3 per day.

There were many terrible things said about the north by southerners but one thing they couldn't argue with was the cost of living. The idea that you could go to the pictures, get fish and chips and still have enough left out of £1 to get the bus home, hadn't been true since the early '70's but it was still much cheaper up north than in London.

After a few pints and a lot of talk, they hatched a plan that would work for both of them. Modern Man would sneak Jack into the flat. In return, Jack had to come up with a plan to release Modern Man from the grip of the Timeshare Bandits. After much more beer Jack had a Eureka moment.

'I have a foolproof plan. I'll be your replacement. You recruit me and I'll give bogus bank details. By the time they try to recoup the training fee, I'll be long gone. It'll work. I know it will.'

'You'll be alright. You're off to America. What if they come after me?'

'Come to the States too. Yeah! There's bound to be some sort of job you could do.'

Modern Man was up for it immediately. He had absolutely no doubt that it was a sensible career move. It would certainly broaden his horizons. Developing management skills could wait. Large quantities of beer can do that to a young mind.

Shortly after closing time they staggered back to the dingy flat, only to find they had been locked out. This wasn't good. In fact it was a disaster because Modern Man didn't have a key.

There was nothing else to do but head for the bright lights of the West End. In the other city that never sleeps, this was the best place to spend the night. It was lively and they had the stamina to survive a warm summer's night on the streets of London. They weren't going to be kicking their heels all night, not with the kind of entertainment that was happening in Leicester Square and around Soho.

By five in the morning the cafes were starting to open up for the early trade and they spent an hour planning how Modern Man could be recruited by the same camp as Jack in less than three days. Jack had the phone number and office address of the agency that had set up his job, so he called it from a payphone in the café. Not surprisingly the office wasn't occupied at six and it went to an answering machine. Jack left a message to say that he would be at the office at nine sharp and had found an excellent individual to work at the same camp.

It took almost the entire three hours to find the agency office and they didn't have to wait long for a harassed looking woman in her early thirties to arrive for work. Before she could hear Jack's message he launched into an ad hoc speech about how good this guy was and how the camp director was going to love him. In fact, he recommended that she phone him now, there was no time to lose, what with the flight only being a few days away.

One brief look into her eyes told anyone brave enough to risk it, that she wasn't a morning person. Patience was clearly a virtue that passed her by and her fuse was shorter than her spiky red hair.

'Shut up you jerk!' was her opening salvo and it went downhill from there. 'Don't you know anything at all? It's quarter past nine here, which means it's quarter past four in the morning on the East Coast. Do you really think David Goldstein is going to be pleased to hear from me, because I don't? Anyway, he has no more requirements for overseas staff this year.'

Another dream lay in tatters and Modern Man couldn't help but show his disappointment. She then rewound the answerphone messages and listened to them one by one in the back office. All Modern Man and Jack could hear through the closed door was her say, 'Shit, shit, shit.'

She came out with a mug of coffee a few minutes later and looked at Modern Man for the first time. She handed him a form to fill in and asked him what he had done with his life so far and how he came to know this idiot. Modern Man talked up his academic achievements and his work experience. Rather sarcastically she asked if he had any Nobel Prizes or Academy Awards. It appeared she was well used to outrageous exaggeration from almost every candidate she interviewed.

Modern Man didn't rise to the bait.

'Do you have a British passport? Are you really available immediately?'

'Yes to both,'

'Do you know where the American Embassy is?'

'Why, is that important?' he enquired, thinking this may be a general knowledge question.

'Because you need to be there in less than an hour to apply for a work visa. Some moron fell off his skateboard yesterday and broke his arm. That was one of the messages on the machine this morning. Clearly he can't teach rock climbing with a broken arm, so he can't go to Camp Redwood. You can though, if you get your act together. It's not the same camp your idiot friend's going to. Big bonus for you, in my opinion!'

At no point in the interview so far had she asked if he had any knowledge or experience of rock climbing. That was a good thing because he would have to admit that he had none and that may have derailed the whole project. Modern Man was curious whether she had forgotten to ask that elementary question or whether it didn't matter. Surely it must matter to someone, he mused. His internal dialogue fizzled out at that point because she was firing more instructions at him.

The gist of it was that Modern Man had a load of forms to fill in. She would fax his details over to the camp with an explanation about the reason for the change of applicant. Hopefully, Benny Weisman, the owner of Camp Redwood, would come back to her within an hour with approval. She knew Benny would be OK because she was giving him an easy solution to a problem that he didn't even know he had yet.

The problems Benny did know about came in the form of about three hundred over-privileged rich kids arriving in a fleet of yellow school buses from the swankiest addresses in the New York metropolitan area.

To Benny, one Limey rock climbing instructor was much like another. Having a few staff from Europe was seen as adding a certain something to the quality of the experience for the kids. Even though these kids came from wealthy families, very few of them had ever been outside the USA.

Modern Man filled in the forms. After he signed a contract of employment he was despatched to the American Embassy. Since he had been on the jobs trail the day before, he actually had his passport with him. This was a stroke of luck because without it he would not have been able to apply for the visa and that would have been the end of this rapidly unfolding opportunity.

As Jack had applied through the college he had been to several meetings and a presentation by someone who had spent the last ten years working on various camps. The guy was a high school teacher so he could spend the entire summer holidays in the States being paid by both the education authority in Britain and the camp. He was annoyingly smug about his 'decade of double bubble.'

Despite that, the guy had been quite entertaining about how to squeeze the most out of the experience. Particularly on the subject of seeing as much of the country as possible on a few dollars per day. The key seemed to be sucking up to parents who lived where you wanted to visit.

He advised that on parents' visiting day, they should chat to at least one family whose kid they liked and who lived in the Hamptons or had an apartment on Madison Avenue. 'The idea behind this is, if you run out of money they'll pick you up, wherever you are, and take you back to their mansion. They'll probably treat you like the aristocrat they believe you really are. With a bit of luck their chauffeur will even take you to the airport to catch your flight home to Blighty.'

The guy strongly emphasised that they would be doing the parents a favour. 'New Yorkers are a naturally generous and giving people. You gave them two months without their kids so they feel the need to repay you for this kindness,' he said.

The only real downside was that this type of work didn't pay very well and about 90% of what they would earn was deducted at source to pay for their flights. In return, accommodation was provided, along with all the food they could eat while on the site. They also had the opportunity to stay in the country for up to a month after camp finished. However, they had to decide before setting off when to return to home. It was a bit of a guess how long the money would last and most people overestimated their budgeting skills.

Jack gave Modern Man all this background information on the way to the American Embassy. The visa section was in the basement with a separate door. A queue had already formed even though they would not start processing applications for another hour. Jack hung around for about fifteen minutes then made his excuses and wandered off.

Standing on his own in a line that was not moving brought home to Modern Man exactly how tired he was. The only interesting things to look at were the other people in the queue and a few embassy staff who used an entrance nearby. Most of his fellow applicants were students, presumably there for the same reason he was. Beyond that, there were a few businessmen and a handful of over-optimistic guys from the Middle East.

Modern Man thanked his lucky stars that those guys were behind him in the queue because he expected their applications would take a bit longer to be dealt with than the average. Eventually the door was opened and a huge US Marine stood guarding the entrance. Everyone knew he was a Marine because his uniform shouted it out pretty loudly and his rifle with fixed bayonet reminded them all that access to the Land of the Free was not a foregone conclusion.

As the line shuffled forward ever so slowly, Modern Man had time to study this Marine. He stood to attention and didn't move anything except his eyeballs. His entire demeanour suggested that he took great pride in guarding a small but significant piece of American territory overseas. It also implied a very tight specification when selecting people to be allowed to do that particular job. A sense of humour was clearly superfluous. As Modern Man failed on all those criteria, he mentally scratched that from his list of possible careers.

When Modern Man's turn came, his documents were examined and his application scrutinised. No doubt his background was also being checked on any number of databases of undesirable aliens. As he had no criminal record and not so much as a parking ticket against his name, the application was approved. Modern Man's passport was given a full page stamp showing he was entitled to enter and work in the United States for up to twelve months from the date of issue.

Proud and somewhat relieved, he returned to the agency office to check what progress had been made. The woman was less stressed than before and seemed to be on top of things. Modern Man suspected the affects of cigarettes and coffee had a lot to do with this change of state.

She had a reply from Benny Weisman at Camp Redwood which loosely translated as, 'Yeah, whatever, send the new guy.'

'When do I fly out?' Modern Man asked.

'Oh, right, Sunday. I think. Let me check. Yep, seventeen forty-five from Gatwick to JFK. Any problem with that? You are available immediately, aren't you?

Modern Man was a little stunned by the immediacy of it all but acknowledged that he had no business or social engagements in the near future.

'Are you OK with returning on September sixth? That's when the other guy was going to come back and it would make it simpler if you could manage that.'

Modern Man felt obliged to keep things as straight forward as he could for her. After all she had provided him with two months work and three weeks holiday in the USA in the space of half a morning.

'Sure, whatever,' he mumbled.

The woman clearly appreciated his flexibility and sent him off to the airline booking office with the change request forms, the original ticket and receipt. As he waited to be served he noticed that the return flight wasn't landing at Gatwick, it was flying into to Manchester. That was alright but he didn't want to be back living with his parents again.

Shortly after lunchtime he had a plane ticket to New York and a contract of employment. The downside was he had less than £5 in change in his pocket. On the upside, he was going to have a holiday in America!

He diverted to a branch of his bank and first asked, then demanded and finally begged for an extension to his overdraft in order to withdraw some money from the cash machine.

Since he could produce a contract of employment that stated he would earn $1,500 he was granted additional funds. Thankfully, the contract didn't state quite so clearly that $1,200 of that would be withheld to pay for his travel.

There was only one nagging problem left to sort out and he had a plan for that.

Modern Man managed to gain access to the flat that evening. Within a couple of hours, he and Jack fell asleep in the dingy living room, part way through a conversation that was going nowhere, anyway. In the cold light of the following morning, Modern Man reviewed his clothing options and picked out a combination of trousers, shirt and tie that would make Jack smart enough for the timeshare recruitment event. On impulse, he put the rest of his meagre wardrobe in a bin liner and left it outside the back door by the bins. All Modern Man had left were the clothes he stood up in. He thought he was being decisive. Making a clean break and starting a new phase of his life. Was it the right thing to do? Only time would tell.

At the presentation Jack managed to find a seat fairly near the front. So far, so good. When it came to the sign up, Modern Man was nowhere to be seen. Where the Hell was he?

Jack was faced with a desperate middle-aged chap who wouldn't take no for an answer. He followed his part of the plan and gave false details. He realised that Modern Man would then have to actually recruit someone for real, but hey, that was his problem.

Modern Man was assigned to a young guy at the back of the room. He didn't want to stitch up the lad but he had to get out, so he quietly told the new guy it was a scam.

'Don't give your real name and bank details,' Modern Man said under his breath.

The new guy was sceptical but caught on eventually and signed with an unintelligible squiggle. Modern Man's parting advice was, 'It's a dog eat dog world, pal. Now run for your life.'

After that little melodrama he was good to go and had to be because he still needed to be at Gatwick Airport the following afternoon. He and Jack parted company, for the duration of the summer, at least. They were working on different camps and it really wouldn't be practical to try to meet up in the States.

At this point he thought he ought to call his parents and let them know what was happening. He hoped they'd be pleased he had a job lined up and be excited for him about his adventure. He also knew they'd find something to worry about. They had a solid track record of pointless angst that he truly hoped wasn't lying dormant in his genes, should he ever have kids of his own.

4. Visiting Uncle Sam

As he waited to check in for the flight, there was something about him that was different to every other passenger. He was the only one without any luggage. Not even a carry-on bag. Most people were too wrapped up in their own little worlds to notice his lack of baggage but to the airport security staff this was a great big red flag. He might as well have had a machine gun under his arm as far as they were concerned.

With quiet confidence, two smartly dressed gentlemen appeared, one on each side of Modern Man. The one to his right quietly asked, 'May we have a word with you in private?' They were so polite that Modern Man found himself obliging before he knew what he was saying. After thirty minutes of firm but not overly aggressive questioning, a search of his clothes and an intimate examination of his previously private places, they were satisfied that he was what he said he was.

It was an experience that would forever haunt Modern Man. The memory of being probed by a man wearing a boiler suit and rubber gloves would stay with him to his dying day. There was a moment during the interrogation when he felt that it might actually be very soon, but it passed and he regained his composure.

With only a few minutes left before boarding the aircraft, Modern Man changed some of his precious £20 notes into US dollar bills and headed for the departure gate. The 'plane was the biggest he had ever been on. Not that he had much prior experience of air travel. He'd been on a BEA Viscount from Manchester to Jersey and a Dan Air Comet to Oslo on family holidays in days of yore, and that was the sum total of his flying experience.

This aircraft was massive by comparison to those older jets. Two aisles, ten seats across and what looked like more passengers in the departure lounge than it could possibly hold. He had an aisle seat on the left hand side of the cabin. This was both good and bad. Good, that he could get out and stretch his legs if he wanted to and bad that he had to get out of his seat when either of the other two people wanted to escape for a while.

He had never previously heard of the airline he was travelling with but that didn't bother him. He understood why when a stewardess started making announcements over the public address system. The accent was unmistakably American and having watched countless episodes of *Kojak* on TV, he reckoned she was a New Yorker. The adventure was properly underway now, it was real.

Once they were airborne and the fasten seat belts sign was switched off, things started to happen. A bar trolley appeared in the aisle and was pushed straight past him. It seemed to take forever to make its way back to his row, by which time he was desperate for a drink.

He'd been told that alcohol was about twice as potent on a plane, apparently it was something to do with the reduced air pressure. Whilst it was intended as a warning, he chose to interpret it as a cheap way to get drunk. Then the stewardess told him how much a can of beer cost and he decided that a free orange juice was probably a healthier option under the circumstances.

He received the standard professional smile from her, which he interpreted as, 'She fancies me.' Was it the coiffed hair in a French Roll or the uniform? No, it was the whole damned package and he had another six hours to do something about it.

She would be busy for a couple of hours with the meal service and all the other things she'd have to do. Maybe during the duty free sales he could catch her eye and subtly hint that he'd like to spend some quality time alone with her. Deep inside his brain connections were being made. His optimistic hopes were being intricately twisted into a three dimensional fantasy in wide-screen and full colour.

What a powerful tool the human brain is, when put to good use, he thought to himself. It was a brief thought that he briefly managed to squeeze in during a smoking break between the fourth and fifth imagined sex sessions with her. They were in a suite at the Park Plaza; deep red satin sheets and a magnum of champagne in the ice bucket. He had a huge Cuban cigar and she drew deeply on a Lucky Strike. This was odd because he didn't fancy smokers. She was smokin'!

When he returned to the real world the stewardess was holding a bag of nuts to go with his drink. He would have taken it from her but he was holding a bag of nuts too. In what he thought was a cool movement he reached for the nuts but knocked his tray table. The plastic beaker of orange juice tottered and an embarrassing disaster seemed inevitable. Deft hands from the stewardess settled the juice and placed the nuts on the table. A quick wink and she floated off to the next row.

Modern Man hadn't really paid much attention to the other two people in his row. Aircraft seats being the way they are, it's almost impossible to get a good look at the people sitting alongside you without it being rather apparent that you are staring at them. Next to him was a well-built guy with dark curly hair and uncommonly small ears. Modern man introduced himself and they shook hands, the way the British do, although it turned out to be a rather clumsy gesture in such a confined space.

'Which camp are you going to?' the guy asked.

'Redwood,' said Modern Man, somewhat relieved that he could remember. 'How about you?'

'Sioux Springs, to coach basketball,' he replied.

Modern Man was not tall, in fact, although he would never admit it, he may even have suspected he was below average height, and yet he was looking this chap in the eye. At least he had been. He found himself unwittingly scanning down this bloke's chest all the way to his legs that disappeared somewhere under the seat in front of him. The guy clocked what Modern Man was doing and said rather smugly, 'I'm six foot seven. People always ask.'

'I bet you're not comfortable though, are you?' Modern Man responded without thinking through the implications.

There was a girl in the window seat who was almost totally obscured by the guy between them. They both leaned forward to introduce themselves and Modern Man felt an immediate connection. He was sure he saw something in her eyes that mirrored what he was thinking. She was good looking with a nice smile and, from what he could see of her, looked slim and about his height.

He suggested to the basketball giant that they swap seats, half hoping that the next time the trolley rolled by it would sever his legs at knee level. 'Not so smug now are you stumpy?' played out as an internal monologue.

It should be a simple process to switch seats with the person next to you. In the space available and with about a hundred spectators and all the stuff that people bring with them 'just in case,' it is not straightforward. The innocent non-mover was almost certain to get a bum in their face at some point.

Luckily for Modern Man she got unnaturally close to the basketball player's rear and wasn't impressed. Athletic he may be but the owner of the source of all sunlight: apparently not.

Modern Man decided it was time to be cool and take it slow. He hadn't forgotten the stewardess but he had to admit to himself that his chances there were limited. He focussed all his attention on his new neighbour and tried to think of something sophisticated to say.

To his surprise she started the conversation. 'Did you say you're going to Camp Redwood?'

'That's right. I am'

'As in Camp Redwood, about two hours north of New York, in the Catskill Mountains?'

'I think so. To be honest, I'd never heard of the place until a few days ago. I was looking for work in London, so I'm a bit vague on details at the moment.' Modern Man thought that sounded pathetic and wished he hadn't said it.

'That's where I'm going. What will you be teaching? I'm Sylvia by the way.'

Modern Man introduced himself then answered, 'Rock climbing.' It was becoming more convincing every time he said it. He was even beginning to believe it himself. 'How about you?'

'Oh, music and drama. I was also there last year. I produced and directed a show for each age group and they performed it to the whole camp. It was fun but hard work. I expect it'll be the same again this summer,' Sylvia said.

They chatted away for an hour or so about the camp and what to expect. She told him what the kids were like, the food and the bunks. She tried to explain the character of the boss guy, Benny. After that the conversation was all about the two of them. Where they had been at university and what course they had done, and so on.

There was absolutely no crossing of paths in their earlier lives. Sylvia was from Bicester in Oxfordshire. She studied at Bristol University where she was awarded an upper second class degree in Music. She then went on to complete a Post Graduate Certificate of Education before becoming a primary school teacher in Clifton. Modern Man had never been to Oxfordshire but knew something about Clifton because it featured heavily in engineering folklore. Brunel's Great Western Railway, Clifton Suspension Bridge and all that stuff was in his memory somewhere. After a year in teaching the gloss had started to wear off and the ever-increasing testing rather than teaching was all that the other staff talked about. Modern Man was no psychologist but he could tell she wasn't destined to spend her entire career in the classroom.

Sylvia had very little knowledge of the north of England but neither did she have the typical southerner's attitude that civilisation petered out around Northampton. She was a good listener and said she liked his accent. She tried to copy it but it didn't come out right.

Sylvia asked him why all northern pronunciation had such flattened vowels. 'That's because we have been dropping our aitches on them for generations,' he said without knowing where that idea had come from but committing it to memory so he could use it again. It made her laugh and that made it priceless. God, she was gorgeous.

Time, quite literally in this case, flew by and before long they were on approach to JFK airport in New York. They flew over Manhattan and close enough to see the Statue of Liberty. He really was in America. Modern Man had gone intercontinental.

Proceeding through immigration took quite a while. Everyone who was going to a summer camp had to show their contract as well as their passport. Their visas were scrutinised along with landing cards and customs' declarations. Some passengers hadn't bothered to complete the forms fully and everyone was delayed as a result.

Others were simply dopey and didn't seem to know where they were going or what they were going to do if they ever got there.

Modern Man was acutely aware that his contract was a poor quality photocopy. Worse than that, his name had been typed over a film of correction fluid that was starting to flake off. Was his summer about to end in a holding tank at Kennedy Airport? Despite the air conditioning he was beginning to sweat.

When he arrived at the yellow line that defines the point of entry to the USA, he waited until called forward. It seemed to be a Federal Offence to put even a toe over the yellow line until advised to do so, such was the ferocity with which people were told to stay behind it.

The Immigration official was a female African American approximately five feet tall and three feet wide. Hair scraped back into a clasp and an expression that did not invite diet and lifestyle advice; well-meaning or otherwise. She checked the big book of undesirables on her desk and found that he wasn't in it. She then glanced at his contract and checked that his passport and visa were valid. In a single movement she returned his paperwork and gave him a dismissive and slightly hostile signal that he was duly processed.

He met up with Sylvia again in the baggage reclaim hall. She was rather surprised that he didn't have any luggage to collect and they walked through the green channel together. Modern Man didn't make it out to the other side. As Sylvia wasn't a relative she wasn't allowed to stay with him while he tried to explain the unlikely circumstances that had led to his travelling light.

She knew he would have a difficult time and also that he had no idea how to get to Camp Redwood. They had found three other staff members on their flight who were also working for Benny Weisman that summer and she needed to look after them too.

The original plan was to make their way to the Port Authority Bus Terminal in Manhattan and catch a bus upstate that evening. As Modern Man was being escorted away to an interview room, she shouted to him not to leave the airport. She would call Benny and come back for him once she'd seen the others onto a bus.

In the circumstances Modern Man couldn't see how leaving the airport was a possibility. His case wasn't helped when the US authorities phoned the camp. They were unable to speak to Benny because he wasn't there and when the administrator, who took their call, checked the list of foreign staff, Modern Man's name wasn't on it. She gave the caller the name of the rock climbing instructor the camp had been expecting.

It was too late in the day to phone the agent in London so they left him locked in the interview room while they decided what to do. His passport and visa checked out. His contract was suspect, no luggage and not much money. He was on the verge of being an undesirable alien and probably guilty of something. There was nothing specific but he wasn't kosher, that was for sure.

After what seemed like a lifetime the door was unlocked and he was told he was free to go. No explanation was given and he was shown out into the arrivals hall as though he had arrived only a few minutes ago. Sylvia was there waiting for him. They hugged spontaneously before realising how brief their acquaintance had been. The subsequent release was a little awkward. She looked exhausted but relieved to see him. Sylvia explained that she had managed to speak to Benny on the phone and he had made some calls. Apparently he knew 'people' the way they do on TV and in films.

The two of them caught a regular bus into Manhattan and walked a few blocks to the Port Authority Bus Terminal. They bought coffee and carried on swapping life stories. There was time to kill before catching the bus upstate.

Sylvia remembered there was a huge Woolworth's store a few blocks away. She decided this was a good opportunity to buy some of the essentials that Modern Man had managed without for the last forty-eight hours. Sylvia didn't feel as though she knew him well enough to tell him how desperately he needed to brush his teeth and change his clothes but she hoped that she would, in time.

The shop was nothing like the Woolworth's he was used to back home and initially he didn't see the point of going in. He had no need for stationery, sweets or a Dire Straits CD. Surprisingly, this one had everything, not literally of course, that would be impossible. It had underwear and T-shirts, sportswear and trainers.

Sylvia helped him pick out enough essentials to suffice for eight days. She explained that he would be set up for the next two months as laundry day was only collected once a week at camp.

Having sorted out a few things to wear and a bag to carry them in, she skilfully steered him down the personal hygiene aisle and didn't wait for him to register his new surroundings. She selected toiletries that she identified as suitably masculine and an aftershave she wanted him to wear, simply because she fancied the guy in the TV advert. Modern man took the hint with good grace and they headed for the checkout.

They made it back to the bus station in time and settled in for a late night ride upstate. As it was a few minutes after three in the morning by their body clocks but five past ten local, they were asleep in no time.

Modern Man woke up as the bus trundled into Middletown. He had no idea where he was or how he got there. The fact that there was a beautiful girl asleep with her head on his shoulder convinced him it was a dream and he would wake up in the damp and dingy flat in London.

With that thought floating in his tired brain, he put a silly grin on his face and tried to force the dream in a very specific direction. It didn't work and Sylvia woke with a start as the bus driver switched off the engine. Looking around she announced, 'Come on. We have to get off here. Redwood is about five miles from here. We'll get a taxi.'

It took them another half hour to find a cab with a driver who was prepared to venture out of town at that time of night. Modern Man couldn't imagine how the taxi driver thought his appearance looked threatening but since he hadn't shaved or changed his clothes in two days he had to accept that being referred to as a 'bum' was not unreasonable. It needed to be explained to Modern Man that, in New York lingo, that term didn't have anything to do with a part of his anatomy. After a little negotiation they agreed to pay up front for the journey and show the driver they had no fire arms or other weapons about their person or in their luggage. Sylvia also took a couple of minutes to phone the camp and let Benny know they would be there pretty soon.

Incredible relief washed over them as they trundled down the last stretch of dirt road and into the small parking lot by the administration building. Modern Man could make out the roof lines of huts, large and small. The place was like a village made out of log cabins. There was also a large house on the opposite side of the road and a huge bear of a man standing on the porch. This was Benny Weisman. He was probably about 6'5" tall, weighed about 230lbs and looked about fifty years old. As he enveloped Sylvia in an all-embracing hug she reciprocated as best she could.

Once Benny had released her he held out a hand and Modern Man shook it and introduced himself in a fairly formal way.

'You British kill me with your manners already. Everyone calls me Benny, so no more 'Mr. Weisman' okay? Camp Redwood tradition dictates that I give everyone a new name within ten minutes of arriving and that name stays with them forever. Yours is, wait a minute, 'Gundog,' because you brought my English Rose back to me.'

Modern Man wasn't sure he liked the idea of being called Gundog by everyone from six year old first time campers through to whiney teenage seniors. Sylvia gave him a look that said 'go with it' so he joined in the group hug and yapped a couple of times then howled at the moon. In his head he was thinking, 'What have I done? This is the boss and he's got a mental age of nine.'

Benny eventually released Sylvia and looked them both in the eye. 'Okay, here's the deal. The kids arrive in two days.' After a quick check of his watch he continued, 'Correction, tomorrow. Between now and then there's a lot to do to get the place ready. Get some sleep; reveille is oh-seven-hundred, breakfast at oh-seven-thirty, staff meeting at oh-eight-hundred. We'll figure out bunk allocations, work duties and go over the rules and regulations then. Gundog, you're in the Staff House tonight. Rose, you can have the guest room in my house.'

Modern Man couldn't believe the degree of jealousy that washed over him and only hoped he didn't show it. As Sylvia turned to pick up her baggage, Benny gave Modern Man a look that told him more than he wanted to know. If the taxi had still been there he would probably have climbed in and left.

The Staff House was one of the bigger huts and had twelve sets of bunk beds in each of two rooms, either side of a central lobby, with a common room behind it. The guys were in the room on the left and the girls on the right. Modern Man found a vacant bed and dumped his gear in a locker. His senses were invaded with the inevitable sights, sounds and smells of about twenty men fast asleep. Then he crashed out, exhausted and added a few contributions to the overall dorm room ambience himself.

He'd never, even for a minute, considered joining the armed forces but this felt like boot camp and when he heard the sound of a bugle it was confirmed. As people around him stirred and groaned he heard them suggest that Benny should attempt things that were certainly inadvisable and probably not physically possible. Suddenly his spirits were lifted and the day seemed brighter.

When the blinds on the windows were rolled up someone noticed him. 'Hey, there's a new guy. What's your name new guy?'

Modern Man introduced himself but they weren't having any of it.

'Nah, what did Benny call you? What's your Camp Redwood name?'

Modern Man shared his new sobriquet with them and waited for the laughter.

'Not bad. I'm Boo-Boo,' said a small round chap with a large mouth and easy smile.

As he was introduced to the others he realised he'd got off lightly and started to wonder what made Benny Weisman tick. Was he a big kid or was it more sinister than that? On the way to the breakfast hut Freddie, Shaggy and Scooby brought him up to speed on a few things that would never make it into Camp Redwood's marketing brochure.

Breakfast was not what he expected. What in the name of all that is holy were they doing serving over-cooked bacon with pancakes and maple syrup? Come to think of it, what was a guy called Weisman doing serving bacon at all? The look of horror and surprise was enough to illicit an answer from his cartoon coterie of fellow diners.

'It's beef bacon, that's why it's darker. Not everyone here is strictly kosher. In fact not everyone here is Jewish. Most of the kids are, and the staff members who were campers when they were younger but it's not a secret Mossad training venue if that's what you're thinking.'

Benny made a grand entrance and the room fell silent. He announced that the counsellor meeting would be in ten minutes. He told them to finish up and be ready to start work. There would be a lot to cover before the kids arrived the next day.

Modern Man was, once again, caught unawares. He didn't know whether he was a counsellor or not. He had lent numerous friends a shoulder to cry on and a sympathetic ear when they had been dumped out of a relationship but he had no formal training in the psychology of trauma recovery.

Shaggy picked up on his quizzical expression and said, 'That's you dude. You're a counsellor, man.'

Modern Man thanked him for the heads up on his generic job title.

The meeting was held in the auditorium; a grand name for a natural hollow in the side of a small hill. It had been flattened at the bottom and narrow terraces formed into benches. It was the only place big enough to hold all the kids and counsellors at once. The meeting was really an advertisement riddled with self-promotion and examination. One giant plug for the camp. About three quarters of the staff had worked there in previous summers and of those, more than half were former campers. Almost all were university students and maybe fifteen of the hundred or so were from Europe. They were mainly Brits but a couple from Israel and a German.

Modern Man glanced around looking for a familiar face but all he saw was a sea of perfect teeth smiling back at him. For one awful moment he thought he had been kidnapped by the extremist wing of the Donny Osmond fan club. In fact it was another mental adjustment he had to make; shifting 'good dentistry' from the rare to the normal column.

Modern Man was starting to understand the differences in the use of English in the States. The word 'please' was rarely used in New York and 'sir' could be inflected to show absolutely no respect at all. That had certainly been his experience at the airport. Why did bad things happen to good languages he wondered?

Benny called for attention, welcomed returning counsellors and had each new person stand up to introduce themselves. Not with their real name of course, that would be normal, oh no, they had to tell everyone what Benny had called them. There were the identical twin girls who were to be known as Pixie and Dixie. They were going to teach dancing. The odd looking guy, who was probably about forty and apparently an ex-cop from the Bronx, was the new security guard. Inevitably he was labelled Officer Dibble.

Modern Man got to his feet, announced himself as Gundog and told everyone he was part of the Nature Group. This solicited a low groan from the crowd followed by half-hearted applause. Benny then talked up Modern Man's experience to a level that totally mystified him. He had never been part of a search and rescue team in the Yorkshire Dales National Park. Neither had he climbed Mont Blanc nor canoed the treacherous white water of the River Dee in Wales. Even so, he was receiving a lot of appreciative nods and glances for these accolades.

Not wishing to rock the boat or cause a problem, he decided it was best to go along with it for now. After all, there were some good looking girls here who might be sufficiently impressed and gullible enough to…. No, wait a minute, what about Sylvia? She knew he hadn't done any of those things.

Modern Man was too wrapped up in his turmoil to pay attention to the rest of the introductions. If he had he would have realised that he wasn't being singled out for special treatment. All the new foreign staff members were being bigged up in the same implausible way.

He would learn later that it was called a 'Benny Boost' and was part of the chemistry of this weird guy who ran the place. Apparently, in his head, it meant that he owned a bit of you. Having put you up there at the beginning, he could drag you down at any time of his choosing and humiliate you to maximum effect. It might work with the younger kids but none of the staff bought it.

'Bunk allocations,' Benny announced. This was the decision that could make or break the whole summer. The camp was split into boys' side, girls' side and staff house. The kids ranged in age from six to sixteen and were bunked by age with two staff members per cabin with a maximum of fourteen kids in each cabin.

There were advantages and disadvantages with most age groups. Since none of the staff were parents themselves, they had no idea what they were letting themselves in for the first time. The youngest campers needed a maid/valet and occasionally suffered homesickness and/or bed wetting. On the upside they could be relied upon to be asleep fairly early. This left a reasonable amount of time for socialising.

The middle age groups were quite cheeky and arrogant. Occasionally, disobedient too. They lacked courage in a one-to-one confrontation and were incredibly accident-prone in those circumstances. By the time they reached their mid teens they were a bundle of raging hormonal volatility. One minute 'King of the Hill' and the next they were in agony about acne. The demands to be cool and respected were too much for some of them and surfaced as public aggression and private depression. As almost all of them came from incredibly wealthy backgrounds, their only frames of reference were money and power.

After the big speech Benny split the staff into small groups. He gave each team a worksheet to talk through. They were instructed to put a short presentation together and deliver it to the others. It was supposed to be about the psychology of play and developing social skills, for the kids. For the staff it was an opportunity to bond as a group. For Benny it was a chance to identify the natural leaders and followers he had hired.

Modern Man did his best to keep a low profile but there was a moment when someone made such a lame statement that he couldn't stop himself from pointing out the blatant short-comings of their argument. This intervention earned him the privilege of presenting their collective thoughts to the assembled masses. As a result he felt duty-bound to pay attention to what everyone else had to say.

When the time came Modern Man found it surprisingly easy to stand up in front of his peers and talk off-the-cuff. It helped that all the female staff loved his English accent and he did appear to have some talent for public speaking. He spoke for just a minute without hesitation, deviation or repetition but with a tiny amount of sarcasm. He couldn't stop himself.

Benny wanted to speak to all the new foreign staff at the end of the meeting. He assigned maintenance duties to the Americans to keep them busy for the next few hours and out of his way. He started off by welcoming everyone and explaining some of the key differences in language and culture.

His favourite phrase to the Brits was, 'You may have invented the English language but we kinda improved on it. If ya know what oi'm sayin'?'

They all knew it was his favourite phrase because he frequently repeated it in one form or another. The guys who had been there before said afterwards that it was word-for-word identical to the previous year.

Modern Man decided this was the time to 'fess up about his rock climbing skills, or lack thereof. Benny couldn't have cared less.

'OK, so we don't do rock climbing this year. Most of the kids hate it anyways and I only make 'em do it if they've pissed me off. I got other stuff they can do in that situation. Can you walk?'

Modern Man was a bit taken aback by this question but said, 'Yeah, I can walk.'

'Great, you can do hiking trips in the mountains. Every kid does an overnight at some point during the summer. The older kids do a three day trip. They bitch about it before they go, all the way through it and for at least a week afterwards. They say they hate it but it's one of the highlights of their summer. Come on, I'll introduce you to our own version of Grizzly Adams.'

Benny led Modern Man to a log cabin standing alone at the edge of the woods. He didn't knock on the door, he strolled right in and yelled, 'Hey Grizzly. Got a Limey for ya. Meet Gundog.'

The person that stepped into the room from somewhere out back looked as if they could have effortlessly slipped into ZZ Top. She had the approximate dimensions of Dolly Parton and could have been any age between about thirty and sixty. Her skin was creased like leather, hair wild and unkempt and she had a voice like Ethel Merman.

'This here is Shawnee,' said Benny, 'but everyone calls her Grizzly. She's head of the Nature Group that you've become the newest member of.'

Modern Man didn't know whether to shake hands, say 'How!' or simply nod. In the end he settled for a vacant expression and what he hoped was non-threatening body language. She looked like she probably ate small trees right out of the ground.

Benny left them to become acquainted and she talked him through the program of short, medium and long hikes along the marked trails in the Catskill Mountains. The camp also had an assault course in the woods as part of the outdoors program. The Nature Group held barbecues for the whole camp every Friday night on the lake field. Modern Man thought he could handle the job reasonably well and was feeling comfortable with the surroundings.

Grizzly then asked him, 'Do you want to shoot hoops with me now?'

He had heard that recreational drug taking was very common and more accessible than alcohol for anyone under twenty-one years old but he was stunned that it was offered as openly as that.

'I er, I don't know. What does it involve?' he managed to steer his tongue around while his brain went into over-drive. He tried to consider the possible ramifications firstly of popping pills and secondly of being caught.

'Come on out the back and I'll show you. I need to fetch something from my bedroom first.'

At this juncture Modern Man realised he had totally misunderstood what shooting hoops meant. He didn't find her at all attractive but she was his immediate boss and it was his first day so he supposed he could go through with it if necessary. He'd certainly never done it outdoors before. That would be breaking new ground.

When Grizzly returned with her hair tied back she led him through the back of her shack and down a path into the woods. Modern Man certainly wasn't going to make the first move, he would follow her lead.

After a couple of minutes they reached a clearing containing two full sized basketball courts. There were a few staff avoiding work duties and Grizzly made a big deal out of introducing him to the rest of the Nature Group team. Modern Man was so relieved that shooting hoops was a colloquialism for an informal game of basketball that he let out the loudest fart of his life.

In polite circles everyone would have totally ignored such an indelicate bodily function from a visitor but this was a group of students. 'Man, you'd better check you didn't follow through on that one. There're trees down behind you. My name's Dave but everyone calls me Crockett. Good to meet you.'

The fart was a tremendous ice breaker and the rest of the group introduced themselves in a more conventional manner when the moment had passed. All the others seemed to know each other pretty well and he soon discovered that they had all worked together the previous summer. There were a couple of girls called Shelley and Bobbi and three lads, Crockett, Mikey and Eric.

'What crazy name did Benny give you?' Mikey asked.

'Oh, Gundog. What's that in aid of?'

'Excuse me?'

'What's it for? Why does he do that?'

'It's just his way of putting one over on you. He's a control freak. Rumour has it, the entire camp ground is bugged and he has a load of radio gear in his basement.'

Modern Man immediately thought of Sylvia and wondered if Benny had had her in his basement last night. He desperately hoped not. She was far too good for Benny but she may have been powerless. After all, only a few minutes ago Modern Man thought he was going to have to get down and dirty with Grizzly. Thank God that was a misunderstanding. He'd have done it, of course, but even so...

Shifting mental gears Modern Man asked the group what zany names they had been given. Shelley was Penelope Pitstop from *Wacky Races*, Mikey was Mr Peavley from the *Hair Bear Bunch*, Bobbi was Joni from *Happy Days* and Eric was Batman. Dave used to be Robin but Crockett was a much better fit. However, Modern Man was immediately suspicious that Batman and Robin may have a history. If they did he decided he didn't want to know.

Grizzly had told Modern Man that the Nature Group was considered fairly low on the food chain of camp staff hierarchy and they kept to themselves a lot of the time. Her back porch was their unofficial hang out and totally contrary to camp rules. There was always beer in her fridge for which they all chipped in $10 each week.

'I've been here the last ten years and Benny knows it works best if he leaves me to organise all the comings and goings. No kid has ever been lost or badly hurt so we stick with the same trails year after year and everyone's happy.

'Some of these kids are so pampered, this is the farthest they have ever walked without shopping bags. At home most of them have their own maid. Their parents don't give them a lot of attention and by the time they're teenagers they may be on their third 'mom'. Almost all of them are good kids but they have no idea what the outside world is really like. Whatever you may think, it's not your job to tell them. They'll never have to experience it so they don't need to know. Got that?'

Modern Man was a little taken aback by the forcefulness of Grizzly's speech. She was practically yelling in his face by the end of it and her body language was totally offensive. Then she smiled, gave him a cold beer from the fridge and asked him about his background. She wanted to know about his childhood and what it was like growing up in little old England. He obligingly told her about his upbringing. When she'd heard enough she showed him the shortcut back through the woods to the Staff House.

His bunk mate in the Staff House turned out to be Dieter the German footballer. His English was perfect, albeit heavily accented. For the first few hours all Modern Man could think about was that episode of *Fawlty Towers*. It was hard for Modern Man not 'to mention ze vor'.

Dieter was from Munich and had played for Bayern's youth team before progressing to the university to study sports science. He was very proud of his home city and talked at great length about the Olympic Games held there in 1972. He boasted how the university was right next to the main stadium and rapidly becoming the leading centre for sports science in West Germany.

Without taking a breath he segued into the might of the national football team and their magnificent world cup win in Munich in '74. There was the pace of Beckenbauer and the power of Breitner. Not forgetting the record-breaking striker, Gerd Müller and the safe hands of Sepp Maier in goals.

Modern Man felt the need to retaliate, chipping in with, 'Yeah, but we still beat you in '66.'

The fact that he had no first-hand knowledge of the event was immaterial. He was English and his team had won. Dieter held up his hands in mock surrender, acknowledging that his enthusiasm for his sport may have been too much, too soon.

The following day a fleet of yellow school buses rolled up the road and stopped at the main gate of Camp Redwood. When the doors opened dozens of screaming kids flew out and ran around for at least half an hour. Even outside the noise was incredible and unrelenting. They had only been travelling for about two hours, having been picked up at various points in New York City then north on Highway 17.

Modern Man was sitting on Grizzly's porch when the announcement summoned everyone who bunked in the Staff House to report to the parking lot. When he arrived, he was amazed to see a mountain of trunks of the kind people used to take on steam ships in years gone by. There were hundreds of them. Three-hundred to be precise.

One trunk for each camper and they all had to be delivered to the right cabin as quickly as possible. There was a dodgy looking pick-up truck and a few hand carts to help them but muscle power was the order of the day. It was a daunting task and Modern Man broke the ice by asking if the kids tipped well. Apparently not.

In every cabin there were nails being hammered into the walls to enable the display of sports souvenirs for New York's Major League teams and a few mementos of home.

The language of American sports was yet another whole new learning experience for the first-time counsellors from outside the US. Most startling for the Brits was that the US version of football was a girls' game. Modern Man could instantly draw parallels with some of the overpaid drama queens seeping into the English First Division. He was, and always had been, more interested in rugby than 'sacker' as he was encouraged to call it.

A hooter sounded across the camp ground and, like iron filings to a magnet, there was a rush towards the dining hall. Officially, there were two sittings for every meal. Unofficially, it was a scramble of first come first served and Modern Man became an expert scrambler in no time. He could easily beat the fattest kids for speed. On the rare occasion when he was unable to make the first sitting by legitimate means, he cunningly used the phrase, 'Excuse me, old chap, I think you're in my seat.' That only worked on those counsellors who had a positive response to manners.

'Beat it, Nature Boy,' was the alternative response, instigating a tactical withdrawal by Modern Man. After a while he figured out that verbal aggression was rarely followed up and almost never sincere. New Yorkers were a truly interesting species to interact with.

For the first couple of weeks Modern Man worked the assault course in the woods with Mikey and Shelly. It needed three of them to work together as there were safety ropes on everything. Order had to be maintained and a safety harness had to be worn by all participants. The ethos appeared to be that the kids wanted to have fun and a bit of danger to make it exciting. Not enough danger was lame and sucky, too much danger was grounds to sue. It was a fine line some days and the threats of legal action ebbed and flowed.

Modern Man never topped the leader board on Grizzly's back porch though. Eric specialised in reckless endangerment of minors and didn't feel he had done his job properly unless at least one camper wet themselves each day. Most of the kids toughed it out but a brave minority swallowed their embarrassment and bitched to Benny. He would raise it with Grizzly and she would smooth things over.

Modern Man's first overnight hike was with two cabins of freshman girls. They used the school and college naming convention for age groups in camp. There were freshmen, sophomores, inters, juniors and seniors. Freshmen were six or seven years old by the look of them. They were totally wrapped up in who was their current best friend, what was cool and what sucked.

He and fellow Nature Group Counsellor, Bobbi, were to take the girls and their bunk counsellors on a walk through the woods, pointing out anything "interesting." The kids were up for it to start with. Then they were told they had to carry their own sleeping bags and anything else they wanted to take with them. To some, this was an entirely new experience and over-packing was rife.

Bobbi led the way from their cabin door down a path into the trees and Modern Man brought up the rear. The pace was pretty slow and the requests to stop for a rest started about five minutes in. After a quarter of an hour the girls were fully unionised. A shop steward had been elected and industrial action was imminent. They knew the problems this caused as most of their fathers' were employers.

Bobbi had seen and heard it all before. She was totally unfazed by their talk and carried on walking. On the agreed signal, all the girls sat down and refused to take another step. Their bunk counsellors tried positive methods first; encouraging and motivating then cajoling and finally threatening.

Bobbi called for quiet and announced that under the Ninety-Third Amendment of the Constitution of the United States of America the girls were perfectly within their rights to refuse to continue with this non-elective activity. However, they should also be aware that she, Modern Man and their bunk counsellors were also entitled to keep going and headed off down the path.

Modern Man had no idea how many constitutional amendments had been enacted but doubted that the fickle needs of small children was specified in such detail. He ushered the bunk counsellors together and gently but firmly nudged them along the same path that Bobbi had taken. Within a few minutes they were out of sight.

The resolve of the girls was quite impressive. It wasn't until Lori Weintraub announced that she needed the bathroom that they realise they hadn't considered that contingency at all. Privacy wasn't a problem, there was no one else around but they didn't bring any toilet paper with them. Lori started to cry and that set off a few of her friends.

Bobbi, Modern Man and the bunk counsellors were less than twenty feet away, hiding behind a fallen tree and watching and listening to their charges. Bobbi reached into her backpack and pulled out a new toilet roll still in its wrapper. Treating it like a hand grenade, she threw it in a high arc. When it landed in front of Lori it appeared to have fallen out of the sky. The crying petered out and was replaced by confusion then a bit of fear crept into the equation.

One of the bunk counsellors couldn't take it any longer. She circled round the back of them and took Lori by the hand, led her a little way off the path and helped her through her first real outdoor experience. As all the other girls watched in amazement, Bobbi broke cover and announced that they had to keep move on before the bears got hungry and picked up their scent on the wind. This was enough to quicken the pace of even the most reticent hiker.

After about an hour of walking along wooded trails they broke out into a clearing where there was a little beach on the lakeside.

'OK kids, this is where we camp tonight' Bobbi announced. 'We'll need wood to make a fire to cook dinner. Go back down the trail we just came on and collect sticks and branches off the ground.'

The girls were so happy to take off their backpacks that they actually ran back into the trees and brought back one twig each. Modern Man stifled a smile and told them they would need more than that. He then set about making a shelter that would hold all of them. He had brought two huge tarpaulins and some rope from the camp stores. One tarp was a groundsheet and the other was suspended between convenient trees to form a roof. They weren't expecting rain and sleeping in the open was normal. There would be mosquitoes and creepy crawlies but nothing dangerous, certainly no bears.

The next rebellion occurred when some of the girls realised they were sitting by the same lake the camp was on and they could have completed the journey in about ten minutes if they had taken a direct route.

Bobbi nipped this one in the bud by asking them if anyone knew what day it was. After a bit of discussion they settled on Friday. 'That's right. And what happens on Friday?' she asked.

The groan was a well rehearsed, 'Service,' they mumbled back.

As almost all the kids on camp and a fair number of staff were Jewish, there was a traditional religious service every Friday at sundown.

'Do we have to go?' they whined.

Bobbi's response was inspired. 'Well that depends. If you were on an overnight hike away from camp you couldn't attend because you wouldn't be there. However, if you were just a few minutes walk away then you would be expected to go. So what's it going to be? Are we on an adventure in the woods or are we on the edge of camp? You decide.'

The unanimous verdict was for an adventure, no service and the mood shifted instantly to euphoria.

The Shop Steward was in a dilemma. Whilst she was delighted that they didn't have to go to the service, she wanted more for her people. When the cacophony died down she stood four square in front of the huddle of staff and said, 'We don't want to go to bed at seven-thirty.'

Bobbi turned to Modern Man and he took it as his cue to respond. 'OK. Stay up all night if you want to.'

He didn't know where that crazy idea came from and the bunk counsellors gave him a collective death stare that told him in no uncertain terms how he had just undermined all the work they had done so far that summer. The Shop Steward gave the universal seven year olds' sign of success by pulling the imaginary train whistle. She was back in charge; her people were behind her and they were going nuts again.

What had seemed like a totally rash relaxation of camp protocol turned out to everyone's advantage. Modern Man built the shelter while the food was being prepared. Everyone sat down to eat Cowboy Stew. Most had complaints about their dinner but there was nothing else on the menu. Only the reckless went hungry. By this time, the kids were running out of energy.

As darkness descended they sat round the fire for a while toasting marshmallows on sticks. The pink and white balls that didn't burst into flames and fall into the fire were sandwiched between chocolate covered biscuits and eaten. Modern Man learned that these were called 's'mores' and were quite tasty, if you were the sort of person who sprinkled sugar on candy floss.

After that they tried a game he was much better at. See how many marshmallows you can stuff in your mouth at one time. Putting them in was easy, it was afterwards that was the difficult part. They stuck together so he couldn't pull them out and chewing a huge mass of sticky goo was incredibly hard on the jaws. The kids were in stitches laughing as he turned blue, struggling to breathe. After that they sang a few songs and the tempo wound down and heads started to drop.

The bunk counsellors helped the girls to unpack their sleeping bags and figure out who they were sleeping next to. This took well over an hour because it was complicated. It required shuttle diplomacy, delicate negotiations and a few Kleenex.

Modern Man kept his distance, he had nothing positive to contribute at this stage so he collected some decent sized logs and built up the fire for the rest of the evening.

By half past seven the kids were asleep. As long as the counsellors stayed pretty quiet and didn't abandon the immediate area, the rest of the night was their free time. It wasn't cold and there was no likelihood of low temperatures in July. The fire kept the bugs away to a certain extent and Modern Man looked around him and only then did he actually realise he was in the company of five pretty good looking women.

While he was mulling over which ones were a 'maybe' and which were a 'probably not', Bobbi did something totally unexpected. She produced a full bottle of bourbon and six plastic tumblers from her backpack. One of the other girls pulled a plastic bag from her pocket and started rolling a joint while Modern Man sat there with his mouth open and pupils fixed and dilated.

'What's up Gurndawg? Don't you guys know how to party in England?' Bobbi said.

'Well, I erm haven't ever, erm. Not like, erm. What about the kids?' was the best he could do for a response.

'Screw 'em. Spoiled little bitches,' chimed in a bunk counsellor called Alicia Schwartz.

'You should know since you came here six years straight,' responded her co-worker and former bunk mate, Jody Spellman.

Only Marissa turned down the party invitation. It was a mixture of early-onset maturity and paranoia at being caught and fired. Her father would be furious and her mother would probably die of shame, she explained. 'They're from The South, you know.' Apparently that covered it as far as the other girls were concerned. Marissa stayed around the camp fire for an hour or more but when the effect of drink and drugs took hold of the others, she withdrew to the shelter to read a book.

'It's probably *Gone With The Wind,*' one of them giggled. 'She's convinced her ancestors are featured in it.'

Marissa was used to the cheap jibes and rose above them as she floated on a cloud of serenity over those vulgar Yankees.

Being at the top of the 'probably not' list, Modern Man wasn't disappointed to see her leave early. Bobbi, Alicia and Jody were piling into the bourbon but Modern Man was lagging behind. The taste was unfamiliar. He'd had plenty of Scotch whisky before but this was his first time on the American variety. He thought he liked it but wasn't certain yet. Nor did he know what kind of hangover it would give him.

The other girl was much quieter. Her name turned out to be Lana. After she had rolled the joint, she lit up and passed it around then immediately started work on another one, which she kept to herself. She didn't contribute much to the conversation and appeared more than happy to sit there doing her own thing. She was the other 'probably not' in Modern Man's head.

For a while it looked like Bobbi, Alicia and Jody would be promoted to 'almost certainly.' He decided to pull back for a while to let them decide amongst themselves who would have the pleasure of his company for the rest of the night. Modern Man didn't want the fire to die down during the night, telling the girls he intended to find a big log to see it through until morning he set off into the woods. He thought that was a fine coded message, the sort that women used and would therefore, understand and interpret correctly.

When he came back Lana had gone to bed, Bobbi and Jody were nowhere to be seen and Alicia was sobbing quietly by the fire. What the hell had happened? He'd only been gone for ten minutes. Modern Man sat down beside Alicia and gently tried to extract some sort of story from her. What with the accent and the irregular breathing and his sketchy understanding of the many things that made girls cry, he was no wiser. Still, he had a plan for the night and a few tears weren't going to throw him off course. He put his arm around her shoulder and drew her in close. She put her head against his chest and the floodgates opened. No wailing like they do on news footage of car bomb carnage in the Middle East or natural disasters in the third world. This was a fairly dignified emotional release.

Modern Man offered her his handkerchief but when he tried to get it out of his pocket he couldn't. He had to half-stand up and when he did he saw, in the light of the fire, that the front of his trousers was damp. Alicia had cried so much it looked like he'd had an 'accident'. This was combined with the inevitable 'semi' of holding her close, smelling her hair and being vibrated by her heaving body as she wept. He hoped she hadn't seen what he'd seen but how could she not.

She didn't merely let go of him, she practically threw him away and only a reflex response stopped him falling into the fire. He immediately became the source of all that was wrong in her world. She called him every uncomplimentary name he had ever heard of and several that he assumed were Hebrew and reserved for the most ardent anti-Semite and in the most extreme of circumstances. Modern Man thought about trying Marissa or Lana but he would have to wake them first and, well he wasn't confident he could pull it off in those circumstances, not even with Lana, who was probably off her head, even then. There was still some bourbon though.

The kids started to wake up soon after sunrise. The unfamiliar surroundings scared some of them and excited others. All of them were noisy. Modern Man opened his eyes and his head exploded in pain. His pillow was hard and square and made of glass. It had a black label with white squiggles on it and it had the cap screwed on firmly. It was, alas, also empty, which meant he had drunk almost half of it. Self-preservation kicked in from somewhere and he pushed the bottle deep into his sleeping bag before any of the kids saw it.

Gingerly he crawled out of his makeshift bed, stumbled down to the water's edge and stuck his head into the lake for as long as he could hold his breath. Slightly revived, he set about preparing breakfast, which was a meagre offering as they'd only brought bread and jam and a juice box for each child. They would be back on camp in time for the second serving of breakfast in the dining hall. The direct route back was the favoured choice as the kids had a full day of activities ahead of them. They'd completed their overnight adventure and the novelty had worn off. Walked in the woods, slept in the open, got the tee-shirt.

At some point in the night Bobbi and Jody had returned to the shelter together and woke up spooning. It could have been perfectly innocent, what with it being a confined sleeping area and rough ground. It was certainly hard to achieve any level of comfort and frequently changing body position was normal. But he sensed there was more to it than that. Alicia wasn't ready to give them the benefit of the doubt. There was clearly an atmosphere but Modern Man still didn't catch on.

Marissa was all business. She was a 'make the best of things' kind of girl and Lana just groaned and shut the world out for as long as possible. It was down to Marissa to help the kids wash and dress whilst uttering quiet threats to her fellow bunk counsellors. They would pay for this. Jody eventually pitched in with Marissa and Bobbi helped Modern Man make jam sandwiches. Alicia joined the breakfast crew and Lana did very little of value from her sleeping bag. As soon as the youngsters were eating and drinking Modern Man dismantled the shelter and dowsed the last embers of the fire with water from the lake. Packed and ready to go they trooped bleary-eyed back to their cabins.

While Modern Man and Bobbi were stowing away the tarps in the stores their eyes met and the big question was asked and answered without a single word being spoken. The look in Bobbi's eyed said, 'Hey, I am what I am. Get used to it. Girls do it for me. Guys don't.'

Modern Man mulled this over in his head while he rolled up the large tarpaulin they'd slept on. In his limited understanding of the female end of the gay spectrum, there were two types. There the ones that wore dungarees and *Doc Martin* boots and the ones in porn films. Bobbi didn't fit into either category and this troubled him greatly. Could there really be lesbians who looked normal? This was a tricky one to take in.

On top of that Jody looked normal too. Better than normal, she was good looking and had all the bits in all the right places. Okay, not model material but certainly worth trying for. How could she be gay? That wasn't fair. Why couldn't the gay ones all be fat and ugly? That would be much simpler for everyone. God, this made it all terribly complicated. Maybe if they let him watch he would understand it better. Not even worth asking, he realised. Definitely worth thinking about. He let that idea germinate.

Having been on duty overnight, he was entitled to the rest of the morning to himself. There wasn't much of it left by the time all the gear was stowed away and he'd cleaned himself up. Shaving being the last step back towards feeling human again.

There were plenty of activities in progress and he wandered around the camp watching his colleagues coach various sports. There were races in the swimming pool and water skiing on the lake. All in all, it was a pretty good place to spend the eight-week summer season, if you were a kid with rich parents, which they all seemed to be.

It wasn't until visiting day, five weeks after the kids arrived at camp, that Modern Man realised how rich these people were. He'd heard stories of course, but who would believe a seven year old when they told you their dad was the CEO of the world's largest insurance company? When the father arrived by helicopter with an entourage of assistants, it was evident he was a 'someone' pretty high up in a 'something' that was doing better than OK. Arriving by aircraft was the exception rather than the rule. Modern Man guessed that once one of the parents arrived like that, they'd all be at it. Next year, Benny would need to build a landing strip and hire an air traffic controller for the day.

The majority of the parents arrived by car and Modern Man was assigned to the lake field overflow parking lot. He was happy to spend an hour or so telling these wealthy individuals where to stick their flash cars. Most, of course, totally ignored his directions and parked wherever they wanted to. One even managed to rip the sump off his sports car by driving over an exposed tree stump. No one laughed. Well they wouldn't would they? That would be so rude. The guy's wife certainly wasn't laughing and a full scale domestic erupted in the confines of a very small vehicle. This day had real potential, Modern Man thought to himself. Potential for what exactly, he wasn't sure but it wouldn't be like any other day on camp so far.

Once the need for parking assistance tailed off Modern Man returned to the assault course. He came across Grizzly diplomatically explaining to an over-enthusiastic dad that, no matter how much he wanted to, it really wasn't possible and that she recommended he watch how well his talented son managed to complete the course in record time. She managed to avoid saying that being about 6'2" and around 230lbs, he wouldn't fit into any of the safety harnesses and could easily destroy some of the obstacles if he were to fall on them. This was not a day for hard facts, it was all about ensuring next summer's advanced bookings remained healthy. Benny had been very clear about that when he had briefed all the counsellors the day before.

During the course of the event Modern Man had chatted to numerous campers' family members about life in England, life at camp, life in general and how wonderful their kids were. This had netted him over $200 in tips and one slightly disturbing Dustin Hoffman moment. The woman in question was called Rosenberg rather than Robinson but it was close enough and her intentions did not need any clarification. She left him with her phone number in Manhattan and the assurance that her husband was away on business all the time. She got so bored you see. She only wanted company. Modern Man had crossed the pond to widen his experience of the world and now it was in Cinemascope.

As the parents returned to their cars there were a few tears from some of the kids. For over a month they had managed perfectly well without their parents but seeing them again for one day was disruptive for some. Benny put on a party for the counsellors that night. It was a thank you for not screwing up. The free beers and pizzas had been earned and were well received.

Sylvia's summer had been extremely successful. She had produced three musical shows, with the help of a handful of volunteers. People had skills and she had the charm to persuade them to participate. Modern Man had been the light and sound man. An Italian-Scottish guy called Angelo was a brilliant artist and painted all the scenery. He swapped his chef's whites from his day job for overalls in the theatre each evening. A girl called Emily seemed to be able to sew anything to anything else with incredible results and Benny supplied the money. Whatever she needed (not wanted, but needed), was delivered in time. After all, the show must go on. The Freshmen and Sophomores did *Oliver!* Inters and Juniors put on *Bye Bye Birdie* and the Seniors production was *West Side Story*. All the kids took it seriously and what they lacked in talent they made up for in self confidence.

Tradition had it that the staff put on a show for the kids in the last week of the summer. Anyone with any real ability was auditioned out at an early stage. The whole point was to demonstrate how much more talented the campers were. To ensure there was a huge gulf in ability the staff were not allowed more than one rehearsal. Another tradition allowed some of the Seniors to direct the production, inevitably this dragged down the quality even further. It was their final year as campers and this was their swan song. Some took it more seriously than others and despite repeated hijack attempts by Juniors, the boards were well trodden.

The audience was almost entirely Jewish and, as it was the height of summer, the understandable choice was *White Christmas*. Modern Man could neither sing nor dance, so he took the role played by Bing Crosby in the film, Captain Bob Wallace. Phil Davies was played by Dieter, the German football ace and the Haynes sisters were Jody Spellman and Sylvia. Jody and Dieter had chemistry. It was the sort of chemistry you see when acid meets alkali. They fizzed and burned with mutual loathing. Modern Man and Sylvia tried hard to jolly things along but the tension was impossible to conceal. The kids thought it was part of the act but it looked real enough up close.

There was an unlikely combination of accents: northern English, southern English, Scottish, German and Park Avenue, New York. This made for an interesting acoustic dynamic. That combined with Dieter's insistence of always pronouncing it, 'Vite Krizmaz,' really put the tin hat on it. Some productions can be so bad they are good but this wasn't one of them. It was all bad but the Seniors who directed it started preparing themselves mentally for Broadway. They believed in themselves and that would see them through, ably assisted by daddy's money and connections.

The day the fleet of yellow school buses rolled into the parking lot was one of great joy for many and sadness for some. The kids were going home. The summer was over as far as camp was concerned. The last task for Modern Man was packing and lugging trunks. Cabin walls were stripped of memorabilia and the various items, that had been lost under beds since June, were returned to their owners. There were no tears. This was a part of camp routine for all the kids, whether first-timers or seasoned veterans. There were a few hugs and open invitations to visit were distributed. These were offered and accepted with good grace but neither party had any intention of fulfilment.

One by one the wagons rolled down the dusty road towards the interstate. Immediately after the final school bus disappeared from view, Benny's voice boomed from every loudspeaker on campus, 'All staff report immediately to the auditorium.' The tone was severe, had they screwed up in some way? They were about to find out what crimes and misdemeanours had been committed. When they were all assembled Benny stormed onto the stage with a face like thunder.

'When I gathered you together the day before the kids arrived I told you I wanted them to have the best summer they'd ever had. Remember that? Remember, do you? Well I have to tell you, I'm not happy. You people have caused me a lot of problems. Problems that are will cost me money and I hate spending money already.'

'Before they left I asked a lot of kids if they enjoyed camp this year and do you know what they said? "It was the best. It was the best ever." Every single one of them had a great time at Camp Redwood. Do you understand what that means? Next year I've gotta do even better, otherwise in twelve months time all I'll be hearing is, "Yeah, it was okay but last year was really something." I ain't having that hanging over my head all winter long.'

'Anyways, you did good and I'm proud of you all. Go down to the lake field now where there's a barbecue starting. You'll find beers and wine and pizza and stuff. Before you leave, stop by the office and pick up your pay checks. I'd hate you to forget them in the excitement and end up having worked for free all summer. No really, I would hate that.' Benny finally put a huge smile on his face and even the dumbest amongst them realised they weren't actually in trouble. It was just Benny, being Benny.

Grizzly had known what was coming and had taken a detour on the way to the auditorium to start the barbecue. As soon as the rest of the Nature Boys and Girls arrived, they took up their stations flipping burgers and serving the hooch. As the sun set behind them, the party atmosphere gained momentum. A few couples drifted off to their favourite secluded locations for one last time but the numbers didn't dwindle significantly and the alcohol had its usual effect.

Now that the kids had gone, so had the rule book, for one night only. They could pretty much do what they liked providing no damage was caused. For some, that meant skinny dipping off the dock or smoking joints but for most, it made no difference. The small thrill of breaking some of Benny's many rules no longer existed. Instead, they behaved fairly normally by the standards of university students. Addresses were exchanged and plans made for the remaining time before they had to head back to college. Most of them had at least two weeks of vacation left and wanted some down time before returning to their studies.

Sylvia only had a week before her flight home. Modern Man had almost three. Neither had much money to spend, meaning a trip to the Bahamas wasn't a viable option. They spent the majority of the evening together sitting on the grass of the lake field, chatting. It was as though the conversation they started two months previously had never been interrupted. They had both consumed a fair bit of beer and wine and for Modern Man the temptation was there to take things a bit further. Something in his head stopped him though. He didn't know why but he went with it and she seemed to read his mind and visibly relax. Damn. If she knew what he was thinking that could be very inconvenient, he thought to himself.

Sylvia had several offers of accommodation in and around New York for her time off but hadn't committed to any of them.

'Let's go to Boston,' she said. 'I've always wanted to go there.'

'Okay,' Modern Man replied. In truth, he would have accepted an invitation from her to the New York City mortuary, if she'd suggested it.

The following morning they hitched a ride with Jody back to the city and caught a Trailways bus to Boston. Jody had offered to lend them one of her cars but they said the bus would be more of an adventure. Jody clearly didn't see the attraction of public transport but she had learned from experience that the Brits could be a bit eccentric.

Modern Man and Sylvia arrived in Boston late in the afternoon and found a cheap little hotel that claimed rustic charm but in truth was in need of a few repairs. To them it didn't matter. It was a few minute's walk from a subway station. From there they could travel downtown easily enough. The only thing Modern Man knew about Boston was that it featured pretty heavily in the War of Independence. He wasn't a big fan of baseball but liked the way the yanks did sport and the Red Sox were a Major League team.

Over the next few days they were immersed in all things cultural. A day of art galleries and museums was followed by walking the history trail through the old town and ending with a night at the theatre. Sylvia explained to him that he should see real actors practice the art, in case he was under the impression that their one-night show of *White Christmas* qualified on some level. Modern Man had always studiously avoided culture in all its forms. He had no need for it and didn't see any reason to complicate his life with such confusing issues. After all, the experts didn't seem to be able to agree what was good and what was awful, so what chance did he have.

With her it was different. Her enthusiasm wasn't exactly infectious but it made her happy when he said something positive and that took him a step closer to his ultimate goal. Sylvia was of course, aware of his objective but was keen to ensure he was prepared to make a significant investment in the relationship before she did what she had been intending to do. It was an intention born while she waited for him to clear customs at Kennedy Airport almost two months ago. She wasn't the kind of girl who wanted to be anyone's statistic.

On their last evening in Boston they went to the ball game. Drinking beer and eating hot dogs was good fun. The game, however, was very confusing. What exactly was going on? Modern Man attempted to explain the intricacies of a game he knew little about. The people in the row behind them intervened and took it upon themselves to explain to Modern Man and Sylvia the rules and tactics as they happened. The concept was simple – the batter hits the ball and runs round all the bases before the other team could throw the ball back to the base he was running towards. Why complicate it so much with all those statistics? Modern Man figured out that HR was Home Run but what the hell was an RBI?

Even with their limited knowledge and the best efforts of the fans around them, who had to explain what Runs Batted In meant and why they were important. It was a new experience and a spectacle. It was fast, the crowd was totally engaged in the game and there was genuine excitement in being at a big live event that went on longer than any opera Sylvia had ever been to. And she'd done the whole Wagner Ring thing on more than one occasion.

Modern Man was reminded of one of the old football commentators' clichés, 'At the end of the game we'll have a result.' Unlike football there were no draws in baseball, they carried on playing until one team beat the other, however long that took. It seemed that the American sports fans needed winners and losers. It's hardly surprising that the USA is one of the few former British colonies where cricket never became popular.

Back at the hotel they made their last night together a memorable one. For Sylvia it was something special that had meaning and was the perfect blend of tenderness and raw animal passion. For Modern Man it was the end of a long and patient wait but well worth it.

Sylvia caught a bus back to the city and met up with Jody for a late lunch. After a shopping fix in Bloomingdale's the girls headed off to the airport together. Jody's line of questioning and desire for detail was a bit too intense for Sylvia. She wasn't ready to share so much so soon, it wasn't in her nature.

Modern Man stayed in Boston. Having waved to the back end of a departing bus he mulled over some of his previous sexual partners. Sylvia was special and he hoped she thought he was special too. He would phone her in a couple of days and try to assess if she really wanted to carry on seeing him when they were both back in Britain.

In the meantime he had to work out how to survive for the next twelve days with $17.49. He couldn't stay in the hotel any longer, it was too expensive. After an hour or so wandering the streets he sat on a bench on Boston Common with his head in his hands. He was close to tears at that point. He simply didn't know what to do. The emotional nosedive from the previous night with Sylvia, to being alone and skint twelve hours later was a lot to take in and deal with.

After half an hour on the park bench feeling sorry for himself, his bum was numb and he was no closer to having a plan to see him through to his flight home. The next thought that popped into his head was the fact that he didn't have a job waiting when he returned to Britain or even anywhere to live. He'd used up all the goodwill of friends before he came out. This was a bad situation. He stood up and walked around the Common trying to think of a solution.

Free thinking in the mind of a young man is a dangerous concept. Too much TV and not enough real life experience. Holding up a drug store was his first thought. That's what good but desperate men did. He would have to be careful not to shoot anyone. Not having a gun, this shouldn't be a problem. Could he buy one? Would a toy gun work? How about a banana in his pocket? No that was ridiculous. The whole idea was barking mad. He needed somewhere to stay but the city jail wasn't a real option.

The cops were unlikely to release him or drive him to New York to catch his flight home.

How about begging on the streets? No one knew him here and this was a posh banking district with rich people who would feel sorry for him. Perhaps he could make out he was a Vietnam Veteran and play the sympathy card that way. The fact that he had been in his early teens when that war finished was a detail he wasn't prepared to entertain.

'*Two hours of pushing broom buys an eight by twelve....*' wafted through the air as he wandered past a country and western clothing store. He didn't feel like the *King of the Road* Johnny Cash was singing about but it did give him an idea. He could actually work for money. He could do that, he had a work visa in his passport.

With the confidence of youth he marched up to the reception desk of a smart city centre hotel and announced that he was immediately available for work of any kind.

'We're not hiring,' came the reply. The guy hadn't even bothered to looked up.

On his third attempt Modern Man was lucky. He had a vague idea what a janitor did but he was about to find out for sure. He wasn't stupid. When he was given a mop and a bucket he realised his academic qualifications were not essential for the role. A certain amount of form filling, however, was required and when it came to his residential address the whole thing unravelled pretty quickly. It turned out he needed a mailing address or he wouldn't be allowed to work. The Bell Captain came to his rescue and told him there was a shelter for the homeless a couple of streets away. If they had room for him that would suffice as a residential address.

The building was in a run-down area and looked awful. If he'd thought it through he would have realised it was hardly likely to be in the stock broker belt. The guy in the office said they had a room but it had no windows. Modern Man asked if it had an electric light and the guy said, 'Sure.' Modern Man took the room and used $15 as a security deposit. He climbed the stairs and unlocked the door.

Whilst factually correct, the guy had omitted some significant detail in his description of the room. Technically, it did have a window. It had a window frame but no glass. It was tiny, with a single bed that had seen better days and a small locker like you see on cop shows. It would have to do, at least for a couple of nights. Modern Man returned to the hotel and started work on minimum wage. His duties were explained by the head of housekeeping, 'Mop up wherever you're told. Smoking's not allowed any place, cursing or chewing gum in guest areas of the hotel ain't allowed either. Don't talk to the guests unless they speak to you and don't arrive late or leave early.'

After a few hours he was ready to quit but with no real alternatives, he decided to stick with it. His co-workers were only a few rungs off the bottom of the socio-economic ladder meaning the conversation during his meal breaks wasn't inspiring. After six days on the job he was paid in cash and entitled to one day off.

He did his best to spend as little as possible during his free time and when he showed up for work the following day they were genuinely surprised to see him. Clara, one of the chamber maids explained that most people don't come back once they've seen some money in their hands. Modern Man said that he had thought about taking a Caribbean cruise instead but it was lost on her.

When the time came to leave, he asked the head of housekeeping for his final wages.

'You get paid at the end of the week, like everyone else.'

Modern Man informed him that he had to go to New York as a matter of urgency and could really do with the money.

'Sounds like you're running out on me, son,' said his line manager.

Modern Man couldn't come up with a credible alternative so he simply nodded.

The guy took a crumpled twenty dollar bill from his pocket and said to Modern Man, 'You've done a good job, been reliable and haven't caused me any problems. I appreciate that, I really do but life's tough kid.'

With that he put the twenty back in his pocket and said, 'Get out of here before I kick your ass. If you ain't here on payday, you don't get paid. It's real simple.'

For the third time in a matter of months, Modern Man realised he'd been shafted. Would he ever be streetwise?

Modern Man only had enough cash left to buy a bus ticket to Kennedy Airport, New York. As he wandered round the terminal he noticed that there must have been a hundred places serving food in its various forms. With no money to buy any, he was relegated to swooping on leftovers as other travellers had their fill. He also figured out that families were the best bet. They bought kids meals to keep their children occupied even though they weren't hungry. After a bit of stalking, he managed to pick up a few part eaten chicken nuggets and some cold chips.

When he finally boarded the plane he was still desperately hungry. He pestered the stewardess for peanuts as soon as he was in his seat. His apology and mitigation that he hadn't eaten all day didn't endear him to the stewardess and he had to wait for the bar trolley like everyone else.

The flight wasn't full, which meant there were enough meals on board for him to have two dinners and he wasn't above begging to make sure he had them. Reasonably sated he sat back and fell asleep. He was shaken awake by the same stewardess and told to fasten his seatbelt for landing. He had slept through breakfast. That was annoying.

Thankfully he had no problem entering the country. A British passport and the normal amount of baggage didn't raise any suspicions with the authorities. He was home, penniless and more than a bit surprised to see a familiar face in the arrivals hall. How had she known what flight he would be on? His mother simply smiled at him, the way mothers do sometimes.

Modern Man emerged from the woods convinced that he was mentally stronger as a result of his early job difficulties. He was also enriched by his time in the States, the friendships he made and his time with Sylvia. That could only have been good for him.

Maybe the problem stemmed from the next phase of his life; the part where he had to stand on his own two feet for more than a few months at a time.

5. All the Right Moves

On the journey from the airport to the family home Modern Man was still half asleep and more than a little bemused by events. As a result he was totally unprepared for the barrage of questions his mother fired at him. Like all good interrogators, she started with a simple open question in the hope that he would spill the beans. 'So, tell me all about it,' she said.

When that didn't work his mother seamlessly and quickly cranked up the intensity, 'Did you have a good time? Did they feed you well? You've lost weight. I thought you might have grown a beard. You're wonderfully tanned. What was the camp like? How many children were you looking after? Where did you sleep? Did you make lots of new friends? Where did you travel to after camp? Did you get into trouble? Did you get anyone else into trouble? Did you have a girlfriend over there? What was her name? Was she American or British? Are you going to see her again? What's her name? How old is she? Is she a student or does she have a job? I bet she's a teacher. They're the only ones who get long enough holidays to go gallivanting off to America for the summer while the rest of us have to work.'

Modern Man closed his eyes and said, 'I had a great time but right now I'm knackered, so you'll have to wait, otherwise I'll have to repeat it all to Dad when we get home. I take it he knows where I've been all summer?'

'Of course he knows where you've been. He only gives the impression of being totally self-absorbed, he's actually very proud of you, you know. It's just that, he doesn't know how to express it, that's all.

With that exchange over, his mother had to focus on her driving as the traffic increased on their approach to the town centre. She concentrated on driving and Modern Man attempted to jump start his brain and organise his thoughts. He was more than happy to share stories about taking rich American kids hiking and camping in the hills of upstate New York but he wasn't prepared to say anything about Sylvia. Mainly because he wasn't really sure what the situation was. He knew that they had connected and that the time they'd spent together had been really good, especially their last night in Boston before she had to catch her flight home.

When they pulled into the driveway of the family home, Modern Man's mother took charge of operations as she always did. Even though she had never travelled further than Western Europe and endured no more than a one-hour time change. She was the self-proclaimed expert on dealing with jet lag.

'Go to bed now and sleep for two hours then stay up until your normal bedtime tonight. What is your normal bedtime these days?' she enquired.

Modern Man's life did not have quite the routine that his parents' had and he had no notion of a time at which to go to bed. It depended on factors like alcohol consumption and what was on the telly at the time. He liked to think of himself as spontaneous. Not having the resolve to argue, he dropped his baggage in front of the washing machine and headed for his old bedroom.

Things had changed in his absence and even through such tired eyes, he could have sworn he saw a sewing machine on his desk and flowery fabric heaped on a chair in the corner. Whatever. His bed was still there and with clean pillow cases and quilt cover, it looked very inviting. After three months of camping trips, he knew that washing his face and brushing his teeth would only wake him up, so instead he stripped down to his boxers and climbed in. It took longer than he expected to nod off but it was the sleep of the dead when it finally arrived.

His resurrection was down to his mother shaking his shoulder whilst screwing up her face as if there was an awful smell in the room. There was a bit of a pong and he was the cause of it. The dog breath and body odour were combined with the inevitable gaseous exchange following a transatlantic flight. 'Oh really, you could have left the window open,' she pointed out.

Modern Man looked around and for the second time in only a few hours, he pondered the presence of a sewing machine and flowery fabric in what used to be his room.

'What time is it?' Modern Man enquired.

'One o'clock. I've made you some soup, come down when you're ready. Oh, and there was a phone call for you a little while ago from a girl called Sylvia.' She left that one hanging in the air. God she was good at this.

Modern Man couldn't figure out how best to respond. He was groggy and still exhausted but determined not to give too much away. The tiredness actually helped him out on this occasion. If he had been sharper he would have reacted to hearing Sylvia's name but in his current state his body language was at pre-school level, struggling to communicate on a consistently coherent level. 'That's great,' he said, leaving enough ambiguity in his answer to cloud whether the thought of soup or Sylvia prompted the response. Two could play at this game, lady.

Modern man intended to be as cool as possible. He'd been working with a couple of guys from Colorado and a girl from California on the camp and they seemed to be cool personified. He hoped more than anything that some of that had rubbed off on him. He'd studied them avidly over the course of the summer and now was his opportunity to emulate their behaviour as best he could.

He took the soup and bread and immediately realised that whatever he had to endure from his mother was at least partially offset by the quality and quantity of food she could provide for him.

She hovered, ready to continue questioning him and this time he recounted a heavily edited version of his trip. He decided there was no need for them to know about the strip search at Kennedy Airport, the freely accessible cannabis or the threat of dismissal for skinny dipping in the lake. Nor had he decided how much to reveal about Sylvia. He had to tell them something, there was no escaping that. The fact that she'd phoned him the day he arrived home had to be a good thing. Unless she had called him to dump him. But why would she do that? She could wait for him to call her and then be all cold and distant on the phone. He knew that technique from previous girlfriends. No, it had to be a positive move and he was desperate to talk to her again. Being cool was harder than he anticipated.

He was totally unaware for how long he had been silent and was jolted out of his introspection when his mother hit him with a painfully direct question,

'Who's this Sylvia girl, then?'

He'd have to wing it and hope he didn't say anything he would regret later.

'She was on my flight out and we discovered we were going to the same camp, and we got talking. Naturally we travelled up there on the same bus...'

'You went on a bus? Didn't they send a car for you? Buses are dangerous. All sorts of crazy people travel on buses, especially in New York. You could have been mugged or killed or worse,' his mother interjected, showing classic signs of anxiety after the fact.

Modern Man wondered what could be worse than being killed. His experience arriving at Kennedy airport was certainly a contender.

'Calm down dear, he's a big lad. He can look after himself. Nothing happened or he wouldn't be here to tell the tale, would he?' his father said, breaking his silence of several hours.

'Mum,' Modern Man continued, 'your knowledge of New York is based entirely on episodes of *Kojak* and *Cagney & Lacey*. If you haven't noticed, several million people live and work there. Yes, of course there's crime but not on every street corner. Perhaps you should start watching *Fame* and maybe you'll start believing everyone dances on the fire escapes and dumpsters in the back alleys.

'Buses are as safe there as they are here. Besides, it was a long distance bus like the Greyhound and Trailways ones you see in films. It wasn't the notoriously homicidal number ninety two that'll run over anyone with dirty underwear.'

Modern man hoped that this digression would throw her off the scent but she was straight back to full attention and wanting to hear more about his adventure and his girl.

'She's not my girlfriend, mum. Not yet anyway.'

Oh bugger, how did that slip out? His mother sat there with a self-satisfied smile on her face. She'd prised information out of him that he'd been determined not to divulge. Damn it!

He went on to tell them all about the activities available on and off camp and how the Nature Group crew were the cool guys everyone wanted to hang out with. He impressed them when he described in detail how he'd helped out on the theatre productions. They were absolutely amazed he'd visited Woodstock to see where the famous pop festival had taken place. They didn't think he'd have even heard of it, let alone know where it was. Reliving it all over again and enjoying it as much in retrospect, he told them he'd taken loads of photos and wanted to have them developed as soon as possible.

His dad brought him back down to earth with a hell of a jolt. 'I don't suppose you have any money left do you? He paused, then hit him with, 'Any job prospects in the pipeline or thoughts in that direction?'

His mother leapt to their son's defence. 'Oh, really! He's only been back in the country for a few hours, give him a chance,' she chastised her husband of nearly three decades.

Modern Man knew his dad was right. He couldn't afford to return to being comfortable living at home again. Come to that he couldn't afford anything. He was totally skint. In his pocket he had $3.85 and a tatty ten pound note he'd kept in case he'd needed a taxi from the airport. The job search would have to begin again first thing on Monday morning.

He'd tried the serious Sunday newspapers' Appointments sections before and they were a complete mystery to him. Some of the adverts were extremely specific in their required skills and experience. Modern Man wondered why they didn't phone up the one or two people in the world who could possibly fit the profile exactly. Even the small ads, with their codes and abbreviations were baffling. No, he needed a different approach. He would take a trip into Manchester and see what he could find there. It wasn't exactly a detailed plan but it had potential. Manchester was a big city and..... Well, he'd think of something when he was there.

The phone rang and despite his best efforts to combine speed of reaction with cool detachment, his mother beat him to it.

'And who shall I say is calling?' he heard from the hall. 'Cynthia? Oh, Sylvia, just a minute, dear, and I'll get him for you,' she said.

Modern Man was up and out of his chair in a flash. There really was no point in attempting to be laid back now, his cover was blown and he knew it. He took the phone from his mother and shooed her away.

Almost an hour later he returned to the living room with a hot, sweaty ear and a warm glow inside. His old man had nodded off in his chair and Modern Man's mother was preparing the evening meal. His parents were rather old fashioned and he didn't know quite how to tell them that he had arranged to stay with Sylvia in Bristol for the weekend.

He couldn't be brash about it because he would have to ask them to bankroll the trip. If he was too coy they would thrash him with stories about there being a war on when they were his age and beside people just didn't do that sort of thing in those days. He'd never watched the whole of *Brief Encounter* but he suspected that Trevor Howard's and Celia Johnson's characters had done, or intended to do, exactly what he was planning that coming weekend.

In the end he settled on a white lie. The shade of white that a school shirt turns after a dozen chemistry practicals or a couple of hundred times through the washing machine. Okay, it was more of a grey lie combined with economical measures of truth, resulting in a highly implausible story.

He cleared his throat and announced that Sylvia had told him there was a very nice Bed & Breakfast place a couple of doors along the street from her flat. She knew the lady that ran it and had been offered a good deal on a single room for the weekend. 'Most of their trade is during the week, you see. Usually business people, I believe. Sylvia's been told it's very nice. There's even a colour TV in the room but no phone, so I won't be contactable.'

He'd made the classic mistake inexperienced liars often succumb to. He'd talked too much. Far too many irrelevant details had been added and all the time he'd been staring at a spot high on the opposite wall and not once looked either of his parents in the eye.

Modern Man was totally stunned when they agreed to his proposal and was then hit with a real kicker of a condition. He had to invite Sylvia up to stay with them. His mother liked the sound of Sylvia's voice and wanted to meet her. This was all moving too fast for him. Involving parents was such a huge risk. There were a great many nightmare scenarios to be foreseen and mitigated against. The logistics alone would take hours of planning.

Why couldn't they let him do what he wanted to do and turn a blind eye if it bothered them so much? He hadn't realised, at that point, that blind eyes and deaf ears were the refuge of parents of that generation and they knew exactly what he was up to. Far from openly giving him their blessing, which of course, they would never do, they were secretly relieved he wasn't 'batting for the other team.' The dream of having grandchildren one day moved a step closer.

There were plenty of things wrong with the railway system in Britain in the '70's and 80's. However, it was much simpler then to find out when trains were supposed to depart and arrive. Buying a ticket didn't require checking price comparisons and special offers. Modern Man went to his local station and within five minutes had a return ticket to Bristol Temple Meads, changing at Birmingham New Street. With his Student Rail Card discount it wasn't desperately expensive if he travelled 'off peak' which he always tried to do anyway.

On the Thursday evening, Modern Man was in his bedroom packing his gear for the weekend when his father stepped in. Something was clearly bothering the old man as he stood with his hands rammed deep into his trouser pockets and rocked back and forth like an unsupported drunk waiting for a bus.

'I, er, wanted to, er, have a word with you about this girl of yours. Have you, er, ever. Well do you know what you're doing in the, er, you know. Are you prepared? Don't want any surprises down the line, if you get my meaning.'

With that he pulled a square packet from his pocket and tossed it onto Modern Man's pile of clothes waiting to be packed. 'Just in case you get lucky,' he muttered, as he turned, red-faced and left the room.

Modern Man picked up the pack of three condoms and put it in his wash bag next to the pack of twelve that he had bought on the way home from the station. He wasn't anticipating the need for luck this weekend.

He hadn't really thought through the idea of buying contraceptives in his home town. It never occurred to him that someone he knew might work in the chemists on the high street. Supposing it had been a girl he had always fancied, or even a friend of his parents from their church, but he doubted it. It was, in fact, a boy who had been in his class at school who had tormented him at every opportunity.

That bastard Briggsy always seemed to be on the fringes when something embarrassing had happened to Modern Man in his teenage years. He was always there, mocking. Always ready to put him down with a smart arse quip and now Briggs was standing between him and paradise.

Modern Man waited until the shop was devoid of other customers then stepped boldly up to the counter and handed his purchases to the cashier.

Briggs looked up with a cheap grin on his face. 'There's a 'use by' date on these you know,' he said. 'It's just that, well, twelve! I mean, optimistic or what?'

As usual when Biggs was around, Modern Man had no pithy comeback and could feel himself go scarlet. 'You'll need to redirect all that blood somewhere else if you're going to get much use out of these, you know.' Eric was warming to his theme and there were other people in the shop by then.

Modern Man threw money at the counter, grabbed his box of delights and left as quickly as he could. He had no need for his change, he needed to escape, catch his breath and stop his heart racing.

He had arranged to phone Sylvia from Birmingham when he changed trains. That way she would be able to meet him at the station. With this in mind, and her being a teacher, he thought he ought to be reading a book that would impress her. One of the classics perhaps, but which one?

English Literature had been so boring at school that he knew little and cared less for this improbable fiction. He'd played fast and loose in exams, inventing quotes when he couldn't remember a real one, not wisely but well enough to scrape a pass. He'd always suspected that no one really knew Shakespeare as well as they claimed. Lord, what fools these mortals be.

In the end he decided to be true to himself and bought a thriller that he would enjoy. He'd already seen the film that was based on the story and that had been brilliant. It ought to mean the book was good too. Frederick Forsyth knew how to hold a young man's attention with technical detail about military hardware and spectacular action sequences. He'd toyed briefly with reading one of the great romances like *Lady Chatterley's Lover* but quickly dismissed the idea. It wasn't his own feminine side he wanted to keep in touch with, if indeed he had one, which he seriously doubted.

The journey south was nice enough and he lost himself in the story until the train pulled into New Street, Birmingham. He didn't have a huge amount of time and still had to find out which platform his connection would depart from.

He was travelling to Bristol. What he had neglected to discover was the train's final destination. He stared up at the massive departure board looking for a Bristol bound train. There wasn't one. He had screwed up. He'd never see Sylvia again. It was all over. She'd blame him, of course. She'd ask the sort of questions that his mother would ask, that all women asked in these situations. The ones that start with, 'Why didn't you...' and finish with, 'What were you thinking?'

Writhing in mental torture a familiar sounding voice broke through his inflated sense of despair and caught his attention. 'Cun-I-elp-yow?'

Modern Man's brain did one of those weird time-warp connections and he was transported back to his college days and a strange but wonderful one night stand with a girl called Amanda. She wasn't the one standing next to him in a British Rail uniform but it could have been Amanda's mother. It was uncanny how alike they sounded.

'Er, Bristol. I'm going to Bristol but I can't see it up there anywhere,' Modern Man told her ample chest.

There was something about a woman in uniform that always did it for him. He was powerless to resist and he knew it. By this time, so did the British Rail employee, who decided to take it as a compliment. In fact, it put a spring in her step and a wry smile on her face for quite a while afterwards. She reminded herself that she still had 'it', choosing not to dwell on how much supporting superstructure was required to keep her most noticeable physical attributes above the equator.

'It's the Exeter St. David's train you want. It leaves in fifteen minutes,' she told him in an unnecessarily husky voice which Modern Man chose to take as sexually predatory and made a rapid retreat to find a phone and call Sylvia.

She was at school, of course, and wasn't ready to share his existence with work colleagues yet. To overcome this they had devised a series of coded messages that he could leave with the school secretary.

As Sylvia lived in a house converted into flats, it would be perfectly reasonable for a tradesman to need access to her flat to complete repairs on the property. Modern Man left the message that the plumber would be arriving at quarter to five and hoped she'd be there to let him in. The secretary was a little bemused that Sylvia was uncharacteristically enthusiastic to hear this and speculated what awful sanitary conditions Sylvia must have been suffering, in silence, for days, if not weeks. And why did the plumber have to come from up north? Surely there were a sufficient number of plumbers in Bristol to go around.

Modern Man found his platform and waited patiently for the train to arrive. When it did, the train was quite busy but he found a seat and returned to his book. The second leg of the journey passed fairly quickly and he amused himself trying to imagine how the locals pronounced the names of the towns he passed through on the way. Modern Man was of the opinion that he was a master at mimicry, particularly English regional accents. He'd yet to find anyone who agreed with him. As a result he restricted them to an internal monologue these days.

The train slowed on its approach to Temple Meads station and Modern Man gathered his gear together and stood up. He stretched and let a cheeky fart loose as he bent down to pick up his bag. He didn't want that making a dash for freedom when he was with Sylvia.

As he was stepping out of the carriage he saw a guy in a suit with a briefcase in one hand and a bunch of flowers in the other. Modern Man had an idea. No, he wouldn't try to buy the flowers from the man, or even mug him for them. He would give

Sylvia the slip and buy some for her. It was a big station, there was bound to be a florist somewhere on the concourse.

There was indeed but Modern Man wasn't about to part with that much beer money for a few daffodils. He canned that idea immediately and concentrated on finding his girl. It was harder than both of them expected. There were a lot of arriving passengers and loads of people milling around. Sylvia spotted him first. Inevitably it would be easier for her because he was wearing clothes that she had picked out for him that summer in America and his fondest memories of her didn't include any clothes at all.

Sylvia moved towards him and he saw her when she was a few feet away. Modern Man dropped his bag and threw his arms around her in an all-encompassing embrace. It was the real deal, properly romantic and then the kiss. They went the same way and the crash of noses made them both wince briefly. She subtly realigned her septum and reconnected the kiss. Sylvia had a tear in her eye that was not entirely due to the pain he had inflicted on her seconds earlier. It was a moment, one of those moments that women cherish all their lives and men pretend to remember, when prompted.

They reconnected on several levels. For Sylvia, it was about finding a potential soul mate. She had been imagining romantic walks in the park and candlelit dinners with him for a few weeks now. For Modern Man, it was about remembering one night in Boston and what led up to it. That and hoping he could recreate in the next couple of hours what took him two months to accomplish in the summer. Like most women, Sylvia could read his mind fairly easily, whereas he hadn't a clue what she was thinking about, nor did he really care. He believed he was in control of the situation and she was happy to let him think that.

When they finally unwound their embrace, they noticed people were staring but in a nice way. Sylvia's cheeks flushed for a moment but she quickly regained her composure. An elderly lady shed a tear at a memory briefly rekindled, while her husband winked mischievously at the young couple. Part of the old chap missed the thrill of the chase but he was in no doubt that he had picked a damned fine filly for life's great steeplechase. A damned fine filly indeed.

It seemed perfectly natural to hold Sylvia's hand as they walked out of the station to the bus stop. It would be quite a while before he realised why it felt natural, even though he had never held hands with a girl before, this was okay. In fact, it was better than okay, it felt good. Conversation came easily as they waited for the bus to arrive. She suggested what they might do and where they could go. He didn't have any preference and was content to agree to everything she suggested.

The bus dropped them at the end of Sylvia's street and she pointed out the Bed & Breakfast place he wouldn't be staying at, unless he was genuinely concerned about her reputation. Modern Man confessed to being torn between his honour as a gentleman and his wanton desire as a red-blooded male. She faked outrage and disbelief at the appalling implication then gave him a look that told him everything he wanted to know. It was in the set of the eyes, the slight tilt of the head and the lips. Those lips were open to negotiation.

Modern Man was ready and eager to declare his opening stance and move on her initial position but he had overlooked the fact that she worked with children. She dealt with instinctive physical needs on a daily basis. She was an expert and he was out of his depth. She was calling the shots and that was all there was to it.

Initially, he was frustrated at having no control or even much influence over unfolding events but he soon realised that she had planned a really nice evening for them. Being with her was too special to ruin with a toddler tantrum. She prepared a fantastic dinner and he opened a bottle of wine, again something that he rarely did, still being pretty much a beer drinker by habit.

His parents drank wine. Not real wine but stuff they made themselves from a kit and unusual fruit or vegetable combinations like elderberry and quince or parsnip and red cabbage. Apart from looking like puke and tasting, well 'different' was the best he could come up with, it was pretty potent stuff and he occasionally joined them in a glass or two in the evening. He also secreted a couple of bottles in his bedroom, for those important times when drinking alone was the only answer to a question best left unasked.

The first bottle of wine lasted through dinner and the second took them through the rest of the evening. Sylvia told him she had rented a video from the corner shop. His heart sank at the thought of sitting though a historic costume drama. She threw him a life line by choosing a classic James Bond film. Modern Man was mightily relieved by her choice. He would have sat through pretty much anything short of *The Sound of Music* or *Doctor Zhivago*. Those two movies had been forced on him as a child and the memories still inflicted psychiatric damage.

He was totally unaware how skilfully he was being manipulated. He thought Sylvia was being considerate, when, in fact, she too wanted a night to remember. She was well aware that planting images in his head of the sophisticated womaniser would heighten his performance in a way that would benefit both of them. Modern Man just liked the film.

In the end they both got what they wanted and the neighbour in the flat upstairs learned more about their appetites and stamina than was strictly necessary for a middle aged spinster. Sylvia didn't know Miss Dearbourne desperately well but feared this was no longer a two way street. Perhaps the gift of a house plant would keep salacious gossip to an acceptable level. Sylvia didn't want to be the scarlet woman of the street and she wanted even less to be thought of in the same terms as Irene Dearbourne.

Saturday morning started much as Friday night had ended and it was almost lunchtime before they were ready to set foot out of the door. Inevitably, Irene was click-clacking down the communal staircase in her leopard print stilettos at that exact moment. Despite her low-cut blouse and exposed ample décolletage, she managed to project a disapproving look with her pursed lips and furrowed brow. When Sylvia wasn't looking, Modern Man blew Irene a kiss. She sniffed with disdain and the look that followed implied, 'I could have you for breakfast, little boy.'

Sylvia saw the reaction but not the cause and decided she was better off not knowing. There was still a fair bit of boy left in this man of hers. On the way down to the vestibule Modern Man had mentally undressed Irene, checked her out and imagined her as a French maid, gangster's moll and police woman. He had imagination when he wanted to. Somehow Miss Dearbourne seemed to sense what he was thinking and her hips swayed knowingly.

They spent the day sightseeing and shopping the sights and shops and found a great little place for a late lunch. As afternoon drifted into evening they wound their way back from the city centre through the university district to Clifton. Sylvia hadn't planned to cook on Saturday night so they changed and went to a nice restaurant for dinner. Modern Man had a credit card but didn't want to use it. Nor did he want to appear as hard up as he really was. Sylvia noticed his dilemma and discreetly paid the bill on the way back from the ladies room. Modern Man was unaware of this and when they decided to leave he thought they were doing a very slow and controlled runner. How incredibly sophisticated this girl of his proved to be.

If the neighbours had been disturbed on Friday night they were almost bounced out of the building on Saturday through Sunday, such was the vigour and raw energy exerted by the pair of them. Some ignored it while others assembled in dressing gowns on the landing outside Sylvia's front door. After a few minutes there was a sweep stake going with bets available on both duration and recovery time. It wasn't only the men in the building, there were ladies of a certain age who claimed some sort of inside knowledge in these matters and they cleaned up. The guys didn't really mind, they were lost in admiration and more than a little envy, as Sylvia had been noticed on more than one occasion by all of them at sometime or another.

Sunday started rather later than planned. A leisurely breakfast followed by a trip to the zoo. It was Modern Man's idea when he remembered all the things his mother had suggested they do and until then they'd only really done what his dad had hinted at. There could be awkward questions if he couldn't account for at least some of the daylight hours of the weekend. There was no hurry, his train didn't leave until late afternoon.

As they walked through the reptile house he recalled the condition his mother had imposed on him coming down here, he had to invite Sylvia to their house for a reciprocal visit. There was never going to be an easy way to phrase that. In the end he blurted it out.

Sylvia was genuinely surprised and thought it was far too early in the relationship. She was having a relationship, even if he was merely having sex, great sex but still only sex. She had underestimated him in that thought. Even though he would not say it out loud for quite some time, the connections were being made in his brain and he was almost ready to accept that this was turning into something big and important.

He was a long way off using the 'L' word. It was one four letter word that rarely came out of his mouth. He settled on 'significant' as the best way to describe her position in his thoughts. He was a bloke and a northerner so he didn't do dreams and aspirations. He dreamt, of course, but not those sorts of dreams, not like girls have.

The silence between them was broken when they wandered past a cage of monkeys, screeching and doing unspeakable things to themselves and each other. Modern Man and Sylvia both laughed out loud when they realised how little difference there was between the two species. The bunch on the landing the night before hadn't exactly been silent, especially when one of them scooped the jackpot. Modern man had watched the victory dance through the spy hole in Sylvia's front door. It disturbed him somewhat that a stranger was profiting from his youthful stamina.

'It'll have to wait until the half term holiday,' she said, thinking out loud. Then adding, 'Last week in October, in case you've forgotten when that is.'

Teachers always know exactly when the next holiday is, how long it lasts and when the one after that is. For people who spend their working life with children and talking about their pupils in their spare time, it seemed strange to Modern Man that they were totally focussed on holidays. He had a lot to learn.

It wasn't far off but he knew it would be difficult to have to wait that long before seeing her again. They would phone of course, probably every evening to begin with, then less often he thought. Maybe taking turns and occasionally not speaking for days on end because they presumed it was the other person's turn to call. Then they'd argue and not speak and one of those bastards in the building would comfort her. One thing would lead to another and before long Modern Man would be out of the picture. That sensitive comforter guy would be in her bed every night. He'd move in to her flat. Oh God, this was bad!

'I'm going to move here and get a job in Bristol,' he said.

'Just like that?' was her immediate response and it didn't come out the way she had hoped. It sounded dismissive. She quickly added, 'That's fantastic' and planted a lingering kiss on his lips by way of distracting him from analysing her verbal reaction.

It worked of course and he responded, briefly forgetting that they were in a public place surrounded by families with young children.

Sylvia knew very little about engineering of any variety but she knew Bristol and its history. There were both old traditional manufacturing industries and the fast growing technology sector popping up all over the city and surrounding area. He was qualified and enthusiastic and she was fairly confident he would be able to find something suitable. Once back in her flat they worked on his CV and she gave him some tips about application letters. His grammar and spelling were dreadful, she'd have to work on those. This was now a team effort with a common goal. They were totally wrapped up in the whole job application thing and he almost missed his train as a result.

Parting was tough and there were tears. Hers not his, he wasn't a total wuss. He found a seat and lost himself in thought for the entire journey home. By the time he arrived he had a plan to research companies in and around Bristol. His mission was to find out who was recruiting at graduate level. He wanted to send his CV with a covering letter to a fairly wide spectrum of engineering businesses. It was a plan with one major flaw. He had no idea how to do it.

His parents read the *Daily Telegraph* and that had a job section on Thursdays. The newspaper called it 'Appointments,' like the Sundays he'd tried previously. He doubted his current skills and experience would lead him to being appointed to a key senior management position. He had no idea what a, 'Globally focussed, employee-driven, macro-economic, forward-looking enterprise,' was. He had a good idea where they felt the, 'beating heart of the financial capital of Europe and the world,' was though. Maybe he'd be ready for that in two or three year's time.

His mother directed him to the library in town. 'It's all in there. Ask Dorothy, she'll sort you out.' Dorothy was the church secretary, his mother's close friend and known as a bit of a gossip.

First thing on Monday morning he presented himself at the library as Dorothy was going for her lunch break. It had been a hell of a weekend and he had needed a lot of sleep on Sunday night.

A serious woman who was an archetypal librarian, a walking cliché in tweed and sensible shoes stepped forward and enquired how she might be of assistance. Modern Man explained that he was a graduate engineer and was looking for work in the Bristol area. He needed help to research potential employers. She cocked an eye and felt the need to point out that he was more than two hundred miles from Bristol and might be more successful in a library that was actually in Bristol.

'If you can't help me then say so,' he said with more volume and irritation in his voice than he intended.

'I didn't say I can't help you. Follow me, the reference section is this way,' she replied, her voice now dripping with attitude.

Modern Man hadn't been in the reference section of this library since primary school. He had associated the library and everything in it as a source of boredom ever since he'd had to do those dreaded projects about far off countries in the British Empire. In fact it came a close second to church in the list of places he least liked to be in his home town. Now that he had a mission it was different. This place was going to help him get out of here and start living his own life.

While these thoughts had been swirling round in his head the librarian had been droning on about the Dewey Decimal Classification Systems. She wittered away about it being used by the library services worldwide to enable users to quickly and easily find the texts they needed. Modern Man suspected that if he had been paying attention he would be asleep by now. He simply asked her where he would find the information he wanted. She showed him and left, with scarcely concealed contempt for his ilk.

A couple of hours working at the library table had produced a reasonably long list of large engineering companies with a presence in Bristol. He didn't have contact names or even phone numbers but it was a start. He went home and called Directory Enquiries to discover the numbers. They were very helpful to start with but less so when the operator realised it was more than one or two numbers he wanted. After about six she asked how many numbers he wanted and told him that twenty three was simply too many. He countered with the obvious question, 'Isn't that what you're there for?' and was promptly cut off. He redialled and spoke to a different and more accommodating purveyor of digits and eventually had a call list to work with.

It was too late to start phoning these companies that day so he resolved to make an early start next day and called Sylvia instead. They discussed their weekend together in great detail and were both excited and relieved that neither of them detected any hint of regret in the other's voice. For her, it was actually happening. For him it was a whole new experience.

Modern Man told her what he had achieved so far and Sylvia said she had been through the phone book and noted down some company names and numbers but admitted that she didn't really understand what it was that he did. He thanked her for taking time to do this and he was delighted that she had wanted to. After an hour his mother made an appearance to announce that his evening meal was ready. He dreaded to think how much of his conversation she had heard and he and Sylvia quickly exchanged goodbyes.

A couple of days later Modern Man received a letter. That in itself was a rare event but a letter from a girl was a whole new experience. Not just any girl either. This was Sylvia, a girl who still wanted to be associated with him after sleeping with him, uncharted territory indeed.

He would have to rely on instinct from here on in. None of his mates would be of any help now. The ones that did see any action in that area were always looking for the next girl before the sheets had cooled down. Modern Man didn't want that and the more he read the letter from Sylvia, the more he wanted her.

He was having sensations he had never had before and apart from the total lack of familiarity with what was happening to him, he was incredibly content with everything. There was no anguish nor uncertainty nor fear. It was all positive, except for the nagging doubt that it was, in fact, a dream. He felt sure he would wake up in a compromising position with the evidence of sexual self-sufficiency all around him.

The actual content of the letter was a combination of skilfully crafted narrative and clumsily girlish giggly-flirty nonsense. Sylvia carefully referred to the activities of the weekend in a cloaked manner that should his parents have intercepted the missive, she wouldn't be made to sound like a cheap whore and gold-digger, but to Modern Man it should push all the right buttons. It certainly had with her when she wrote it.

The hardest part was deciding how to finish it. Should it be 'Love Sylvia' or even 'All my love Sylvia,' so much could be inferred from the use or avoidance of this emotive four-letter word. Was it dismissive not to use it or too risky at this stage to introduce it, albeit reasonably obliquely, to the relationship?

Once the word was out there, it had to be reciprocated and with equal or greater sincerity. If it came back too quickly, was it love on the rebound? If it came back too slowly then it smacked of obligation not infatuation. In the end she side-stepped the dilemma with a suitably affectionate, 'Missing you,' and three kisses. As an after thought she also enclosed the page of notes she had made about technology companies in Bristol, Bath and surrounding areas.

Modern Man read the letter again and again. He analysed it, mulled over particular words and phrases she had used and tried to decipher any hidden meanings and nuances, either intended or accidental. In the end he settled for the clear message that she was into him as much as he was into her and that made him extremely happy.

He knew he had to take that positive energy and channel it into finding a job down there. The information she had sent him was incomplete but very useful all the same. He spent the next day on the phone and two days after that writing letters of application.

Whilst he was in a huge hurry to launch his career, the companies he had written to seemed to have no sense of urgency whatsoever. The day after posting his letters he was ready for interviews. He had a suit, of sorts. It was a suit and it had fitted him less than a year ago but now it was a bit short in the legs and tight round his chest. He couldn't blame the dry cleaners because he had never had it cleaned. Maybe it shrank on the hanger in his wardrobe, some of his other clothes had done that during the last few years.

Modern Man was restless, agitated and impatient. His mother was trying her best to be supportive and she really did want him out from under her feet. She tried to take his mind off his predicament by suggesting things he could do around the house that would be useful.

There were a few minor DIY projects that his old man had been putting off for months, if not years. Modern Man tried but his mind was elsewhere, right up to the moment when he gave himself an electric shock while replacing a cracked plug socket. That focussed his attention and he decided that switching off the power at the meter was a good idea after all. He had been trying to avoid the need to reset various clocks and appliances when he'd finished. The threat of death overcame his innate laziness.

By the time his first invitation for an interview arrived he had painted half the back fence, wallpapered most of a wall in the spare bedroom and taken some stuff out of the attic and put it in the garage, ready to go to the tip. He was under the impression that he had been a great help and was a bit put out that his mum didn't shower him with praise and adoration.

The interview was with a large company working mainly in the defence industry. Modern Man's application had arrived at the 'eleventh hour' before they closed their graduate program for the year. Since he was available immediately, his appointment was scheduled for only a few days after his application was processed. He phoned to acknowledge he would attend and then called Sylvia to tell her the good news. He spent the rest of the evening studying a map of Bristol and the company information they'd sent to him.

It wasn't until he was on the train on the journey down that he started to feel nervous. It suddenly hit him how much was riding on a one hour conversation with a complete stranger. His previous interviews had been for odd jobs that didn't really matter to him. This one was important. More than that, it was vital. It was life and death; his life or the death of his relationship with Sylvia. 'Oh My God,' he thought to himself, 'I'm in a relationship.' He was trying his best to steer his desire into determination but was afraid he would end up looking desperate instead.

Sylvia had agreed to meet him for a coffee at the station after his interview. He wasn't there when she arrived. She immediately started to worry that something awful had happened. After nearly forty minutes of anxiously hanging around she saw him jump off a bus and run up the station approach. She was instantly annoyed and simultaneously pleased to see him. Totally mixed emotions overloaded her and she berated him, without really understanding why. He took it on the chin. The fact that she was still there made the uncharacteristic outburst bearable.

The interview hadn't been an hour; it had lasted for the entire afternoon. He told her all about it over the worst cup of coffee he had ever drunk.

'I had two face-to-face interviews. There was some sort of psycho test or something. Then there was another test of basic numeracy and literacy. Finally, some bloke with a beard gave a presentation about the company training scheme,' was his summary of the day's events, in between slurps of coffee. 'They said I should hear within a week if they're going to give me a job.'

He slept for most of the journey home. Mental fatigue took him down within ten minutes of the train pulling out of Temple Meads and he dozed fitfully for a good two hours. Not for the first time in his life, he woke up and he had no idea where he was or why he was there. It was one of those surreal moments when there was absolutely nothing familiar around him. He was on a train. He was wearing a suit and had a briefcase. None of these things seemed at all likely. Eventually he put his world back together and figured it all out. The only real uncertainty left was whether he had interviewed well enough to be offered a job. He would have to wait that one out.

Both his parents were there to meet him off the train. He gave them a run down of his day as they drove home and answered their many questions as best he could. His father was all about career paths and opportunities whilst his mother wanted to know what the staff canteen was like and whether the company would help him find somewhere to live when he started work there.

Each morning Modern Man sat in the hall waiting for the post to arrive and each morning there was nothing for him and the week was almost over. A sense of dread was haunting him. Morose was becoming his default state of mind and he spent more and more time alone in his room.

Seven days after his trip to Bristol he had a phone call from someone who said they were a Human Resources Administrative Assistant at the company he had visited. She told him they would like to offer him a position as a graduate engineer and could he report for work the following Monday. She said there would be a letter in the post that day, confirming the offer in writing but if he could give a verbal acceptance over the phone that would be lovely.

Modern Man briefly forgot himself and gave a very strong affirmative response with a couple of totally unnecessary swear words thrown in for good measure. Realising what he had done, he apologised at least six times to the rather startled woman on the other end of the phone.

She told him it was perfectly alright. 'I've been working with young engineers for many years and I am quite used to their profane language and lack of manners,' she said in a somewhat weary tone. 'Although, I've usually met them in person before it starts,' she added, and then asked if he had any questions at this stage. He couldn't think of anything and was still embarrassed by his earlier outburst. She gave him her phone number, along with the recommendation that if he did think of anything, he should call her at any time up to the end of that business day.

Modern Man put down the phone and screamed at the top of his voice, 'I got the job!'

His parents appeared at opposite ends of the hall and ushered him into the kitchen. His mother put the kettle on. They weren't the kind of people to have champagne chilling in the fridge on the off chance. They'd have the 'good tea' instead of the everyday brand, and they'd have cups and saucers, not mugs.

After recounting the phone call, the interview process and everything he knew about his employer, Modern Man suddenly realised that it was Thursday afternoon. He was due to start this job on Monday morning and that was like, really soon. He needed somewhere to stay close to the work, or on a bus route at least.

His mother suggested the Bed & Breakfast that he'd stayed in when he went to visit Sylvia.

'What?' escaped his mouth before his brain stepped in to save him and deftly converted a serious faux pas into a finely crafted compliment. 'A good idea, Mum. Brilliant. I'll phone Sylvia and get her to arrange it.'

'Why don't you call them yourself? You'll have the number from the last time, won't you?' she enquired.

This wasn't the time for verbal sparring with his mother. He had too many things to think about and do and only three days in which to do them.

'Look. I need to call her to tell her I have the job and she'll want to help. This is something she can do that will sort out one major thing for me.'

'You can't live in a B&B, it'll be terribly expensive. You'll need to find a flat or a shared house or something like that.'

Mother was on a roll and there was no stopping her. The next idea to be floated was a big one. 'How about we all go down in the car? We can spend the weekend looking at flats and exploring the area. And we can meet Sylvia! Can't we dear?'

She had him and they both knew it. He couldn't turn down a free ride and help sorting himself out. He would have to warn Sylvia. Maybe they could say she had to go away this weekend, on a course or visiting a sick relative or something. No, he wanted to see her and if that meant her having to run the gauntlet of his mother's enquiring mind, then so be it.

Sylvia was, of course, delighted with his news and even okay with the whole parents-in-tow part of the surprise weekend package. She was happy to book them all in to the Bed and Breakfast place and even went along with his suggestion that they infer he'd stayed there on his last visit. She didn't know the owners well enough to ask them to blatantly lie but she thought she could sway them towards gentle exaggeration.

Modern Man tried to explain to Sylvia what his parents were like but it was difficult. They were probably listening in to his side of the conversation and he neither wanted to offend them nor scare her off completely. He settled for whispering, 'Old fashioned, eccentric and staid,' when he felt he could get away with it and left her to devise a strategy to deal with them the following day.

After his experience of packing to go to college, Modern Man politely but firmly refused to accept any gifts of household items that were offered to him. He had the perfect response in that he didn't actually have anywhere to live yet and would be imposing on Sylvia to store some of his stuff until he had a place of his own. In the end his luggage amounted to two suitcases, a rucksack and a couple of boxes. It wasn't the sum total of his worldly goods but it wasn't much to show for over twenty years of life, love (occasional) and the pursuit of happiness either.

As they motored south, in the family car, his mother regaled him with tales of her youth in the West Country. His dad had heard it all before and knew all the stories but featured in none of them. He hadn't known her in those days and, on the strength of her whimsical anecdotes, was very relieved about it.

He was a proud Yorkshireman with a full set of down-to-earth attributes. He had an economy with words which meant any question he didn't want to commit an answer to could be handled by responding with, 'Appen.' Derived as a short-form of the common English word 'happen', it infers no commitment to, nor confirmation or denial of an action or event that may or may not have occurred in the past or be about to occur in the near or distant future, to which the individual is either responsible for or bears witness to. It's a five letter word that can confound and frustrate, bewilder and antagonize. Its real value is as the equivalent of the Fifth Amendment of the US Constitution, to protect against self-incrimination.

As Modern Man's mother's stories became longer and more detailed, her accent drifted back with them. She clearly remembered conversations the way she first heard them and to repeat them any other way would be incongruous to her way of thinking.

As they approached the city of Bristol, she was obliged to stop reminiscing and start navigating. She insisted she had no need for a map as this was her territory. Admittedly there did seem to be a lot more houses than she remembered and ending up lost was practically inevitable on all family expeditions. Modern Man's only advice to his dad was to head downhill. There was a kind of logic to this simplistic approach as there was a major river running through the city and it had docks and stuff like that. The old man could relate to this and followed his instincts instead of his wife's directions.

Eventually they found themselves in the city centre and parked up. Modern Man located a public phone box and called Sylvia. She gave him directions to a nice pub and told him she would take the bus and meet them there in about half an hour. Modern Man reported back to his parents and they gladly went along with this plan. He ordered a pint for himself and his dad and a bitter lemon for his mum. It was at this point that she realised she'd been nominated as the driver for the rest of the evening.

Totally unnecessarily, her husband twisted the knife by saying, 'You know this area better than us. It seemed like the best thing to do.'

There was a look from her and a shrug from him. Modern Man was very glad he wouldn't be in the car for the return journey up north because his mother didn't take prisoners. The old man would be held hostage for several hours and on the receiving end of a committed tirade.

His mother wanted background information on Sylvia.

'What do you want to know about?' he asked.

Her somewhat predictable reply was, 'Well, everything. Obviously! Where does she come from? What are her parents like? Is there money in the family? What's in her past that we should know about?'

Modern Man was in a difficult position now. If he didn't tell her anything, she wasn't above asking Sylvia these direct questions herself. He didn't want to be sarcastic or facetious because that would create a difficult atmosphere and Sylvia could walk in at any minute. She was bound to sense any tension and that would only make things worse.

With no other options open to him, he had to resort to honesty. 'She's from Bicester in Oxfordshire. Her dad's a solicitor in the town and her mum used to be the secretary at the practice. Actually, I haven't met them yet. I have no idea what they're like. She has no brothers or sisters and as far as I know, and I can't imagine, she has any skeletons in the cupboard. Maybe we'll find out when we clean it out and stow all my stuff in there.' It just slipped out, he couldn't stop himself. His mother had no right to even suggest Sylvia had 'a past' as she called it. Mother took the rebuke on the chin and realised, too late that her protective instincts had gone beyond all reasonable limits, again.

Modern Man checked his watch. He couldn't remember exactly what time he'd phoned Sylvia, so he wasn't sure when to expect her. He knew half an hour really meant at least an hour but he couldn't help being anxious. He wanted them all to get along. Life would be far easier if they hit it off. He failed to appreciate that what little independence he enjoyed in his life would disappear in a heartbeat if his mother and girlfriend truly bonded.

When Sylvia walked into the pub heads turned and conversations ground to a halt. She looked stunning. It took her a moment to spot them and weave a route between chairs and tables to where they sat on the far side of the room. Modern Man's dad was slow to catch on and did a real double-take when he eventually realised it was Sylvia.

'Close your mouth, dear, and stop staring,' his wife murmured as Sylvia approached their table. Modern Man stood up. He was immediately hit with a tricky question of etiquette. Should they hug, kiss, hug and kiss? Definitely not shake hands. Hell, the whole pub was watching. Men were jealous of him, women were impressed by her. Sylvia took the lead and offered a cheek for him to peck. To his credit, he read the signal correctly and an almost imperceptible, 'Aawh' hung in the air for an extended moment before people returned to their own worlds.

Modern Man made the introductions and wondered how his old man would respond. Thankfully, he stuck out a hand and shook hers warmly. His mother did the same, which surprised her son a little and he tried to determine what that meant while he was at the bar ordering Sylvia a glass of wine.

They had a couple more rounds of drinks then they all piled into the car for the short trip to the B&B. Sylvia rode shotgun, helping out with directions when the situation required it. Modern Man and his dad sat in the back, both with silly grins on their faces. Each knew what the other was thinking and it was a rare moment of bonding between them.

The B&B was a town house with two double rooms on each floor, apart from the attic which had two singles. The proprietors had thoughtfully put his parents in the room immediately below him and no one was booked into the other single. Modern Man was curious why the proprietors thought he needed to know that. Sylvia suggested they unpack then come round to her flat for a while.

Modern Man's mother decided it was late and they should call it a day. 'You two go. We'd only be in the way. We'll see you straight after breakfast. It'll be a busy day tomorrow,' she said.

Modern Man and Sylvia were half way down the stairs when Sylvia suggested she nip home and bring the wine to his room; that way there was no danger of him being locked out. In the end they walked round together and returned almost straight away with the wine and a couple of glasses. They sat and chatted for a while but couldn't ignore the noise coming from below. It was a gentle rumble with a rhythmic knocking.

They looked at each other and Modern Man said, 'You don't think they're, you know, doing it, do you?'

'Either that or rearranging the furniture to get a better view of the bridge.'

Modern Man would never know and his father didn't feel the need to ask what had put his wife in the mood. He was just grateful and assumed she was stirred by happy memories spent in this part of the world.

If only they knew, and his wife was determined they never would, that she had fallen in love for the first time in a house very similar to this one. She'd been seventeen and at the twenty-first birthday party of her best friend's cousin. She hadn't been drunk but had sipped a couple of glasses of *Babycham*. It had been enough for her to drop her inhibitions when the opportunity arose and she'd surprised herself. She never did see the boy again and didn't even know his name at the time, although she did find out eventually.

Whilst the sensations she'd experienced then had been incredibly powerful, she resolved to put that particular genie back in the bottle. Such a loss of control couldn't be good for a respectable young woman like herself. She was glad she'd risked it, and the fact that no one knew, even if some suspected, enabled her to keep her reputation intact.

Stifling giggles, Modern Man and Sylvia finished the wine and she left him in his room trying hard not to visualise what was happening one floor below. He didn't sleep much that night and his dreams were unusually cryptic when he thought back over them.

Breakfast was served from half past eight and, true to form, his parents were up at seven-thirty sharp, showered, dressed and ready for the day to begin. For once Modern Man was also up when he said he would be. They discussed how best to cover all the required tasks, while munching through the Full English cooked to perfection.

Armed with a street map, they worked out which flats on their list were handy for the city bus routes. Sylvia joined them about an hour later and advised on certain districts to avoid, however reasonable the rent may appear. His dad spent a lot of the day sucking his teeth at the price of anything worth considering and was becoming a bit of an embarrassment to them all.

After looking at a number of hovels and a few penthouse suites they found something in the Bedminster area that would fit the bill. It was affordable, it was reasonably straightforward to commute by bus and it was a furnished studio flat in a converted end of terrace house near the shops.

His dad stumped up the first month's rent and a deposit of a further month's rent. It had taken most of the day to complete this mission but it was one major step towards his independence and Modern Man was mightily relieved about that.

His mother was worried, naturally. She worried that he wouldn't be able to look after himself, that he may be burgled or mugged. She worried that the job wouldn't work out and he would still have to pay the rent with no money coming in. She unburdened herself over the course of the evening and felt much better for it. Modern Man and his dad didn't have anything like the required imagination to come up with all the disaster scenarios that she had laid out in front of them and Sylvia was too polite to rubbish all of them as somewhere in the range of improbable to highly unlikely.

They had a pleasant meal together in the same restaurant that Sylvia had taken Modern Man to on his previous visit. His mother started to question her but a gentle kick under the table from both the men in her life was sufficient to convey the message across that this wasn't the right time for that. Sylvia took it as no more than genuine interest and was happy to talk about her childhood and upbringing, her career and her time at summer camp in the States with their son.

His mother had one of those brains that retained detail and as Sylvia spoke she was cross-checking Sylvia's version of events with those her son had divulged on his return from camp. She knew they were holding something back and she would find out what it was, eventually. A mother needed to know these things.

They spent Sunday morning assessing what was required in the flat. The women decided it needed a good clean and together they scrubbed the place thoroughly. An inventory was taken of kitchen utensils and a shopping list was prepared. They bought enough food to keep Modern Man happy for the first couple of weeks. That was all there was room for in the tiny fridge and cupboards. It didn't take long after that to put away the few possessions he had brought with him.

His parents eventually left them making dinner and set off in the general direction of the motorway north. Inevitably, they were lost within minutes but managed to find a local inhabitant whose accent was decipherable. With his directions they found the road that would lead them to the motorway.

Modern Man and Sylvia played house together for a while. It would take two buses for her to return to her flat in Clifton and she was torn between setting off before it was really late or rising early in the morning for a quick dash back to her flat then into school. In the end she left him watching a film on TV and had another rather tearful parting. There was no phone in his flat. He said he'd call from the public box on the corner in an hour, to make sure she was home safely.

Most of his first day at work was filled with administrative things that there hadn't been time for between the interview and his start date. He was instructed that this was a defence establishment and he may or may not be involved in work that was secret. Either way, he was required to read and sign the Official Secrets Act and must, on no account, talk to the press or anyone, including friends and family, about his work or other projects in the company.

Modern Man was shown to a desk with a phone on it. He had a big swivel chair and a two drawer cabinet next to it. Everyone else had the same, it appeared. In fact, there were people at similar desks as far as he could see. It was a huge room with a walkway down the middle and clusters of workstations geometrically spaced for optimum advantage. There were a few offices along the back wall and windows along the other side. Some people had shoulder-height partitions round their desks but most were facing someone else.

His manager had one of the offices and called a meeting after lunch for all the graduate trainees. There were six of them altogether. Most had started the previous Monday and one trainee the week before that. They appeared to be a nice enough bunch and, although still a bit nervous, Modern Man was starting to relax. The manager explained that the approach to training was a mixture of learning and doing. They would be sent on courses from time to time but would also be assigned to a senior engineer. They would have tasks to complete, deadlines to meet and reports to write. It sounded a bit like college and Modern Man reckoned he'd be alright if it was.

After the meeting he was introduced to his mentor, a senior engineer called Brian. Modern Man was expecting a wizened old bloke in a tweed jacket with elbow patches, NHS glasses, a pencil lodged behind his ear and a pipe to fiddle with. What he was given was an arrogant young fellow who sneered at him, had a bone crushing handshake and enough contempt to fill an Olympic sized swimming pool.

Brian was introduced as one of the rising stars of the department and Modern Man was told he should learn as much as possible from him. As soon as the manager left them alone, Brian laid out how it would work between them. 'Right, let's get one thing straight here and now. You are a new graduate and therefore, by definition, know nothing of value to anyone. I am a senior engineer, which makes me God and you are my bitch, got it Dickhead?'

Modern Man arranged his facial features into the most gormless expression he could conjure up at such short notice and, in the style of a country bumpkin, said, 'Come again?'

Brian's response was to glare at him, pass three huge lever-arch files to Modern Man and end their first exchange with, 'Read these.'

Modern Man took that as his cue to return to his desk. He was glad he hadn't crumbled but wondered how he was going to work with this guy, Brian. He decided the only way to handle it was to be as good as he could be and leave him with nothing to complain about. Although more worldly wise, than many of his contemporaries, Modern Man still had a little of the naïveté of youth: bless him.

By the end of the afternoon he was almost half way through the first file. It was an overview of the project he would be involved in. Never having been an avid reader of anything, he was quite slow and found he had to repeat several sections before he had any idea what they were about.

In the context of engineering documentation there is no room for flowery prose or engaging dialogue. It's not a novel that requires a fast-moving narrative. To call it dry would be an insult to all the exciting things that happen in a dessert on a hot sunny day. Modern Man hunkered down and ploughed on. Page after page of monochrome monotony, occasionally interrupted by a graph or pie chart. These were the oases he had to look forward to. He had to confess to himself that he'd thought working on defence projects would be more exciting than this.

As Modern Man was preparing to finish his first day, his manager came over and said, 'Don't worry, the first day can be tough but work hard, meet your deadlines and you'll start to enjoy it.'

Modern Man felt that eventuality was highly unlikely but he wasn't about to give up after only eight hours. He'd give it a week, at least. After all, he wasn't a quitter. The last thing he did before leaving was to phone Sylvia at her flat. She invited him over for dinner and he was out of the office like a shot. The day was about to improve big time.

The conversation over dinner was mostly about his first day at work. She sympathised about Brian, knowing only too well what it was like to work for an overbearing jerk. The headmaster at her previous school had tried a few times to charm her into bed and when he finally gave up on that he decided to make her life a misery instead. Sylvia's last words to him, when she left the school were to point out that he was crap at being charming but had certainly found his true vocation when he was being a complete bastard. It was a gift and came naturally to him, she'd informed him.

The washing up didn't feature in the events of that evening. The TV wasn't switched on and to avoid another awkward meeting with her neighbours, they tried quiet sex for a change. Modern Man occasionally whispered things in her ear that made absolutely no sense. It added nothing to the otherwise highly pleasurable sensations she was having. He had stamina and was trying a few new moves on her which she appreciated. She too, had been doing a little research of sorts, to enhance these close encounters.

When it was all over and they had caught their breath, lying in the warmth of each others bodies, she couldn't contain her curiosity any longer and asked him what he had being whispering to her.

'Ah, yeah,' he said, a little embarrassed. 'That was the primary requirements for the landing gear release mechanism on the Agile Combat Aircraft. But I shouldn't have told you that. Now I'll have to kill you.'

'Okay,' she said 'but do it gently,' and spread-eagled herself across the bed. 'Now I know what you were saying, but why?'

Modern Man thought for a moment then responded with, 'You don't need to know, but you'll reap the benefit, believe me, in fact we both will.' Eventually the penny dropped and she smiled lasciviously.

Modern Man showed up for work the next day wearing the same clothes. In most offices that would be noticed and there would be speculation, innuendo and covert gambling. These were engineers. Wearing the same clothes day after day was an indication of nothing more exciting than poor personal hygiene. It wasn't exclusively a male environment but the majority of women were eventually dragged down by the immense gravity of indifference and saw no reason to knock themselves out sartorially when no one noticed.

As each day passed, Modern Man became more comfortable in his workplace. He started to have a feel for how projects progressed in a big company. He noticed who was helpful and who could look busy without actually doing anything. The shock of the first encounter with Brian was history and his mentor eased up a bit. Brian still referred to him as his bitch and called him Dickhead from time to time. Modern Man accepted this as something he had to live with and tried not let it annoy him.

He never bothered to have a phone installed at his flat. He didn't see the point, he didn't spend much time there, not awake anyway. He paid the rent on time, had no complaints and wasn't complained about. He spent all his spare time with Sylvia and life was good.

Weeks turned into months and Christmas was approaching fast. Modern Man still had to keep his side of the bargain and invite Sylvia up north for a weekend at his parents' pleasure. He thought that having them meet her when he moved into his flat would be enough but apparently not. They were determined to inflict their brand of hospitality on the poor girl and there didn't seem to be anything he could do about it.

He was yet to meet Sylvia's parents. They knew about him, of course, and they had been to visit her but she had persuaded him to stay out of the way. Her father had an unfortunate habit of scaring away her boyfriends.

Sylvia's father didn't spend any significant amount of time in court these days but still had the ability to ruthlessly cross examine any young man he considered unworthy of his daughter's attention. Her mother was more accommodating but would never do something against her husband's wishes. Consequently they had been drip fed information about Modern Man. Sylvia had shown her parents the occasional photograph and mentioned him in conversation from time to time. Sylvia wanted her father to accept him and hoped he might one day actually learn to like Modern Man but she knew it would take time. Time she was ready to invest.

Plans had to be made for the Christmas holidays. Modern Man wasn't entitled to many days leave so had to use them wisely. Sylvia, being a teacher had a full two weeks over Christmas and New Year. In previous years she had always decamped from her flat and returned to her parent's home in Oxfordshire, to rest and be pampered. It was also a tradition to meet up with old friends from her school days.

This Christmas would be different. It was a high risk strategy, but she decided that her father would be bound by good manners and her mother would ensure that he behaved decently towards a house guest during the Festive Season. She discussed it on the phone with her mum. Certain rules were laid down by her mother.

'You're an adult now and I don't want to interfere but you have to understand this is our house. Don't be caught doing anything to embarrass your father. Be discreet, for Heaven's sake.' Sylvia got the message before her mother rammed it home with her closing statement, 'The spare room has been decorated. I'm sure he will be comfortable in there.'

Sylvia was also aware that they had to put in more than an appearance at her boyfriend's parents' home. The simple idea that they could spend Christmas at one house and New Year at the other was fine until they had to make the big decision. Neither family would be happy to sit down to Christmas Dinner without their child.

The phrase, 'But it's Christmas!' would be ringing in their ears until Easter. Modern Man suggested they do a bunk and go to Tenerife instead. He wasn't really serious and the idea was killed with a look from Sylvia.

After mulling over the pros and cons they settled on her parent's for Christmas and his for New Year. Modern Man then had a flash of inspiration that would make it turn out incredibly well.

'How about you take your fiancé instead of your boyfriend? Would that work?'

She looked at him with a mixture of disbelief and confusion and said, 'Are you asking me to marry you?'

'Yes, I suppose I am,' he said.

6. Flights of Fancy

'I've had enough of being a teacher. I want to do something else,' Sylvia said, shortly after they passed the Worcester exit on the southbound M5 motorway. Modern Man was driving with one eye on the road and the other flitting between the temperature and fuel gauges in his Fiesta XR2. He played a sort of Russian roulette with petrol and coolants when it came to motorway driving. He objected to paying the few pence extra per litre at the service areas. He would wait until the warning light came on then take the next exit and find a filling station.

Sylvia did not find this an endearing quality in her fiancé. She filled up her car when the tank was half empty. She had a battered old Renault 5 that she'd christened Florence. She also had a flirtatious relationship with the owner of a small garage. He was prepared to perform any number of miracles to keep Florence roadworthy. He would do pretty much anything to ensure Sylvia brought that little car back to him. She'd flash him a smile and then negotiate all the profit out of the work he'd done on the car. His fantasies about Sylvia weren't desperately creative but they saw him through the day.

'What do you have in mind?' Modern Man asked her. He still wasn't giving her his full attention and driving far too close to the car in front, in her opinion.

'You know how, on the flight to the States, you couldn't keep your eyes off the stewardess? And before you ask, yes, I did notice. As did she, and most of the other passengers in the adjoining rows. Anyway, that got me thinking and I've been doing a bit of research for myself. After all that investigation I did for you, I simply carried on doing it for myself, you see. Bristol Airport is being expanded this year and that will mean more flights to more exotic destinations.'

'Teaching is rewarding but the administration is becoming ridiculous. It's changing the job and I don't want to be one of those middle aged grumps you see at the NUT conference on TV. I certainly won't ever be cheering and jeering at the behest of some left wing wannabe politician. And you'll never see me wearing a tent and matching cardigan,' she added.

She paused for breath and Modern Man took the opportunity to leap into the temporary void.

'You want to be a trolley dolly? Are you serious? Early starts, drunk punters trying to grope you as you walk down the aisle. Constantly jet lagged. Duty free booze, hair up all the time, full make up every day, high heels, uniform. Right! You have my full support.'

Once again Modern Man had delegated logical thought away from his brain and had no control over his mouth. Sylvia was a little taken aback. What started as a typical tirade of chauvinism had somehow morphed into a ringing endorsement of her plan. She had intended to drip-feed him with positives over the coming weeks and months but that no longer seemed necessary.

'So, you're okay with it then?' she asked, still a little confused by his verbal gymnastics.

'Absolutely. No problem. Bristol Airport's down the road. Go for it,' he beamed.

This was a huge relief as she had already applied and had a pre-selection interview scheduled before the spring term started. She would have to polish her French language skills to an acceptable standard and Modern Man would be no help in that department, struggling as he did, to understand the chimps in the tea advert on telly, 'Avez vous un cuppa?'

Sylvia hadn't exactly lied to him but she had been more than a bit misleading by focussing on Bristol Airport's imminent expansion. She had also applied to the big carriers based at London Heathrow. She would be happy to settle with short haul charters to Spain, Portugal and the Euro-Med region but her ambition was to fly the long haul routes to Africa, Asia and Australia. That was what she really meant by travelling.

Some of her friends had taken a gap year backpacking to 'find themselves' and ended up living in squalor for a while in a Bangkok hostel, having run out of money. Sylvia had no intention of finding out what she would be prepared to do in circumstances like that. It didn't bear thinking about. Whatever they did, they never talked about it. Not to her anyway.

She had known Madeleine since primary school and even when very drunk one Christmas, all Sylvia managed to coerce out of her was, 'What happened in Thailand, stays in Thailand. I don't want you to think less of me than you do already.'

Sylvia worried for her friend and imagined things ten times worse than what may have happened. Close to tears, they both hugged and managed to move the conversation on to which of their contemporaries looked fatter. Soon they were giggling about who had a stupid boyfriend or had totally lost their dress sense. There was plenty of scope in the pub that evening, as most of her school year group seemed to be home for the holidays.

Cheered by the failings of others, they resolved never to mention it again. Sylvia remained curious and wondered what she would do if push came to shove, with her back to the wall? She hoped she would never be in a position to answer that particular question. Ignorance wasn't bliss but sometimes it was a hell of a lot better than cold hard facts.

Modern Man went back to driving and Sylvia did her best to put those dark thoughts out of her mind. She was suddenly cold and shivery. She had to force strong memories of happy times to the front of her mind. Make no mistake, she had plenty to choose from. Especially over the last few weeks and months. She was in love and going to be married for goodness sake. How much better could it get? They hadn't set a date or anything. They hadn't really had a chance to plan any of it. It had been such a rush.

Sylvia's parents were delighted, of course. If they had any reservations they had the common decency to keep quiet about them, at least when she was within ear shot. Even her father, who she feared would take an instant dislike to the love of her life, had hugged Modern Man. There was a tear in daddy's eye and his voice had cracked a little.

Sylvia's mother made a fuss of her fiancé, naturally. She tried to do everything for him and ended up doing nothing of value. Her father opened a bottle of fine champagne and they celebrated in style. Once that was polished off, the men moved on to brandy and Sylvia and her mother worked their way through a Chablis Premier Cru and saluted that with a large Baileys over ice. The next day's headaches would be off the chart but none of them cared. They were celebrating and that was that.

The reception from Modern Man's parents had been less flamboyant but equally enthusiastic, albeit in a more down-to-earth kind of way. The hugging was full-bodied and not far short of indecent assault in his dad's case. Sylvia took it in good spirit. This wasn't the time to put a dent in her future father-in-law's crown jewels. She knew that was his wife's privilege and was sure it would be performed with a flourish, whether literal or metaphorical in execution.

They all trotted off to the pub and the old man made sure everyone knew his son was engaged to the most beautiful girl in the world. He was on the verge of buying a round for everyone in the place but some rapid calculations led to the usual conclusion, 'Stuff 'em. They could all buy the happy couple a drink instead.' The landlord didn't care who paid as long as someone converted this outpouring of emotion into actual money he could put in the bank. Another night of serious drinking followed and the hangover fairy visited pain and suffering on them all.

No one could face the traditional 'hair of the dog' remedy but settled for the flesh of the pig and offspring of the hen in the form of a full English breakfast. The more time Sylvia spent with Modern Man's parents, the more she realised why he was the way he was and also how much he had managed to adapt and grow into a more complete individual. They were good, decent people and she would love them, as much as anyone really loved their in-laws. Her concern was when his folks met her parents. Somehow, she just couldn't see them hitting it off. They would have to meet fairly soon, otherwise it would become awkward. She'd need to invite both sets of parents to Bristol. It wouldn't work unless it was on neutral territory.

Sylvia had decided that she didn't want a formal engagement party. That seemed terribly old fashioned. She told Modern Man how she felt and he didn't appear to be bothered in the slightest. He said he would have a few beers with his mates, probably a weekend in London, something like that. He wasn't asking permission, merely stating an intention. He knew the rules had changed now the relationship had been formalised but he wasn't about to turn meek overnight. Sylvia was relieved, as that meant she could have a shopping trip with her friends, and a totally clear conscience.

By the time he parked the car outside her flat, it was late and they were tired. Modern Man stayed over and they slept in the next day. The neighbours were becoming accustomed to seeing Modern Man around the place, and even Irene Dearbourne was warming to him. She had swapped around her bedroom and dining room and was sleeping more soundly as a result.

One of the presents Sylvia had been given for Christmas was a personal stereo player. It wasn't much bigger than a deck of cards and the sound quality was really good. She wandered round the flat listening to a cassette of conversational French and repeating the occasional sentence rather loudly, much to Modern Man's amusement. Her interview was coming up in a few days and she needed to be ready for it. She had very little information about the procedure. All she knew was that it was being held in one of the large city centre hotels and the time she had to be there.

When the day arrived, she spent ages trying to decide how much make up was required. She knew what she intended to wear, that was sorted but the cosmetic issue was a tricky one. Too much was, well, too much! None at all looked like she didn't care. In the end she was in danger of running out of time and decided to stay with her usual favourites. Thankfully it wasn't windy so her hair wouldn't be a disaster.

She walked through the door of the hotel's main function room with a couple a minutes to spare. She showed her letter of invitation to a liveried administrator and was given a name badge to wear. At exactly ten o'clock the doors were closed and anyone who arrived afterwards was turned away, no matter what their mitigating circumstances may have been.

An ugly scene developed when one angry latecomer screamed, 'I was only late because your bloody airline cancelled my flight at the last minute and I had to drive.' The young lady in question completed the withdrawal of her application with a string of expletives that hung in the air like a nasty smell.

There must have been two hundred people in the room, seated in rows facing a raised platform. A middle aged woman, not in uniform, stepped up to the lectern and silence broke out across the room. She introduced herself as the head of cabin crew recruitment, welcomed them all and thanked them for being punctual. Those who could not arrive for interview on time were unlikely to arrive for work on time and since delayed flights cost the airline a lot of money, she had no use for such people, she explained.

The talk went on for about half an hour and included some of the rules and regulations. She stressed the no-alcohol on company time on numerous occasions during her speech.

They were then split into groups of ten and given a task to do. There were observers with clipboards, hovering near each group, eavesdropping on conversations but not interfering in any way. Any sign of teamwork breaking out or natural leaders being identified was duly noted. Sylvia's group were mainly sheep in sheep's clothing, apart from one girl who put herself forward as team leader and started issuing orders in a fairly random way.

The task was to come up with a 'brand' for the airline. They had to identify a target demographic and create a suitable theme and marketing approach that would most appeal to them. Two of the group would present the team's idea to everyone. Bossy Boots hadn't read the brief properly before she started ordering people around and she was clearly creating tension in the group. Being polite and not knowing each other, they exchanged quizzical glances and set their eyebrows to 'furrowed' but no one summoned the courage to step up and take her on.

No one except Sylvia, that is. She had spent the last few years dealing with stroppy and unruly children. Bossy Boots was just a little older but clearly out of the same mould. Sylvia skilfully talked her round to a different way of approaching the task. She didn't front up and go for the straight cat fight. Sylvia was more subtle than that. She initiated a non-confrontational dialogue that appeared to be supportive and yet managed to win over the agreement of the other people in the group.

The group worked together and eventually some of the others put forward ideas and suggestions. Once the natural inertia had subsided Sylvia let herself slip into the background a little. She didn't want to be regarded as the other dictator. It came as no surprise that the group consensus deemed that Sylvia should do the presentation, or that her co-presenter would try to steal the show and take any credit on offer.

The result was rather confusing for the audience as Bossy Boots went off on a tangent to explain the rationale behind 'her' ideas. Sylvia let it go, in full knowledge that nothing was to be gained by interrupting. They were given polite applause and returned to their seats. One by one the other groups put forward their ideas. None were outstanding and some were truly appalling, which made Sylvia feel a little better.

A buffet lunch followed and this in itself was something of a deliberate challenge. There was a wide choice of finger food, as well as soft drinks and wine. There were no tables and chairs in the room, making it quite a feat of dexterity to hold a floppy plate and a drink whilst trying to fork food to the mouth without it landing on the floor. Sylvia was too nervous to eat a lot anyway and didn't want to appear greedy.

For those who took the wine option, their day was over. One by one they were invited by an interviewer to, 'Come for a chat,' out of earshot of anyone else. They were politely reminded that drinking on duty was not permitted. The job required them to resist the temptation to consume alcohol despite it being in plentiful supply on board the aircraft. Naturally they felt hard done but they had no valid defence.

Sylvia would have loved a glass of wine at that moment. The day was proving to be quite stressful. However, the thought occurred to her that there are occasions when drinking is totally unwise and during a job interview is definitely one of them.

She resisted the temptation and was rewarded with the sight and sound of Bossy Boots being escorted from the room proclaiming her innocence by stating she was only holding the glass for someone else. It wasn't actually her wine at all, she insisted.

There was more drama to follow when one of the few boys at the interview was being ejected. There were tears and insults flew, before he fired his parting shot. 'You're just a frump with your fat legs and bad skin. As for your hair, call that natural!' There the hissy-fit ended. Sylvia thought to herself, 'Hell hath no fury like a bitter young queen.' The other boys distanced themselves from the event and quietly bitched about their erstwhile departed chum.

There were a couple of guys there who weren't obviously gay and Sylvia chatted to them for a while. They were blokes who wanted to travel and hadn't realised that being straight men might place them in a minority. Having noticed they were surrounded by pretty girls and that most of the other chaps only seemed to be interested in each other, the guys hinted to Sylvia that it could work out very nicely for them. Sylvia told them she was engaged but wished them luck all the same.

The afternoon started with each of the remaining applicants giving a short presentation about themselves and focussing on why they wanted to be cabin crew members. Some people folded under the pressure of speaking to such a large audience and others waffled on for so long it was like watching the Oscars.

There was another presentation about the company, detailing the lifestyle of flying staff. While that was happening the interviewers were identifying which applicants they were interested in talking to on a one-to-one basis. By the end of the presentation they had a list together and it was read out to the assembled audience.

'The following applicants should remain in the room,' one of them said. 'If your name is not called, you have been unsuccessful on this occasion. We thank you for your interest and for coming along today.'

The first name to be called resulted in a one-woman cheer. The lady in question was immediately embarrassed for such an inappropriate response and tried desperately hard to be invisible. Subsequent responses were more restrained in deference to those around them, still waiting and hoping. As no one knew how long the list was, the tension grew unbearably. It could stop at any moment. Dreams would be crushed and ambitions that had been nurtured since childhood, dashed. It all hung in the balance.

Sylvia's name was called and those around her seemed genuinely pleased for her, if more than a little envious in some cases. A bond had developed between a small group of them and she had been the reason for it. She was shown into yet another room. This time there was an interview panel of three uniformed staff.

They asked the usual background questions about career to date and why she wanted to fly with their airline. Without warning one of them switched to speaking in French and asked her a few questions related to travel and that sort of thing. Sylvia was a little surprised by the sudden change but managed to engage the right part of her brain after a short pause.

She had never claimed to be anywhere near fluent but felt she did reasonably well in the circumstances. After a few minutes they returned to conversing in English and without giving any clue to how she'd performed, thanked her for attending. That convinced Sylvia she had blown it. It had been a mentally demanding day and she was in desperate need of a large glass of wine, which she poured as soon as she was in her flat.

It was a brown envelope that arrived a week later. Thin, franked and Sylvia knew before she opened it that it wouldn't be good news. The airline thanked her for her interest and wished her well in her future career but were not in a position to offer her a role in their Cabin Crew team. No reason was given, not even a hint as to what she could have improved on. She wasn't about to fly but the letter did. She screwed it up and launched it across the room into the bin. Quite aerodynamic really.

The disappointment was tempered a mere two days later with an invitation to an interview with the national carrier. British Airways hadn't recruited flying staff for several years and appeared to be in terminal decline in the late 1970's. The BOAC and BEA merger seemed to have created a monster that gobbled up state funding and spat out indigestible food on a global scale.

Radical action was essential if the airline was to survive and in the early eighties it was beginning to show positive results. Sylvia had never been a BA passenger; it had always been out of her price range. She'd flown Pan Am once, returning from summer camp the first year she worked in the states. Even tired and hungry, she was aware that they were more attentive and somehow slicker than the budget carriers with whom she usually crossed the Atlantic.

This interview turned out to be an entirely different experience. There were only six applicants attending and it was held in the company headquarters at Heathrow. They were offered tea and coffee, had a pleasant, non-confrontational chat on a one-to-one basis, then a group discussion about what made good cabin service. It was chaired by the interviewer, who made sure everyone spoke, whether they wanted to or not, and who also managed to make notes about candidates.

There were five girls and one rather shy young man. Sylvia wondered if that made it harder for the girls. Would they recruit in equal numbers between the sexes, making this guy an almost dead cert? Could they do that in these enlightened days? She had no idea and had now lost the thread of the discussion taking place around her. It was a sort of pink noise as each of the girls raised the volume a bit to make sure they made their point.

The interviewer had steered the conversation around to personal qualities and customer contact skills. Too Shy Christopher was given the floor. Up to that point he'd only made one significant contribution. He grabbed everyone's attention when, in an unlikely Lancastrian accent, he blurted out, 'Hang on now, don't suppose you've considered….no stupid idea, sorry.'

It looked like he'd messed up his big chance to impress. The conversation picked up again and was eventually brought to an end by the interviewer. The applicants were thanked individually for attending and told they would be contacted within seven days. The next stage would be a second round of interviews, for those who had been successful on this occasion.

Sylvia came away from it feeling she'd done herself justice and if it wasn't to be then she would have to accept it with good grace. As it was, grace was not required. She was invited to return for a second interview and converted all the excitement and nervous energy into indecision about what to wear for the call back. As a primary school teacher she was not required to have an abundance of suits and her personal preference in smart casual clothes was definitely not appropriate for interviews. Shopping was required but Modern Man was not. She took her best friend and they spent a day in Bristol playing dressing up.

Modern Man had much to learn about his role in the relationship. He mistook her readily offered opinions about his choice of clothes to be a two-way thing and she was too polite and too much in love to shoot him down in flames. She knew he would catch on eventually and was prepared to wait it out

The second interview consisted of three face-to-face meetings with managers from various departments. Sylvia didn't know what to expect so prepared for the interviews as best she could by researching the company. Her enthusiasm for the job increased enormously when she discovered all the fantastic locations she could be flying to.

The Cabin Crew manager asked her what she knew about the airline and had to interrupt her after almost ten eloquent minutes of facts about the company. The Human Resources interviewer asked her about her family background and current domestic situation. She used phrases like 'current partner' and 'significant other' instead of coming out and asking if she was living with a boyfriend or girlfriend. When Sylvia said she had recently become engaged the facial expression changed to grave concern.

The HR manager went to great length to explain that some partners found it hard to deal with the lifestyle of flying staff.

'Long haul crew are away for up to three weeks at a time, then home for six or seven days, then away again. It's very disruptive,' she said.

Sylvia immediately wished she'd stayed quiet about being engaged but then realised she had a sizeable diamond on her finger and that may have prompted the question in the first place. Better than being caught in an obvious lie, Sylvia decided.

The occupational psychologist ran her through some psychometric tests and asked lots of oblique questions. Sylvia assumed there was some point to this but couldn't imagine what it was.

On the train back to Bristol Sylvia fell asleep and could easily have ended up in Swansea if she hadn't been woken by a crying child in the Box tunnel, shortly before they passed through Bath. On reflection, she thought she had given a good account of herself but she was still anxious about the outcome. Her feelings had shifted from ambition to burning desire and she desperately wanted the job. Teaching had been good but like so many things in life, it was about knowing when to stay and when to move on. For her, it felt right to do this now.

Thankfully, the recruiters agreed and Sylvia was offered a position on a long haul 747 course. They knew she would have to work a term's notice and had a course starting after the Easter weekend. Sylvia bounced around the flat screaming like a mad woman and Irene Dearbourne was not amused. She stamped heavily on the floor of her flat immediately above Sylvia's. Such was Sylvia's level of excitement that she shouted, 'Sorry Irene,' through the ceiling.

Modern Man was delighted for her, of course, but it didn't take him long to realise that Sylvia would be away a lot of the time. 'What the hell,' he thought to himself, 'I'm engaged to a British Airways Stewardess,' and that was pretty cool for a junior engineer.

Sylvia hadn't really explained too much about the lifestyle that came with the position because she didn't really know what it would be like herself. There'd been snippets of information at the interviews but none of it made much sense. There had been talk of smart hotels, allowances and slip stations down the routes. This was a whole new language to learn.

It was going to be tough to concentrate on teaching for the rest of term. Maybe she could have her class do a project on flying. They could draw and paint aeroplanes, write about interesting countries and the maths class could be about currency exchange. Science could bring in time changes and the great circle route used in global navigation. Now she was going too far, they were only six years old, she reminded herself. At that moment she wasn't particularly far ahead of them.

February and March usually flew by but that year they, dragged their heels. On her last day at school the children became extremely excited because there was a party and then they all cried when they realised why. There were hugs and smudged mascara, flowers and cake, promises to come back and visit and to send post cards from exotic locations. Emotionally drained, Sylvia returned to her flat and once again dinner took the form of a Chinese takeaway. She had a little over a week before her course started at the Heathrow training centre and a lot to do, although she couldn't think exactly what at that precise instant. The airline had provided a hotel room for the first week of the month long course, explaining that after that she would need to either commute daily or find a place for herself near the airport. The thought of travelling there and back every day didn't appeal and the cost would also be an issue she couldn't ignore.

Sylvia was the type of woman who liked to have important things planned ahead. She could be spontaneous with trivia but not the big stuff like where she was going to sleep that night. She had an elderly aunt who lived in Surbiton. Although she hadn't seen her for some considerable time, Sylvia was sure that a bed would be made available if required.

She phoned her parents with the news about her job and her problem with accommodation. They knew Sylvia had applied and they had mixed feelings about it if they were honest. They weren't to her face, of course. They simply didn't understand why she would want to give up something as secure as teaching and do this, 'glorified waitressing job.' That was how her father saw it.

She'd been such a sensible girl until now. Her mother mused that perhaps it would be the end of Sylvia's relationship with this northern lad and that she'd meet a nice pilot chappy and marry him instead. A broken engagement would be embarrassing but far better than an unsuitable marriage. Only time would tell.

Her parents were sure Aunt Elizabeth would be happy to have a lodger for a short while and offered to call her on Sylvia's behalf. Sylvia asked that they didn't. Once an arrangement had been made she would be committed to it and Sylvia preferred to have her options open.

Aunt Elizabeth was her father's first cousin and had never married. She worked her whole career in the civil service in Whitehall and had once reached the semi finals of Mastermind; her chosen subjects being the Crimean War and the life and works of Florence Nightingale.

Unfortunately, when speaking with a BBC researcher there had been some confusion and Florence Nightingale became Anne Nightingale, the Radio 1 disc jockey. Aunt Elizabeth didn't score well enough in her specialist subject round to make the final.

She never watched the program again after that. The memories were excruciatingly painful. She switched her allegiance to University Challenge and the rather dishy Bamber Gasgoigne. She found high intellect very attractive but sadly had little to offer in terms of physical attributes herself. Nevertheless rumours persisted in the corridors of power that in her day she'd oiled the wheels of diplomacy on more than one occasion. She would deny it to her dying day, naturally. However, for Queen and country, one did what was required of one and one didn't make a fuss about it afterwards.

The first day of Cabin Crew training was taken up mainly with administrative bits and pieces and their passports were collected by one of the instructors. They needed all the necessary visas to work in American air space and enter various Middle Eastern countries. It was also essential to verify that each new crew member was actually who they claimed to be.

There were sixteen on the 747 course and another twelve on a parallel Tri-Star course which also started that day. A few of them knew each other, having previously worked together in charter airlines. That seemed to grant them a license to squeal loudly at regular intervals and jump up and down hugging each other.

There were three instructors running Sylvia's course and they explained the structure and content of the next four weeks. Two and a half weeks would be spent learning cabin service, followed by three days of aviation medicine and a week of safety equipment and procedures.

Sylvia couldn't decide if two and a half weeks felt like too much time to learn how to push a trolley or if there was a lot more to it than she had realised. In the end she accepted that they probably knew what they were doing and she should let them do their job. She was excited, as they all were, but not to the level of high pitched squealing. Not yet anyway.

Of the sixteen on the course, eleven were girls and five were boys, although two of the boys looked as if they might be girls on the inside. They also behaved as if they were a couple; subtle but noticeable if you knew the signs. And she did.

Of the other three guys, one clearly believed he was on this earth for the benefit of all womankind. He couldn't pass a single shiny surface without giving himself an admiring glance. By the end of lunch on the first day he had approached at least half of the girls in search of a night out, 'to get to know each other.' None of them was playing ball this early in proceedings. Clearly, no one wanted to be labelled as his first conquest.

The other two boys looked scared witless and said nothing all morning or during the breaks, not even to each other. It was as if female company was a totally alien concept to them and they had no idea how deal with it. Most of the girls ignored them, not through bad manners, simply because the rest of the group were more interesting and responsive. Sylvia wondered how these boys had passed through the interview stages and been selected.

During the afternoon session each person had to stand in front of the others and present a five minute talk about themselves. The brief was to cover their previous jobs and what they hoped to gain from their flying career. Five minutes didn't seem like much but it would be an age to stand in silence with only the odd, 'Erm,' thrown in from time to time.

Sylvia had no problem with public speaking. Standing in front of people had been the main part of teaching. She was confident and spoke clearly and at the correct speed. Many of the others either spoke too quickly, showing their nerves, or over-compensated and droned on at a snail's pace. The Gigglers giggled through their presentations, as one would expect. Lover Boy stood with his feet too wide apart for good taste. The couple 'outed' themselves, as if everyone hadn't figured them out by then and the two quiet boys both trembled uncontrollably. Instructors made notes throughout and were generally encouraging in their comments and appraisals.

By the end of the first day Sylvia was prepared to believe that it would take two and a half weeks to cover what was in the training manual. It wasn't simply food and drink, there was a lot more to the job than that. There were duty free sales involving foreign currency exchange. Galley stowages had to be learned and cocktail recipes memorized. On top of that, there was a whole vocabulary of terms to become acquainted with. She quickly realised that she couldn't go far wrong if she put 'air' in front of every word in common parlance. It wasn't a larder, it was an air larder. If the prefix wasn't 'air' there was a fair chance it was either 'cabin' or 'flight.'

At the end of the session transport was laid on to take the class from the training centre to the hotel. It turned out to be one of the big chain hotels on the Bath Road. Checking in took quite a while but they all agreed to meet in the lobby in an hour to find somewhere to have dinner together.

Thankfully they were given a room each. Sylvia couldn't face the idea of sharing with any of the girls on the course. She didn't actively dislike them but was looking forward to a bit of alone time. Her room was the biggest hotel room she had ever stayed in. There was the usual phone by the bed and even one in the bathroom. She wouldn't be answering that one under any circumstances.

Sylvia showered, changed and went down to the lobby to meet up with the others. Not surprisingly she was the first to arrive. At least she hoped she was the first and that the others hadn't already left or that she'd been the only one to bother. After a few minutes a girl called Charlotte arrived. Sylvia hadn't spoken to her before as their paths hadn't crossed at any point. They chatted about the events of the day and Charlotte complemented her on her presentation.

Charlotte had left university the year before and didn't know what to do with a degree in Archaeology and had drifted into banking. She'd been a PA to a middle ranking manager in an investment bank in the City. After a couple of weeks Charlotte realised that it wasn't for her. If her boss worked late she had to work late. He was for ever changing his schedule and expected her to be some sort of mind reader. He travelled quite a lot but Charlotte had never been able to venture further than the post room. Her salary had been enough to live on but no more.

'You made it sound pretty impressive in your presentation,' Sylvia said.

'I learned a lot about spin in a short time,' was the instant retort.

The rest of the girls showed up eventually and they all trotted off to the coffee shop together. The crowd from the Tri-Star course were already in there and a bit of light-hearted banter ensued. There was friendly rivalry between the fleets. 747s had more of the exotic routes but Tri-Stars covered the Middle East which was more lucrative for the crews. It was a strange quirk of the salary and expenses structure with its roots in the mists of time.

Eventually the manager of the coffee shop had a quiet word with both tables and they settled down and scoured the menus. In the fullness of time they made their selections from the menu. The company was paying for their rooms but they had to cover all other costs themselves. Compared to some of the hotels on the airport strip, it wasn't expensive but Sylvia couldn't envisage every night following this pattern.

When the bill arrived for the table the mistake was clear to all but a couple of the Gigglers, to whom it appeared, almost nothing was crystal clear. One bill, eight diners. Some had starters, most but not all shared the three bottles of wine and the selected main courses varied in price from a few quid to more than a tenner.

The two girls at opposite ends of the table went for their calculators. First to draw would apportion the costs as they saw fit. There would be winners and there would be losers and a tense silence fell on this dimly lit corner of the room. The three people seated on either side of the long table pushed their chairs back a touch. No one wanted to be caught in the crossfire.

Their waiter stood behind the saloon doors, knowing this was not the time to intervene. He'd seen too many of these situations get ugly, friends turned on each other and claret was spilled. A tense silence descended and a freak wind blew a balled up paper napkin along the entire length of the table. This town needed a sheriff, and quickly.

Charlotte stepped in and the tension cranked up a notch. She was an unknown quantity. Could she restore law and order or would she crack under pressure? Her first action was to deputise Sylvia and then she broke the deadlock by announcing that splitting the bill equally was quite clearly unfair. Her French Onion soup and diet Coke was a quarter of the price of Sarah's Lamb Printemps and lashings of Haute Médoc.

A murmur quickly built up into a disconcerting rumble as each individual had to decide whether to back Charlotte or allow the shoot out begin. It was tough for some, they weren't all natural decision makers.

While Charlotte had their attention, Sylvia had a small notebook and pen in hand and was writing down who had what, sneaking an occasional peak at the bill and apportioning costs appropriately. At the critical moment when Charlotte needed support, Sylvia announced how much each of them had to pay.

The calculator cowboys were sceptical that she could do that much maths in her head and checked the figures. Reluctantly they both backed down when they realised she had also factored in a 7.5% tip into her costings. The waiter unclenched his buttocks and moved in to collect the spoils.

A sense of relief washed over the table as they went their separate ways. Some to the basement night club and others back to their rooms.

For Charlotte and Sylvia, it was a moment of indecision. Should they succumb to the temptation of the lounge bar and have a drink together or simply acknowledge that a bond now existed between them. Sylvia was first to speak, 'I need to call my boyfriend,' she said. 'Phone me for breakfast?'

Day two of training started with a trip to Uniform Stores to be measured and kitted out. There were two noticeable absences; the two boys who had hardly spoken the previous day. They had finally plucked up the courage to talk to the training manager, if only to say, 'It's not what we thought it would be like. We don't want to do this anymore.'

The training manager and the three instructors tried hard to persuade the boys to stick it out a bit longer but their minds were clearly made up. On the evidence of the first day, none of the instructors could see them being particularly useful on an aircraft, especially if there was an emergency situation. They wished the boys well and let them go.

The uniform fitting made it all real. Day one had been interesting but this was exciting. They were starting to belong. None of them had thought in advance exactly how much uniform they would be given. Four skirts, six blouses, two jackets, four summer uniform dresses, three in-flight tabards, one uniform handbag and one hat. It was going so well until they were issued with the hat. It brought back memories of *Bill and Ben the Flowerpot Men* from *Watch with Mother* on the BBC. It was bound to make a mess of the hair and frankly, looked stupid. The boys had proper peaked caps that made them look like officers in the Navy or Air Force and they were quite sexy in their tailored uniforms.

Lover Boy was swaggering about the room, revelling in the number of mirrors available to him and offering compliments to any of the girls whom he thought may respond similarly. The other two boys were happy to admire each other and fussed over details to the point where it took them much longer to be fitted than anyone else.

There would be alterations, of course, and strangely enough each person had to organise their own. The girls were used to adjusting hem lines but for the boys, well, where were their mothers now they actually needed them? The couple had a friend who was a tailor in Ealing, which meant they were sorted. Lover Boy decided it was an honour he would bestow on one of the girls, but which one? It was tough because quite a few had been giving him the eye. They thought they were being subtle but he knew the signs. They all wanted him. They couldn't help themselves.

He didn't want to embarrass the others so Lover Boy made his approach discreetly. It was only fair to protect the chosen one from the inevitable jealousy of the rest of the herd. Sylvia and Charlotte clocked his approach from across the room and watched with great amusement as he split Giggly Bianca from the group. They weren't sure how he managed to peel her away because this was a bunch that seemed to do everything together.

By the time they boarded the coach and returned to the training school it was lunchtime. The afternoon session would be role playing in a mock up of an aircraft cabin and galley. This was new territory to all but the handful who had previously been crew on other airlines. There were three of them and they expected it to be exactly the same. They couldn't have been more mistaken.

One of the instructors acted as a passenger and had two of them working the bar trolley. He asked for a drink that he knew they wouldn't have, to test their mettle.

The response he received was, 'We ain't got none of that stuff, pick somefink else.'

The course hadn't covered the section on reading body language at that point but even without that degree of tutelage, they all knew that Tania had made a serious error. Martin, the instructor displayed every physical manifestation of shock and outrage that is possible for the human body to exhibit. He would later acknowledge, at his own performance review, that he over-reacted on that occasion but at the time he couldn't contain himself. Something in his stressed brain made him lapse into transatlantic parlance as he managed to string together the single sentence, 'Run that by me one more time.'

'What?' said Tania, in an aggressive-defensive tone.

'Repeat exactly what you said to me when I asked you for my drink.'

'Oh that. We haven't got any. What do you want instead?

Martin was struggling to regain control; he was in a tail spin. His emotional altimeter was rotating faster than he could imagine was possible and his career as an instructor was about to crash and burn immediately after take off. Why had he opted to be an instructor when he could have carried on flying as crew full time? What had possessed him to spend six months a year trying to instil professionalism into a bunch of no-hopers like these. Yes, he was able to spend more time with his family but he missed the shopping down the routes and had noticed that his colleagues treated him differently when he was on the aircraft. However, using the breathing exercises his singing teacher had taught him, he managed to recover his composure before speaking again.

After a few minutes of careful contemplation he said, 'Tania, that's not how we speak to passengers in this airline. The correct response would be, "I'm sorry sir, we don't carry that particular brand, I'm able to offer you 'blah' instead." In that way you are helping them make a decision rather than rejecting their initial request which may be taken as a rejection of them personally. Do you understand the difference, Tania?'

Her uninspiring response was, 'Yeah, suppose.'

Martin passed out small cards with the name of a drink on them to half the group, who he seated in the mock up. The other half took it in turns to work the bar trolley. Everyone was nervous that Martin would throw another fit and Lover Boy risked everything when he took it too far with, 'I say, old bean, care for a snifter before luncheon?' Martin was about to give him both barrels when he realised that this injection of humour had relieved the tension and Martin wagged a finger instead. He backed this up by a rueful smile. Lover Boy's stock soared and he basked in the glow.

By the end of the second day the group had splintered into factions. There was no attempt to dine en-masse, which was a relief to the Coffee Shop manager. Sylvia and Charlotte went to the pub over the road and had bar meals and the others split in different directions.

Lover Boy worked his magic on Bianca and whether she did or she didn't was immaterial as everyone thought she must have. Even her friends did nothing to dispel the rumour.

Sylvia and Charlotte swapped life stories and by the end of it, Sylvia had a place to stay for the rest of the course. Charlotte had a one bedroom flat in Hammersmith but it was big enough to accommodate the pair of them for a while. The tube station was a bit of a walk away but that kept the rent down and Hammersmith was not too bad an area. Not spectacular but affordable.

At the end of the first week they had a test on everything they had learned so far. They were each told their score in a one-to-one interview with the lead instructor. It was an opportunity to find out how they were coping and to raise any issues they had about the course.

The test was harder than anyone expected and included questions such as, 'Where in the galley would they find baby food? How many varieties of whisky were loaded in the economy galley bar out of London Heathrow and what seat row number is immediately aft of Door 4 Left on a 747 aircraft?'

No one failed the test but a few were shocked out of complacency and some of the performance reviews were far from glowing endorsements. Sylvia had a few things to work on. Her classroom time with young children had rubbed off on her and she tended to talk to passengers as six or seven year olds, she was told. Charlotte was surprised to hear that the instructors found her too accommodating at times, frequently running back to the galley for something that could wait a few minutes and as a result her bar service was a bit slow.

They all went their separate ways on Friday evening. Sylvia caught a train from Paddington, Charlotte went back to her flat and Lover Boy made no secret of his intention to party with the Gigglers. Bianca must have given him a reasonable report because they appeared to be up for it.

Good luck to them, Charlotte thought. Since she'd left the bank her former boss had been bombarding her with requests for a date, sending her flowers, perfume and lingerie. He was married and he knew, that she knew that he was. Charlotte decided it was his life he was ruining not hers and finally returned his call. He was outside her flat a couple of hours later. He took her to a trendy restaurant in the West End where they drank, chatted and drank some more. At the end of the night they went to Charlotte's place and she made good on his investment. At some point in the early hours he whispered in her ear that he'd better go home, he was playing golf first thing Saturday morning. When Charlotte woke up she wasn't sure if she'd been dreaming, but no, it had happened and she had a feeling it would happen again and that was okay with her.

Sylvia peered wistfully out of the train window as she travelled towards the setting sun, finally arriving at Bristol Temple Meads. Modern Man was there to meet her and their embrace was like the first time. She had missed him, of course she had, but she had also been totally wrapped up in her new job and hadn't realised how much he would have missed her. He laughed it off with tales of long drinking sessions with his work mates and curry and porn nights but she knew he'd probably done none of those things. At least, she hoped not.

Their weekend together was a hectic combination of animated story-telling, sleeping, shopping and laundry. In less than forty-eight hours he knew all about her first week in the training school and the other people on her course. Sylvia was telling him about the instructors and what she had learned, when he butted in and said, 'Put the uniform on.'

After a little bit of encouragement she obliged and they did a bit of role playing that would never find its way into the training manual of that or any other airline.

Sunday evening came round far too soon for both of them. She was excited at the prospect of returning to London but being home, even for such a short time, reminded Sylvia how much she loved him, it, the whole situation.

Self-doubt rarely featured in Sylvia's life but it made an appearance later that Sunday evening when she faced an hour and a half of soul searching on the train to London. Was she doing the right thing with this career change? She'd read her mother's mind when she'd told her about the job. It was her mother's eyes that gave her away. Teaching was secure, they knew that. It couldn't be denied that security had value but flying was going to be exciting. Wasn't she entitled to do something exciting with her life? Would people think less of her as a result? Did it matter what people thought? On some level it certainly did matter. Sylvia remained in this tormented state during the journey.

Charlotte met her at Paddington Station, which was a huge relief. She couldn't image how she was supposed to manage on public transport with all her luggage.

'Where did you park?' Sylvia asked.

'Oh, I didn't come in the car, I came on the underground. I managed to park right outside my flat this afternoon and didn't want to lose that spot by using the car this evening,' she replied.

Sylvia looked stupefied, to her this made no sense at all. To any big city dweller it would have sounded perfectly reasonable. The tube wasn't terribly busy and it only took another fifteen minutes to drag her case along the pavement to Charlotte's flat.

It was a converted Victorian townhouse and thankfully Charlotte's flat was on the ground floor. Luckily for Sylvia, Charlotte had bought a sofa-bed when she moved in and with a bit of reorganising, managed to convert the small living room/kitchen into a living room/kitchen/bedroom with en-suite metropolis. Sylvia's flat was huge by comparison but she decided this wasn't the time to share that nugget of information with her new landlady.

That thought spurred Sylvia to bring up the potentially difficult issue of rent for the next three weeks. She didn't want to assume anything and Charlotte didn't want to talk about it. Consequently, they made absolutely no progress on that front. To fill the awkward silence, Sylvia suggested that they could split petrol costs and she would buy the food and cook the dinners while she stayed and see if that worked. Charlotte agreed immediately and pulled a bottle of wine from the fridge, indicating that it was a done deal.

As they sat and drank their wine Sylvia couldn't help noticing things about the flat. She knew it was rented which precluded any great expectations in terms of décor. It was basically clean but it was tidy in a way that suggested a hurried attempt to find a place for things that had never had a place before. When Charlotte opened a kitchen drawer to find a corkscrew, Sylvia could have sworn she saw a pair of tights in amongst the knives and forks. She must have been mistaken.

'Who would do that?' she thought to herself.

A casual glimpse through the open bedroom door revealed a knot of clothes stuffed under the bed and a line of shoes making an escape attempt from an overcrowded wardrobe.

In the course of conversation they figured out a morning routine that would prevent them being in each others way and eventually went to bed. It was a fairly quiet street and the sofa-bed was soft and comfortable but the sleep was fitful for Sylvia. She would have to find a way of tidying up, without insulting or upsetting her friend. The following morning they both managed to be ready and be out of the flat reasonably efficiently.

Week two started with a detailed look at the duty free bar and introduced the topic of foreign currency exchange. Everything was priced in pounds sterling but there was a bewildering array of currencies that could be accepted. Many of which they hadn't previously known existed.

Once again they were seated in the mock up cabin with a cue card each and took turns to serve each other. Sylvia was somewhat taken aback when Lover Boy asked for a litre of whisky, a model aircraft and a stewardess doll.

'I want to pay in Omani Riyals and have my change in Thai Baht,' he said with a twisted grin on his face.

'It doesn't say that,' Sylvia snapped back at him and grabbed the cue card out of his hand.

Before she could read it the instructor yelled, 'STOP! We don't talk to our passengers like that, Sylvia, do we?'

She was mortified. 'It doesn't say that. He made it up to embarrass me in front of everyone,' she jabbered.

The Gigglers did what they did best but the others waited quietly to see what would happen next. Sylvia still had the card in her hand and slowly read every word. It was exactly as Lover Boy had said, although the smarmy expression was his own ad lib and one, it seemed he was especially proud of.

This brief melodrama knocked Sylvia's confidence for the rest of the day. No amount of explanation from the instructor that this was a reasonable request was going to convince her and there was a moment when she thought it was time to pack in this crazy idea and retreat to the classroom.

'Everyone has a wobble at some point and yours is out of the way now,' one of her instructors explained during the lunch break. 'Seriously. People, who fly frequently, do make requests like that. The simple rule is if you can do what they've asked then you should do so. If you don't have any Thai Baht in your cashbox, tell them. Most people will accept either British Pounds or US Dollars.'

By the end of the week Sylvia's confidence was restored and she scored particularly well in the test that covered exchange rates, time changes and timetabling questions. She had also built up a tolerance to Charlotte's natural untidiness and Charlotte, to her credit, had made an effort to clean up her act while she had a guest staying. Having said that, the girls were relieved to have their own space for the weekend.

Week three was more of the same for the first two days then the focus moved on to aviation medicine. The training was carried out by a nursing sister from the company's own medical unit. The whole group was stunned to hear how many people managed to schedule serious medical conditions to coincide with long haul flights. There were heart attacks, strokes, ruptured ulcers, 'D and V....'

The Sister stopped speaking when she noticed there was an epidemic of quizzical expressions infecting the class. 'Right, for those of you not medically trained, it's diarrhoea and vomiting. Something that we'd like to avoid in the confines of an aircraft cabin.'

The next thing she asked was if any of the trainees were former nurses. Two of the Gigglers put their hands up and unbridled astonishment bounced round the room. Sister quizzed them for a few moments to establish their bona fides and when satisfied, continued with the class.

She clocked Lover Boy as a fine example of someone who needed medical attention and selected him as her 'casualty.' She used him to demonstrate how to place a body in the recovery position. He was also her victim in explaining the treatment of a fainting passenger. Sister may have been a little more enthusiastic than necessary when she pushed his head between his knees. His red face clearly indicated increased blood flow to the brain and that was the whole point of the exercise. Lover Boy was about to return to his seat, only to be restrained for a little longer. He had yet to be used as a casualty requiring bandaging and splinting.

The trainees were split into pairs to practice on each other. Sylvia and Charlotte worked well together but the two remaining boys on the course bickered over details, both convinced they were right and the other wrong. It was their first public spat. The medical course was intense and serious. Failing the test would mean failing the whole crew training course and out of a job. Sister mentioned this at least three times each day, lest they should forget. None of them did fail and by Friday afternoon the mental fatigue had taken its toll on the entire group.

Sylvia caught her regular train home to Bristol and Modern Man was there to meet her. They picked up a takeaway en route but she was too tired to play doctors and nurses with him. They did couple stuff on Saturday and it was clear to her that he was really missing her during the week. He didn't have to say it and she knew he wouldn't want to, in case it made him sound pathetic. Modern Man was a northerner and emotional outpouring was too much to expect from him. She left him on Sunday evening with the comforting words that this would be the last week in the training school.

Safety Equipment and Procedures filled the entire week. The what, where and how of every safety feature on this huge aircraft was drummed into them. They took turns practising evacuating down the inflatable slides from the full-sized aircraft mock-ups.

There was a lot of classroom time learning the contents of various stowages, memorising the locations and how to use the different types of fire extinguishers and smoke hoods. There was a place for everything and everything was in its place. If the trainees didn't know where each and every one of those items of emergency equipment were to be found then they would fail the course.

They learned about arctic survival as the London to Tokyo route via Alaska flew over the Arctic Circle. It was the instructor's favourite part of the course because there was always one person who asked why they went so far out of their way. He loved showing off his big globe. He would have that person stretch a piece of string between London and Anchorage. Once he proved his point he would suggest they transfer to European Division where the curvature of the earth would be less of a problem.

The final Friday consisted of tests all morning, one after another. Lunch was a nervous affair, no one appeared really confident that they had nailed all three tests. The pass mark in the Safety exam was 90%. That didn't leave much room for silly mistakes or indecision. It was also time limited. You had to be quick and correct. The instructors frequently reminded them that quick and correct was the only way to be in an emergency situation. It was a tough one to argue against and after the Arctic Circle string debacle, no one was ready to take that one on.

Sylvia and Charlotte had lived together, worked together and studied together. Thursday night had been one long question and answer session and although both girls were nervous, they believed they were as prepared as they could be. On Friday afternoon they would find out if they were flying or job hunting the following week.

The final day of the training course was laced with tension. It was the kind of tension that only comes with life changing moments. Moments that are out of the hands of the individuals whose lives may never be the same again. It was that big a deal. They were on the verge of a career of international travel to exotic locations. The possibility that it might be withheld at the last moment did not sit easily with any of the trainees.

Their instructors were well aware of the stress and did nothing to alleviate it. Each trainee was called in to a one-to-one meeting to have their performance analysed, scrutinized and circumcised. Shortly before the end, the instructor cut to the chase and told them whether they had passed the course. The instructors were aware from experience that the reaction of those who failed was to have been cut down and stitched up. For those who passed, it was a tingling sensation of new experiences and a release from previous constrictions.

Sylvia had passed and her new life was about to start. Charlotte had also passed and the hugging could begin in earnest. In fact they had all passed and the Gigglers became squealers for an unfortunately long time.

The last hour of the day was the Wings Ceremony when they were presented with their single-wing badge and certificate. It was a combined event with their colleagues on the Tri-Star course that had run in parallel with the 747 course. Remembering that drinking alcohol in uniform was strictly forbidden, the fully fledged crew members celebrated with a glass of fruit juice each and the sage advice that they should make a habit of drinking water, juice or soft drinks at work. One of the girls on the Tri-Star course broke the awkward silence that followed the remark by inviting everyone to a party at her boyfriend's wine bar in Kensington.

It was an invitation well received by those who were staying in London but a good few would be heading home and that could be anywhere in the country for long haul flyers. Sylvia made an instant decision to stay for the party. Charlotte gave her a nod of approval that it was okay to stay at her place for another night. Sylvia made a mental note to phone Modern Man.

The final event of the Wings Ceremony was the distribution of their first roster as operating Cabin Crew. It was a single A4 page with times, dates and three-letter airport codes. They had covered some of the codes in the course but Sylvia could only stare at hers, she couldn't figure it out at all.

There was a real buzz in the room as people excitedly exchanged details of their trip. Charlotte was going to Los Angeles on Tuesday, Lover Boy was heading for New York and one of the 'boys' could hardly contain his excitement at being handed San

Francisco. His partner made a feeble attempt to be happy for him but clearly felt that Miami wasn't going to rock his world to the same extent.

Eventually the spotlight fell on Sylvia and Charlotte asked, 'Well? Where are you going?'

'I don't know. Where's BGI?'

'Bridgetown, Barbados you silly cow!' was the first response.

Followed by, 'Bitch,' and a range of other insults with varying degrees of venom and playful insincerity. Handing out their first trip details turned out to quite divisive and had been left to the end for that very reason.

Sylvia had been rostered the best trip of the group. She hadn't come top in the exams and was curious why she had a week in the Caribbean for her supernumerary flight and others had night-stops or double-nights in various US locations.

She asked one of the instructors. His confusing reply was to wink and say, 'Rostering is a mystery to everyone. The rules are complex. You take what you're given. My only advice is never complain and don't try to bribe them. They have a huge influence over your life and they're audited frequently.'

Sylvia's trip was scheduled to leave Heathrow on Sunday afternoon for a week away. If she went to the party that evening she'd have less than twenty-four hours at home before leaving Modern Man again. It could be a difficult conversation with her fiancé but she wanted to go and it had to be done. She made the call and told him about her trip and the party. She even tried to make it sound as if the instructors had organised it, obliging her to attend. He was surprised that she had a trip so soon and a bit miffed that she was going to a party without him.

She detected some disappointment in Modern Man's voice and, in an effort to appease the circumstances, said, 'Come to the party with me.'

He realised immediately that he would be the odd one out and quickly fabricated an alternative arrangement. A darts match with the guys from work sounded credible on the spur of the moment. Perfect. When he put the phone down he called a couple of lads from the office and suggested a game of darts and a few pints. He'd sold himself on the idea as soon as he'd said it.

The party was good. The tension from the day had been converted to excitement and most people who could, turned up. All the talk was about flying. Crews being moved around the world like chess pieces on a global board game. Not to mention the shopping, parties and promiscuity from Anchorage, Alaska to Adelaide, Australia. How much was true and how much was exaggeration was impossible to tell.

Unbeknown to Sylvia, Charlotte had arranged to meet her ex-boss at the party. From the moment he walked into the bar Charlotte became detached from the group. They were totally wrapped up in each other for the rest of the night.

One of the Tri-Star guys gave Sylvia his best chat up lines. He wasn't put off in the slightest by her being engaged, in fact it seemed to be a major reason for his approach. He was good looking and she was a little bit drunk. He was charming and she was flattered by his compliments. She found herself wondering if she could, even though she knew she shouldn't. It was very unlike her but so much about her had changed in the last four weeks. He moved in for the first kiss and she found herself going along with it. It was one hell of a kiss and he obviously had no intention of stopping there. She was in a trance-like state, practically an out-of-body experience, unable to control her responses.

She woke up in Charlotte's bed shortly before noon on Saturday. She had the hang-over from Hell and couldn't remember a thing from the previous night. There was a note from Charlotte on the dressing table.

'Gone food shopping, back about two-ish.'

Sylvia had to pull herself together if she was to catch her train to Bristol. She also needed to piece together the events from the night before. She remembered talking to a guy in the wine bar in Kensington. She thought at the time he was one of the lads from the Tri-Star course but was less certain as she mulled over the few details she could pull from her rather woolly brain. Faint stirrings of panic began in her stomach. He had certainly looked like crew. He had been mingling with them and talked the talk. Then… Oh My God! She'd let him kiss her. How had that happened? She didn't let total strangers do things like that, even when drunk. In fact she became more reserved not less, it was the way she was wired. Had he spiked her drink? More to the point, if she'd let him kiss her, what else had she acquiesced to? Sylvia was frantic. She desperately wanted to eradicate the memory but at the same time, she had to know what had happened.

As she showered she checked herself for scratches or any other signs that she had been man-handled, quite literally man handled. There was nothing. She didn't know whether to be relieved or more anxious.

Showered, dressed and ready to go she checked her handbag. It was a reflex thing she did before leaving her flat. House keys, car keys and purse, check. There were loads of other things too. It was a woman's handbag after all.

There was also a crumpled piece of paper. It had a phone number on it and a name, Karl. Under the phone number was a short message.

'Call me when you wake up. It's important.'

Sylvia dialled the number and immediately hung up. She was trembling uncontrollably. Sylvia tried to think logically but there were too many conflicting emotions colliding in her brain. She dialled again and this time let it ring.

A croaky voice said, 'Yeah?'

'Is that Karl?'

'I think so, who's this?'

Sylvia explained about the note in her handbag and the party and then stopped, realising she still had no idea who this guy was or if he was The Guy.

Karl engaged his brain and told her what had happened. The Guy wasn't crew, he was a ringer who'd been listening in on their conversations. Karl didn't know how or why The Guy had targeted Sylvia but suspected he'd spiked her drink. Although Karl hadn't really spoken to Sylvia at the training school, he'd seen her whole pattern of behaviour change when she had been talking to The Guy for about fifteen minutes. At first he decided it was none of his business but when he saw him attempting to leave with her, Karl and the Tri-Star lads decided it was time to step in.

'The Guy tried to make out he was your fiancé and he was taking you home but he knew almost nothing about you. Nothing significant anyway. He had hold of your hand and tried to pull you towards the door. You stumbled and threw up all over his suit. Nice one! It was a smart move, he lost interest in you almost immediately. Charlotte told us you were staying at her place, so Ritchie and I brought you back in a taxi. Ritchie had an early report for his supernumerary trip to Amman this morning, that's why he wasn't drinking at all last night.'

Sylvia put the phone down without even saying thank you or goodbye. She couldn't believe what she'd just heard. At the other end of the conversation Karl was still talking. If Sylvia had still been listening, she'd have discovered that Charlotte had her own problems. It transpired that Charlotte and her ex-boss had been confronted by his wife and the man wouldn't let Charlotte leave the wine bar. The ex-boss was using her as a human shield to protect himself from injury, in addition to the many vicious and vitriolic insults being fired his way.

Sylvia caught the train to Bristol. Deep in thought for most of the journey, she eventually realised that Modern Man didn't need to know any of it and thinking she'd been abandoned by her friend, decided Charlotte could burn in Hell.

7. A Supporting Role

Modern Man's manager was nothing if not a patient man. He had a kindly nurturing personality. He was man who forgave much but forgot nothing. When he gathered a new crop of graduate trainees together for the first time he would deliver, in a Churchillian fashion, one of his favourite speeches. 'Some are born engineers, some become engineers and some have engineering thrust upon them.'

The real message, left unsaid but equally clear was, if anyone was there for the wrong reasons and didn't cut it, they would be out on their ear.

Modern Man's one-to-one interim appraisal with his manager had been, on balance, optimistic. Modern Man hadn't caused any dramatic failures in his first few months, nor had he accomplished anything brilliant. After discussing his progress so far and throwing a few adjectives around for a while, they agreed to settle on 'solid' to describe his performance. Modern Man had hoped for something better and cheered up slightly when informed that some people's career's peaked at 'solid' before returning to mediocre and occasionally plummeting to unreliable. At which point the door was held open for them until they realised their professional future lay elsewhere.

Modern Man had become immersed in a large defence project and was experiencing a wide range of disciplines as well as working with external subcontractors. Up to this point his focus had been entirely on his job until, and with the undeniable aid of a mug of strong coffee and a chocolate *Hobnob* biscuit, he had a Eureka moment. These were exactly the same skills required to plan a wedding. His wedding. Sylvia would be relieved that he was taking some of the load off her shoulders. She had such a lot to think about at the moment, with the new job taking her away so much and the constant jet lag wearing her down.

The brainwave hit him while Sylvia was away on a trip. Much as he wanted to, he couldn't share his brilliant idea with her immediately. Anyway, that couldn't be helped. He decided to press on regardless. He could only imagine how delighted she would be.

Like most guys, Modern Man had no idea how much planning was required for a wedding. As far as he could tell, it was a case of vestments, vows and victuals. No doubt there'd be some other trifling details to take care of and he'd tackle those when prompted. He also knew there was a fairly long list of 'do nots' as well. Turning up drunk or failing to turn up at all are the biggest but there are numerous others. Some of these are only disclosed when the offence has already been committed. Phrases like, 'Why would you think that was okay?' and, 'Wasn't it obvious?' would be rained down with venom and disbelief.

His company training had taught him the vital importance of securing the best possible deal for the country and the tax payer, in all matters of defence procurement. Quality was important but the tendency of suppliers to see government contracts as cash cows was a real issue. Hard negotiating was rewarded with long term contracts and improved profitability for his employer. These were transferable skills he could carry forward into this more personal project. He had watched and listened as the buyers held out for the last few pennies per unit and was confident he could do the same.

Armed with pen and paper and alone in the flat, he jotted down the essentials as he saw them:

Church – almost definitely, although a registry office might be cheaper (suggest it). Can't imagine that a parish priest would be difficult to beat down on price. Even if he brought the organist with him for moral support they would be like lambs to the slaughter.

Flowers – yeah. She'd probably want some of those to brighten the place up a bit. Nothing over-the-top though. A little posy to carry should do the trick. He recalled, as a little lad, he'd always given his mum chrysanthemums on Mother's Day and she'd always been chuffed to bits. Lots of different colours and not too expensive either.

Dress – No idea what they cost. Could it be as much as a couple of hundred quid?

Photographs – Dad had a nice camera and was very proud of his Dales landscapes that he'd had blown up to poster size and framed. He'd be made up if he was the official photographer at his son's wedding. Brilliant, no cost involved there, probably not even the film and developing.

Guests – Sylvia had talked about a small family event. Off the top of his head, there'd be her mum and dad, not sure about aunts, uncles and cousins, best friend (probably as bridesmaid), a few mates. His own his family. Twenty to twenty-five people tops.

Reception – She probably wouldn't want the pub's function room or the work's social club, although both were very reasonably priced and usually available if you gave more than a week's notice. Maybe one of the city centre hotels would be a good idea, especially if they threw in a room for the night to sweeten the deal. Phil in Marketing could do the disco and maybe the canteen manager could do the buffet. The hotel was bound to hike up the price to compensate for the free room he'd negotiated.

Honeymoon – This would be the big one. Now Sylvia was flying, they would be able to go anywhere they wanted for nothing. Australia, New Zealand, Hawaii, Africa. All of these places were worth considering, so perhaps a round-the-world tour was the answer. If they kept accommodation costs under control by staying in backpackers hostels in the Far East and motels in the States they could do it. It would be a fantastic adventure. Sorted!

Sylvia's world had been turned upside down in the last seven days. She had made it home to Bristol in time to do little more than laundry and pack for her first real trip as a long haul stewardess. She couldn't help but freak out a couple of times about recent events that had to remain confidential. She also wondered if she had made a huge mistake with this career change. Modern Man had been supportive but not particularly useful on her brief sojourn to the flat. However, he had known her long enough to recognise the simultaneous manifestations of excitement and anxiety and was forever making her cups of tea. It was a useful alternative to asking what was up with her.

When the time came, he drove her to the station, saw her onto the train and came to terms with the reality that the mental image of her in uniform would have to satisfy him during her frequent absences. He pondered this as he walked to the car park.

For the best part of an hour Sylvia fretted about what she had forgotten to pack. She checked her hair, makeup and passport at least once every fifteen minutes until she heaved her suitcase off the train at Slough and was ready to take a taxi to Heathrow. The driver knew exactly where to drop her, which she found rather odd and odder still that he seemed to know it was her first trip. 'The Knowledge' clearly extended beyond the road network of London and its environs.

Sylvia signed in at Crew Reporting and went to the briefing room at the appointed time. She was last to arrive and had to stand even though she wasn't late. There were three people sitting around a table at the front of the room and eleven more seated facing them. Sylvia felt strangely at home; it was like a tiny classroom.

The Cabin Service Officer introduced himself as Ronnie and his two Pursers, Bob and Michelle. Bob would be in charge of both First Class and Business Class and Michelle in Economy. He also took the opportunity to welcome Sylvia as a supernumerary crew member straight out of the training school. The reaction to this news was mixed. An extra pair of hands was welcome if she turned out to be useful but a drawback if she would always be in the way. Sylvia put on a brave face and smiled while her guts twisted and writhed inside her.

Each of the fourteen crew members selected a working position on the aircraft in order of their seniority. Three people worked in the first class cabin, one person worked on the upper deck serving business class and the flight crew, five were allocated to Galley 2 on the main deck and the remaining five in the Rear Galley.

They were transported straight to the aircraft via a security checkpoint where all their staff passes were scrutinized. About thirty minutes later the passengers would start boarding and this vital half hour was spent preparing the cabins and galleys for the flight as quickly as possible.

For everyone else, it was a routine. For Sylvia, it was an opportunity to prove herself useful. She had always been a compiler of lists, sometimes written, often committed to memory. She spent a few minutes organising her mind then set about following the pre-flight cabin checks they had been taught. In the training school she had been commended for being thorough and methodical. In the real world she was confronted with, 'Done that,' every time she started a task or checked a stowage.

Clearly downcast, she slumped into a seat near the galley and immediately received a ticking off from the captain who had only ventured into the realms of economy when he heard there was a shiny new stewardess in his crew. Apparently sitting in a passenger seat was a heinous crime and the day was slipping from bad to worse with every passing moment. Michelle, the purser, respectfully yet firmly informed the captain that Sylvia was on her first trip and couldn't be expected to know everything. The captain blustered a bit then strode off to the familiar territory of the flight deck. Michelle told Sylvia not to worry, she probably wouldn't see him again as captains rarely ventured into economy in case a passenger tried to engage them in conversation.

Sylvia was informed that Captains and First Officers usually restricted their visits to the first class cabin. Flight Engineers could turn up anywhere but were less hung up on status if it meant they could have female company, she learned.

'They're not all crusty old farts,' Michelle added with a twinkle in her eye.

Sylvia didn't really know how to interpret that last remark but her musings were immediately interrupted by an announcement over the public address system. 'Passengers will be boarding in the next few minutes.' All the crew took their positions in the doorways to welcome and guide passengers to their seats.

Over the course of the following quarter of an hour overhead bins were crammed with carry-on bags. Seatbelts were fastened, adjusted and unfastened and air blowers fiddled with. A few crew call bells were tested and, assumed to be pressed in error, reset by Michelle without the passengers' knowledge. Eventually the flood of people became a trickle as the last few seats were occupied.

The flight was full, the destination was the Caribbean and there was genuine excitement amongst the crew as well as the passengers. A week in Barbados was not a trip that came up very often. Apart from one evening when they were to shuttle to Trinidad and back to Bridgetown, the time was theirs to do with as they wished. It was unreal. She was being paid to lie on a beach, drink rum punch and go shopping.

Before any of that could happen there was about ten hours of cabin service to contend with. Michelle gathered her team in the galley for a final briefing. 'It's a holiday flight. Keep them happy but watch out for those drinking too much. There are quite a lot of families on board, some of them aren't sitting together. See if the people around them are happy to move. Sometimes I think check-in do this on purpose! One more thing. Sylvia, you can do the safety demonstration instead of Laura.'

Laura was delighted but Sylvia was filled with dread at the thought of over a hundred people staring at her while she fumbled with an oxygen mask and a lifejacket. It had to be done and there had to be a first time, no matter how embarrassing it may be. She knew the worst bit would be pretending to blow into the tube to top up the air in the life jacket and she blushed terribly at that instant. Sylvia made it through the rest of the demonstration without any other incidents and strapped-in for take-off.

Over three hundred tonnes of aircraft rumbled down the runway gaining speed and eventually left the ground. Sylvia was taken by surprise how soon after take off the other crew members had released their harnesses and were setting up bar trolleys in the galley. Michelle realised that the most efficient way to use Sylvia was for her to act as a runner, restocking the bar trolleys as they moved through the cabin, rather than serving on the first bar round. There would be plenty of opportunity to do that later in the flight.

Sylvia hovered behind Laura as she expertly and deftly served each passenger with incredible efficiency of movement. Laura had the ability to make each of them feel special. The connection was brief but real.

Alcohol was chargeable but soft drinks were free. Most people wanted simple things like gin and tonic, beer or wine and most paid in pounds. Sylvia felt totally useless. Laura didn't need help. Mike, the steward on the other end of the trolley was equally capable and Ritchie and Donna, working the other aisle, didn't need anything either.

Michelle's head popped out of the galley and a quick flick told Sylvia that at last, she was needed. Now she could do something useful. Michelle had her prepare the galley for a quick pit stop for the drinks trolleys as they passed by.

Apart from a brief respite while the movie was shown, the crew were constantly busy with the needs of the passengers. It was all a bit intense for Sylvia and once the afternoon tea service was over they were descending towards Bridgetown International.

Like most Caribbean airports the facilities were fairly basic. There was no air-bridge to walk through into a cool terminal building. Instead, a battered pick-up truck towed a set of stairs to the side of the jumbo jet and the ground staff opened the aircraft door.

As usual, there was an unofficial race to be the first passenger off the plane. There was no prize other than self-congratulation and if lives were lost in the struggle, so be it. Inevitably the queue for immigration was something of a leveller. There were two officials on duty and no detectable sense of urgency in either of them. Suitcases arrived in the fullness of time and whilst some passengers became hot and bothered about it all, most accepted it for what it was and soaked up the mood and rhythm of the islands.

A minibus took the crew to their hotel, which was a relief for Sylvia as she hadn't given a moment's thought to where they would stay or how they would travel from the airport to the town. It seemed ridiculous, on reflection, but it suddenly struck her that she couldn't remember the instructors saying anything about crew accommodation down the routes.

As the transport pulled up under the canopy of the Hilton Hotel, Michelle nudged Bob who tapped the foot of the guy in the row in front and before long they were all giggling, all except Sylvia who was staring open-mouthed and wide-eyed.

She looked around the minibus, clearly astonished. 'Are we staying here?' she mumbled.

Captain Crusty looked at her severely and said, 'Yerse, but if it's not to your taste I'll take it up with London when we return.'

To his credit he managed to crack a smile and Sylvia managed to breathe, which was fortunate as fainting would have been too embarrassing.

It took quite a while to check-in the whole crew and after exchanging room numbers they all wandered off, leaving their suitcases behind. All except Sylvia who went over to the neat row and pulled hers out of line. The Bell Captain, courteously but firmly, told her to leave the bag, it would be delivered to her room and she should tip the boy.

'It's okay, I'll take it myself.'

'No, miss, the boy will bring it to your room,' was the firm response.

Michelle appeared by magic and discreetly mumbled to Sylvia, 'The bell boys need the tips. Go with it.'

Another mistake. Sylvia was feeling rather depressed.

'We're all meeting for drinks in Bob's room in about an hour,' said Michelle. 'Put on your party dress and come along.'

Sylvia hadn't packed a party dress as such and this was yet another concern for her tired brain to deal with.

It took a while but her suitcase was eventually delivered to her room and she was finally able to shower and change. She had brought one smart outfit and it had survived the journey without needing to be ironed. It turned out Bob's room was immediately opposite hers. When she heard voices, Sylvia peeped through the spy hole in her door and saw some of her fellow crew members arrive in shorts and tee-shirts. The whole party dress routine was a stitch up. Bastards!

She changed into beachwear and joined the room party. It wasn't long before her yawns out-numbered spoken words and Sylvia had to call it a day. As she was leaving the room Donna shouted, 'Nine o'clock in the lobby for breakfast,' to which Sylvia nodded.

The curtains were heavy but the Caribbean sun found its way in and Sylvia woke up. It had been hot in the room and the air-conditioning was tricky to control. In the end she had slept naked to try to keep cool. Yawning and stretching she pulled back the long curtains to find her room had full length windows looking directly onto the beach and adjacent to the hotel coffee shop. No nets, no blinds and plenty of witnesses. She could only hope that none of them were her crew colleagues. Since it was **just** after six in the morning she hoped she had been lucky and quickly pulled the curtains closed again.

After several moments of flustered indecision Sylvia put some clothes on and thought she might explore the hotel complex. There was no reason to rush as she pottered round her room doing girly stuff first. After four weeks in the training school and staying at Charlotte's, it was a pleasure to have some time alone.

Eventually she left her room and found her way back to the hotel lobby. It looked totally different in daylight. She wandered through to the pool deck and glanced into the coffee shop, nervously looking for familiar faces and feeling very relieved when there were none. The pool deck opened onto the beach and there was a building down by the water's edge. Sylvia made her way down the path through the palm trees and found that the building was in fact a beach bar.

It was all a bit much to take in so early in the morning and the possibility that it might be a dream was both real and scary. What if she woke up and was in a staff meeting at school with everyone staring at her. Sylvia gave herself a mental slapping, then a physical one to be certain.

Sylvia could hardly contain her excitement, she was indeed in Barbados. She was standing barefoot on white sand, surrounded by palm trees and watching the clear blue waves crash onto the beach. She couldn't believe she was being paid for this. She didn't normally do guilt but at that moment she realised she hadn't given her fiancé a single thought in almost twenty-four hours. If he had been here with her it would have been perfect. It was pretty close to perfect without him and she knew she would have to adjust to enjoying new experiences like this on her own.

After walking on the beach for a while and checking out all of the hotel facilities it was almost time to meet the others for breakfast. Sylvia sat in the lobby and waited but no one turned up. Was this another prank at her expense? At quarter past nine

Donna and Ritchie arrived simultaneously and maybe even together but not necessarily so. Within the next ten minutes Mike, Laura and Michelle had also shown up. By half past they all decided no one else was coming and headed off to the hotel coffee shop.

'Is this how it works?' Sylvia asked.

'What? Oh, galley-centric socialising. Yeah, sometimes,' was the consensus reply. 'On a busy flight out of London you often don't get a chance to talk to the people working in the other galleys and if you haven't flown with them before and you get on with the people in you're working with.... Yeah, it happens.'

On the flight over, while the other three had been on a break, Laura and Mike were on duty in the galley, serving passengers on an ad hoc basis. In between swapping news and gossip, they extracted Sylvia's entire life story with a series of probing questions.

Sylvia wasn't used to being asked for such personal information by people she had never met before. In any other situation it would seem rather rude but to stewards and stewardesses it was as natural as breathing. Laura realised Sylvia was uncomfortable and explained the interest in new crew, especially finding out what career they had given up to start flying.

Michelle, Donna and Ritchie were quickly brought up to speed and over the course of breakfast Sylvia learned as much about her colleagues as they knew about her. Eventually the conversation moved on to relationships and her recent engagement dominated the conversation for quite a while. Losing interest, Ritchie and Mike excused themselves to play tennis.

Michelle was divorced. Laura had been married to a pilot for a couple of years and Donna was, to use her own words, 'Enjoying being single.' That only added weight to Sylvia's suspicions about Ritchie's and Donna's arrival when they all met for breakfast. Still that was none of Sylvia's business. Having divulged most of the details about herself the previous day, the focus then moved on to her future husband. The girls were genuinely interested and not in the least judgemental.

Michelle warned that whilst she was very happy for her, Sylvia should be aware that the job could be difficult for partners to deal with. Donna chipped in that it was perfectly possible to live two separate lives, for which she was flashed a disapproving look from Laura. Anxious to move things on, Sylvia asked Laura about her wedding and how difficult it had been to plan it while being away so often.

At midday they moved the conversation from the coffee shop to the beach bar. In her old persona, Sylvia would have been taking copious notes, such was the rich vein of information she had tapped into. Laura was a global wedding shop compendium. For almost thirty minutes she regaled the relative merits of varieties of orchids that could be purchased in Singapore. She then drifted into a long story about invitations being printed in Hong Kong and the Noritake china dinner set she bought for herself in Sri

Lanka. Michelle stayed with it but Donna had become bored and went off to watch the boys play tennis.

It was too hot for the girls to even consider eating lunch so they settled for a jug of rum punch and three glasses instead. The afternoon rolled by in much the same way the morning had and the alcohol, warm sea breeze and lingering fatigue from the previous day all took their toll on Sylvia. She drifted back to her room and fell asleep for six hours.

Sylvia woke refreshed but very hungry. She picked up the room service menu and was horrified at the prices they charged. That was the clincher. She went to the coffee shop instead. It was dark outside and still pleasantly warm as she strolled along the illuminated path. The clicking of crickets, maybe they were cicadas, added to the whole incredible experience. This was the life - and she was actually living it!

Sylvia felt a little self-conscious dining alone but at this late hour the coffee shop was quite quiet presumably because all the serious romantics were in the restaurant. They were probably staring deep into each other's eyes with hopes and dreams. Short-term or long-term, depending on the gender of the dreamer.

The following day she joined the economy galley's synchronized sunbathing team. Practically all of the crew were stretched out on loungers round the swimming pool, some were reading but most were listening to personal stereos; headphones plugged into their ears. *Sony Walkmans* and the like were the current must-have accessory but severely restricted the usual babble of conversation and tall tales of adventures in far-away places.

The stories tended to start with, 'Have you flown with....? What're they like?' and ended with an embarrassing event or something akin to a diplomatic incident being narrowly avoided.

The crew clearly took tanning very seriously and Sylvia was keen to acquire some colour. She was also thinking through the possibilities that her conversation with Laura had opened up. She knew cheap flights wouldn't be available until she had completed a full year with the company but there was no rush to the alter for her. Besides, the idea of a small family wedding had never been a serious consideration. Why would any girl want to scale down the biggest day of her life? It made no sense at all. She certainly wasn't about to compromise, no matter how long it may take. Certainly, not now that she was beginning to appreciate that the world was her shopping mall.

A fleeting thought told her not to bring a pad of note paper and pen out to the pool with her. Her colleagues had been merciless on their ribbing of her minor misdemeanours so far and she wasn't about to give them any more ammunition. She still had a sharp mind and reliable memory despite the dramatic increase in alcohol consumption in the last month.

Some of her colleagues mistook her expression of concentration as a mood and bitched about her not being able to take a joke and typical of the new intake. 'What were they doing in recruiting these days? When I started flying....,' peppered the selective memories of an ageing and bitter element, upstaged by these youngsters. Sylvia was totally unaware of the idle resentment that she had done nothing to deserve. It seemed that being twenty years younger and having a fantastic figure and pretty face were criminal offences.

She was too wrapped up in an article in Harpers & Queen about a young dress designer who had escaped from Cuba on a small boat. He and a few others had been picked up by the US Coast Guard and, because his father was politically active in his homeland, the designer narrowly avoided being deported back to a life of oppression. As a result he was given asylum and eventually managed to be acquire US citizenship.

He had a small studio in Manhattan's lower east side and was making quite a name for himself creating wedding gowns. There was one picture and instantly Sylvia knew this was the guy who would design her dress. A primary school teacher in Bristol could only dream of such things. A long haul stewardess could actually make them happen.

As the sun set in paradise, people drifted off to their rooms to shower and change. Arrangements were made to meet in the hotel bar at seven o'clock and decide which restaurant to dine in that evening. Sylvia hadn't eaten a thing since breakfast. After a couple of drinks she was quite tipsy. They all were.

The hotel bar was cosy and informal, situated on a terrace that looked out over the sea. A grand piano stood in the corner but no one was playing it. Michelle asked the waiter, who served them, why there was no music and he informed them that the regular pianist had called in sick. What possessed Sylvia to say she could play the piano was a mystery to her but it was too late to back down. She was literally carried to the instrument by Mike and Ritchie.

As the daughter of a country solicitor she had a fairly old fashioned upbringing that included piano lessons from the age of six. There was no doubt that it was a bonus when she was a primary school teacher. In a luxurious hotel, basking under a Caribbean sunset and an audience with great expectations, it was the source of serious self-doubt. She could certainly play the instrument, that wasn't the problem. If there had been any sheet music she could sight-read, but there wasn't. What the hell, go for it, she thought and hit them with the opening bars of *Nellie the Elephant.* Always a favourite with children. Strangely enough they loved it and most sang along.

This gave Sylvia some desperately needed thinking time. She followed up with *Puff the Magic Dragon* then drifted into *Bridge over Troubled Water* and a medley of Motown hits. A standing ovation from her crew colleagues ensured Sylvia would be the subject of future tall tales to be recounted round swimming pools from Los Angeles to Auckland. 'Did you here about one of the new crew who pushed the hotel's resident pianist off his stool and played pop classics on a *Steinway* grand piano for three hours straight?' She couldn't decide whether Miss Arkwright, her piano teacher would have been proud or ashamed of her impromptu performance.

Eventually they found a restaurant that would take a booking for seventeen people at ten minutes notice. They piled into a fleet of taxis and headed into Bridgetown. Fantastic seafood, loads of wine and the attention of several guys clearly wanting to make a move on her was both flattering and a little too much to take. A handful of the crew staggered to a club to dance the night away but Sylvia managed to extricate herself from the persistent grasp of her suitors and return to the hotel tired but triumphant. It had been a great day.

It was a bit of a wrench to work the shuttle flights to Trinidad and back to Barbados the following evening but it meant that another crew would be in the hotel for a few days and that meant more socialising. The aircraft arrived from London and most of the passengers disembarked in Bridgetown. Sylvia's crew then took the remaining passengers on to Port of Spain. They were on the ground in Trinidad for a couple of hours while the plane was cleaned and restocked for its flight back to London via Barbados.

Michelle explained that maximum working hours prevented one crew from working all the way from London to Trinidad. Another crew were scheduled to take the two short shuttle flights and a third crew, who had also been staying at the hotel, would board when the plane returned to Barbados and the fresh crew would take the aircraft on to London. Sylvia hadn't even noticed there'd been another crew in the hotel. They'd noticed her though. Some of them had been having an early breakfast, before heading out on a fishing trip, when she had exposed herself to the world on her first morning.

The purser who took over the rear galley from Michelle turned to Sylvia and grinned, 'Nice to meet you. Didn't recognise you at first with your clothes on.' Despite the early stages of a sun tan Sylvia's blush was spectacular. Donna's eyes were out on stalks and more than a few passengers would have something to talk about on the long flight home. Sylvia told Donna in confidence what had happened and she told everyone else.

After a few more days lazing in the Caribbean sun it was time to work her passage home to London. An important part of the hotel's role was to phone each crew member one hour before they were due to depart for the airport. Sylvia had realised when they operated the shuttles earlier in the week that an hour wasn't enough for her to do all that was necessary, without rushing. By the time the call came she was already drying her hair.

The entire crew assembled in the hotel lobby with one exception: the guy working in the first class galley had gone sick at the last minute and was not fit to work. It sounded like food poisoning, based on the groaning noise that was emanating from his bathroom. A doctor was called but it was clear, he was in no fit state to travel, even as a passenger.

The Captain and Cabin Service Officer decided that as they had one extra cabin crew member anyway, Sylvia would have to fill in. A bit of shuffling of operating positions secured her a place in the economy cabin and a more experienced crew member would take the role of galley chef up front, in first class.

There wasn't a spare seat on the plane and Sylvia performed admirably in the circumstances. By the time the crew strapped in for landing at Heathrow she was exhausted. The passengers disembarked slowly and somewhat chaotically as many of their in-flight essentials had found ingenious places to hide during the hours of darkness. Once the last person was out of earshot Michelle thanked Sylvia for her hard work and reassured her that the job got easier with practice.

Her desperate need for sleep on the train journey home was interrupted by being shaken awake just as she was sinking into the deepest of somnolence. She fumbled for her ticket and proffered it, bleary eyed, to the woman standing over her. Oddly, this person did not take it and clip it, scribble on it or even check it was valid, she asked Sylvia what the baggage allowance was on European flights. Still half asleep, Sylvia went to move her cabin bag off the seat next to her, assuming that was what she had been asked to do. The woman then repeated her question with added gusto and a little irritation, appending it with, 'My son has a business trip to Madrid and needs to know how heavy his suitcase can be.'

By this time Sylvia had gathered her wits, and although she heard the question, she couldn't imagine a situation where anyone would do such a thing. She managed to check the almost automatic reaction to point out the major breach of protocol in interpersonal communications between strangers. Suddenly the penny dropped. She was in uniform and therefore public property. She confessed to being unable to answer with any degree of certainty, recommending a telephone call to the airline or a visit to her travel agent. The woman stormed off declaring she would never fly with Sylvia's airline as their staff were all clearly incompetent.

The need for rest conquered Sylvia's annoyance and she drifted back into the land of nod. A rush of cold air through the carriage during a prolonged stop at Bath Spa woke her and provided sufficient time to organise herself before arriving at Bristol Temple Meads. Naturally Modern Man was there to meet her. In fact he'd been there for the previous two trains arriving from London as he had no idea how long it took from the time the aircraft landed to her actually being on a train heading west. He was ready for the full on platform greeting and was a little deflated when she didn't respond with the same level of enthusiasm.

'Take me home,' was all she managed to say and was lucky to get the last word out as her fiancé was more than ready to reconnect with her on a physical level. He had plenty to learn about her new lifestyle, as did she.

Having been away for a little over a week in total, she was entitled to a few days off before her next trip. Another roster had arrived in the post while she was in Barbados. It was a Miami night-stop. Really a three-day trip when you considered the overnight flight back into London. After a long bath and an even longer sleep she started to feel human again. Modern Man decided a Chinese takeaway was the best idea for dinner and phoned in the order. He also picked up a bottle of wine when he went to collect the meal. He hoped a few drinks would put her in the mood. He was already there and trying to keep a lid on it.

For Sylvia the following day started before dawn. Wide awake much earlier than she would normally be, she was forced to accept that sleep would evade her until she adjusted to the time difference. She looked across at Modern Man who had a silly grin on his face. She could guess what he was dreaming about. It wasn't difficult. The same thoughts occupied most of his mind when he was awake.

She made tea and toast and settled down happily to her huge pile of post. It had slipped her mind how many catalogues she had requested before her first trip. Everything from cakes to cars. She was at that blissful stage in her wedding planning that she could, and would, totally ignore the price of everything. She'd have whatever she wanted: cost didn't enter the equation. Daddy wouldn't even attempt to deny her anything on her big day.

Sylvia's mother had said, 'Leave it to me, I'll talk to him.' This had become the recurring closing remark of many of their phone conversations and Sylvia knew her mother had all the necessary skills to make the right things happen in the right way.

Modern Man eventually stumbled out of the bedroom and joined Sylvia on the couch. When he realised what she was looking at he produced his week's work on that subject with a flourish.

'I've been thinking about the guest list and the table plan for the reception,' he said as he passed her an A4 notepad. 'These are the people I want to invite and who I think should sit together at the meal.'

She hadn't met many of his school and college mates but would always remember some of the stories he told about their 'adventures'. Die-Bitch, Jack-Six-Pack, Kinky Matt and Jan, Silent-But-Deadly-Alex, Double-D-Amanda.

'Wait a minute, didn't you go out with Amanda?' she asked.

'Yeah, and she dumped me on my birthday.'

'So why invite her?'

'I really want to rub her nose in it. Show her what she let go,' he proudly announced.

'Not at my wedding,' Sylvia responded in a way that did not invite a response.

Mortally wounded, Modern Man retreated to the kitchen to make himself some breakfast. 'Her wedding? Wasn't it "their" wedding?' he mused, as the toast burned under the grill and he put a tea bag in the same mug as a spoonful of instant coffee, before adding cold water from the kettle. She'd changed in that week in the Caribbean, really changed.

8. The Final Countdown

Modern Man continued to make suggestions and initiate activities related to the wedding. Their wedding. However, with the benefit of several years teaching five to seven year olds Sylvia had the necessary skills to let him believe that his contribution was both welcome and valuable. She also managed to torpedo any firm arrangements he made before they became binding contracts and to come up with sufficient mitigating evidence to suppress any wounded pride or ill-feeling on his part.

His parents wanted to help as well but Sylvia had persuaded Modern Man's mum that since the wedding would be taking place in her home village in Oxfordshire and her mother didn't go out to work any longer, everything was in hand.

'Well if you're sure dear,' was the comforting response.

Modern Man's dad was clearly delighted that he wasn't stumping up for it and had no desire to be involved in any aspect of the planning phase. That was evidently women's work and, since time immemorial, the onus to pay for the wedding was on the bride's father. These were important traditions that should be upheld in an ever-changing world, particularly since he'd had the good sense to sire a boy not a girl.

Sylvia was relieved that one more potential banana skin had been avoided. Her future in-laws were good people and she didn't want to upset them unnecessarily. Her father rather uncharitably referred to them as common stock but as a dyed-in-the-wool southerner that came as no surprise to her. He now saw Yorkshire as a worthy county cricket opponent and industrial hinterland. As a young man it was the source of painful memories of National Service at Catterick Garrison.

Planning her wedding was progressing well. The date had been determined by the availability of venue she wanted for the reception. It was a delightful country house hotel in rural Oxfordshire a few miles from Bicester. So popular, in fact, that they were prepared to bide their time to celebrate their big day there. There was a lot to do in the many months in between. Sylvia had no need to rush. Attention to detail was absolutely critical.

The vicar of St. Mary's beamed at the idea of a local bride using his church, instead of the usual stream of optimistic outsiders looking for a suitable backdrop for photographs. He'd baptised Sylvia as a baby, Confirmed her as a young teenager and took great pride in his small part of her Christian upbringing. He was also keen to meet the chap who had stolen her heart and almost insisted that they visit him the next time they were over to see her parents.

Sylvia was proud of her man and loved him unconditionally. She was also aware that he could misrepresent himself as a first impression. Consequently, she was working on his social skills as a background task, treading carefully, or so she thought.

A New York nightstop barely gave her enough time to track down the Cuban designer. She phoned him from the hotel and although he was fully booked with appointments that afternoon, Raoul agreed to see her when she explained the circumstances. He would be working late again but his growing reputation was more important to him than leisure time. The ride on the subway was no worse than it would be in London at rush hour but the district where Raoul had his studio was like something out of a TV cop show. The duration of the ten minute walk from the station to his building was more nerve wracking than her first day of teaching practice.

Raoul showed her a number of wedding dresses at various stages of creation, 'Each gown is created for the individual client and therefore totally unique.' He had a number of well practiced phrases that clinched deals. This was always the first one he used. Sylvia didn't ask about the cost. If she had he would have politely curtailed the meeting and thanked her for her interest, explaining that he was unable to take on any more work at that time. Raoul had no need for the price-conscious consumer in his business model.

She explained that the nature of her job would make future meetings difficult to plan more than a month in advance. She would call him every time she was in the city and meet if it was convenient. Her wedding date was suitably far in the future for him to take the commission and she left his company an extremely happy lady. Once back in her room she called her mother to share every detail. It was way after midnight in Bicester and although always pleased to hear from their daughter, a phone call in the early hours was not normally a good thing for any parent to receive.

Sylvia's father answered the phone and struggled to hear what was being relayed to him as his wife kept asking, 'What's happened? Who's died? Which hospital was she in?' All this whilst attempting to get dressed and grab the phone from her husband.

'It's Sylvia for you, she's excited about something or other.'

With that her father drifted back into a deep sleep and her mother took the call in another room. Sylvia recounted every detail of her meeting with Raoul, the dresses she had seen and the fact that he would be creating her wedding gown. The call lasted about twenty minutes but the repercussions would reverberate for a lot longer. Neither woman slept much more that night. Sylvia was very excited and her mother, also wrapped up in it all, was devising a way to persuade her husband to buy into the project. He would have no problem with the concept but an unknown cost was a loose end he would have to be caressed into gently.

Sylvia's flight back to London the following day was the early departure from JFK. It was unusual in a couple of ways. First, weather conditions often meant it picked up a strong tail wind to add to its normal 500mph ground speed, shortening the scheduled flight time by as much as an hour. Second, it was daytime all the way across the Atlantic and almost none of the passengers fell asleep.

Added to that was the fact that as a rule New Yorkers were not regarded as the most easy-going laid-back punters which meant the cabin crew had no breaks. It was continuous service from take-off to landing and for this reason it was nicknamed 'The Daylight Maniac.'

The crew in the rear galley didn't exchange the usual chit chat of home and family. There simply wasn't time to engage in frivolous banter. Sylvia only discovered that one of the guys was driving back to Cardiff when they were strapped in side-by-side for landing. He asked where Sylvia lived and after learning that she was taking a train to Bristol, offered her a lift in his *Porsche*.

She had been non-committal at the time in case he was looking for more than a bit of company on the motorway but the thought of public transport and worse, the travelling public, swung it. At that moment she'd rather be taken roughly up the M4 exit ramp than spend another two hours as public property. In the end she had nothing to worry about. She phoned her fiancé to tell him not to drive to the station as she'd accepted a lift and would be back in the flat considerably sooner than if she'd taken the train.

Modern Man was beginning to pick up the rules of engagement when Sylvia arrived home from a trip. It was a different kind of tired to anything he had really experienced. After the summer camp he'd been wrecked for almost a week but could take as long as he wanted and needed to recover from the jetlag. Sylvia had a few days at home then she would be away again for another dose of long days and short nights. As a consequence he tried not to overload her with information and questions as soon as she walked through the door.

He'd learned to his cost that the job had usually taken her reserves of patience and goodwill and it wasn't up to him to find her breaking point. It also went down well with Sylvia if he could leave for work without waking her. That pretty much guaranteed the following night he would get what he had been missing most while she'd been away. Simple incentives with big rewards worked for him.

Once Sylvia had caught up on her lost sleep she would regale him with the stories and folklore of the job. She didn't believe half the tales she had been told but they were great anecdotes and for some reason an exotic location made the implausible possible and the mundane interesting.

On the journey down the motorway the previous evening, Eric 'the *Porsche'* had told her about a twenty-three day trip down to Australia and New Zealand that he'd been on a few years ago. On the way out they'd stayed in Abu Dhabi and Singapore. From Sydney they worked some shuttles to Adelaide and Melbourne, before heading off to Auckland. The return leg of the trip called in at Perth and Bombay.

By the time they landed in India they had quite a bit of money in their pockets. The consensus was to have a big blow-out on their last night. The entire crew turned up for dinner. After a decent meal most of them headed off to another hotel that had a night club popular with airline crew. By the end there was only a small group who didn't want the night to finish. Eric said he'd gone to bed at about four in the morning but wasn't the last to leave the room party.

He recalled being woken about three hours later by a strange noise outside and pulled back the curtains to see a baby elephant in the hotel swimming pool and several of the hotel staff attempting to move the beast off the premises. Something prompted him to check his wallet. He was surprised to find he didn't have as much cash left as he thought he should have.

Over the course of the day and a number of conversations with the main suspects, they pieced together what they thought might have happened. Dennis, the party animal from Gloucester, had claimed that he could buy anything at a discount and challenged his equally drunk colleagues to test this claim. They went into a huddle for a few minutes then each thrust $50 in his hand and told him to buy an elephant.

If he succeeded he would get another $50 but if he failed they each got double their stake back. He took the challenge and they didn't see him again that night. Each of the five crew members who had challenged him found a note pushed under their doors when they woke up. It simply said, 'UOI $50,' and was signed in very wobbly writing, 'Dennis.'

Modern Man laughed to the point of near incontinence and was ready to chuck in his career and go join the global party. Sylvia knew he didn't have the temperament for the working part of the job but promised that as soon as she qualified for her travel concessions she would take him on a trip with her. She'd only recently discovered how that worked and it took a bit of explaining for Modern man to fully understand.

'I think I get it. You work on the flight and I'm a passenger? When we get where we're going the hotel is free and we can do what we want, yeah? You get money we can spend and on the flight home you work and I'm a passenger again. Is that right?' he asked.

'Basically, yes. It's not completely free, only the room is paid for, not food or anything charged to the room. We have to pay the staff travel rate for your ticket and you are a stand-by both going and coming back, remember, you're not guaranteed to get on either flight,' she added.

Modern Man had tuned out after 'yes' and was dreaming of the Caribbean, Thailand, California and sun-kissed Pacific islands.

Having lifted his spirits with this far off opportunity, she decided this was a good time to tackle an issue that had been bothering her for a while.

'Who do you have in mind to be your Best Man?' she enquired nervously.

It was one of the few decisions that she felt she could influence rather than control but too much was at stake, she couldn't let him have a completely free choice. Men could be incredibly stupid when given the opportunity.

'It's a tough one,' he said. 'I've a lot of good mates to choose from.'

Sylvia's response came from a loving place but crashed and burned on impact. 'It needs to be someone responsible. I'm not having my day ruined by tales of drunken pranks and debauchery dressed up as an after-dinner speech.' She hadn't intended to phrase it quite like that but the damn had burst and the words flooded out.

The reaction took her completely by surprise.

'Your day?'

She was steeled for him defending his friends to the hilt but this was a real shocker.

'I thought it was going to be our day?'

Sylvia felt trapped. There was no easy way out of this one. She had been totally wrong-footed and was embarrassed. Modern Man was ready to take the advantage and propose the most unsuitable Best Man he could think of. However, a logical thought managed to gate crash the emotional part of his brain. He realised that he would be the subject of all the stories, both real and fabricated. These anecdotes would be made public at his wedding and that was just dumb. It was time to take the moral high ground.

'I haven't decided but rest assured that it will be a wise and noble man well versed in the etiquette of such an important event.'

Sylvia really didn't know how to interpret this response so she withdrew from the confrontation and moved onto safer territory.

'I think ties would be better than cravats with the morning suits. What do you think?' she asked rather tentatively.

This time it was Modern Man's turn to be surprised. She hadn't solicited his opinion on anything thus far and his answer was based totally on the fact that he had no idea how to tie a cravat, nor any desire to wear one.

'Ties would be good,' he replied. 'Do we have to buy the suits or can we rent them? I suppose your father has his own, would we need to find ones that match his.'

'No sweetie, he doesn't have a morning suit. He has a dinner suit. And by the way, one hires a morning suit, you rent a flat.'

Modern Man was sinking fast but had to ask the obvious question, 'What's the difference?'

Sylvia dug deep into retained knowledge acquired from her father and pronounced, 'Hiring pertains to the temporary acquisition of personal services, whereas renting implies payment to the first party for the use of land or property by the second party.'

'No, I meant what's the difference between a dinner suit and a morning suit, silly?' he said.

'Oh that's easy, the jacket of a morning suit has tails and a dinner suit is darker and can have shiny lapels,' Sylvia replied.

In the fullness of time and after a lot more questions and answers they were ready to venture into the city to find the shop belonging to the brothers Moss. Modern Man had never been measured for a suit before and his only awareness of the world of tailoring was from watching television. *Are You Being Served* had been part of his parents' regular sitcom diet and he wasn't looking forward to meeting the real Mr Humphreys. His catchphrase, 'I'm free,' was about as subtle as Mrs Slocombe's frequent references to her pussy. It had to be done and he would take one for the team if necessary.

Measurements were taken without any inappropriate touching and all important questions were answered by Sylvia after five seconds of silence from Modern Man. This was deemed sufficient time to indicate he didn't understand what or why he was being asked.

The entire transaction couldn't be completed until all five men in the wedding party had been kitted out. Her father would pick up his suit in the Oxford branch and the other four would be handled in Bristol. Modern Man expected this to be a complication that they would not entertain but apparently it was quite normal and no problem at all.

Once they were out in the street and heading back to the car Modern Man asked why they needed five suits. He knew there would be her father, himself and the Best Man but who were the other two for?

Sylvia read his mind and said, 'Groom, father of the bride, Best Man and two ushers.'

It seemed highly unlikely that they would be selling ice cream and popcorn in the church, consequently Modern Man had no idea why they would need ushers. Once again Sylvia tapped into his thoughts. She explained that the ushers directed guests to either the bride's side or groom's side of the church for the service. Some of the wedding party would be meeting their guests for the first time at the reception and it was the ushers' duty to make those introductions. Modern Man was curious how she knew all this stuff but wasn't about to ask. He'd had enough education for one day.

The passage of time is a curious thing. At some moments the wedding day felt so far away it would never happen and on other occasions it seemed to be almost upon them. Sylvia felt she couldn't possibly have everything organised in time.

Her job quickly became second nature and before long she was returning to cities she'd been to before. Almost half of the 747 routes were transatlantic enabling her to speak to Raoul often enough to be reassured that her dress was coming along nicely. They did have one interesting call where he needed her to check the measurement across the back of her shoulders. His assistant had spilled her latte on his original notes. He fired her, of course, but he had to make the call even though he was embarrassed to have to do so.

She had a tape measure in her handbag. It was a girl thing. The act of trying to run the tape round the back of her neck, holding one end on the point of her left shoulder and pinching the tape where it passed over the point of her right shoulder whilst lodging the phone between her cheek and collarbone didn't happen as well as she'd hoped. She would have to call him back. In the intervening few minutes Sylvia stood in front of the bathroom mirror to do the job properly. This, like everything else, had to be right or the whole day would be a disaster.

Sylvia's brain had found a rather creative and unusual way to count down to her Big Day. She became aware of this while doing the weekly shop. 'Sell by dates' kept catching her eye. At first it was the kind of food that hardly needed a 'best before' because tea bags and dried pasta could probably outlive her, if kept away from moisture and mice. As more and more items on her shopping list could be safely consumed by her as a married woman, she took another virtual step towards her wedding day.

She had a bit of a wobble at tinned custard and her stomach was doing somersaults by the time red pesto crossed the great divide. There was still a great deal to do and hardly anyone she could rely on. Her mother was too excited to be of any great help and forever lunching with her friends instead of checking progress on her own to-do list. Sylvia calmed down considerably when she collected her dress.

On the flight out to New York she had told one of the girls she was working with that she was collecting her wedding dress in Manhattan that afternoon. By the end of the conversation they were both so excited Sylvia simply had to take this girl with her to pick up the dress. Once at Raoul's studio she had a final fitting in her wedding gown and it was perfect. After much clapping and squealing Raoul was declared a genius. A status to which he was becoming familiar. Her father did the necessary credit card transaction over the phone. After which he was in desperate need of a large whisky. Single malt, naturally.

At cottage cheese Sylvia was back in control and reverted to a more conventional device to track time, commonly known as a calendar.

Periodically Modern Man attempted to participate in the planning process. Sylvia listened, evaluated and then rejected his suggestions. Convinced, as she was, that she had everything under control, she had no use for enthusiastic amateurs.

Having learned her lesson when broaching the subject of a Best Man, Sylvia was far more cautious in her choice words when she enquired about his plans for a stag night. She instantly regretted asking when he replied, 'Oh, I'd forgotten all about that!'

He hadn't of course, but he wasn't averse to messing with her head from time to time. She was in a hole but despite herself, she kept digging.

'Who is going to be your Best Man? You never did say if you'd decided.'

'I am proud to announce that it's to be my old school friend Martin Missleton,' Modern Man announced, as if addressing an assembled audience of local dignitaries who were awaiting the outcome of significant democratic process.

This was, in his opinion, a master stroke as Sylvia had never met Martin. She knew they went way back and had taken phone messages from him from time to time but he had never visited Bristol while she had been there. Wisely, on both their parts, Modern Man had enjoyed his lads' nights out when she was away. She trusted him not to chase other women and had no desire to see him test his resistance to alcohol and kebabs, with or without extra chilli sauce.

The little devil sitting on Sylvia's shoulder whispered in her ear, 'He's doing this to annoy you. He wants to spoil your day. The day you've been dreaming about since you were a little girl. He's going to embarrass you in front of all your family and friends. You will be humiliated if you don't nip this in the bud.'

She involuntarily flicked the collar of her blouse and muttered, 'No he's not,' under her breath.

Modern man heard this and took it as a challenge to his only decision in the entire wedding planning process. He was on the verge of going into a full scale rant and got as far as, 'My Best Man. My decision,' when he saw tears rolling down Sylvia's cheeks.

The shock of seeing her cry for the first time removed the powers of speech and logical thought. It was too overwhelming and highly illogical. God dammit, women were complicated machines with no user manual. He decided to keep quiet and let her explain. Unfortunately for him, she couldn't.

Modern Man decided that the men of the bridal party should meet together before the serious stuff was under way. Martin had taken a different route to the rest of his mates. College didn't suit him and he dropped out at the end of the first year. He'd passed his exams but decided to start working and earning instead of watching children's television most afternoons.

Martin was totally sold on the idea of being paid monthly but wasn't completely on-board with the contractual requirement of regular and useful work in exchange for this financial compensation. In the early days he tried to pull occasional 'sickies' with an array of fictitious diseases and family crises but to his dismay his employer had hinted that he didn't believe him. It was outrageous. The boss had practically called him a liar. To his face.

A free and frank exchange of views followed and Martin was at the point of a toddler tantrum when the boss told him he was actually good at what he did. He had a bright future if he would only use his creative energy in a positive way, rather than conjuring up schemes to avoid getting out of bed in the morning. At that moment of heightened awareness an attitude changing switch was flicked in Martin's brain. The planets aligned momentarily and he became a responsible adult.

Modern Man was aware his friend had changed but wasn't up to speed on the circumstances that caused the monumental shift in attitude. He assumed it was a gradual thing, the usual slow-dawn of maturity that most guys go through. It wasn't important anyway. What mattered was that his old mate could be relied upon to do what he said he'd do and be where he said he'd be.

Choosing a Best Man had actually been much harder than Modern Man had expected. On the face of it, it should have been straight forward. Pick a close friend who is dependable and responsible. As no one sprang immediately to mind he took it to the next level. Who could support him at the front of a church for half an hour without making stupid jokes? Who was capable of standing up at the reception and making an after-dinner speech without enough Dutch courage to leave The Netherlands in bored sobriety for months afterwards? After a short process of eliminating everyone else he knew, Martin, was the best candidate.

He also had to choose a couple of ushers and decided to go with his college mates Jack-Six-Pack and Dai Beech. They had stayed friends throughout their courses and met up at least once a year for a few beers and a curry. He noticed he was starting to feel the effects of the vindaloo-morning-after to a greater extent than he ever used to do.

He'd never had particularly spicy food when he lived at home. His dad couldn't stand it and was quick to remind anyone who challenged him on the subject that there was nothing exotic about food that left you being burned at both ends.

Like many families in the 1970's, they had gone through a painful period of being the guinea pigs of some experimental Cordon Bleu and wider European recipes tried out by an apprehensive wife and mother.

The old man put a stop to it all when his wife had added a tiny amount of paprika to his Lancashire hotpot and told him it was Hungarian goulash. After that it was meat and two veg, occasionally fish and chips but none of the peculiar foreign food. His dad was a creature of habit and viewed consistency as an indication of strength of character.

Modern Man suggested that Sylvia's father should meet Martin, Jack and Dai before the big day. He had an ulterior motive, of course. He didn't want her old man inviting himself to the stag night. Modern Man was sure her father wouldn't want to attend. He was equally certain that the women would want him there to 'keep an eye on things' as they would put it.

Her father was as straight-laced as one might predict a respected Home Counties solicitor to be but he was not ignorant of the ways of the common man. In his younger days, working for a small law firm in Oxford, he had gained court experience defending the strange behaviour of many young men the worse for drink. He was at a loss to understand why these chaps felt the need to adorn statues of war heroes with traffic cones or argue volubly with inanimate objects like lamp posts. The attraction of stealing items of police uniform also baffled the him. However, his job was to defend them as best he could and that's what he did.

It took a few phone calls and a bit or organising regarding travel arrangements but eventually the night out was planned. Modern Man picked a nice old country pub with a good selection of real ales and food that wasn't too expensive to dent the beer fund. He even booked a taxi to collect them at the end of the evening. What could possibly go wrong?

Sylvia's father drove across to Bristol on the Saturday afternoon and managed to park his Jaguar right outside the flat. Sylvia told him he was lucky to be able to find a spot as close but he didn't consider luck to play any part in it. He saw it as entitlement. Modern Man started to worry that the whole idea of them getting to know each other was a terrible mistake. It would be better if his future father-in-law only thought Modern Man was an incompetent fool rather than having it proved beyond reasonable doubt. However, it was far too late to change the plan. He would have to hope for the best.

Over the course of the next hour the guys arrived and they called for a taxi to take them to the pub. Sylvia's father had offered to take them in the Jag but the thought of a totally sober witness to what may or may not happen was not worth a thirty minute ride in a supercharged V8 motor car. They all declined politely.

Sylvia's father never been a beer drinker, preferring the taste of wine but thought he'd better try to meet the lads half way. He bought the first round of drinks and tried to break the ice by asking each of them about themselves. He genuinely thought he was showing interest in the young chaps as individuals. However, they felt as though they'd been cross-examined in the witness box.

For Martin, in particular, it was difficult. It had taken many years to suppress the memory of his conviction for urinating in public but this brought it all flooding back. He quickly excused himself and spent as long as it took in the gents' toilet to regain his composure and dry his trousers. By the time he returned to the table the conversation had moved on.

More rounds were bought and consumed and they were all starting to relax. From absolutely nowhere, Martin asked Jack what his real first name was. They all knew the initial was 'C' and that Jack was his middle name and actually it was really John but he had been called Jack from an early age,

'It's Charles, after my granddad,' he said, feeling the need to qualify what he felt was a rather old fashioned name and a serious impediment to the cool image he tried hard to portray.

Martin burst out laughing and his mirth was directed straight at Modern Man.

'Your ushers are Charles and Dai!' he spluttered.

Both Jack and Modern Man took the joke reasonably well, having little option in the circumstances. It certainly broke the ice regarding his future father-in-law's presence. He was in hysterics. The guys never considered for a moment that Sylvia's father might be nervous in their company. Why would he be? He was a bit up tight to start with but loosening up by the minute.

After four pints his middle-aged bladder was struggling with the sheer volume of liquid that it was being forced to contend with and the number of trips he was making to the lavatory was not going unnoticed. It was time to move the battle onto more familiar territory and he returned to the table with large single malt whiskies for everyone. This killed the conversation stone dead.

To a man they simply stared at the small tumbler in front of them as their addled brains recalled the last time they had succumbed to Scotland's most potent revenge on the English, even counting The Bay City Rollers. *Shang-a-Lang* wasn't even a proper word, how could it be a song lyric, let alone the title of a hit single.

Not so many years ago they had all downed whisky with total disregard for its finer qualities and suffered the mother of all hangovers for days afterwards. The old man read their minds and decided it was time to pass on some wisdom. He discouraged the addition of mixers like cola and ginger ale but allowed, even recommended a small quantity of water to release the flavours.

His tutorial lasted about ten minutes, during which he informed his nervous young charges about the differences between malts from the Western Isles and the Highlands. The noticeable smoky and peaty tones and the subtle influence of the spring water in the final taste.

The guys sniffed, swirled and sniffed again. Finally, and under close supervision, they sipped. There would be no chugging on this occasion. They were no longer ignorant and this knowledge would be with them for the rest of their lives. He had fulfilled his responsibilities to those who had educated him in the same way all those years ago.

Despite serious reservations based on experience, the guys could not deny they were enjoying the whisky. It warmed rather than burned as it went down their throat and the after taste was exactly as they had been told it would be.

'That was really nice, thanks,' said Martin. 'Who's for another pint of Old Gutmangler then?' he enquired.

The boys returned to quaffing beer and Sylvia's father nursed his malt for a couple more rounds.

When last orders was called by the landlord there was a moment's hesitation as a non-verbal communication passed around the group, followed by a brief shake of each head. A further trip to the gents followed. It was a pre-emptive strike. They all knew that stepping out into the cool night air when they left the pub wouldn't be good for them, if they hadn't been before they went.

The taxi was waiting and the driver was visibly relieved to see a responsible adult was part of the group he was taking back to the city. His many years of night-shift experience driving cabs had taught him to lay the law down before the car moved and if his customers weren't prepared or able to adhere to his rules, the deal was off. It was not a long list of instructions, simply a requirement for advanced warning of any unexpected evacuations of bodily fluids or solids so he could let them out before they let it all out.

The journey passed without incident or accident until they were about five minutes away from the flat.

'Shtop the car. NOW!' was barked loudly in the driver's right car.

He stamped on the brake and skidded to a halt, reached behind him and opened the passenger door. In a single fluid movement the driver grabbed the shouter and launched him onto the pavement. Dai managed to curl up into a sort of combat roll and quickly got to his feet. He turned to his astonished friends and said, 'Kebab anyone?'

Sylvia's father declined and while the lads piled into the shop to order their take-aways, a curt nod to the taxi driver was all it took for him to quietly slip back into the traffic and continue on their journey. It was a win-win situation. Sylvia's father didn't mind paying for the taxi in exchange for an earlier return in relative comfort. The lads clearly wanted something to eat and the taxi driver had no desire to have a car smelling of eastern Mediterranean fast food for the rest of his shift.

His daughter was not impressed when her father arrived at the flat alone. 'Where are they? What happened? Are they in trouble? What have you done with them?' she babbled.

'I'm more concerned about what they have done to me,' he muttered.

When she paused her tirade to breathe, he told her they had stopped at the kebab shop on the main road and they waved him off. He took that as an instruction to continue the journey alone. It was a version of the facts that he intended to stick to.

About half an hour later the guys arrived. They were loud, clumsy and brought in a fog of pungent gases that no domestic air freshener had a hope of dispersing, let alone neutralising. Sylvia was relieved, if not pleased, to see them all.

Modern Man's planning of the evening hadn't gone beyond the primary objective of going to the pub and it was a sign of his advancing maturity that he had actually considered booking the taxi back.

However, accommodating a significant number of extra bodies in a fairly small flat with limited facilities had been left to Sylvia. While the men folk had been out 'bonding' she had borrowed camp beds and sleeping bags, moved furniture and morphed her living room into a dormitory. She had also warned her neighbours above and below, as a precaution.

A moment of inspired genius had prompted her to complete her night time ablutions before they returned as she could only guess what her bathroom would be like after the inevitable assault on its dignity. She truly hoped they were all good shots and tried not to over-think the consequences if they weren't.

She'd actually had a nice evening on her own. A couple of glasses of wine, a book she was really enjoying and her music choice on the stereo. Bliss! It was only interrupted by her mother on the phone, offering advice on how to deal with them when they returned. Sylvia realised she had never seen her father properly drunk. He'd been 'merry' on numerous occasions but not drunk. She wouldn't have given it a thought if her mother hadn't planted that seed of worry in her head. A seed that had germinated, taken root and was maturing into a fully fledged panic attack at a startling rate.

Her options were clear. Organise, manage and direct or get as drunk as they would be and to Hell with the consequences. She chose the former and began running scenarios in her head. Hope for the best and plan for the worst was a mantra that she had lived by for most of her young adult life.

In the end there wasn't a problem. No one was sick. They were loud for a while but the alcohol had its usual effect and they were asleep fairly quickly. Some fully-clothed, others in various states of undress and apart from the snoring and farting, they were pretty quiet. The breakfast menu consisted of tea, coffee, toast and paracetamol. A couple of them had rather guilty expressions which concerned Sylvia hugely. She knew they were well-brought up boys which meant their misdemeanours could be quite serious if they felt ashamed of themselves. She needn't have worried, it turned out the sleeping bags were machine-washable.

By mid-afternoon the lads had all left. The flat was tidy again and her father was back to his usual self, supplying unsolicited advice to her. His contrition had been a transient state unfamiliar to them both and the return to more familiar territory was strangely welcoming for Sylvia. She would always be his daughter, she knew that, but she wouldn't always be twelve years old. She hoped he would eventually acknowledge that she was capable of making good decisions for herself. To make amends for any inconvenience, real or imagined, that he had caused, he took Sylvia and Modern Man out for an early dinner before pointing the Jag towards the Cotswolds.

Sylvia' friends wanted a hen night to send her off into married life and she was too busy with final arrangements for the wedding to put up a spirited objection. It would have been a major disappointment if they hadn't done something for her. She had, after all, instigated several of her dearest friends' events. The rub was that Sylvia had always known what was going to happen at these events. She wasn't desperately keen to be on the receiving end of her friends' excessive exuberances.

Sylvia was not in control of this one and that worried her. She was no prude but the idea of a male stripper was not what she wanted prancing around at the back of her mind. It was the twinkle in the eyes of her girlfriends when they had told her it was her 'special night' that nagged at her brain. She would be happy with a nice meal in a smart restaurant.

It turned out to be a bit of a wind up. Six of them went for cocktails then on for a meal and finally dancing at a night club. They didn't embarrass her and instead, protected her from unwelcome advances from the handful of guys who tried to join the party. Some of the girls were more than happy to take the bullet for Sylvia if the man in question was up to scratch.

Modern Man's actual stag night also passed without serious incident. The boys were definitely the worse for drink but there was no sign of lipstick or whiff of cheap perfume on any of them. They'd settled on a drinkers' pub with proper beer rather than a trendy place. There was a strange sense of déjà vu when Matt spent far too long at the bar when it was his round. It was like the first day of college all over again. He was trying to extract the bar maid's phone number from her. In many ways they had grown up and moved on but individually they were much the same as they had always been.

The following morning Sylvia, once again, dispensed medicine and breakfast for what seemed like hours. In the face of repeated requests she also acted out the aircraft safety demonstration, miming the seatbelt, oxygen mask and life jacket parts. However, she refused point blank to put on her stewardess uniform to do it. Never-the-less, 'Emergency exits are located here, here and here,' earned her a standing ovation from the boys and they were given a demure curtsy in return. Why guys got such a kick out of the explanation of aircraft emergency procedures was a mystery to her. She had no idea how a tight white blouse over a perfect figure and arms outstretched would grab every man's attention; or maybe she knew exactly what was going through their minds and she just didn't want to dwell on it.

With only a week until the wedding, Sylvia was nervous about not being nervous. She was fairly confident that everything was in hand. Lists had been checked, rewritten and checked again. They were leaving the flat on the Tuesday morning to drive across to Oxfordshire. Packing the car was carried out with military precision to ensure nothing was left behind. There were separate bags and cases for the hotel and her family home. The dress had its own shipping case packed by Raoul in New York and checked twice each day since to ensure it had not evaporated, shrunk or been eaten by vermin.

Modern Man was to stay with her at her parent's home until Friday afternoon then move into the hotel where the reception was to be held. His parents were travelling down on Thursday and also staying at the hotel. A grand pre-wedding dinner was booked for the evening of their arrival and a final rehearsal in the church on Friday afternoon. Absolute perfection was the minimum required standard and they all knew it. There was tension.

Modern Man's dad drove down with his wife. The rest of their family were taking the train together and staying at a more modest hotel. The motorway was busy with the usual combination of British and European articulated lorries and homicidal white van drivers. Add the nation's sales reps in their trademark fleet cars and frequent outbreaks of road-rage were almost inevitable.

With all this traffic lane-hopping around him, the last thing Modern Man's dad needed was a lecture on his behaviour over the forthcoming weekend. Not that he was surprised when it started. A long list of, 'don't say this, keep your opinions to yourself about that and under no circumstances mention the other,' lasted through Staffordshire and into Birmingham where the traffic ground to a halt.

Once the car was stationary, he could reduce his level of concentration on the road and turn to his wife and say, 'Eh?' He had learned through their many years of marriage that he could annoy the hell out of her in many ways but it was his own personal goal to do it in the least number of syllables. This was a new personal best and he was an even prouder man for delivering it on the way to his son's wedding. An event that had already taken his pride off the scale.

The wedding ceremony itself met everyone's expectations. Sylvia's dress drew gasps. Exactly as she'd hoped for and Modern Man looked dashing in his morning suit. She was glad he was slightly nervous, it would stop him being flippant. One of her many concerns that day. All the boys looked fabulous but ever so slightly uncomfortable in their formal wear. Her father, on the other hand, seemed totally at ease in this regalia. It was as if he had been born in top hat and tails. Behind this facade he was a basket case. It was essential that this day should be a total success. It was clearly the event of the year for this part of the county and it had to be flawless in every way. He would not be able to relax until breakfast the following morning.

Every conceivable combination of relatives was photographed outside the church. Several group ensembles of the entire congregation meant the day was recorded in minute detail. While all that was taking place the smokers were able to cluster behind a buttress and bond as the group of social pariahs they knew they had become.

Eventually the fleet of cars headed for the reception and more photographs were taken of the wedding party at the hotel. There was only one more onerous task for some of the men in morning suits to worry about. Sylvia's father, Modern Man and Martin had to make after-dinner speeches and all three were extremely stressed about it. This made it almost impossible to enjoy the fabulous meal that everyone else was tucking into. Albeit in a kind of relay, since the top table was starting dessert at exactly the same moment the awkwardly single guests at the far end of the dining room were finishing their soup.

For Modern Man in particular, the nerves were building up. He couldn't use alcohol to calm himself. He too had very clear instructions from his better half. His head was spinning, his intestines knotted and, although he actually had no evidence to support this hypothesis, he was pretty sure his DNA was unravelling. A psychologist could have identified all these common symptoms and explained the root cause in great detail but thankfully there wasn't one present.

A well-informed observer at the event would have picked up the signs and realised that under such stress people revert to type. That's exactly what happened. Sylvia's father spoke eloquently with apparent confidence. Occasional Latin phrases were included to point out his educational credentials and his fluent prose was delivered in the style of a closing address to a crown court jury.

Modern Man's speech was completely different. That came across like an engineer's report on the suitability of two pieces of equipment to interface successfully in a larger and more complex machine. There was more emphasis on the commissioning period than Sylvia's mother was comfortable with but nothing that would inflict lasting damage on the relationship with her son-in-law.

Best Man Martin delivered a marketing campaign that would leave no one in any doubt that Modern Man and Sylvia were as strong a brand as Rolls and Royce, Rogers and Hammerstein or Marks and Spencer. He had a different speech prepared up until the stag night when Sylvia had taken him to one side and reminded him of her father's profession and that any libel, slander or defamation would be dealt with extremely severely. Should he choose to go down that route he would need a very good solicitor but in the short term, an equally adept proctologist to remove her stiletto. Not that she'd want it back, of course. Sylvia was hugely relieved that her threats had found their mark and joined her mother in wiping away a few tears from time to time.

The Toast Master invited the guests to enjoy after dinner drinks in the lounge while the dining room was cleared and the evening's entertainment prepared. Despite their best efforts, Modern Man's mates were unable to spike his drinks or indulge in any pranks that they had half-heartedly planned during the course of the day. Sylvia informed Martin, Dai and Jack that they had fulfilled all their obligations to her complete satisfaction and they could change out of their finery if they wanted to. They took this as official clearance to party and set about their new task with great enthusiasm.

The first dance was, of course, a waltz, with only the newly-weds taking to the floor. Modern Man had a surprise for his new wife and led her across the floor faultlessly. At the far end they spun all the way back. He later confessed that he had been practicing at work. Every time he left his desk he would take a circuitous route around chairs, printers and photocopiers. Left, right, slide; right, left, slide. He didn't do the arms, that would have looked ridiculous. If he happened to be carrying something he would imagine he was holding her and try to fix the axial point of rotation at the notional centre of gravity between their bodies. He was an engineer and it was important to be as accurate as the limiting factors allowed. An unbalanced load would cause excessive stress on the bearings and he didn't want his to be worn out before their time.

After considerable applause Sylvia's parents, Modern Man's parents and Martin, accompanied by the bridesmaid, joined them on the floor. Within a few minutes everyone, who wanted to be, was up there doing their best not to crash into anyone and failing miserably. In the fullness of time the dance became a disco and the older people left it to the youngsters to own the floor for the rest of the night. There were a few instances of 'dad dancing' that always set a wedding aside from any other social event but nothing too embarrassing to spoil the night.

As with every other contributor to the day's activities, the disc jockey had been briefed by Sylvia. She gave him a general play list and a run down on the type of music that would not be tolerated. 'No punk, nothing cheesy and no head-banging stuff,' she told him. He chanced his arm with *Viva Espania* which she wasn't too impressed with but he found himself at the wrong end of both barrels when he played the *Birdie Song*. It wasn't only the music she hated; it was the stupid dance that went with it.

By the end of the night a few of her girlfriends had laid the foundations of relationships with some of his mates thereby increasing the odds that the cycle of weddings would continue. Sylvia was happy for them. She'd come to know the guys over the last couple of months and they were nice lads who would benefit from the kind of influence her friends could supply. Martin was with her bridesmaid, Sophie. Jack and Charlotte had been conspicuous by their absence for several hours and Dai had been cornered by Fiona. He was clearly enjoying her company and Matt was getting on very well with the barmaid. She had finished her shift at midnight but stayed on, with Sylvia's permission, as a guest for the last hour or so.

The newly-weds enjoyed a leisurely breakfast in their room before leaving for Heathrow. The hotel had put on a limousine as part of the package and Modern Man was very impressed that his new wife had negotiated such a stylish addition to a perfect day. She was clearly learning a lot from him.

The location of their honeymoon had been a difficult choice. He wanted to travel longhaul to an exotic white sandy beach with palm trees whilst she wanted to explore some of the ancient European capital cities. In the end they reached a compromise and went to Vienna for four days of culture then ten days on a Greek island for a bit of sun. She convinced him that he could have his Caribbean dream when she was rostered a working trip there. It would be easier that way, with the hotel and airport transfers covered by her employer.

They checked-in their baggage at the airport and Sylvia resisted the temptation to flash her crew ID badge. The purser, on her last trip as a single girl, had advised her against it. She had heard some of her colleagues claiming to have been upgraded to Club class on the strength of their being flying staff but she was told it was terribly bad form and could just as easily work against her. Instead, Sylvia dropped into the conversation that they were on honeymoon and hoped that the clickety-clack on the keyboard was recording this important information. They wouldn't find out until they boarded the aircraft.

Once on the aircraft and settled into their business class seats they spent a few moments silently reflecting on the events of the previous day. Sylvia then raised a rather important question that they hadn't previously discussed.

'Do you like children?' she asked her husband.

Modern Man ran through all the joke answers he'd heard to that question. 'Yeah, I used to go to school with them' and, 'They're okay but I couldn't eat a whole one.' Unusually for him, he decided to play this one with a straight bat. 'I suppose. I've never given it much thought, why?' he said.

This wasn't really the reaction she was hoping for but pressed on regardless. 'I think I might be pregnant, that's all.'

Modern Man breathed in sharply but the corresponding exhalation was significantly delayed while his brain processed this new and alarming data. He thought he had married a girl who only dealt in certainty and this was quite a big thing to be unsure about. He opted for silence in the hope that some sort of explanation would follow but it didn't.

The aircraft powered up and tore down the dotted line on the runway. Modern Man spent this time absorbing the information and trying to assess its impact. Sylvia felt better for sharing it but wasn't sure how he had taken the news. She hadn't planned to tell him like that. She wanted to be sure one way or the other first but she couldn't keep it to herself any longer and that few minutes of silence had to be filled with something, so she'd unburdened.

After what seemed like an age Modern Man turned to her with a frantic expression on his face and said, 'On the honeymoon, we can still have sex, right?'

Modern Man's hike through his life history had so far turned up nothing. Not the slightest inkling of a potential cause of his physiological discord. These had been blissfully happy times.

By now he'd totally lost track of time and didn't really care either. There was nobody at home waiting for him, thinking he may have had some horrific accident and be lying at the roadside covered in blood.

Besides, he was in need of solitude, so much so, he'd even walked past the pub. Normally the smell of great food wafting from the kitchen and the peals of laugher emanating from the bar would have drawn him in for a pint or three.

Away from the gravitational forces of The White Lion, Modern Man was able to pick up the threads of his personal diagnostic retrospective, whilst also putting one foot in front of the other. Who says men can't multi-task?

9. The Inner Child

This was the '80's. It was the '60's for the generation who had heard all about that fab and groovy decade from their parents. Witney was *saving all her love for you* and Dire Straits were *getting money for nothing and chicks for free.* It was a very good time to be alive, if you lived in the right bit of the country and had some money in your pocket. If you didn't then you weren't invited to the party. Modern Man was there but occasionally felt he spent too much time in the kitchen talking to the host's inebriated mother. It was a sneaky feeling he had from time to time.

Modern Man didn't want to know the details of how a woman could be uncertain about being pregnant. He assumed they must know, one way or the other. They seemed to know everything else about their bodies, why not this? Sylvia, on the other hand, was in turmoil. She desperately wanted him to be supportive and didn't realise that he would be, if he knew what he was meant to be supporting.

For him it was fairly straightforward. If she was, great and if she wasn't then they would carry on as if the conversation had never happened. He knew he shouldn't but he asked the question anyway, 'How can you not know if you're going to have a baby?'

She tried to explain about being late but he didn't understand the inferences and she wasn't about to discuss that aspect any further. She continued with the usual female trait of expressive subtlety that only other women understand, thereby confusing her new husband even more but acquainting a number of her fellow passengers and air crew with the information intended only for him.

As the 'Fasten Seat Belts' sign was switched off and the cabin staff launched themselves into the galleys, the penny kind of dropped in Modern Man's head. He'd had a few minutes of thinking time since the roar of the engines drowned Sylvia's voice and he could take in what she had actually said, not said and implied. It took some unravelling but he got there and held her hand while she composed herself. At the first opportunity she nipped to the loo to splash cold water on her face and check her appearance.

She hadn't told the operating crew that she was a stewardess but she suspected they had guessed. She had 'the look' and familiarity with procedures. Even so, she didn't want this little episode to be flashed around the planet at crew parties.

'Do you know Sylvia something, ex-teacher from Bristol? Well, she had a barny with her husband before the aircraft had got to cruise altitude.....' was how it would start and after being retold a few times she would be labelled as a total diva. It was just the way of the world she lived and worked in these days. While Sylvia was re-applying her mascara, Modern Man was on the receiving end of some unsolicited advice from the unfortunate passenger who occupied the window seat in their row. The lady was probably in her sixties and didn't appear to be bound by the international convention of blindness and deafness on witnessing a domestic dispute in public. She spoke with quiet authority and didn't invite interruption or contrary opinion, so Modern Man let her 'advise' him.

In the normal scheme of things he would have politely cut her off at the earliest opportunity but he actually needed help here and what she was saying might carry some weight. In the short time they had alone, he was brought up to speed on the conflicting emotions a woman experiences when she believes she might be pregnant for the first time. Peppering her lecture with frequent instances of, 'Young man', 'Naïve,' and, 'Insensitive,' did nothing to endear her to him but it held his attention and he learned more on the subject of pregnancy in three minutes than in his entire life so far.

For the rest of the flight he and Sylvia elected not to talk about it, focussing instead on their time together during the honeymoon. This was far easier for Modern Man than it was for her. There were far too many ways for her to be reminded. The subject loitered at the edge of the thoughts, refusing to be ignored. The in-flight meal consisted of oven-baked breast of chicken with cherry tomatoes and baby carrots. As they flew over the Alps the captain announced that he would deliver them at their final destination within a few minutes of the scheduled arrival time.

Before leaving Vienna airport she bought a pregnancy testing kit and as well as her change, she was also given a disapproving look from the middle-aged woman at the cash till. Sylvia smiled and made a point of showing her wedding ring as she put the cash back in her purse.

Apart from drastically reducing her alcohol intake, Sylvia didn't hold back in any way. Modern Man enjoyed the city a lot more than he expected to but the time in Greece was what he had really been looking forward to. He had a pretty good physique himself and noticed a few second glances. That was nothing compared to the way his new wife was turning heads in the resort and on the beach. Modern Man had the hottest girl on his arm and he was milking the envy of other guys. In his head he was mocking them for their poor taste in women but he managed to maintain an expression of cool nonchalance. He wanted these onlookers to believe it was perfectly normal for him. Always had been and always would be.

Sylvia had grown quite skilful at reading his mind but she misinterpreted it this time. She thought he was checking out other women, not judging them on a scale of dog to Sylvia. Normally she would have gently rebuked him but something held her back on that occasion.

There was an uncertainty that she hadn't experienced before. She knew she had a good figure but her she inadvertently redrew that image with a huge stomach and fat ankles. Worse still, in this recurring image, she had a burger in one hand and a cream cake in the other. Whatever was happening to Sylvia's body, her brain was working overtime preparing her for the next forty weeks.

By the end of their two-weeks away, Sylvia had bought and used three more pregnancy testing kits and had a majority decision in favour. That might be enough to win an election or a boxing match but she still wouldn't fully accept the likely verdict. Her doctor confirmed it beyond doubt and that was what she needed to hear. She followed the doctor's advice of keeping the news to herself and confiding only in her husband until the critical twelve week milestone had been passed. It was a wise precaution as family and friends would probably go bananas when told.

Modern Man made an observation that she hadn't considered up to this point. 'I've never seen a pregnant stewardess on a flight,' he said. Several minutes of searching through her contract and manuals revealed that she must report her condition as soon as it was confirmed by a medical practitioner. With a little trepidation, she phoned the fleet office and was told that she was 'grounded' with immediate effect. There was a procedure (naturally). She wasn't the first stewardess to find herself in this situation. They managed to make it sound rather sordid she thought. Or perhaps she was being over-sensitive. It was difficult to be sure of anything anymore. She was told to report to the Travel Shop in the city centre and that she would be expected to work 9 'til 5, Monday to Friday.

Since Sylvia had been employed by the company for more than two years, there was an entitlement to maternity leave. She'd seen that it was in the contract but hadn't paid much attention at the time. At some point in the future she would be entitled to a 'return to work' interview, if she wanted to continue flying after her baby was born. That seemed so far in the future that she couldn't even guess how she would feel then. Sylvia was disappointed that she wouldn't be going to New York any time soon. She wanted to show Raoul her wedding photos. On The Day, the dress was all that the women wanted to talk about. Of course, the men's minds had been occupied by a slightly broader range of topics.

The first ultrasound scan was a fascinating experience for Modern Man and a nerve-wracking one for Sylvia. There was a computer monitor displaying a picture of blurred grey shades. As the probe was moved over her bare stomach, the picture changed to show an area of lighter grey but still very fuzzy. The radiologist froze the image and started using various tools to mark and measure the distance between one blob and another, explaining to them what she saw and what she was doing. Neither Sylvia nor Modern Man could make out anything that looked remotely human but went along with it, nodding sagely but saying nothing in case they revealed their ignorance.

At the end they came away with a postcard-sized photograph of the grey blur and a rather shaky conviction that it showed their unborn child. Modern Man claimed to understand the science of ultrasonic imagery and started to explain it to Sylvie but she had already upped-sticks and inhabited fairyland. Now that she believed she was going to have a baby, her hormones had a meeting and unanimously decided to have some fun at her expense.

Like most people before they have children of their own, Modern Man and Sylvia paid little attention to the huge marketing effort that was aimed at new parents. All the books and magazines, not to mention the large sections of department stores and a growing number of megastores purpose made for baby and kids' stuff alone.

Unfortunately, Sylvia was the kind of person who needed to know everything there was to know about something in order that she could make an informed decision. She regarded it as being thorough.

Modern Man didn't think that way at all. His approach was to find out what he needed to know to take him to the next stage, reassess the objective, then gather more information based on the required outcome. Whilst it was their baby, it was her body and that seemed to be the trump card when their strategies conflicted. This was going to cost a fortune. He could see that coming but there was nothing he could do about it without causing a huge argument.

They had experienced a few spirited debates during their relationship and had usually managed to keep to reasoned argument rather than dipping to a no-holds-barred slanging match. As the pregnancy progressed, Sylvia's ability to process logic diminished. In her head she knew what she was trying to say but the words just wouldn't form. Frustration muscled in and weeping soon took over as the default response to any conflict. She was in bits and it was completely unlike her, or the person she had been before all this happened.

It wasn't a permanent state. There were days when she couldn't be happier. She watched the bump increase in size. She noticed how her eyes shone and her lips were somehow fuller and her complexion more rosy. She was having a baby and it was the most natural thing in the world. On days like that she cried for other reasons. She'd well up if an elderly man gave her his seat on the bus. Hell, there were TV adverts that could start her blubbing. It was rather embarrassing but people seemed to understand.

Sylvia attended all her check-ups and scans. Modern Man accompanied her when he could and they both went to the antenatal classes. She was taken aback that he actually wanted to go. He was taking a genuine interest, not making corny jokes and was being more supportive than she could possibly imagine. Was he over-compensating for something? Did he have a secret agenda or guilty conscience? This was so out of character, he must be up to something. Her hormones performed a quick victory dance before messing with her head a little longer. They hadn't had this much fun since they made her fall in love with this guy. That had been a hoot.

Modern Man wasn't reading the books and magazines that his wife was devouring avidly. He glanced through one or two at the beginning but they were so obviously written by women for women that he decided to do his own research. Some of his colleagues delighted in telling him how his life was over. 'Kids change everything,' and, 'Bought a Volvo yet?' were the kind of comments he had to tolerate.

One of the project managers shared some useful advice with him, covering the 'what' and 'when' of his immediate future. Along with the benefits of structuring evenings and weekends around the needs of the baby. 'Identify tasks, plan ahead, build in contingencies and allow for the unexpected,' he said. He could so easily be talking about an engineering project and Modern Man suspected the guy's entire life was organised and tracked on spreadsheets. Still, it was valuable guidance and he felt sure he would use some of it in one form or another.

Sylvia's advice, on the other hand was coming to her from experienced mothers, some of whom were unaware that the world had moved on since they had their children twenty years previously. The thought of doing pelvic floor exercises with a group of other women didn't appeal to her at all. On the other hand, neither did a lifetime of mild incontinence. By the time she was assigned to a midwife, she had a list of concerns to raise with the trained professional. That reassurance enabled her to take these horror stories at face value, reacting appropriately to each tale of woe. Her hormones eventually took a break from screwing with her brain. They didn't want to trigger any major physiological events that may actually harm her or her child. They were human after all.

Being pregnant made Sylvia think about God for the first since she'd been a little girl. The meaning of life and the possibility of a greater scheme of things had rarely crossed her mind before she discovered she was expecting a baby. Wandering around the supermarket together she abruptly stopped and asked Modern Man, 'Why are we here?' She'd shared some of her musings with him and he picked up the thread of a recent philosophical conversation they had stumbled through in the early hours of that morning. He had no answer, no theories and very little interest in the topic so he went for bland platitudes, somewhere between biblical and evolutionary without really committing to either.

'No, why are we in Sainbury's?' she said. 'What did we come in here for? My mind's gone totally blank.'

He wondered if dementia was a side effect that no one had warned him about.

Sylvia's due date arrived and Modern Man was ready to take the Superhero role in his wife's hour of need. A bag was packed ready, her parents were on stand-by and his parents were attempting to keep a low profile by only phoning twice each day. He had informed the young telephone operator at work that any call from his home was urgent, he had to be found. The switchboard girl was only seventeen years old and wasn't sure how to respond to such instructions but the words 'medical emergency' penetrated the ditzy exterior and she wrote the details on a yellow sticky note.

By late afternoon, nothing had happened and he considered the possibility that Sylvia might have passed out in the flat while waiting for a taxi or ambulance. He didn't know which of the emergency services to call. Maybe he should phone all four of them, in case it was more serious than he'd anticipated. On reflection, the coast guard could sit this one out. It was unlikely that she'd attempted to row across the Severn Estuary to Wales to seek help.

He had done no useful work all day. Sympathetically, his boss sent Modern Man home before he wet himself. Despite the rush hour traffic he was home in record time and found his heavily pregnant young wife in the kitchen. There was a strong curry smell and a lot of steam. Pans were bubbling on the stove.

'I've made a curry for dinner. It's supposed to kick things off, apparently,' she said cheerfully.

Sylvia's hormones were back at work and had passed a message to her brain that the more powerful the curry the sooner things would start happening.

He'd had some fierce curries at college, usually after a skin-full of beer but this was practically nuclear. If NASA were given the recipe they'd have an astronaut on Mars by the following weekend. Even the rice looked as if it were trying to retreat to the edge of his plate.

While Modern Man tried to look thankful for what he had just received, Sylvia was shovelling it down her throat like a time-served stoker on the Titanic. He would actually welcome an iceberg right now, or at least part of one. Not wishing to seem like a wimp, he asked her, 'Isn't it burning your mouth?'

'Oh yeah, it's killing me but this baby is due today and I want it to happen. No price is too high. One more thing, we're in this together. If I have to eat this, so do you.'

It was definitely an order, not a request, so he manned up and got handy with his fork. There would be consequences. He only hoped he'd be in a position to deal with them in private.

Sylvia's hormones realised far too late that they had over done it. They should have known her by now but they forgot how she was sometimes. They had to capitulate before any real damage was done to her gastro-intestinal system so they invoked the vomit protocol before sending a message downstairs that it was a go situation. She rushed to the bathroom and puked up as her water's broke. Her hormones were back in control and many high fives were exchanged between them. She felt thoroughly wretched for a few moments then realised what had happened. Sylvia called for help and her husband was at her side in a flash. He surveyed the scene and immediately threw up in the sink. It was self-inflicted in his case. He wasn't going to wait for that time bomb to go off. He had important things to do.

Sylvia was driven to the maternity unit by her husband who was like a man possessed. He ignored a red traffic light, the usual decorum at roundabouts and any use of indicators before making turns. His driving would have been enough to bring her into labour if she wasn't there already. He had phoned ahead to say they were on their way and expected a reception committee at the door.

At the last minute he decided that a handbrake turn in the ambulance bay was not required and settled for a controlled stop in front of the Accident & Emergency entrance. There was no crash team, no gurney and no nurses looking frantic. No one had shown up, this was appalling service. Modern Man prised his enormous wife out of the back of the car and she waddled towards the door. Inside they were courteously redirected to the maternity unit where they were attended to immediately.

Sylvia was examined in a cubicle while her husband sat, then stood, then paced a bit and fidgeted in the waiting area. Sylvia emerged with a nurse and was taken to the labour ward. Modern Man was surplus to requirements at this stage of the proceedings. He wasn't invited to join them on the ward and was advised to go home. The nurse assured him they would phone in plenty of time when things started moving.

'When will that be?' he asked.

'Baby will come, when baby is ready,' was the rather patronising and childish reply.

There was nothing else he could do except follow these simple instructions.

Modern Man returned to his car in time to see a two-man clamping crew unloading their gear. He thought he'd left plenty of room for ambulances but apparently that wasn't the point. He'd parked where he shouldn't have. He quickly weighed up his options. He could open negotiations with the clampers, simply accept his fate or, by far his favourite, make a run for it. The clampers' van hadn't blocked him in and the two guys hadn't associated him with the vehicle at that moment.

There was an overwhelming temptation to combat crawl along the path before plastering himself flat against a wall. He could peep around the last corner then make a run for the car. Screeching away in a cloud of tortured rubber smoke and exhaust fumes, like they did in films. Spectacular but also somewhat unnecessary. It wasn't as though the clamping crew had weapons. Without saying a word to them, he walked briskly up to his car, got in and drove smartly away while the clamping guys stared at each other. No one had ever done that to them before so they didn't know what to do.

Back in the flat he sat by the phone for the first hour then picked up the receiver to check there was a dial tone. There was. The phone was working. It started ringing when he was in the bathroom on a mission that couldn't be rushed. Sylvia's nuclear curry was doing unspeakable things to his insides. The phone continued to ring ringing and eventually he picked up only to find that it was his parents asking for an update. Modern Man told them what the situation was and they accepted that he would call them when there was some news.

The real call came at about half past five the following morning. The nurse told him that Sylvia would be taken to a delivery room in about half an hour and he could join her there for the birth. Modern Man thanked her and quickly showered, dressed and drove to the hospital.

The delivery room was nice and bright and Sylvia was hooked up to a bank of monitors. A middle aged midwife was in attendance and Modern Man was relieved to see her. He still had a thing for women in uniform but this wasn't the time for any kind of fantasy. Even if it had been, this particular woman wouldn't have featured in any of his. Although she was calm and businesslike Sylvia was clearly nervous. Modern Man desperately wanted to be a useful part of the team and not an embarrassment in his lovely wife's greatest moment of need.

He asked the midwife how he could be helpful. She showed him which machine was monitoring Sylvia's contractions. 'That machine records the intensity of each contraction and displays it on the screen,' she explained. 'They start before Sylvia will be aware of them and it really helps her if she can breathe correctly, during them and between them.'

Modern Man assumed the responsibility. He had an important job in Mission Control and failure was not an option. He was shaken out of his private daydream by a scream worthy of the bitch-troll from the gates of Hell. It came through the wall and must have originated in the next delivery room. The midwife registered the look of concern on Sylvia's face and said, 'Don't worry dear, some people can't handle the discomfort without sharing their experience. I'm sure you're made of sterner stuff.' Sylvia certainly hoped she was. Her husband did too.

As the frequency of the contractions increased, it became evident that it was all about to happen. Words of encouragement flowed soothingly from the midwife. Modern Man held Sylvia's hand and concentrated on his job of telling them both when the next contraction began. Sylvia focussed on her breathing and pushed when she was instructed to. The midwife seemed satisfied with both their performances. Another

171

scream came through the wall prompting a wink of support from husband to wife. She was coping admirably and he was incredibly proud of her.

The delivery was text book. No cord-round-the-neck problems and no need for surgical intervention on Sylvia or the baby. Modern Man stepped out of the way to let the midwife do her stuff. There was one massive problem when he saw his son for the first time. He re-ran all the antenatal classes in his head on fast-forward but at no point had this vital piece of information been passed on. It must be serious, why wasn't the midwife reacting? She too must have seen it. The boy was blue for crying out loud. Had Sylvia had an affair with a Smurf? It was all too much to take in. Modern Man's own hormones weren't going to miss out on all the fun. They enjoyed messing with his head almost as much as Sylvia's had enjoyed their playtime.

Another scream, but this time it came from the baby. Modern Man knew about this one. It was the first and vital inflation of the lungs and the skin colour changed to ever so slightly pale yellow. The newborn had quite a lot of spiky dark hair and was bruised around the eyes and nose, as if he was wearing a dark mask. In that moment of uncertainty one thing was beyond doubt. They would call him Robin: Boy Wonder had landed.

The yellow hue was transitory and he soon took on a more normal skin tone. Modern Man was invited to cut the umbilical cord, which he did with a flourish. However, he was horrified at the force used by the midwife to detach the placenta from his exhausted wife. He had to assume that part of the training for midwifery involved tug-of-war competitions at village carnivals. He really feared for Sylvia's internal well-being. It wasn't as if you could stick a plaster in there if it tore.

After the post-delivery checks Sylvia was handed her baby and tears of joy, relief and exhaustion trickled down flushed cheeks. Even after more than twenty years in the business, the midwife would feel emotional from time to time and this was one of those occasions. Not all deliveries went as smoothly and the last one she attended had been still-born. Modern Man and Sylvia were too wrapped up their own special moment to wonder why this woman left the room so abruptly.

They didn't notice straightaway that it was a different member of staff who took over a few moments later. There were photographs to be taken, naturally. Sylvia knew she had looked better but didn't have the strength to put up a spirited fight. Boy Wonder was the star of this show and a roll of film was exposed in a matter of minutes.

Sylvia was then whisked off in a wheelchair to a private bathroom for a long soak. Meanwhile Modern Man set to work. His project manager colleague at work had given him a gem of a plan to stay ahead of the game and keep the parents and in-laws sweet for the rest of his life. He took the camera to a one-hour processing service and ordered a double set of prints. The previous evening, while waiting for the vital phone call, he had addressed two large envelopes, one to his parents and one to hers.

He added a short note that simply said 'Here's your first grand………' with enough space to add 'son' or 'daughter' once that was known.

The hour was passed in the pub at the end of the road, where he had a quiet pint alone at the bar. He wasn't ready to share yet. This was a special moment and he wanted to spend it alone with his thoughts. He had a son now and that was a special feeling for a man. It wouldn't have been any less special if he had a daughter but he knew it would be different, somehow.

When the photos were ready he split one set between the two envelopes and kept one set intact that they would treasure forever. He reasoned that it didn't matter that the grandparents were sent different pictures because they wouldn't know what the others had received. This was another tip from Project Manager Paul. At the Post Office he even paid the extra for guaranteed next day delivery. Hang the expense, this was a big moment in all their lives.

Once home he started working through his phone list. Sylvia had busied herself over the last few days putting together a list of people to call then recompiling it in the order that they should be contacted. This was important because as soon as one friend knew they would start calling other friends and a pecking order of who knew first would be unofficially established. She didn't want anyone to feel they had been the last to know. Such a delicate act of diplomacy occupied her fully for two days and Modern Man had strict instructions not to deviate from the order when the time came.

Visiting the maternity ward also had to be controlled and the hospital had recruited a couple of nurses who looked like the offspring of a no-nonsense wrestling promoter and a grizzly old street cop. Throw in zero-tolerance to disobedience and anyone would be forgiven for thinking the inmates of Alcatraz prison had an easier time than the friends and families of these new mothers. No more than two visitors to a bed at any one time was the mantra they announced every thirty seconds or so.

Modern Man did exactly as he had been told. He phoned in the right order and explained the visiting hours and required protocol. To a woman, all of Sylvia's friends ignored the rules completely. They piled up to the hospital like a hen party recently informed of a late-opening wine bar across town. On the way most of them bought flowers although some decided on chocolates or blue balloons instead. Quite a few also picked up 'Congratulations' cards. They tried to rush nurses Stallone and Schwarzenegger at the door of the maternity ward but their tactic failed and the defensive line held. Chastised but still excited, they eventually succumbed to the Noah's Ark Rule and went in two-by-two. They had to draw lots each time to decide who went next as none could agree any other way.

Modern Man had happily stayed at home. He would visit in the evening when it was quieter. When he arrived, Stallone and Schwarzenegger had been assigned to the Accident and Emergency department. There had been a big football match on and it was expected to be busy. As he entered the maternity ward Modern Man's brain was forced to dismiss the images his eyes were sending to it. He blinked a couple of times. His brain processed the new data and eventually accepted that he was looking at eight smiling women with at least one breast exposed.

This was a new experience. Never before had complete strangers exposed themselves to him without significant amounts of alcohol first and even then, not all at the same time. He wanted to stop staring but he couldn't. His brain wanted every detail to file away and bring back to him in moments of sadness in the future. He'd thank his brain for it eventually but right now he was gawping and that wasn't cool.

Sylvia's bed was at the end of the ward and she was watching with some amusement. She had seen several new fathers have the same experience during the course of the day and wasn't offended or upset. Her man was normal and it was okay to react to such unusual situations like that. If he made a habit of it he'd be in trouble but she guessed he knew that. She'd deal with that problem if it ever came up.

When he saw her he snapped out of it and gave her his total attention. Boy Wonder was asleep in his cot at the end of her bed and Sylvia was engulfed in flowers and cards.

'I can't believe no one came to visit you this afternoon. I phoned them all, honest. Unbelievable!' he quipped sarcastically.

She had managed to have a bit of sleep during the day but still looked very tired, even so, that raised a smile.

She'd phoned her parents and was informed they were coming over the next day. They intended to stay in a hotel so Modern Man wouldn't have to do anything for them. He silently hoped the photographs would arrive before they set off otherwise his master stoke would be worthless. Little did he realise that giving them a grandson was enough to keep them sweet for the rest of their lives.

For the next three days Sylvia and Boy Wonder became acquainted in the maternity ward. She learned his different cries that meant feed me, change me, pick me up and put me down. He learned that she would do anything he wanted, in the limited scope of their combined capabilities. For Boy Wonder at least, life was good.

Modern Man spent this time shuttling between the flat and the hospital. He had missions to buy various baby boy things now the gender was known and even managed to cook a meal for himself instead of relying on takeaway dinners every night.

On the fourth day of his life, Boy Wonder was discharged into the long term care of his parents. They were assigned a midwife who would call in daily and could be reached by phone during normal business hours. They should phone the ward if necessary during the night or go to A & E if it was a real emergency.

The maternity ward sister had given this briefing hundreds, if not thousands, of times and she had a pretty good idea which new mothers were ready and those who would have to learn fast. She looked into the eyes of Sylvia and Modern Man and said with true sincerity, 'Just one more thing. If at any time you feel you can't cope...'

Modern Man interrupted her, 'We know. Speak to the midwife.'

'No. What I was going to say was, "We don't do returns or refunds." Now go, before I decide to keep this gorgeous little chap for myself.'

10.   Part Time Single Parent

Modern Man and Sylvia stood and stared at the car seat on the kitchen worktop. Their baby was fast asleep and looked content. Neither spoke nor moved for several minutes. Their car was parked outside with the doors open, boot lid up and passers-by left in no doubt that a baby lived in one of those flats. The vehicle was loaded with stuff.

There was a knock at the door, which was unusual. Normally they had to buzz visitors into the building first. Their upstairs neighbour, Irene, was standing there with some of their shopping from the car, in fact, as much as she could carry.

'You left your car open. I've shut the doors and the boot but there was too much to bring up in one go,' she said.

She'd seen them arrive home and was actually delighted to have an excuse to see the baby. Irene knew her sleep would be disturbed by the little fellow over the coming weeks and felt entitled to meet her nocturnal tormentor face-to-face. Sylvia led her into the kitchen where Modern Man was now beaming with pride. She looked at the baby, looked at Modern Man and without thinking it through said, 'Oh isn't he a handsome fellow! He looks nothing like his father.' Realising her faux pas, she made her excuses and left.

Modern Man hadn't been listening. He was in a world of his own, looking forward to doing dad stuff at various stages of his son's future life. This boy would be the cleverest, coolest kid to walk on God's Green Earth. He'd be a natural athlete, have great taste and maturity beyond his years. All the way through school other kids would do anything for him, simply to be around him. Boy Wonder wouldn't take advantage of them, there'd be no mean streak, no manipulation of lesser beings and the girls would love him all the more for it.

As the boy became a young adult the girls would be desperate to be his favourite. Modern Man knew he may have to help out his son by occasionally thinning the pack and selflessly diverting their attention away from Boy Wonder and towards himself. He was ready to make that sacrifice. He'd do whatever it took to make sure his progeny had the best possible life.

Sylvia was on a different planet altogether. While her husband was flying through the future, her focus was on the present. Her emotions were polarized. There was great joy and pride in being a mother. Along with that, was immense relief that there had been no complications in the birth itself. Overshadowing both of those was a massive heart-wrenching fear that she wouldn't be able to cope.

What if she couldn't feed her baby? What if there was something wrong with him and the doctors had missed it? What did she know about being a mother? How could she possibly be any good? What if she turned out to be a rubbish mother? It was all too much for her and the tears cascaded down her cheeks. Her shoulders slumped and her knees gave way. She dropped to the living room floor and sobbed.

Modern Man was more than a little confused by this. None of his matey briefings by the guys at work had prepared him for this situation. In his head it was a natural thing for the female of every species to instinctively know how to raise their offspring. Vets didn't have to run antenatal classes for rabbits, hamsters or budgies so why did women make such a big deal out of it? Weren't humans the flagship of evolution? After a few seconds of watching his wife being crushed by self-doubt, he realised that she needed help and she needed it immediately.

In the normal run of things he would make Sylvia a nice cup of tea but he sensed tea wasn't going to be enough. The next stage would be a large glass of wine but he knew alcohol was incompatible with breast feeding. He tried to get in touch with his feminine side and imagine what was causing this monumental distress but nothing sprang to mind. She was babbling incoherently so he wasn't picking up any clues from her either.

He eventually settled on soothing platitudes on the grounds that he couldn't make things worse and doing nothing was definitely not a viable option. Modern Man joined her on the floor, held her and let her cry herself out. For this Sylvia was both infuriated and grateful. Why wasn't he able to see the potential problems ahead? Was he going to be any help at all or was she on her own?

Oh My God, what if she actually did end up on her own? What if she snapped? She might push him too hard and he would leave her? She'd be a single mother, relying on state benefit. She'd find herself living hand to mouth for the rest of her miserable life. That brought more tears, more babbling and what Modern Man interpreted as anger directed at him for some reason. Maybe she did want a cup of tea after all. He was seriously confused now.

The outcome was resolved by Boy Wonder waking up and demanding attention in the way babies do. It was a two pronged attack assaulting both the aural and olfactory senses. The noise was loud and piercing but the smell was totally over-powering resulting in major indecision regarding the priorities of nappy changing and feeding as both appeared urgent. It would prove to be a defining moment in this three-way relationship and Modern Man stepped up both literally and figuratively. He hauled Sylvia up onto the sofa, threw her a muslin and extra cushions then set about his first solo nappy change. It was like the day he passed his driving test and went out in the car for his maiden voyage. He knew what he should be doing and deep in his brain he knew how to do it but there was so much to think about and react to, the pressure was horrific.

He had wipes and a changing mat and cotton wool and antiseptic cream and about a thousand new nappies in bomb-proof plastic wrapping. He also had a biodegradable bag to put the dirty nappy in but he didn't have a plan. It was a rookie mistake and he beat himself up over it for a while then organised his thoughts. After a moment's disbelief at what he saw in the nappy, he wrapped it up and put it in the sanitised disposal bag. That stank nearly as much as the nappy but in a more clinical way.

Collateral damage was wiped away and then his brain froze. Was it powder or cream? A combination of both sounded unlikely. Might the wrong one be classed as a catastrophic failure with long term implications for his child's health and well-being? He doubted it and tossed a virtual coin; heads for cream, tails for powder. Based purely on the result of that imagined event, he powdered Boy Wonder's tail and applied the new nappy securely but not too tightly. How many times had the midwife repeated that at the antenatal class? Enough to be firmly lodged in his brain for sure. With a proud flourish he presented his son to Sylvia for her part of the deal.

It may have been natural but that didn't make it easy or straightforward, even when both parties were willing. Breast feeding was a bit of a hit and miss affair at first. Sometimes Boy Wonder took it immediately and other times he kind of danced around it for a while before giving up and crying. It was hard for Sylvia because she didn't know what she was doing wrong. Eventually she found a method that worked for both of them and the relief was simultaneous.

The overwhelming fear of their baby's imminent death prevented both parents from sleeping that first night. Boy Wonder was in a cot at the end of their bed and every few minutes one or other of them would drag themselves out of bed and check their baby for signs of breathing.

Sylvia's parents had the good sense to phone before visiting the flat. They hadn't forgotten what it was like to be new parents and realised that all the gadgets in the world didn't lessen the anxiety that serious mistakes were being made and damaging the child. Sylvia's mother took one look at her exhausted daughter and suggested that the new grandparents should take the baby for a walk. 'We will be out for at least an hour,' she proclaimed and more than hinted that they should go back to bed. Everything else could wait.

The flat was a mess, there was new baby stuff still in carrier bags and Sylvia would rather have tidied up first. Before she even started putting things away the fatigue had overwhelmed her and she crashed out. Modern Man kicked a few of the bags behind the sofa and followed her into the bedroom. He was even too tired to think about sex. Another first in this new world he had entered.

Conflict was inevitable at some point and even after some well-needed sleep Sylvia's batteries were nowhere near fully recharged. She was grateful for their visit and didn't want to be prickly but sometimes her father was impossible. His old school attitudes regarding the responsibilities of men and women were bound to infuriate a saint.

Her mother frequently interjected with, 'What your father is trying to say is that in his family...' before being railroaded into silence by her father's continued diatribe on the role of women in British society. The fact that he was raised, in part, by a nanny was irrelevant in his mind. The nanny was a woman, ergo, it was woman's work.

Modern Man decided it was time to step up. He boldly interrupted his father-in-law by stating that he had changed a nappy that morning. The reaction was not what he expected. It wasn't as if a standing ovation was anticipated but, 'What do you want, a medal?' And this from Sylvia too.

That was uncalled for and she looked embarrassed as soon as the words were out. Sylvia's mother took the bullet for her by adding, 'Or a chest to pin it on?'

Modern Man took the hit to his ego but recovered quickly and with his best Dustin Hoffman impersonation said, 'Are you trying to seduce me, Mrs Robinson?'

It made no sense at all but it did kill off a potentially difficult moment and laughter filled the room. Even Modern Man's father-in-law managed a prolonged smile. He knew he had over-stepped the mark and was preparing a financially based apology to support his grandson's long term wealth.

Sylvia's parents were staying in a hotel in the city for the benefit of all five of them. For the remainder of the weekend her mother did everything she could think of to make Sylvia's life easier. She even took it upon herself to train Modern Man in the arts of laundry, ironing, dusting and cooking. None of these were new skills to him. He simply chose not to exercise them on a regular basis. He felt that it was enough to know how to. If he showed too much expertise, he might be expected to take on these chores on a permanent basis.

He asked a few stupid questions to carry the illusion that it was all new to him and as far as he was aware, his fake ignorance had been convincing. By Sunday evening, as her parents were leaving, appropriate storage locations had been identified for all the new baby equipment and, thankfully the flat was tidy again. There were no dirty clothes in the laundry basket. It was never going to be more than a temporary state but a welcome one, all the same.

Modern Man's parents were just as eager to see their grandson as Sylvia's folks had been but his father's role as fixture secretary for the amateur rugby league club meant that they couldn't travel during the season. He had to ensure that two teams from different clubs and a referee, preferably a qualified one, turned up at the same time and the same place every Saturday afternoon. It sounded simple enough to Sylvia until Modern Man pointed out that some of the blokes who played this game needed help tying up their boot laces.

Modern Man's mother referred to most of them as steam pigs, an odd and yet suitable metaphor for these earthy individuals. She would have been quite happy to leave her husband behind and see her grandson without him but she didn't, it wouldn't have been right. The only solution was Boy Wonder's first road trip.

With the kind of spatial awareness that is second nature to a good engineer, Modern Man packed a lorry load of baggage into their small hatchback car. He secured Boy Wonder into his high tech seat and gave Sylvia at least a dozen opportunities to check they hadn't left anything essential in the flat. As soon as they drove onto the motorway Boy Wonder started to drift into a deep sleep. Sylvia managed to wriggle into a comfortable position in the front passenger seat and dozed off fairly soon afterwards.

Modern Man didn't mind, silence was golden, mainly because he wasn't being instructed on his role in a future event or debriefed on a recent failure. He knew deep down that his wife didn't mean to be so critical but every single detail? Really? Was he such a social liability? Surely not?

They didn't normally stop at motorway service areas on the way to his parents home. A full tank of fuel was sufficient for the journey and, unless there was a need for a toilet stop, there was no reason to break the journey. Not anymore. First stop was a nappy change near Dursley in Gloucestershire. That was quite quick and with hindsight should have included a feed while they were there. The feed was demanded vocally, almost as soon as they were back on the M5, resulting in another stop a few miles north of Tewkesbury. Modern Man began to wonder if he would be back in time for work on Monday. Maybe they should cut their losses and abandon the trip right there and then. Two more stops north of Birmingham were all that was required to see them through the journey. It had taken a couple of hours more than usual but he guessed he'd have to get used to that. All being well, it would improve with time.

They were welcomed with open arms. Quite literally in Sylvia's case. Modern Man's mum had been watching through the front windows for at least half an hour, anxiously waiting for their arrival. Sylvia handed over the baby to his grandma and graciously accepted her father-in-law's over-enthusiastic embrace. She had become used to his ways and he, in turn had almost learned what level of physical contact was acceptable. It was a work-in-progress for both of them.

Modern Man's parents had been fore-warned by their son that Sylvia needed to be in control of all things baby related and that meant pretty much 'all things.' He made it especially clear that even suggesting an alternative to anything she asked for could be interpreted as challenging her as a mother and that could be suicidal for his parents.

His mum pointed out that they had some experience, having raised him perfectly well. Modern Man decided this wasn't the time to reveal any Freudian demons that may be lurking within him and reminded his mum that her own mother-in-law criticised her frequently and heartlessly. That was enough to close the discussion. Sylvia would be in charge, or at least believe she was. His old man had no intention of being told what to do in his own house by two women and took Modern Man to the pub as soon as he garnered the necessary permissions.

Sylvia talked the new grandma through the use of baby equipment that was alien to her and to her credit, Grandma managed not to point out that in her day you simply got on with it, with what you had or were given. It was a wonder to her the human race had survived without all the paraphernalia considered essential these days. Boy Wonder was loving all the attention and smiled up at these two funny faces staring at him, in between wiping away their happy tears.

By Sunday afternoon the baby had been introduced to his northern roots and even had a sneaky taste of local beer when his mother and grandma were distracted. Granddads were incorrigible by nature, it seemed.

The five of them had walked the moors together, all wrapped up with hats and scarves. They'd visited Modern Man's old haunts and established a strong relationship across three generations.

Packing the car to return home was rather disorganised and resulted in a few small but important items of baby equipment being left behind. Modern Man's folks had sneakily added several items to the huge pile of bags they'd brought with them. A pile Modern Man was trying to load into the car in exactly the same way he had for the northbound journey. When they unpacked the car at the flat they discovered they had been given a few things that would be of absolutely no practical value at all to them but freed up a bit of space in his parents' back bedroom.

After a few months, which seemed like no time at all, Sylvia received her 'back to work' letter. She had to decide whether to resume her flying career or be a full time wife and mother. It would be tough whichever option she chose. There were still places on the route network that she hadn't been to and really wanted to see.

She had to weigh up the benefit of cheap flights that would enable them to have fabulous family holidays, against the pain and guilt of abandoning her baby for days at a time. How would her husband cope with a full time job and being a part-time single parent? Both sets of grandparents were too far away to be called on each time. In some ways that was a blessing. After long discussions of the pros and cons, backed up by Modern Man's assurances that he would be fine, they decided to source a child minder who would take care of Boy Wonder while Sylvia was away and Modern Man was at work.

Modern Man was to handle evenings and weekends and Sylvia would take the option of short trips which would limit her time away to a maximum of ten days. She signed the return portion of the letter before she changed her mind and posted it straightaway. Once again Sylvia was in emotional turmoil. Was she being selfish in trying to have it all? Would her baby even recognise her when she came home after each trip? Maybe she should phone the fleet office and tell them she'd changed her mind. They'd understand. She wouldn't be the first.

Finding a suitable child minder turned out to be easier than they thought possible. They agreed that the Yellow Pages may be perfect for identifying emergency plumbers and even driving instructors. However, choosing a total stranger to help raise your child should not be based on the size of the advert or the ability to pick a company name that would appear first in an alphabetical list. They asked their Health Visitor for advice and she told them of a former colleague for whom shift work had become intolerable and had set up a small nursery on the edge of the city.

Modern Man and Sylvia made the phone call, mentioned the recommendation of their Health Visitor and arranged to call round. It was in a part of the city that quite suddenly switched from urban to rural. From the back of the building open countryside stretched as far as the eye could see. The city stopped at the front gate and the noise and traffic stopped with it. The place was perfect in every way.

The proprietor, a Mrs Dunkins, showed them round and explained the procedures and security features. Sylvia felt obliged at that moment to mention the biggest stumbling block of all. The nature of her job. It would mean they weren't looking for a straight Monday to Friday week in week out. Sylvia was really concerned that this would be unacceptable and the whole thing would fall apart there and then.

A dismissive wave of a chubby hand from Mrs Dunkins appeared to confirm Sylvia's worst fears. Mrs Dunkins then turned to face Sylvia and said, 'A number of my clients are stewardesses. I understand the way it works. Keep me informed a couple of weeks ahead of time and we'll be fine.'

Sylvia almost wept with relief. They finished the tour in Mrs Dunkins's small office and discussed the practical details of fees.

Modern Man had already renamed her in his head as Mrs Dumplings and to his horror she looked him square in the eye and said, 'Call me Plum. It's a name I picked up at school during my first gym class. My chubby face was flushed red with exhaustion after a couple of minutes and stayed that way for the rest of the morning. I didn't like the name at the time but never managed to shake it off so I decided to embrace it. It rather puts the boot on the other foot, wouldn't you say?' Modern Man needed air.

Sylvia hustled him back to the car as quickly as possible. She was embarrassed for and by him but she hoped he would learn from the experience.

'You nearly ruined everything, you idiot,' she scolded.

'How was I supposed to know she was a mind reader?' was all Modern Man managed to utter in his defence.

'She read your face, you don't have a mind. You moron.'

It was tough to take but he had no choice. She was right.

They returned to the flat to find a trip roster had already arrived in the post. Sylvia had a Miami night-stop leaving in four days time. She also had a return-to-work interview the day before that and a couple of million other things to think about.

The interview wasn't the formality Sylvia had been expecting. She felt as if she was applying for the job all over again. They even quizzed her on the safety equipment and procedures. Her brain wasn't used to working like this again, it was scary. Thankfully she passed and was cleared to fly the following day.

Whilst sitting on the Bristol bound train, she organised her thoughts. Not only did she have a trip to pack for, she also had to ensure Boy Wonder had everything he would need for his first day at the nursery. On her return to the flat she discovered Modern Man was on his second attempt at assembling his son's essential kit for nursery. Sylvia took over and her husband observed.

He allowed an extra half hour for the detour to the nursery on his way to work but it turned out to be insufficient. Late leaving the flat meant more traffic and additional anxiety. Modern Man was never late for work, never late for anything. Drop off at the nursery was not like the 'drive-thru' lane of a fast food outlet. He felt he should stay for a while to make sure Boy Wonder was settled.

Plum was almost pushing him out with reassuring words and surprisingly strong arms for a woman of her stature. He found it hard to concentrate on his work that day and had the phone in his hand several times, ready to make that quick call to check everything was okay with his son. At the end of the day, the pick-up was much easier. Boy Wonder had enjoyed a busy day with different toys and was asleep in his car seat in no time.

The evening routine was a simple procedure of bath, bottle and bed. Modern Man was ready to indulge himself in all three but had to step up and provide them for his son. Bottles of formula milk had to be made up with boiled water that had cooled down and an awful lot of bottle shaking. If the water was too hot or too cold the formula didn't mix properly. He learned those lessons fairly early on. He filled the kettle and waited for it to boil. That was quite quick. Waiting for it to cool to the required temperature took an age. He used that period to prepare for bath time.

Boy Wonder was in his play pen and, although secure, was not being entertained and that bothered the little chap. He enjoyed being the centre of attention and made vocal demands if he felt overlooked. Modern Man broke off his current task and played with his son for a few minutes. This brought the happy smile back to the lad's face but didn't move the evening routine along any further.

Modern Man returned to the kitchen to continue preparing bottles and bathwater. Annoyingly, the water in the bath cooled down far too quickly and the kettle much too slowly. The kitchen was mission control and Houston, he had a problem. He couldn't put Boy Wonder down for more than about thirty seconds at a time before he started to cry and in such short intervals he couldn't make up a feed or fill the baby bath tub or collect fresh towels from the airing cupboard. In the end Modern Man had to let the boy cry while the jobs were done because time was marching on relentlessly.

Boy Wonder was asleep in his cot by half past nine and Modern Man finally was finally able to make some dinner for himself. He was ready to crash out by ten but realised that the next day would be at least as bad if he didn't work out a better routine. He started to think like an engineer and identify tasks that could be completed well in advance. He needed to identify the bottlenecks in the process and overcome conflicting requirements.

The next evening went much more smoothly and he felt pretty pleased with himself. The following day Sylvia would be back from her trip and she could take over, under his now expert tutelage.

The aircraft was full out of London and the economy cabin was bursting with eager holidaymakers. Florida was now the destination of choice for the generation who had grown up with fortnights on the Spanish Costas. It was quite common for first time travellers across the Atlantic to underestimate the effects of alcohol consumed at altitude. That and the fact ten hours or more in the air could be both boring and physically tiring meant Sylvia and her colleagues were on their feet serving and clearing away drinks for most of the journey. Passengers were liable to become irritable with each other and tempers could fray in such confined surroundings. It wasn't the ideal return to work that she had been hoping for.

When she finally walked into her hotel room, Sylvia peeled off her uniform and took a quick shower before crashing out in her bed. Apart from a couple of bathroom visits she stayed in bed and mostly asleep until her alarm clock woke her almost twenty-four hours later. To be ready for a flight, Sylvia normally allowed herself ninety minutes. Shower, hair, make-up, pack the suitcase and be down in the lobby in plenty of time for the journey to the airport.

The standard phone call was always one hour before pick up time and even with the extra thirty minutes she'd allowed herself, she wasn't as prepared as she would have liked to be. Still bleary-eyed after too much sleep, she faffed around wasting valuable time. Eventually she found her way into the shower and started washing her hair, only to be interrupted by a knock on the door. She had forgotten that a Bell Boy came for suitcases quite a while before pick up. The hotel management didn't want to be held responsible for delaying a crew and potentially an aircraft departure.

Sylvia rinsed shampoo out of her eyes, wrapped herself in a towel and opened the door. The young bell boy stood transfixed with his mouth open. It was his first day in the job and the lad had never seen that much naked female flesh before, not in three dimensions anyway. Sylvia quickly glanced in the full length mirror to make sure she wasn't exposing more than she ought to be and was relieved to see she wasn't. The lad's face was briefly scarlet and all he could do was mumble something about suitcases that made no sense. Sylvia told him she'd bring her case down herself and he left to knock on the next door, optimistic that this wasn't a one-off experience. He'd heard he'd probably see plenty of tips in this job. Maybe he'd misheard. Either way, his first shift was starting well.

She made it into the lobby with five minutes to spare but not with the cool and professional image that she usually portrayed. Sylvia now had about forty-five minutes to pull herself together before they arrived at the airport and a further half hour on the aircraft before passengers were invited to board. The return flight was overnight which generally meant all but a few travellers slept most of the way.

Of those who didn't, there was often a lone individual who wanted to become best friends with the crew. They would make themselves a nest in the galley and talk about their exciting lives back home and the incredible or disastrous holiday they had experienced. Naturally the bonding process required they identify themselves as genuine world travellers, setting themselves apart from the tourists and holidaymakers. Not all lonely passengers could bore for Britain but Sylvia felt she was auditioning those with a realistic chance of a medal, should it ever become an Olympic event.

By the time Sylvia arrived back at the flat she was almost a zombie again. She managed to unpack her case into the washing machine, throw herself into the shower and make a cup of tea without scalding herself or tripping any circuit breakers. Totally out of character she switched on the TV and started watching daytime telly while waiting for her man to bring her baby back home. She had really missed them and wondered how much her son would have changed in the three days she'd been away.

It was after six that evening when they eventually returned and she was beginning to worry that something had happened. Modern Man looked rather ragged and bit her head off when she demanded to know what had taken him so long. He followed this by plonking Boy Wonder, still strapped into his car seat, on the couch next to Sylvia and grabbing a beer from the fridge.

'All yours!' he added with a flourish and sat down in his favourite chair.

In Modern Man's head he had been coping without help for two days and nights and this was the shift change he had been waiting for. Sylvia, on the other hand, couldn't believe that he expected her to do everything when she'd been working all night.

Not a word was said out loud but each knew what the other was thinking and felt betrayed by the one person who should be their life-long ally. Neither ACAS nor a UN Peace Keeping Force would be any help for the next hour or so as they parried and thrust their most compelling reasons for the other person to be more understanding of the situation.

Boy Wonder slept through most of this but when he was ready for a feed he let them know in the usual way.

Modern Man turned to his wife and said, 'Bottle or boob?'

'Boob'

'What about the baby?'

Sylvia gave her husband a look but she couldn't keep it up and it morphed into a smile. She didn't have the energy or, if she was honest with herself, the will to stay mad at him. He seemed to have coped very well on his own and she was both relieved and proud. They would have to figure out a better way of handling her first day back from a trip.

As time passed, their ability to work as a team improved. Modern Man devised new ways of filling the weekends when Sylvia was away. They tried all manner of father-and-son activities to keep busy, simply because it was much harder when his son wasn't in the care of Plum and her team of enthusiastic baby minders. Sylvia found out about things they could do at the sports centre and swimming pool. There was always the zoo.

Shortly before Boy Wonder's first birthday, Sylvia was rostered a trip to San Francisco. In a moment of inspiration she suggested they all go. Sylvia would be working, of course, but staff travel concessions now made it an affordable treat for her family. It also meant the hotel would be paid for by the airline, as would travel to and from the airport in California. She assured Modern Man that crew took their spouses on trips all the time and everything would be fine. He didn't need much persuading. Modern Man had always wanted to visit the American west coast, particularly LA and San Francisco. Sylvia bought the tickets then set out the ground rules of Staff Travel.

'It could be complicated because you are on standby status. That means if the flight is full of fare paying passengers you don't get on. It also means you might not know if you are on the flight until the last minute. If that happens, you may need to run the entire length of Heathrow airport to the departure gate. No dawdling in the Duty Free shops trying on expensive sunglasses,' she told him. 'On the upside though, if the flight isn't full, you might be upgraded but there are no guarantees,' she added optimistically.

On the day of the trip Sylvia dropped Modern Man and Boy Wonder at the Staff Travel check in area and went to park the car before heading off to the crew reporting centre. Modern Man was weighed down with luggage, baby paraphernalia, instructions and Boy Wonder on his shoulders, in the backpack. Although excited, he was also extremely anxious that things might go horribly wrong. It suddenly occurred to him that he'd have to make his way home on public transport with all this gear. Sylvia's parting words had also been a dagger through his heart,

'Don't let any other passengers know you are family of crew. They don't like it, they think you're being treated preferentially.'

He had never felt so alone in such a busy place in his whole life.

At check in he was told to wait until he was called back, probably about twenty minutes before the scheduled departure time. There was nothing to do but loiter in the immediate vicinity. There were quite a few other people doing exactly the same. A captain's wife and his two teenage daughters were amongst them. Modern Man wouldn't have known this had the woman not announced it loudly when attempting to prompt some additional privileges on the basis of her husband's rank. The check-in staff had heard it all before and remained courteous but unimpressed. Based on the information they were told by staff passengers, the company chairman must play golf with every employee and be a close personal friend of all their family members. With that knowledge the playing field remained level for everyone.

Eventually, and with great relief, Modern Man was given a boarding card and directed to a departure gate in a galaxy far, far away. Hot, sweating and out of breath, he and Boy Wonder made it to the aircraft door with seconds to spare. Sylvia was not there to greet them but they were shown to a seat in the front row of the second cabin of the 747 aircraft. The stewardess said she would return to help him with the baby seatbelt when everyone was strapped in.

Incredibly, the seat next to him remained empty and his first experience as a business class passenger was about to begin in style. His fellow passengers seemed less enthusiastic about a baby in the same cabin but none actually asked to be moved away. Shortly after take-off a different stewardess appeared with a carrycot and set it up on the bulkhead in front of the adjoining seat. Boy Wonder was carefully placed inside and seemed content to be at eye level with other people while he played with his favourite toy.

Modern Man resisted the urge to drink large quantities of free alcohol and marvelled at the improvements in flight catering over the past few years. After the meal service, headsets were distributed and a movie was projected onto the screen at the front of the cabin. Modern Man hadn't seen the film before but knew he wouldn't be able to watch it without interruption. He picked up his book. At that moment Sylvia appeared as his elbow.

'Would you like me to look after your baby for a while, sir?' she asked, a little louder than necessary, so those seated nearby would hear.

'Great, thank you,' said Modern Man. 'Do you have children of your own?' he enquired.

'Yes, I have a son about the same age as this little guy, by the looks of him,' she added with a broad smile.

Murmurs of admiration filled the cabin as Modern Man sat reading his book with a rather smug expression on his face. Meanwhile, in the economy galley, Boy Wonder was being treated to gooey baby talk from Sylvia's fellow stewardesses, none of whom were mothers themselves. Eventually, she returned Boy Wonder to his father and carried on the illusion that it was all part of the service.

Within a few minutes the baby was pointing at the ceiling and saying, 'Bah.' This was a new experience and took a while to be accurately interpreted and confirmed. Boy Wonder was actually asking for his bath. Modern Man was stunned but a check of his watch confirmed that he would normally be in bed by now, if they were at home. There are a great many things on a jumbo jet but a bath isn't one of them, even a baby bath. However, a sink works equally well and, even in the confined space of an aircraft toilet cubicle, Modern Man managed to follow the routine they used at home. Buttoned in his sleep suit and sucking on a bottle, Boy Wonder was settled down for the night.

Afternoon tea was served about an hour before they were due to land and the sandwiches, scones and clotted cream went down very well. For Boy Wonder it was a jar of stewed apple, one of his favourites, and he was also ready for something to eat. The jar was polished off in record time so Modern Man decided to try for a second. About halfway through came the first refusal. The mouth stayed closed. The second refusal was a turn of the head. Modern Man used his usual trick of tickling Boy Wonder's tummy then shovelling in another mouthful when he unclamped his jaws to laugh. Success was temporary on this occasion as Boy Wonder spat it out all over his father's shirt and tie. The cabin erupted in laughter and Modern Man became acutely aware of exactly how much scrutiny he'd been under for the last few hours. Boy Wonder giggled, farted and giggled some more. He was having such fun on this flight.

The time difference on the west coast is a brutal eight hours and although Sylvia was able to sleep through the night, both the guys were wide awake in the hotel before four the next morning.

Modern Man decided they had to get out of the room otherwise Sylvia would be exhausted and they would all suffer the consequences. He managed to dress himself and Boy Wonder in the bathroom and they left the hotel room as quietly as they could. The Concierge suggested an all night diner where breakfast was served without the company of druggies and down-and-outs. Modern Man was very grateful for this advice.

It was warm and sunny and the city was slowly coming to life as Modern Man and Boy Wonder wandered down to Pier 39, stared at Alcatraz Island in the misty bay and killed time for a couple more hours. When he thought it would be safe to return to the hotel room they found Sylvia was up and dressed. She didn't usually bother with breakfast, a cup of tea was all she needed to start the day.

Her plan was shopping. If he had a plan it was rejected unheard. She had routines on her trips and some things didn't change under any circumstances. By midday Boy Wonder had some fantastic new outfits. Sylvia had bought an unlikely combination of things not available in Britain at the time and Modern Man treated himself to a forty-niners baseball cap. Very cool. Everyone was happy.

After lunch they took a boat across to the Alcatraz to join a tour then slobbed about in the hotel room until they couldn't keep their eyes open any longer. They all slept better the second night. The following day they were heading for home. Modern Man and Boy Wonder were in Business Class again and didn't even have to run to the gate this time.

Despite some poor sleep patterns when they returned home, there was no denying the trip had been a great success.

Modern Man was looking forward to doing it all again soon but Sylvia was lukewarm to the idea for a reason she didn't want to share with him at the time. He let it go for a while but when a trip to Los Angeles came through a few months later, he pushed for another 'holiday.'

Sylvia filibustered to the best of her ability but when he wouldn't let it go she snapped. 'This might be my last trip EVER. I think I might be pregnant and if I am, I'll be grounded after this roster and I won't go back to flying again. It may be selfish but I want to have this trip on my own.'

11. A Bump in the Road

Sylvia's second pregnancy proceeded without any problems and Darling Daughter entered the world like most babies, bruised, blue and rather sticky. For Modern Man it was the third miracle of his life, the first being that Sylvia had agreed to marry him and the second was the birth of Boy Wonder. The family was complete, the universe was balanced and there were a handful of work mates in the pub waiting to wet the baby's head. With this in mind Modern Man decided that Sylvia needed rest and left her in the care of the midwives.

Boy Wonder was also in capable hands. Nursery nurses were never going to appear in the *Sunday Times Rich List* and baby-sitting was an obvious extension of their day job to earn a few extra quid. Modern Man had grudgingly paid the girl to watch his son sleep in the early days but what little social life he had left became more precious with every passing day and his attitude changed. He could now see that nights out with the guys would be rare and nights in watching TV would be the norm.

After a fairly brutal exchange of views, he and Sylvia had come to an arrangement whereby Modern Man could go out with his mates the evening she returned home from a trip, provided Boy Wonder was ready for bed before Modern Man left the flat. He felt he deserved some time out after being a lone parent for a few days and she couldn't summon up a strong enough argument to throw back in his face. She was far too tired to ratchet up her brain to that level of verbal sparring. They had an uneasy truce and she did try occasionally to persuade him to stay at home.

It is assumed by the health care system that anyone who can manage with one child without the intervention of police, social services and emergency medical assistance, will be okay with two. Sylvia and Darling Daughter were sent home from the maternity unit the day after the birth and added to the list of the community midwife for home visits. Apart from being surprised at being discharged so soon, Sylvia was glad to be back at the flat and sleeping in her own bed. Routines were adjusted to accommodate the addition to the family and the stock of nappies seemed to be taking over the living room. It was becoming clear that they would need a bigger home sooner rather than later. Modern Man was concerned that he would never earn enough to keep up with the current financial outgoings and was sure they were bound to increase appreciably.

Sylvia was still on the pay roll but wouldn't be for much longer. Her employers weren't stupid. The airline had plenty of experience of stewardesses leaving after having children. Sylvia knew this too and whilst she didn't want to pre-empt the event, she wasn't going to cling on with her finger tips to a job that she no longer wanted, not even for the money. Modern Man was impressed by her ethics but concerned that, as a family, they couldn't afford such high moral standards and urged her to stall as long as possible. A letter from the fleet office brought things to a head and Sylvia wrote back the following day tendering her resignation. The Stewardess was now The Homemaker. It had been good while it lasted and she was glad she had taken the plunge but her priorities had changed. A few tears escaped down her cheeks to mark the end of one exciting chapter of her life. She'd certainly miss the nice hotels, the thrill of going somewhere for the first time and, somewhat strangely, the distinctive smell of jumbo jets. Eau de Boeing.

A different and equally distinctive smell knocked her out of this daydream as reality assaulted both nostrils simultaneously. Modern Man appeared in the bedroom doorway like Mr Ben, one of Boy Wonder's favourite kids TV programmes and performed the nappy change. Boy Wonder appeared content to remain soiled almost indefinitely but Darling Daughter demanded a pit stop immediately after an event occurred.

As Sylvia was now a full time mum, she developed her own routines for feeding, changing, bathing and bedtime. Modern Man was ready to amend what he believed to be an excellent and extendable protocol that served both parents and children with care and efficiency. He was a bit miffed that she threw out his tried and trusted methods simply because, 'They wouldn't work with two kids,' even though she hadn't really put them to the test. She was, without doubt, taking over every aspect of the children's upbringing and he was relegated to a secondary role in pretty much everything. Normally that would bother him but then he remembered that she couldn't drink alcohol until she stopped breast feeding and despite her requests, there was no way he was going to give up beer and wine as some sort of ridiculous show of solidarity.

Time passed extremely slowly when the children were very young. Life revolved predominantly around their needs and little else. It was a grind at times but Modern Man and Sylvia ploughed on, stopping wasn't an option. There were occasional birthday parties and as Boy Wonder became a little older there were more activities at the sports centre in which he participated. He especially liked the bouncy castle at Toddler Blitz. It was a crazy couple of hours of soft toys, inflatable objects and a ball pool, every Saturday morning.

Life for Modern Man had changed a lot in the last few years but he was okay with it. More than okay. He loved it. Life was good in a way that he would never have expected. Being married with two children hadn't been part of his future plans as a young guy. Not that he had much in the way of a plan but if he had then this wouldn't have been it. Of that he was certain.

His attitudes had also changed since becoming a dad. Despite his best intentions he was spending considerably less time with his mates. It wasn't due to the influence Sylvia was attempting to exert. Absolutely not. He actually didn't want to go to the pub so often. It seemed like such a monumental waste of money. That wasn't the only reason though. He was aware that he had moved on with his life and the guys really hadn't progressed at all. They were still his mates and he'd do anything for them in times of crisis but his focus now was on being the best parent he could possibly be. His childrens' lives depended on it.

Sylvia had the same priorities but a different approach. She had become a mother to the exclusion of everything else. She hadn't let herself go physically but she couldn't deny her body had changed somewhat over the last few years. Her friends told her it was inevitable but Sylvia was having none of it. She didn't have time to go to a gym, instead she took advantage of the terrain and pushed the fully loaded double buggy up the long hill back to the flat at least twice each week. She made subtle changes to their diet and had completely lost her appetite in the bedroom. She was getting plenty of physical exercise during the day and when she flopped into bed she only wanted to sleep. Modern Man wasn't happy, feeling he had gone without for long enough. Her suggestion that he amuse himself was unnecessarily blunt in his opinion. What did she think he'd been doing for the last two years? He had to do something. Whether or not he had a sex life was now entirely in his own hands.

This was not the time to negotiate, he didn't want necrophilia or turbo sex. These were the alternatives she had resorted to in the past. It was either bore him into early withdrawal or get it over with as quickly as possible. In the end he settled for a long shower and his life would never be the same again after that.

There was a lump, or maybe a ridge but definitely something where there shouldn't be such a topographical feature. They should be smooth and round and reassuring to hold, they always had been before. Modern Man rinsed off the soap and checked again. Nothing.

That was a relief, maybe it was hard skin on his fingers. Third time for luck and no chickening out this time. He had to be thorough, compare left and right, all the way round, well as far as he could reasonably go. There was no denying it. There was a hardness to the right one that didn't exist on the left one.

He told Sylvia in the hope that she would investigate it herself and it may lead on to other things. She took it to be some sort of peculiar foreplay initiative and told him that if there really was something there he should see the doctor. He insisted there was and said he'd make an appointment soon. She suspected he was stalling and the following day she called his bluff and phoned on his behalf.

The surgery was a converted townhouse and the waiting room was probably the drawing room in days gone by. The decor and furnishings created an atmosphere reminiscent of a TV costume drama set in the early twentieth century and this greatly influenced the behaviour therein. Modern Man was trying too hard to convey an air of quiet nonchalance, which no one was buying into.

Sitting there in his own little world, he was trying to weigh up whether it would be better if the doctor was male or female. Both had pros and cons. No man had ever touched that part of his body and the thought wasn't appealing. On the other hand, a man would have firsthand knowledge of how gently to tackle the area in question. If it was a woman, things could go so terribly wrong. Oh the, 'What ifs?' tumbled out one after another. She might be recently divorced, jilted, a natural man-hater, or merely a bit sadistic! As his anxiety went into overload, his subconscious was pricked by his name being called again and again.

The doctor turned out to be male and quite young. Was that a good thing or not? Modern Man had lost all powers of logical thought and reason. At the prompt, to his immense surprise, he calmly informed the doctor that he had found a lump on his right testicle.

'OK, let's have a look at it,' the doctor replied.

He didn't just look though, he had a good feel around and after a few minutes remarked that there was some hardness and a referral to a Consultant Urologist would be arranged.

'It may be cysts on your epididymis.'

It was as if the doctor hadn't intended to say it out loud and he wished he hadn't.

He could see from the blank expression, with a hint of, 'Scared witless,' that clearly Modern Man had no idea what his epididymis was or the severity of having cysts there. Despite a blatant need for more information, the young GP ushered Modern Man out whilst mumbling medical terms in an attempt to reseal the can of worms he'd opened. Modern Man sat in his car slightly stunned as to why Ken Dodd had invaded his thoughts. Tickled he was not by the news the doctor had given him.

'Well, how did you get on? What did the doctor say?' Sylvia asked, as soon as he walked through the door.

'There might be something wrong with my Diddy Men. They're going to use ultrasound to try to find them. At least I think that's what he said.'

'Start again love. What EXACTLY did the doctor say?'

Modern Man did his best to recount what he had been told at the surgery.

The appointment to see a Consultant eventually came through. Modern Man would have to wait three months to find out if it was serious. Three months during which Modern Man had imagined every possible and impossible medical condition that a university library could identify. He had never signed up to the ignorance-is-bliss school of thought and dived in to find out as much as he could as quickly as possible.

With a thirst for knowledge that had been conspicuously absent during his own student days, Modern Man learned how to use a library the way it was intended.

The language of the medical profession had more Latin than he was familiar with but he understood the gist of it most of the time. He was frequently confused, occasionally scared and, temporarily, almost suicidal.

When the appointment with the Consultant came around, it was very straightforward. A few questions followed by another examination. Modern Man had now experienced two men holding his testicles and, on balance, preferred the gentler touch of the young GP to the more confident and forthright approach of the Consultant. On the strength of this the Consultant thought it probably was cysts on the epididymis. 'Cysts don't cause any problems and are not dangerous in themselves. There's no need to remove them surgically. I'll arrange an ultrasound scan and blood tests to confirm my diagnosis.'

That evening he brought Sylvia up to speed with the good news that his Diddy Men were perfectly happy to have a few cysts. It was nothing to worry about after all.

When the time came for the ultrasound scan Modern man had become accustomed to exposing himself to strangers in a medical context. He was secure in the knowledge that they weren't judging him or in any way comparing him to anyone else. It was cool. These guys were doing their jobs, professionals that they were.

'This is Jenny. She will be doing your scan,' said a voice from another part of the galaxy.

Without looking up, Modern Man ran a quick data check. Had there ever been an instance of a male child being given the name Jenny? He remembered Johnny Cash singing about a boy named Sue but that was no help now. Was there be any chance it had been Gerry? As he slowly raised his head it became blindingly obvious that not only was Jenny a woman, she was a young woman. A beautiful young woman. His mind raced back to the time in the doctor's waiting room when he was considering the pros and cons of being examined by a female doctor. He couldn't remember a single pro, other than the base and rather obvious one. Base and obvious as it was, he might be on a sticky wicket here.

Jenny wasn't alone. There was a male doctor and two other women, nurses presumably, although their uniforms didn't exactly shout it out. They were very conscious of the potential embarrassment and requested that first he should lie down on the bed. One of the nurses then covered him with a sheet and requested he lower his trousers and underwear to about knee level. After a lot of wriggling and shuffling

Modern Man was ready for action. The top sheet was carefully pulled back and a clear gel squirted over his testicles. It wasn't especially cold but it was still a strange experience.

As the radiologist navigated skilfully round the vicinity, Modern Man managed to twist himself into a contortion to see the image on the monitor. To him it was about fifty shades of grey. To Jenny it was much more meaningful. Occasionally there was a distinctly curved outline and that coincided with the probe acquiring his undivided attention as it pressed against a particularly sensitive area. It was a bit like having a slightly damp bar of soap pushed a little harder than is strictly necessary to generate a decent lather.

When the job was done, Modern Man was given some of the least absorbent tissue he had ever come across, to wipe away the gel. It was a strangely familiar feeling reminiscent of happier times. More important than that was the possibility of the damp gel soaking through his trousers appearing as though he'd wet himself. It was a long walk through the hospital and he still had blood samples to donate before he set off home.

After a couple of weeks the Consultant hadn't written, he hadn't phoned; didn't he care? Modern Man was beside himself. Was he merely a statistic now? Cast aside and forgotten? Sylvia was not one to let a commitment slide by. She phoned the GP practice and firmly requested they chase up the blood test results. A young doctor from the family practice returned he call and although she couldn't divulge the results of the test, the doctor did provide plenty of background information about the possible outcome and what treatments may be recommended depending on the diagnosis.

The following day the same young doctor phoned Modern Man. Before commenting on the results of the blood test, she acknowledged that she had already spoken to his wife and asked if that had been alright. Modern Man assured her it was fine to talk to his wife, in fact he even did it himself sometimes. The doctor clearly thought Modern Man was in need of psychiatric evaluation but that diagnosis would be left for another day. She told him the blood test results were very good. On a scale of zero to five, his tests had come out at a little over zero. That excluded the possibility of a teratoma, the more aggressive form of tumour but gave no hint about a seminoma being in there somewhere. The next step in the investigation was for another ultrasound scan.

Sylvia was now firmly 'in the loop' and starting to worry that this was really serious. Any sentence that included the words tumour and aggressive were upsetting. The idea that his may be less aggressive than the alternative was of little comfort to her. She tried desperately to suppress the butterflies in her stomach. She busied herself with routine tasks and tried not to think of the awful possibility of being a widow with two young children.

Modern Man's approach to the second scan was a mixture of calm assurance about the process and mild anxiety at what may be discovered. There was no getting away from the feeling that there might be something bad lurking in those grey shadows. The images were both interesting and confusing for the doctor driving the probe. The same area was covered again and again from different angles of approach and increasing degrees of forcefulness. Modern Man wondered if the doctor was trying to erase his entire testicle, such was the force exerted on his crown jewels. This was happening on the left side. Previously they had been more interested in the one on the right.

The right testicle did feature but only to measure a grey area that clearly they expected to be there. The doctor offered no explanation of what had been found, what she was looking for or where things went from there. Modern Man sensed the uncertainty and asked, 'What have you found?'

'I'll write up my report and send it your consultant,' was the rather terse reply.

Modern Man was now very concerned. She'd been quite chatty the last time. This was a major change in her demeanour and it bothered him.

One thing he had learned with certainty was, if you wanted information you had to ask questions. It wasn't that the doctors were deliberately withholding details from him. It was more likely they were reluctant to start a conversation they would find difficult to finish. The weakness of all doctors was interrogation. Medics were programmed from early in their training to answer direct questions with straight answers. Modern Man managed to extract some useful intelligence but was quickly lost by the doctor's inability to restrict the responses to words he understood. Modern Man instinctively made a tactical withdrawal from the exchange before he said something stupid.

Modern Man's journey eventually petered out and although fairly tired, his overwhelming feeling was frustration. He simply didn't know enough to decide whether to be scared, resigned, angry or depressed.

His internal compass had guided him back to his front door. He'd paid so little attention to his surroundings over the last few hours that he could have just as easily walked off a cliff or into the sea. On reflection, living thirty miles inland and surrounded by rolling countryside, neither of those eventualities was a genuine risk. No, his problems were much closer to home and he resolved to face them with dignity. If he couldn't manage dignity, he hoped he wouldn't be a big girl's blouse.

A couple of days later Modern Man was summoned to the urology clinic again. This was unprecedented speed. Previously the appointment timescale had always been measured in months. It couldn't be good news but the Consultant's secretary who made the call was infuriatingly uninformed on the subject. Inevitably the dark thoughts began to cluster in Modern Man's mind. He knew about being an engineer but not so much about how his body worked. If this was a machine they would diagnose the faulty component, identify the reason for the failure and redesign it. Could this Consultant do something similar to fix his body? It was certainly more reassuring to believe that he could than to consider that he couldn't.

Once again Modern Man found himself horizontal and genitally exposed while the Consultant examined him. The Consultant looked grave but attempted a casual tone to his rather odd question.

'Is your family complete?'

What the hell did that mean? None of them were amputees so he said, 'Yes,' because it seemed a safe answer with no likely follow up. The Consultant went on to explain that the results from the ultrasound scan showed a growth had appeared and seemed to have grown rapidly in the left testicle and disappeared entirely from the right one.

'It could have been calcification from an earlier infection, not necessarily an infection in the testes.'

As if that made things any clearer!

The only things that were certain was the uncertainty of what they had found and the fact that it definitely wasn't cysts on the epididymis. Surgery was the best way forward and the Consultant phrased it in such a way that any other course of action would be delaying the inevitable. Modern Man liked to think of himself as decisive and was happy to agree to surgery before spending too much time thinking about what they were considering cutting open.

The Consultant went on to explain that a biopsy was required. It would mean taking a slice of the testicle, freezing the slice and examining it for malignant cells. If there were none the testicle could be sewn up, otherwise it would be replaced by a prosthetic.

'This is done while you're asleep,' the Consultant continued.

'That's a relief. I wouldn't want to watch all that happening,' Modern Man replied, without thinking what he was saying or to whom he was speaking.

The Consultant cracked a smile and mentioned that the test only took about thirty minutes. If the testicle was to be reassembled, it would happen in the same operation, not as a separate procedure. The Consultant explained that reconstruction of the testicle had possible complications. The testicle would be more prone to infection and feel different. Inevitably it would be slightly smaller but there was no danger of it shrivelling up completely. The Consultant also made Modern Man aware of the option of a prosthetic replacement. He described it as like a small breast implant. A silicone filled fake testicle that would be inserted in place of the diseased one.

Modern Man liked the idea of a breast to have and to hold, even a small one but was totally confused by the talk of chopping and changing. 'Are you saying that even if the testicle is alright, I can still have a prosthetic replacement, if I prefer?

'Correct.'

This guy wasn't a born salesman but it sounded better than sticking the bits back together after the biopsy, provided the bits turned out to be healthy.

Modern Man wasn't ready to commit either way on the spur of the moment so asked for time to think it over. He mused that perhaps Sylvia would like to have some input to this potentially huge decision.

'This type of cancer is the only one where we can say with 99% certainty that you're cured.'

There it was. He had used the 'C' word. There was no going back now, death was inevitable. Sooner or later his body would be devoured by mutated cells, painfully slowly or outrageously quickly. Resistance was futile, the outcome unavoidable.

There was a diary open on the desk and the date on the top of the page was the following Thursday. Immediate action was being taken and Modern Man appreciated that. He would be in hospital for a few days, possibly over the weekend. It was neither practical nor reasonable to keep family and friends in the dark any longer. He went home and made some calls. Both he and Sylvia were in dire need of a few drinks before the end of the day.

On the day of his operation he arrived early and was taken through the admissions process. There were forms to fill in, of course, and some of the questions he was asked did raise a metaphorical eyebrow. He never liked talking about religion because he didn't really have one and on this occasion, wasn't in the mood to discuss spiritual hypotheses. Nor was he reassured by the term 'next of kin.' That had a bad outcome written all over it.

The surgical gown was unlike any other item of clothing Modern Man had ever had to wear. The instructions from the nurse were pretty simple, 'Wear the gown, only the gown, no underwear, no jewellery, and no watch. Clear?'

With the opening at the back and only three sets of tapes to hold it together, it took a few attempts to master the technique. He tied all the tapes first and tried pulling the gown over his head. Even with the curtains drawn round his bed, in bending over he managed to show his bare bum to the entire hospital ward and couldn't wriggle into the gown anyway.

His second attempt was to put his arms in the sleeves but then he could only reach the tapes at the back of his neck and once again his rear flank was exposed. He took it off and tied the top two tapes first then slipped it over his head, only to strangle himself when he sat down. 'Knock me out now before I make a complete idiot of myself,' was the only thought passing through his mind.

Whilst waiting in pre-op the Consultant came over to speak to him. Almost unrecognisable in operating theatre scrubs, he asked Modern Man how he felt about having the prosthetic replacement whatever the biopsy showed. This seemed reasonable on several levels. The surgery could be completed in one session and where was the benefit in having a possibly damaged and reconstructed testicle put back in anyway? Modern Man had clearly given the right answer. That was evident from the expression on the Consultant's face.

Before he knew it he was being brought out of a general anaesthetic. To be raised from the deepest of slumber to drowsy rather quickly and then spend several hours in fitful sleep was uncanny. What was much worse was that no one would tell him anything about his operation.

The stock answer from all nurses was the same. 'The Consultant will speak to you during his ward round later this afternoon.'

Modern Man was also half expecting to see a spherical object immersed in clear liquid in a jar on his bedside cabinet. Apparently they don't return body parts as a souvenir of a stay anymore. It seems someone mistook their recently removed appendix, floating in formaldehyde, as medicine to be taken immediately upon waking. This mistake caused immediate complications to an otherwise routine surgical procedure.

The Consultant toured the ward in the late afternoon. He had a small entourage of frightened looking junior doctors with him and a harassed looking ward sister making notes in his wake. Modern Man was expecting a detailed debrief but it was all over very quickly. These guys obviously didn't hang around sick people for fun.

What he did gather was that a small malignant tumour had been removed from the left testicle, which he no longer thought of as his own. So it was official then. Modern Man had cancer. The question was did he still have cancer or had it been confined to his ex-testicle. That would remain the burning question for a while longer because he needed a scan to determine if the cancer cells had spread to any other parts of his body.

While that major development in his life story was finding a part of his memory to call home, the Consultant and his followers were moving on to the next patient. The opportunity to ask any questions had passed and Modern Man was annoyed with himself. How had he let that happen? There was a knowing look on the Sister's face. She'd seen it far too many time before. It was never accidental.

The look said, 'Consultants do it all the time. I'll come back and talk to you and fill in the blanks.'

To her immense credit, Sister lived up to her unspoken word. Modern Man, however, processed what he now knew to be fact rather than speculation and started texting family and close friends with an update. This would have been a good plan if he wasn't still groggy from anaesthetic. He tapped out one message that would do for everyone and saved it. In a flurry of activity, he first sent it to the same person three times, then to two people who didn't know he was in hospital and finally to a few wrong numbers. One of the misdirected recipients was kind enough to offer sympathy and encouragement, by immediate return. There are good people out there, Modern Man thought to himself.

Sylvia visited him after dinner. He'd texted her earlier with a list of essential items that the ward staff were either unable or unwilling to supply. It appeared that, 'May I remind you this is a hospital,' was considered a valid response to whatever he asked the nurses to provide.

Sylvia saw no reason to risk public humiliation. She brought fresh fruit instead of the cans of beer and crisps he'd requested. She also told Modern Man that she'd phoned his parents and brought them up to date with his circumstances. Only during the call did she discover how little they previously knew. Sylvia was both amazed and annoyed that her husband had kept his mum and dad in the dark for so long. It wasn't easy for Sylvia to discuss such things with her mother-in-law. Talking to her about his testicles made her uncomfortable.

Evening slipped into night and Modern Man settled down for what turned out to be about three hours of fitful slumber. A large portion of the day had been spent half asleep. It was hardly surprising that he found it difficult to nod off. There were clicks, bleeps and whirs of heart monitors, blood pressure recorders and all the other machinery that is operating 24/7 in a surgical ward.

The night shift nurses were clustered together in an alcove, each with a mug of tea, texting, chatting to each other or finding some other way to pass the hours between the routine tasks. When they noticed Modern Man standing there, he was given the 'look.' The kind of look an unwelcome stranger is faced with when they walk into a village pub. Somewhere between disbelief and openly hostile but with a side order of curiosity as to what on earth they're doing there.

Modern Man acknowledged his status and moved on. Walking was becoming easier with every step and, although not exactly quick, he was happy to pass the small hours wandering round a hospital that on all previous visits had defeated his sense of direction sooner or later.

Like so many other hospitals he had visited, it was long corridors and signs with arrows to departments where they cured things he had never heard of. The only place with any real activity was Accident & Emergency. Between the hours of two and four in the morning A & E played host to the unlucky, the unwise and the unhinged sectors of the local population. After about half an hour of eavesdropping near the treatment cubicles, Modern Man shuffled back to the safety of his ward and tried to make himself comfortable.

The Consultant appeared with a fresh entourage soon after breakfast. These eager young doctors were like Labrador puppies. Keen to please their master but at the same time desperate not to disappoint him. Modern Man was showered and dressed by this time. He'd learned from his experience of the previous afternoon and was ready with a list of questions. The Consultant still wasn't playing ball and the only clear information Modern Man received was a CT scan would be scheduled in due course and he would be passed on to the Oncology department for further treatment.

The Consultant's parting words as he left Modern Man's bed were, 'Send him home.

Modern Man was happy with that instruction.

The ward sister returned to his bedside after the rounds had finished and answered all his questions. She gave him a letter for his GP and advised Modern Man that he shouldn't drive for a week or so. He would receive an appointment to attend the oncology clinic in about a fortnight.

Modern Man was curious how Sylvia would treat him. Would it be chair-side service like a first class passenger, or would he be silently accused of milking the situation? Only time would tell.

Jack-Six-Pack and Dai Beech both phoned and a few other friends found reasons to drop by over the next few days. They were surprised that Modern Man looked much the same as the last time they had seen him. Perhaps they were expecting him to have visibly aged a couple of decades. He was grateful for their concern but also slightly amused that he was putting them back together emotionally because they were anticipating having to do that for him. The bottom line was that he didn't see the point of being stressed about having cancer because he didn't know he'd had it until he didn't have it anymore. A bit too logical for some, perhaps, but that was how Modern Man decided to deal with it.

On the spur of the moment Sylvia decided they needed a break and booked a weekend in Cornwall for the family. A small hotel she had stayed in as a child was the perfect idyll to forget about this for at least a day or two. Fresh sea air and gentle walks on the beach would do wonders for his body and his soul.

Surgery wasn't the end of the process by any means. The follow up would last five years and consist of regular clinic visits, blood tests and an annual CT scan. There'd probably be more ultrasound as well. The first clinic appointment was to determine how best to proceed and Modern Man actually had to decide which option he wanted to take. He was presented with three alternatives; chemotherapy, radio-therapy or simply to rely on self-examination.

It was time to 'man up' and self examination was clearly the 'cop out' choice, included only to test his mettle. He knew that radio-therapy had something to do with radiation but had no idea how chemotherapy was administered, only that the side effects could be pretty rough going.

Thankfully, the Oncology Consultant had not been off sick the day they taught bedside manner at medical school and was happy to talk through the facts of both types of treatment. The Consultant was also careful to avoid any hint of persuasive argument in favour of one over the other.

Modern Man didn't have the interviewing skills to draw out any hint of professional preference. He was forced to shut out the emotional side of his brain and listen only to the analytical side. He settled for chemo and immediately attempted to forget everything he had been told about radio-therapy unless that started to sound like a better choice later on.

The first computer tomography scan was scheduled for a month or so after his surgery and the results may necessitate a change in the course of treatment he was told. Not a decision Modern Man would have to take, that would be one for the Consultant. The instructions for the scan were straightforward. He should eat a normal meal about an hour before the appointment time and drink as much water as was humanly possible, then some more water. Finally, finish off with a good long drink of water.

Modern Man followed the instruction to the letter and arrived at the hospital in plenty of time for his appointment, only to be presented with a litre bottle of water and the unnecessary reminder to drink as much as possible. The nurse added pointedly that a visit to the toilet was not forbidden but the relief would only be temporary. Whatever fluid was released would have to be replaced before the scan took place.

He was left sitting in the small waiting area with three or four other patients. Inevitably there were stories to be told by the old hands who had been through this hoop many times over the years. In the folklore of long-term sickness, kudos is given to the battlers who have doggedly kept the cancer at bay for more than most. As the stories caught the imagination, the quaffing of water had dwindled to occasional sips and discomfort was becoming an issue.

The actual process of being scanned was another chapter in the book of new experiences. He was asked to lie down on a fairly narrow trolley with a large metal doughnut at the head end. A cannula was inserted in his right arm and a dye injected that would show clearly on the scan. The sensation of that was like nothing he had ever experienced before. Modern Man was quickly aware of a rapidly spreading warm feeling in his lower abdomen. A complete and immediate evacuation using both forward and rear exits seemed inevitable. Thankfully, nothing happened and the nurse put the mop and bucket back in the corner of the room. The sensation subsided as rapidly as it had built up and the relief was measurable.

A voice from the 'doughnut' told him to take a deep breath and hold it. He wasn't sure whether he moved or the doughnut did but it scanned from his chest to his hips and back before instructing him to breathe normally. Job done.

The reward for not embarrassing himself in front of witnesses was a long, satisfying, and most importantly, private trip to the bathroom. It was probably only a minute or two but Modern Man felt he'd been standing there all day before the well eventually ran dry.

Whilst he still maintained that he didn't feel ill and hadn't at any stage of the whole bizarre scenario, he couldn't help feeling a bit anxious during his next clinic appointment. He was about to find out if he was hosting any more cancerous growths. The Consultant didn't hang around with small-talk, he came straight out and told Modern Man that the scan was clear. There were no signs of cancer anywhere and one session of chemotherapy would be a good way of catching anything the scan had missed.

Sylvia had decided to join him for this appointment and whilst Modern Man thought they were finished she took it upon herself to acquire some more details. She quizzed the Consultant about the reliability of the scan results, the possibility of error or misinterpretation, the likelihood that the cancer could return at a later date and any number of related questions. It was Mastermind before his eyes: specialist subject – diagnostic oncology and it lasted for a good deal more than the two minutes most contenders have to get through. Modern Man was quite looking forward to the General Knowledge round to see what she was going to ask him next.

Chemo time came round and Modern Man presented himself once again for a trip into unknown territory. The Receptionist at the cancer unit was suspiciously upbeat and cheerful and this could mean only one thing – His death was imminent. Modern Man was directed to the lift and told which floor his ward was on. The Nurses' Station was staffed and after they checked his details against their list, he was directed to the day room.

The Day Room turned out to be a pleasant lounge with comfortable chairs, a TV and no other people. As time passed other patients and family members arrived and departed; just the room, not life as we know it. Some were chatty and buoyant, others less so.

In a day where surprises should have been expected Modern Man was stunned to be told by a registrar that his chemo would actually take place the following day. He'd received a pamphlet in the post about a week before his appointment. It enlightened him of fascinating information regarding the limitations of available parking spaces for visitors. It also had an interesting paragraph on the location of post boxes within the building and the frequency of collections by the Royal Mail. He went on to read about his need to keep his personal possessions secure and how that was his responsibility, not the hospital's concern.

Considering the information this pamphlet did include, he was amazed to be told at this late stage he'd have to come back the next day. It wasn't as if he had something more important to do but really, it was hardly a minor detail. On reflection the bit in the pamphlet about post boxes may have been an oblique reference he should have picked up on. He didn't know why he was annoyed by this but he was.

Whatever failings in explaining the process had been uncovered, a recognisable effort was made by the Consultant to put right the misconception. He did something that Modern Man didn't think a consultant was capable of. He admitted it was his mistake and apologised.

Modern Man immediately suspected this would end up in the Sunday papers as one of those instances where someone with no medical qualifications poses as a doctor for years and years until they make one tiny mistake and their whole deception unravels. In his experience, consultants just don't do that sort of thing. It's not in their DNA. In fact, in their case DNA actually stands for Do Not Apologise. This one did though. He was either destined for great things or a life of ridicule by his peers. Only time would tell.

The Consultant went on to explain that chemotherapy is not like aspirin. It's not a single drug that all cancer patients are prescribed. Chemotherapy is a complex cocktail of drugs that takes into account the ability of the patient's body to handle them. The obvious aim is to kill off the cancer cells without killing the patient in the process.

To achieve this simple goal, the doctor needs to know what each patient is capable of withstanding and they determine this by testing the efficiency of the kidneys to clean the blood. Each patient is injected with a radioactive marker that can be detected with a blood test and from this the efficiency of their kidney is calculated. The patient's height and weight are added to the mix and from all this information comes the recipe for the chemo drug.

With this new information filtering into his brain, Modern Man settled down with a good book and let the hospital staff do their jobs. It was no great inconvenience to return the next day and far more important that it was carried out properly than rushed.

Modern Man took the opportunity that evening to have a few beers with his mates. It might be quite a while before he was able to join them again. As they sat in the pub talking about everything except cancer and chemo, Modern Man realised they actually wanted to know but had no clue how to ask. For the next half hour he told them everything that had happened. They were guys, they got plenty of details whether they wanted them or not.

Day two started with an explanation of all the possible side effects. This was only for the specific chemotherapy drug that he'd been prescribed and the list seemed endless. The medical profession had a clearly defined strategy regarding the possible side effects of the chemotherapy drug he'd been prescribed. The nurse reeled off a long list of maladies and misfortunes that may befall him.

'You probably won't get all of them and you might not get any if you're lucky.'

At the end of the explanation Modern Man was presented with a consent form to sign, acknowledging that he had been informed of the risks and possible side effects of the treatment. He signed on the dotted line to enable the treatment to begin. As if he was about to say, 'No, let's see what happens if we leave nature to take its course.'

The chemo drugs were administered through a drip into a vein in the back of his hand. Modern Man was impressed with the care taken by the medical staff to ensure that the drip they were connecting to him was the one prepared for him. No assumptions were made about who he was. He was asked to verify his name and address, his date of birth and also his height and weight, as they too were important factors in the complex calculations. This was no time for vanity, he didn't try to make out he was taller and thinner than he actually was.

For the next couple of hours he settled back on the bed and read his book. Occasionally he snagged the cannula in the back of his hand as he turned a page or tried to make himself comfortable.

After disconnecting all the equipment and sliding the lines out of his hands, he was presented with his homework assignment. There was stuff to read about his treatment and the drugs he'd been prescribed. He was given firm instructions regarding the medication he was taking home. He had a three day supply of steroids and five days of anti-emetics to stop him throwing up.

'Take the medicine when you are supposed to and don't stop until you run out.'

More anti-emetics could be supplied if necessary. There was also the phone number of the hospital ward which was staffed around the clock. They really did know about reassurance and assumed that there was some fear and trepidation even though Modern Man knew he was projecting an air of confident self-control.

Even though Sylvia had forewarned the children that dad wouldn't be able to play with them like he usually did, they seemed to sense, in the way children do, that something wasn't quite right with him. He couldn't lift them up and throw them around the way they liked. In turn they gave him more cuddles and brought extra cushions when he was downstairs.

One dose of chemo doesn't make all your hair fall out or cause constant puking. Nor does the patient require industrial strength incontinence pants. For Modern Man the first effect was a feeling not dissimilar to that after a few too many pints topped off with a dodgy kebab. The familiar sensation when you've managed to get into bed but the room is spinning a bit and your mouth starts to fill with rather rusty tasting saliva. It's decision time. Do you hang in there and deal with a savage hangover in the morning? Or drag your sorry carcass into the bathroom and force yourself to throw up, knowing that you're trading tomorrow's bad head and guts for the lining of your throat right now? It's a tough call sometimes.

There was also the need to pee more frequently than usual. He presumed his kidneys were working overtime processing the fallout of the bio-chemical assault on his body. This only lasted for a day or so. The next interesting thing occurred almost exactly twelve hours after the intravenous anti-emetic finished, a little after five in the morning, unfortunately for him. He woke up with a dry, sore throat and heartburn. It was as if the drug that prevented this had worn off and, 'Ping!' the symptoms came back instantly. He eventually drifted off to sleep for about an hour but, after staring at the bedroom ceiling for several minutes, realised he might as well start the day a bit earlier than usual.

The directions for the anti-emetic instructed him to take two tablets four times a day, with food. Fantastic, four meals a day, by order of a doctor. Things were looking up. What he found was that taken after food, instead of before, resulted in immediate and powerful hiccups for about fifteen minutes. That's a mistake he wasn't going to make again. The hiccups lasted for two days and were much worse in the evening. There were a couple of days without them and then the gas changed direction and went out of the backdoor with the same kind of determination that the hiccups had blasted through the main portico.

There was one thing about chemo that was hard to cope with. It was the first time he had ever had a medical treatment that made him feel progressively worse not better. The anti-emetic seemed to last almost exactly six hours, causing him to wake up very early every morning. The sore raspy throat returned as soon as the effect of that drug wore off. If one day started very early then it wasn't easy to keep going till after midnight unless he could have a snooze after lunch. The feeling of a slight stomach upset was never far away and fried food multiplied the effect many times over.

When the drugs were finished, there was a day or two more with the queasy hangover feeling but that did subside. What really took him by surprise was how little stamina he was left with. He was tiring easily and started each day well below his normal energy levels. Without the steroids he'd have been as feeble as a kitten.

A week after chemo he was sleeping properly again although the sore lump in his throat did come back occasionally. Ten days after chemo, Modern Man woke up and immediately felt fantastic. Only then did he realise how crap he had been feeling right up to the day before.

The future would consist of regular blood tests, chest X-rays, physical examinations and the occasional CT scan. There was a clear process. It was being followed and Modern Man was now used to being handled, in every sense of the word, by the Health Service.

Sylvia had been very supportive throughout. She could see the effect it was having on him and was very careful how she phrased her recommendations of what to do and what not to do. A few days after chemo she had asked him how he was feeling. He described how wine seemed kind of bitter and food that he knew he liked didn't taste right. There was a constant feeling of about to throw up, sleep was fitful and during the waking hours he couldn't stand up for long and couldn't get comfortable when sitting down.

'Just like being pregnant then?'

In that instant something changed forever. 99% of the sympathy she had been displaying evaporated and was replaced by a look that said more than mere words can express.

There was no doubt that the experience had aged Modern Man physically and mentally. He had met and talked to people in a far worse state than he and with prognoses that would be hard for anyone to face up to. He realised how incredibly lucky he'd been and joked with his mates about having, 'Diet Cancer,' and, 'Cancer Lite.' Gradually he became familiar with the feel of his prosthetic implant where there had once been a vital organ. Well vital to him anyway. He also made an important decision. He would not become a cancer bore. It happened, he got over it but it wasn't going to define him as a person.

He returned to work, the children continued to flourish and Sylvia stopped worrying about him in that respect. He would still be a cause for concern in so many other ways. Life moved on and they all lived happily ever after.

Like Hell they did!

Printed in Great Britain
by Amazon

22841629R00118